ARTI YOUNG WARRIORS

DAVID HANCOCKS

VALLEY
PUBLISHING

Published in the United Kingdom by Valley Publishing in 2011
First Edition
Copyright @ David Hancocks, 2011
David Hancocks has asserted his right under the Copyright, Designs and Patterns Act, 1988, to be identified as the author of this work.

This book is sold subject to the condition that it shall not, by way of trade or otherwise, be lent, resold, hired out, or otherwise circulated without the publisher's written consent in any form of binding or cover other than that in which it is published and without a similar condition, including this condition, being imposed on the subsequent purchaser.

Valley Publishing
Priory Mill
Nailers Lane
Monmouth
NP25 3EH

www.valleypublishing.co.uk

A CIP catalogue record for this book is available from the British Library

ISBN 978-0-9569093-0-5

Typeset by Daniel Goldsmith Associates, Cheshire
Cover design by John Smith
Printed and bound in the UK by the MPG Books Group, Bodmin and King's Lynn

This book is printed on Vancouver Book Wove, a mixed sources paper, approved by the Forest Stewardship Council (FSC).

To Charlotte

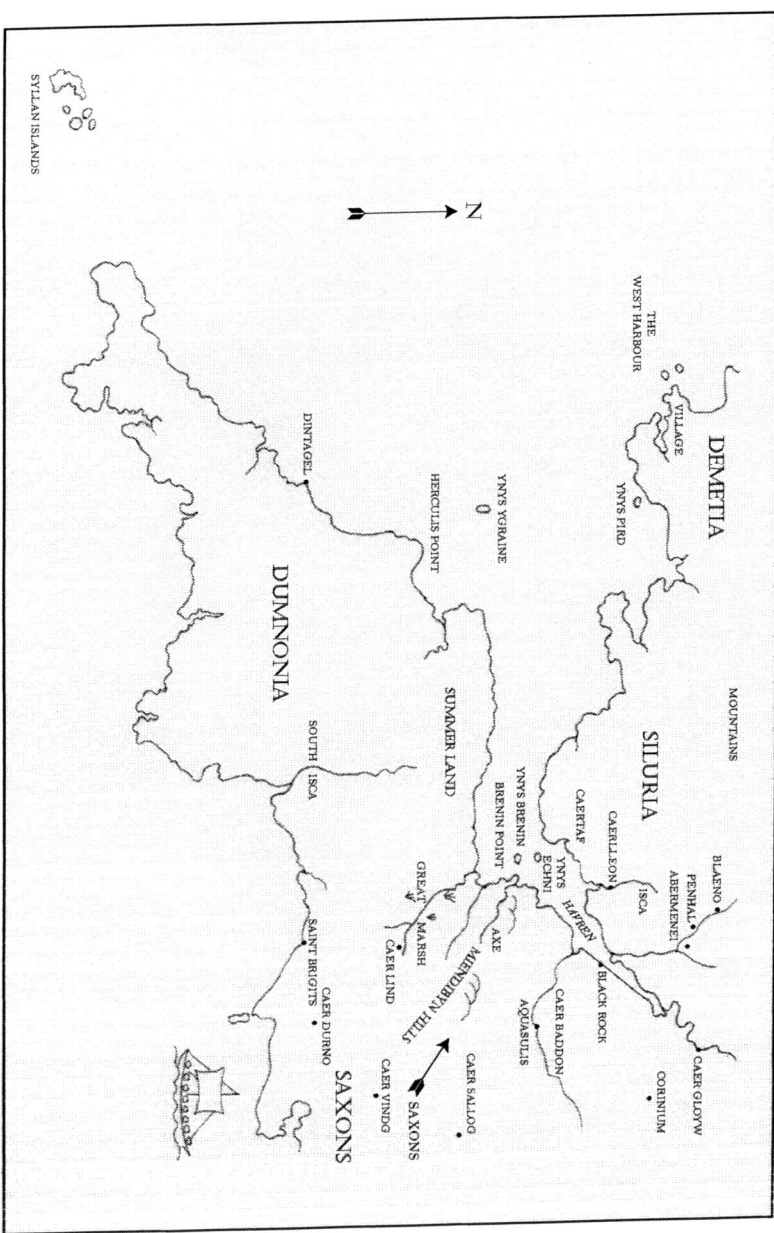

CHAPTER 1

The Decision

The decision had finally been made – Rhys, now sixteen, was going to the monastery school at Caerllion. After weeks of discussion and anguish, the clan would now be relieved to know that Rhys had made the decision to leave Penhal, his grandfather's estate.

It fell upon his younger sister, Olwen, to rush around the settlement with the news; little did she know that Rhys had made up his mind some time ago. He knew exactly what he wanted to be when he grew stronger, and revenge was burning in his young heart. His grandfather's warriors boasted of killing Saxons – soon he would join them.

As she skipped through the doorway of the wood-framed hall into the spring sunshine, Olwen shouted through all the house doorways and waved her stick at the barking dogs. The puppies, especially, thought this was a new game and hurtled through the gateway in front of her. Skipping and running across the field to the river, her first call was to the priest up on the hill. Olwen knew that he would be delighted – it was just what he had been hoping for.

"Rhys is going to school. Rhys is going to school," she shouted. Everybody was going to know. Climbing onto the bridge, she heard the younger children leaving the stockade to join her; they knew that running up to the cemetery, and the priest's small house, would mean honey-cakes and milk.

Ruthall, the priest of Penhal, strode from his garden on hearing Olwen's shouts. His joy was obvious as he scooped up Olwen and hugged her tightly.

"This is a blessed day, Olwen. Brother Cunval would have been so pleased that Rhys wants to be educated." Ruthall glanced across the cemetery at Cunval's grave.

"Are you sure Cunval's not listening?" joked Olwen with a sly grin. "After all, he's only just up there, you know." She pointed to the sky.

"Now then, let's be grateful we're all down here enjoying the springtime, Olwen."

Ruthall was a big man for a priest; the warriors often jested with him as a devout man of God and said how grateful they were that he had been sent to Penhal to save them from the wicked Saxons. He loved the humour of the clan and always responded with a wagging of his finger. "You wouldn't want to go down there when you die, would you?" he would ask gravely, jabbing his finger towards the ground.

"Well, Olwen, when is he off? Is he going up to Blaeno first? Does he know the way? I got lost when I came up here from Caerllion, you know."

All priests seemed to worry too much, thought Olwen; they were always fussing. Ruthall had been at Penhal for just over two years, ever since his predecessor, poor Cunval, had been killed during an unexpected and particularly vicious Saxon raid.

Olwen stared through the gateway of the neat cemetery. The priest's hut at the rear, near the spring, was hardly big enough for a group of people to sit inside. But its mud walls and thatched roof certainly made it cosy in the winter.

Ruthall noticed the direction of her gaze.

"I know what you're thinking, Olwen, how can I live in a cemetery? Well, there are only five graves. Anyway, look, here come the children, let's have some cakes." He greeted the panting children and invited everybody into his adjacent garden. "See, my field beans are sprouting. It's a lovely time of the year, don't you think?" The children heartily agreed, for they were looking forward to the summer and the thought of splashing about in the river.

Meanwhile, back in the smoke and gloom of the hall, Rhys stood tall and adjusted his warrior's leather jerkin. He already had an air of authority about him, gained from his hard training with the warriors. His mother, Anharad, looked on proudly, but with an inner feeling of foreboding. Now that Rhys was sixteen years of age, and growing by the day, she could see something of his father in his stance. She was afraid that this meant he would now want to avenge the death of his father, killed by invading Saxons in a battle far to the east, even though Rhys had been only a boy at the time and could surely hardly remember him. Far closer to home was the death of his uncle, who had brought him up, killed in another battle only three years before. Anharad was not the only widow on the large estate.

Rhys, with the weight of decision-making lifted from his shoulders, strode to the doorway and breathed in the clean air. He was still thin with youth, but riding and training with the warriors had given him strength and agility beyond his years. He smiled in a grown-up, confident way. The older people within the stockade had left their houses to congratulate him, for they were glad that their heir apparent was going to learn to read and write and not just follow the warriors into a life of turmoil and sudden death.

A shout from the field interrupted the happy group.

Gathering in the gateway, they could make out two horses approaching from the eastern forest – it was the Yarl Brochvael and his wife Gwenhaen. Brochvael eyed the gathering suspiciously and heaved himself off his big horse. He grudgingly turned and helped his wife down from her own horse, something he did not normally bother to do. Gwenhaen had already looked into Anharad's eyes and sensed the meaning of the occasion as Rhys took the reins of Brochvael's horse and wheeled the stallion around to tether him.

"I expect to be off within a few days, grandfather," Rhys said.

Brochvael snorted. "So be it! But remember, you will still have to join the warriors at Caerllion to carry on your training. If you ever take over this estate, you'll need to be the strongest of the bunch." Brochvael ruffled his grandson's curly brown hair.

his goal of being a war leader when he was older. Rhys had met three priests in his young life, and he had loved and respected them dearly, but when it came to following the old gods like his pagan grandfather, or the new one God, he thought of how many more Britons the Saxons had managed to kill. As his grandfather loved to point out, the Saxon god, Woden, often seemed to be the strongest in a pitched battle.

Realising that Ruthall's lecture appeared to be over, Rhys turned to the children.

"I must go up to Blaeno tomorrow. Who's coming with me?"

"Are you going to kiss Helena?" Olwen rocked her head back and forth with a big smile, well knowing what Rhys' reaction would be.

"Shut up, you stupid girl," shouted Rhys, red in the face. "You can stay here if you're going to cause trouble." The rest of the children hooted with laughter. The last time they had all travelled upriver to Blaeno and played with the children of the farm, they had spied Rhys kissing the young Helena, daughter of the overseer.

"I'm off," snapped Rhys and ran up the trackway onto the moor. He was flushed at the thought of Helena, and this was exactly why he wanted to visit Blaeno. During the winter visits, he had looked at her in a different light and she seemed to be willing to walk alone with him. The warriors had gruffly told him all about women and it had taken him ages to pluck up courage to ask if he could kiss her. Oh, yes – he could remember that glorious kiss. It had lasted for ages, until they had been interrupted by the sound of children giggling. Later, Helena's parents had smiled knowingly at Rhys, but had said nothing. And now, he desperately wanted to see her once more. The thought of how he would miss her had almost made him decide against going to Caerllion. However, he knew his destiny was to become a King's warrior.

With all these thoughts racing through his mind, Rhys had run the whole length of the trackway. Even Hawk had lagged behind. He stared into the distance, recalling how, shortly after his uncle's death in a battle to the east, two marauding Saxons had attacked Penhal. His good friend, Cunval, had been struck down while defending the children. He glared across the Gwei valley and quietly cursed.

After resting awhile, he became aware of shouts from the woodland to the north; the Penhal warriors were hunting a deer and it was coming in his direction. He climbed an oak tree to get a better view, just in time to see the hunting dogs bring down a stag. He could just make out the leading warrior jumping from his horse to spear the animal through the heart.

A few minutes later, as the band of five warriors rode leisurely through the heather to the trackway, Rhys thought it would be a good joke to surprise them. He pressed his back tightly against the wide trunk.

"Lie down, Hawk, stay there boy," he whispered.

Arteg, the leader, headed the troop; the dogs, as usual, were just in front in case of an ambush. If the Saxons were ever to be intimidated by an enemy, then Arteg, big and powerful in his saddle, would be the man to make them quake. His long spear hung loosely in his hand and his sword flapped menacingly against his muscular thigh. Arteg was Rhys' hero; and he had always pushed Rhys to the limit.

As the troop came up to the oak tree, Rhys leapt to the ground in front of them holding his hands up menacingly. "Stop, you heathens!" he shouted. "This is my land!" The dogs yelped as Hawk sprang at them barking furiously.

Arteg cursed as his horse reared up and nearly threw him. The rest of the warriors burst out laughing; Rhys had certainly given them all a fright.

"So," hissed Arteg mockingly, as he dismounted, "is the height of your ambition to frighten poor, innocent travellers like us?"

"You'll all have to fight me if you want to pass," insisted Rhys, hands on hips. "You were lucky I didn't have my bow with me."

Arteg moved swiftly. He ordered his dogs to pounce, then lunged forward to grab Rhys' ankle as he was stepping backward. Sprawling on the ground, Rhys looked up to see Arteg poised over him with his spear ready to strike.

"Fool… you allowed yourself to be distracted; you're as good as dead."

The rest of the warriors guffawed loudly. Arteg gave a big grin, gathered Rhys up, and threw him onto his horse. Rhys' hands came to rest on the still-warm deer straddling the horse's shoulders. The blood on its hide was starting to congeal.

"If I give you that deer, will you take us to your priest and beg him to forgive us for our sins?" said Arteg in a solemn tone. The warriors found this all very amusing and smote Rhys roughly as they rode by. It was time to return to the settlement for their usual refreshment.

"Well, I suppose so," agreed Rhys. Arteg was much too quick for him with his vice-like hands and bulging muscles. For the last two years he had been training Rhys in every form of combat – galloping and spearing, shooting arrows, fighting on foot with sword or dagger and most importantly, dodging and swerving to confuse an attacking enemy. The warrior band had all experienced battle with the Saxons.

As the troop rode on ahead, Arteg took the reins of his horse and led Rhys along the trackway.

"You still have much to learn, Rhys, but you're good for your age. Remember, you must have complete confidence. Never hesitate. I was only a young soldier myself when your father was killed, but your uncle Catvael was fearless in battle… too fearless. I wept when we brought his body back with us, you know."

There was silence for a while. Rhys wondered how afraid he would be in a real battle – would he freeze in fright?

"You'll get your revenge one day, Rhys, but don't allow hatred to cloud your judgement; always think carefully."

"I've made up my mind, Arteg."

"Yes, I know… you're going to Caerllion, aren't you?"

"How did you know that?" Rhys felt that Arteg had always really wanted him to stay at Penhal, despite continuously whetting his appetite with stories of glorious battles.

"I just knew. It will be good for you to learn how to read and write the Roman language, but you can still train with Arthur's army at Caerllion at the same time. I've been thinking, we can get Ruthall to write a letter to my good friend, Cynan, Prince Arthur's best captain, asking him to train you after school. He'll be able to fix it. After all, you were the best friend of his brother, Cunval, and Cynan will always remember that."

The previous summer, Rhys remembered, Arteg and his warriors had joined Cynan in an expedition to seek out some Saxon raiders near the headwaters of the Tamesis River.

"When we finally tracked down the enemy in open country," mused Arteg, "we rode them down before they could scatter. The Saxons rarely use horses, their strength is in numbers at close quarters with battle-axes and swords. Fortunately, they're not skilful with war-bows, but now they've found it unhealthy to make incursions into our home-lands, they've turned their attention to attacking our coast with their fast longships and making surprise raids at dawn. We never know where or when."

Rhys sat proudly in the saddle. Caerllion might be a bit overwhelming at first, but there would surely be a chance to get close to Prince Arthur, the leader of the King's cavalry, and maybe take part in future expeditions.

"I know I'll have to commit myself to the monastery school, Arteg, but every harvest time I'll be able to return to Penhal and then enjoy the late summer with you and the warriors." He was now too old to play games with the children; he had a man's work to do.

When they arrived at the cemetery, they found the other warriors already drinking Ruthall's cyder. Large quantities had been made from the estate orchards in the autumn and Ruthall, although he could not refuse to share what had been allotted to him, was concerned that the warriors often seemed to end up at his enclosure after hunting or training.

"Here, Rhys," called one of the warriors, "Ruthall is making some more honey-cakes, and with our favourite cherry jam!" Tough training was now forgotten.

The children, despite an earlier breakfast, had eaten all of Ruthall's previous batch of cakes. They swarmed around the warriors, pulling at their beards. One of the warriors had gutted the deer and was busy chopping up some of the still-warm entrails for the dogs. Hawk gratefully joined in.

"Now, Ruthall," said Arteg. "I want you to write a letter for me. I want to send a message to my old friend Cynan." Rhys hoped he could help with the composition of such an important letter.

"I'll just leave these cakes cooking," said Ruthall as he moved two sloping flat stones nearer to the fire. Ruthall always looked so awkward in his long brown tunic, thought Rhys. "Now Rhys, this will be a good chance for you to help me translate Arteg's message into Latin, and, no doubt, Cynan can get one of the monks in Caerllion to read it back to him. I have some parchment and a quill in my hut."

Rhys pulled a face, but knew that the children, particularly, would be watching him with great interest.

"Greetings, Cynan, dear friend," dictated Arteg staring up at the sky. "Could you train Rhys after school…"

"Not too fast," pleaded Rhys as he and Ruthall both struggled to get the words set down correctly. The children crowded around to see the letters being formed. They had all practised scratching their own names onto newly made jars and mugs at the pottery kiln, but writing a complete message was a mystery to them.

Arteg struggled through his letter with help from Ruthall and then the parchment was laid out to dry. "There," said Arteg, clapping his hands with satisfaction, "now, are those cakes ready?"

***

The rest of the day was spent in jousting and archery on the big field. Rhys was now so accurate with his bow and arrows that he almost matched the warriors in target practice.

Arteg walked over to Brochvael, who had been watching from his bench and sipping wine. "Rhys will become a champion within a few years and Caerllion will be just the place to continue his training. I've sent a message to Cynan to take him in hand."

"We'll see," muttered Brochvael through his dirty beard. The old man loved his grandson; he could see his own dead sons in Rhys' features now that he was growing up. "I sorely wanted him to stay at Penhal where we could personally groom him as heir to the estate, but I know that letting him go to Caerllion might well be in the best interests of the family. I only hope he's not sent into battle…"

Arteg sighed. "If he has to go into battle under Prince Arthur, he'll be in good hands."

Brochvael scoffed.

"I remember that young Arthur. An arrogant, spoilt pest of a lad. However, I've heard he's certainly a leader of men now he's been trained by his father, my old friend King Myric. Apparently he's as clever as a raven, as cunning as a fox and as brave as a dog-wolf."

Both men laughed uneasily.

CHAPTER 2

Goodbye to Penhal

The morning mist gave way to sunshine as preparations were made for the journey upstream. Olwen, as the oldest girl, was to ride one of the bigger horses with Fach, the smallest boy, sitting in front of her. Fach, always cheerful despite his malformed leg, grinned proudly at the other children as they were helped onto their ponies by the farm labourers. The labourers were glad to help the children; this was a welcome diversion from their early morning march to the fields for the back-breaking job of ploughing and harrowing.

Rhys swung himself up onto Beech, his own unpredictable stallion. The other warriors had been wary of Beech while he was being broken in, but Rhys was able to talk to him quietly and tell him secretly of his plans to ride east one day. As the dominant horse, Beech, had the lead position and Rhys allowed him to rear and whinny in front of the other horses. After settling him down, Rhys was handed two large jars of wine to strap carefully onto his saddle and some metal tools as gifts for Blaeno. Food and milk were slung across the ponies, and everything was ready.

This was the first spring that Rhys had been put in charge of any expeditions. As a grown lad and a future leader, lately he had been given more and more responsibility by Brochvael. As the party proceeded upriver, Rhys kept a lookout out for any danger from the parts of the bank gouged out by winter floods. The river level was still high and the water looked icy cold.

"There we are, children, the first flowers and buds, there, where it's sheltered." Rhys pointed out the various signs of early spring. Rhys' mother called this the 'magical re-birth of the land' – a saying older than time in the Celtic world.

When they reached halfway, Rhys led the file up a steep slope to gain a high vantage point for their rest-stop. Olwen, as usual, took control of the laying out of bread, cheese, milk and eggs, then finally gave them permission to start eating.

"Don't eat too quickly," she snapped at Rhys, ignoring the fact that Fach was cramming food into his mouth with both hands. Rhys merely shrugged. It had been a while since breakfast and Rhys was relieved when the endless chatter abated as the children ate. Although he had made sure that the horses were tethered so they could graze quietly, he couldn't understand why he felt so edgy. It was true that he hadn't seen Helena for some weeks, but surely he wasn't needlessly nervous? Perhaps she had forgotten all about that kiss. Perhaps she had an admirer somewhere else; there were plenty of other young men in the outlying farms. "Right. Hurry up, you lot," he said, suddenly anxious to be off.

"I haven't finished clearing up yet," scolded Olwen as she threw the scraps to the waiting dogs. "And I want to pick some nice flowers for Helena's mother." Rhys could only shrug once more – she was getting more bossy every day.

On the noisy ride upriver to Blaeno, there was much excitement at the new white blossom of the trees. The river level had now dropped to show a clear gravel bed over the shallows so there would shortly be fresh salmon to cook over open fires. The farm dogs at Blaeno heard the expedition approaching and soon there was a shrieking group of children and barking dogs running towards them.

Rhys made straight for Marc's house and jumped off his horse with such mock bravado that Marc had to catch him as he stumbled and fell to the ground. When he looked up, Helena was emerging through the doorway, looking a little surprised to see the embarrassed figure on the ground. Marc, smiling gently, was quick to speak.

"Welcome, young warrior. Do you need a helping hand?"

Helena, flustered at seeing Rhys, dashed back into the house. Rhys, although embarrassed, couldn't help having noticed Helena's new shape beneath her plaid dress. As for her light brown hair, he couldn't remember it being that long. He quickly grasped Marc's hand in an adult greeting and dusted himself down as the children looked on.

"I think I know why you're here, Rhys," said Marc slowly. Rhys looked away – he knew exactly why he was here. "You've decided, haven't you?"

"Oh, ah, yes, yes. I'm off to Caerllion tomorrow. I thought I'd come up and say goodbye and give the children a good run. I trust everybody is well and healthy?"

From the doorway, Marc's wife Julia said, "Of course, Rhys, that is, all except Helena. I don't know why she's being so shy." Rhys could sense a little awkwardness all round. Fortunately, he remembered the gifts.

"Some wine from the Gwei valley, and I'm sure you can soon make some wooden handles for these tools." With Marc's help, Rhys carefully untied the stout leather strap between the jars and they lowered one each with fitting caution.

"Good. Brochvael promised me some wine after the winter. He must have appreciated those steers I sent him. Now, let me show you our new calves and lambs; it's been a good spring." They led Beech into the paddock away from the farm's own stallions and wandered into the orchard. Rhys glanced around from time to time to see if Helena had yet slipped out of the house.

"Well, Rhys, I'm glad that you're going to Caerllion. I spent many years there as a young warrior, but I never saw much action. Most of the time I was just a city guard. My captain said I was a farmer at heart and couldn't be trusted with anything more dangerous." Marc laughed lightly. "That was probably true, you know, but you Rhys, you're different. I hear that you've been talking more and more about killing Saxons."

Rhys folded his arms and looked down at his boots. "I have to go to the monastery to learn about reading and writing, but I think Cynan is going to help me to train with the soldiers as well."

"I can give you a lot of advice, Rhys. If you don't mind me saying so, you've had a sheltered boyhood at Penhal. When you start living in Caerllion, you'll have older boys knocking you about, and in the college you'll find life very strict. I remember seeing the younger monastery lads being beaten with sticks if they disobeyed their masters." Marc smiled as Rhys winced.

Rhys hadn't envisaged a life of discipline – he had been more interested in seeing the soldiers and the ships. He'd only been in one real fight and that was down in Abermenei when some older boys had picked on him and he had suffered a bloody nose. Still, he wasn't worried about being hurt; Arteg had said it would make him tougher.

Marc looked around and waved. Helena was walking towards them, her hair hanging down over her shoulders. As she got closer, Rhys started to blush. This was terrible – she would notice and think him too young to talk to. What could he say to her? He hoped that his worn leather jerkin and dirty boots wouldn't put her off.

"I've heard you're leaving tomorrow, Rhys." Even her voice was different – very confident and grown up. "I'm glad that you've decided to go to the school at the monastery. Mother says you'll enjoy it once you settle in."

Rhys coughed awkwardly as Marc patted him on the head. "Oh, but he's going to have a rough time, Helena. You should feel sorry for him." They all laughed and shuffled their feet.

"I'll be fine. Ruthall says I'll make lots of new friends and see the parades and the tournaments." Rhys couldn't bring himself to look at Helena as he spoke; her eyes were so beautiful, he could only glance quickly at them.

"Let's go over and check the older lambs and calves," said Marc, "we have to keep an eye on them occasionally during the day in case they get into the river."

Strolling through the orchard, the bees, small birds and clouds of insects built up a loud buzzing noise that was most pleasing to the ear.

"Isn't springtime wonderful?" said Helena. Rhys could only nod in agreement. They arrived at a gate and leant on the top bar smiling at the young animals at play – all was well and the conversation grew more natural. Rhys started to relax.

"Oh. I've just remembered, I've got some hides for Brochvael," said Marc. "I'd better prepare them. Now don't stay too long, Helena." With that he strode back across the orchard. Rhys and Helena looked at each other and smiled. The tension had gone as they both realised that Marc had probably meant them to be alone. At least they were out of sight of the children.

"You'll be gone for years, Rhys. It must be terrible when your grandfather expects you to be a brave warrior. I hope you don't have to go off and fight…" Helena stopped as she realised that this might be bringing back dreadful memories for Rhys.

"It was bad for you too, Helena, when your cousin was killed in the same battle as my uncle. I've got to avenge them. It was only since I last saw you that I've started to feel real anger."

Helena put her hand on his arm and looked into his eyes warmly. "I think I understand. Dear Rhys, I'm going to miss you so much. I was hoping to come down to Penhal in the summer with mother."

"I'll be back for the harvest. I'll come straight up to Blaeno to see you if you like." Rhys put his hand on Helena's and squeezed; this was what he had been praying for. She turned her hand and their fingers intertwined. Did she really like him?

"I'll pray for you, Rhys. My great aunt taught me many things when she lived with us. I didn't take much notice then, but it's surprising how I keep remembering all the advice she used to give me. Perhaps I'm growing up."

Rhys smiled easily. He felt good. "You're more grown up than ever I remember you, Helena. I wish I wasn't going to Caerllion now."

They laughed together as their fingers squeezed tightly. There wasn't much else to say. They watched the lambs running madly from one tree to another and then pressed their shoulders together in a mutual understanding.

"I feel that we'll always be in each other's thoughts, Rhys. I just know that we'll be together one day." Rhys looked down at the ground. He had to swallow a few times – this was, indeed, his own wish.

"We'd better go back now," whispered Helena, letting go of Rhys' hand.

"Can I kiss you goodbye, Helena?" Rhys put his hands on Helena's arms and, drawing her close, kissed her gently on the lips before reluctantly turning away. Their first kiss the year before had been just childish fun, but this was a moment to be remembered.

***

They ran back to the noisy children, who were setting up benches and tables in the warm sunshine. Olwen, as usual, wanted to organise everything and Julia thought it better to agree with her and then make her own adjustments. The boys were more interested in Rhys' training with the warriors and produced bows and arrows to indulge in some archery practice. Two of the Blaeno boys were now thirteen and spoke endlessly of joining the warriors at Penhal after next year's harvest.

"Let's set up some targets, Rhys. Marc said you could use his bow, and we'll use the smaller bows. We killed a hare last winter you know and we nearly got a deer!" The bigger lad could hardly stop talking and Rhys laughed at his enthusiasm.

"Now, you have to stand properly… see. And don't take your eye off the target." The three young warriors had moved well away from the crowd, but Rhys knew that the children would be watching. He hoped Helena was impressed.

"There," said Rhys triumphantly, as the first arrow struck the upturned log with a thud. "You have to have the second arrow ready as the first one strikes."

Rhys fired off six arrows and scored four hits; his constant practice was paying off and cheers rose from the crowd.

The boys, anxious to show off their own skill, shouted loudly as they, in turn, scored an occasional hit. The doors of the barn provided the next target as the group retrieved their arrows and eagerly continued the game. Eventually, the onlookers called them to the tables and the feast began.

"Are Arteg and Helga still friendly?" enquired Julia offhandedly during a lull in the conversation. Rhys knew that she was dying to know all about Arteg's pursuit of Helga, the Saxon widow of his uncle Catvael.

"Of course they are," said Olwen, before Rhys could speak. "Young Cadaer is three now and a terrible handful, I have to watch him all the time. When Catvael captured Helga as a slave, he had no idea she was a Saxon princess, you know, and then he fell deeply in love with her…"

Rhys groaned; he had heard the story so many times. The mention of Helga brought back many memories for Rhys. Catvael, the Penhal war leader, had captured Helga after a battle and eventually her hatred for him turned to love. He had been killed before their son was born and she had grieved for almost a year.

More importantly, Helga had heard of a white-haired Saxon leader who had been at the battle eleven years earlier and who had boasted of killing many Britons. This had tied in with Arteg's account of Rhys' father charging forward on his horse, much too far, and fighting a fierce Saxon with flowing white hair. By the time Arteg and the rest of the Penhal warband had got to him, Rhys' father had been fatally wounded and the Saxon had escaped back to his comrades. Some prisoners had called him The Wolf, a name that haunted Rhys.

"Anyway," continued Olwen, "I'm sure Helga has fallen in love with Arteg and I think they're going to get married and have lots of babies. He shaves his beard every day now, you know." Even Helena looked sheepish as Olwen waved her arms about in her enthusiasm.

Olwen continued her story. "Little Cadaer loves to see the horses and sometimes Arteg puts him up in his saddle and pretends to send him off for a ride. Of course, Helga goes mad and kicks Arteg and then he teases her, but she doesn't take any notice, you know. I don't know what she sees in him. He's a real brute. She'll never convert him to Christianity."

Julia had been listening intently as Olwen was speaking. "Do Arteg and the warriors still worship the gods, then?"

"No!" said Olwen exasperated. "They've finished all that. Mind you, Brochvael still goes into the old shrine sometimes, but no one else bothers now."

Julia turned to the younger children. "We got rid of our shrine years ago when my mad old aunty pulled it to pieces with her bare hands. Mind you, we were all glad really, but we didn't want to upset Brochvael."

"Oh, that reminds me," Olwen butted in again. "Ruthall is coming up to see you soon; he's got some new stories for the children." The younger children clapped their hands – story telling was always something to look forward to.

Helena could see that the older boys were starting to lose interest. "Now that Helga's a Christian, Rhys, do you think that all the Saxons will one day become Christians and stay over in the east? You wouldn't have to fight them, then."

"Perhaps. Anyway, I'm going to make sure they don't ever come here again."

"Rhys can speak their language, you know… can't you Rhys?" Rhys nodded as Olwen took over once more. "Helga makes Rhys talk all the time, because she says that, one day, he will need to talk with the Saxons. And Helga can speak our language pretty well too. Brochvael says that he cannot believe that he has a grandson, who is half Saxon and will grow up speaking both languages."

Everybody laughed; this was, indeed, all very strange. Rhys only smiled; he knew that Helga had dreams of her young Cadaer being a mediator between the two enemies when he grew up.

Marc had been listening with interest. "That sounds good, Rhys. I know there are Saxon slaves in Caerllion, perhaps you will be able to talk with them and get some useful information." Rhys nodded again – he had already considered that.

Once everyone had eaten their fill, it was time for the boys to mount their horses and go exploring. The younger lads complained that they had not been invited, but the two older boys wanted Rhys to themselves – they had much to show him around, the woods and the riverside. Taking up their bows, they promised to bring back some venison, or at the very least a hare. As they galloped off together, Rhys hoped that Helena would notice his expert horsemanship.

The boys, with an excited pack of dogs, explored every likely wood and moor in their search for deer or wild boar. The dogs, too excited to stick to the finer points of seeking out and bringing back their quarry, finished up chasing any animals that came their way. The three boys loved every moment of this wild chase, and although Rhys knew that he would soon be leaving this wonderful life of freedom and fun, he braced himself with thoughts of new adventures in Caerllion.

On the way back to Blaeno the dogs finally raised a young stag from the bracken. Rhys was just close enough to spur on his horse and prepare his bow. As the stag leapt up a bank and then slowed for a moment, Rhys turned Beech and let fly with a deadly arrow. The sharp point pierced the animal through the front ribs and caused it to stumble and fall backwards. The other boys in an instant drew their bows and one more arrow found its mark. The stag scrambled to its feet and tried to run into the forest, but the dogs had now caught up and pounced. In the blink of an eye, Rhys had galloped forward to jump down from Beech with his dagger drawn. He grabbed the beast's antlers with his left hand and plunged his dagger into the baying animal's heart. Death was swift and merciful.

The dogs were reluctantly drawn back and the three boys cut through the stag's windpipe to release a torrent of steaming blood. The carcass was pulled up the bank to allow full blood-letting and the dogs dived into the flowing red mass to satisfy their instinctive craving. For those few moments, the boys had become primitive hunters – their desire to hunt and kill an animal for food was very satisfying. They wallowed in self-congratulation.

"We'll hang it over my horse," offered Rhys. "I think Beech was the real hunter you know!" The two younger boys agreed; they knew that they would have been outrun by the stag had Rhys not been there with his bow.

At the sound of distant barking and whooping huntsmen,

the whole community of Blaeno came out to see their homecoming. They were a little startled when the three horsemen galloped up to them and threw the dead stag to the ground.

"He's ready for gutting," declared Rhys. "We've already bled him."

"Well done, boys. A couple of days hanging and we'll be having a feast. I think you should take a haunch back with you to Penhal." Marc slapped Rhys on the shoulder in congratulation, but he was nevertheless aware that Rhys and Helena were more interested in looking at each other.

Helena took Beech's reins. "I've got some nice herb broth for you, boys, you must be thirsty after all that hunting. And we're just cooking some oatcakes." Rhys was elated – there was no doubt in his mind that Helena was very impressed by the kill.

It was soon time to leave and Helena offered to walk a little way with Rhys. The rest of the children, of course, had to join in, but the couple – now true sweethearts in everybody's eyes – were able to walk hand-in-hand together with Beech trailing dutifully on his reins. There wasn't much to say and a quiet sadness hung over them.

"We'll meet again at harvest time," whispered Helena as she kissed Rhys firmly on the cheek. Rhys felt very pleased with himself as he gazed into her eyes.

CHAPTER 3

The Initiation

The night before his departure, Rhys had not slept well and did not appreciate the excitement around him. As he prepared his horse, everybody wanted to wish him good luck, but some of the women looked as forlorn as if he was going off to war. A packhorse was being prepared for some goods to be delivered downstream to Abermenei and this was Brochvael's opportunity to return some empty wine jars to the governor, Pedur. Rhys had strapped his bow and a quiver of arrows onto Beech, together with two bundles – one with his personal belongings in it, the other containing the few carpentry tools that had once belonged to his friend, Brother Cunval.

After a full breakfast, the time arrived to mount up; Brochvael hugged Rhys so hard he coughed and Arteg gripped his hand until he felt his bones would crack. The children danced around him as his mother tried not to cry, but Olwen stood by quietly.

"Remember all I've taught you, Rhys. You'll be up against some big lads at Caerllion and you'll need to be alert to the wily ones too." Arteg was not usually emotional, thought

Rhys; perhaps it was because Helga and young Cadaer were holding his hand. Rhys nodded to Helga and wished them all well in the Saxon language; he would return at harvest time. Arteg looked on proudly as Rhys jumped expertly into his saddle.

With everybody staring at him, Rhys began to feel uneasy. Now it was time to go, he could not admit or show that he was now a little frightened. Giving a wave of his hand, he spurred Beech onto the trackway that led around the stockade and then followed the river downstream. The children ran a little of the way and then, as they held back a whining Hawk, Rhys was on his own. He had travelled this route many times, but with an overcast sky threatening rain, it had never before felt quite so miserable. He pulled his woollen cloak tightly around his neck.

It was nearly a whole morning's ride down to the town and, as usual, the dogs and the children were the first to spot him. His good friend Conmael galloped across the meadow on his pony to greet him.

"Hail, Rhys, what are we going to do today, go hunting? I've feathered some new arrows. Well, what do you say?"

"I'm going to Caerllion. I've got some things to deliver to Pedur, then I'm off." Rhys looked steadily at his friend, anticipating the shock his words would produce.

"But I thought you would surely be staying at Penhal. How long will you be away?" Conmael was obviously unhappy to be losing his good friend.

"Don't worry, I'll be back for the harvest. We'll have plenty of time for fishing and hunting, then I'll be able to tell you all about the coast and the ships, and I'll be able to teach you to read and write." Rhys laughed as Conmael pulled a face. "Perhaps you'll want to go yourself next year and then I can show you all the sights."

On reaching the town with the children in tow, they all made for the house of Pedur, the town's governor. It was the duty of everybody passing through a town to report to the governor and relate any messages, at the same time taking messages to pass on to their next stop. Rhys was warmly welcomed as usual and given broth and bread. He now had to offer Brochvael's greetings and pass on news of the estate. After that, leaving the packhorse behind, he had one more call to make with Conmael before resuming his journey. The town priest, Tidioc, had his cemetery and hut on the banks of the wide Gwei river. That was where Rhys had first met Cynan, the King's captain who had been badly wounded in the great battle at Corinium and where the two priests, Tidioc and Cynan's brother, Cunval, had nursed him back to health. Rhys wondered if he would meet Cynan at Caerllion, and would he even remember him?

"My goodness," enthused Tidioc striding from his enclosure, "you look more like a warrior every time I see you. Now, don't tell me, you're off to Caerllion. I knew you would." Once more Rhys' hand was gripped in a friendly clasp.

"I can't stop now, Tidioc. I want to get to Caerllion well before nightfall." Rhys wheeled his horse around, not wanting to let Tidioc see the moisture in his eyes. He loved the priests he had met in his short life, but what good would they be in a battle with the Saxons?

Tidioc shouted after him in jest. "Take Conmael with you, Rhys. I can't teach him any more here. Good luck… and give my regards to Bishop Dyfrig."

Rhys and Conmael cantered down the roadway past Abermenei to the river bridge. Rhys was glad of the company, but well before noon they parted – it felt as if it were for the last time. One consolation was the singing of the birds in the roadside undergrowth, although the cackling rooks tending their nests sounded a little forlorn.

Brochvael had given Rhys careful instructions on the landmarks to look out for on his journey; the old Roman road was well worn and easy to follow. The main stopping place was Caer Bigga and as they approached the town gateway, Rhys could see that Beech was in need of water and rest. He dismounted near a stream to let Beech drink and quenched his own thirst from his water flask. Walking on to the gateway, he approached the inevitable crowd of curious children and asked them the way to the town governor. It made Rhys feel important to have to announce himself; it was the first time he had been so far from home. He puffed out his chest and strode purposefully forward, just as Arteg had always instructed him.

The children knew better than to be disrespectful to a stranger with a bow and helped lead Beech through the dirty streets. Some interested townsfolk greeted him; it was rare for them to see a bold young man entering their town.

The governor and his wife strode from their old Roman

quarters on hearing the children approaching and warmly welcomed Rhys. "That's a fine mount you have there, young man. Now, if I'm not mistaken, you're off to join the army in Caerllion." The governor patted Rhys' bow. "Come inside and tell me all about yourself. My wife has some stew and I have some good wine."

Rhys introduced himself and offered greetings from Brochvael.

"Well, well. So you're Brochvael's grandson? Oh, I've just remembered… Brochvael lost both of his sons. I'm sorry, Rhys. You've had some bad luck at Penhal."

The governor's wife put her hand on Rhys' shoulder as he sat down at the table. Suddenly he felt a little lost in this new environment and stared at the floor for a moment.

"I'm really looking forward to seeing Caerllion," Rhys sat up straight again. "I know Cynan, and I've already met Bishop Dyfrig, and when the army passed through after the big battle I saw the King…".

"Well done, well done," said the Governor. "You're just the sort of lad they need in Caerllion. I went into many battles with your grandfather, you know. Well, they weren't big battles like the one at Corinium, but vicious enough. Now, eat first and then tell me all the gossip about the Penhal estate."

As he told the couple all about his training with Arteg, they listened attentively and soon Rhys was in full flow describing the farms on Brochvael's estate and the latest news from Abermenei. He realised that grown-ups loved to know everything that was going on elsewhere. The governor's wife, he knew, would be delighted with the story of Arteg and Helga, so Rhys spun out the whole story. She sighed with satisfaction.

Too soon, it was time to journey on. The governor rose from the table. "I'll walk over the army bridge with you and point you in the right direction."

The two new acquaintances strolled through the town to the bridge.

"Call again at harvest time, Rhys. You must tell me all about your first summer at the school." The governor raised his hand in farewell as Rhys spurred Beech on down the road to Caerllion.

***

The overcast day had developed into warm spring sunshine and Rhys was now looking forward to his first sight of the King's great city. Beech seemed to sense Rhys' excitement as he trotted firmly along the old stone roadway. Hills and woods lay in every direction and the first greenery and white blossom now showed up pleasingly against the green-grey background of the forests.

The afternoon passed quickly and before long the road led gently to a promontory from where Rhys could just see the tiled roofs of what he knew must be the monastery buildings. As he approached the summit of Saint Aaron's Hill, he gasped; never had he seen such a sight. The monastery and its many outbuildings set into the hillside below him was breathtaking, but on the low hillside beyond was the splendour of Caerllion city. There were many red-tiled roofs and the stone buildings and columns dwarfed anything he had seen at Abermenei. Some of the buildings had been lime-washed and shone pure white in the sunshine. A huge stone wall surrounded the centre of the city. There were other buildings across the Isca river and farms and houses on every hillside. Rhys' found his misgivings forgotten as he thrilled to be at his destination.

White clouds against the blue sky over the far ridge line meant one thing. The estuary and ocean were almost within reach. As Rhys gave a low whistle, Beech looked around and whinnied; he, too, seemed to know that this was journey's end and he could smell other horses in the air. The roadway to the monastery was quite steep, so Rhys dismounted and walked slowly down to a walled entrance, at the same time taking in the now distinct noise and bustle of splendid Caerllion city in the distance.

The yard past the gateway was quiet and empty; Rhys looked around hoping to see somebody and proceeded slowly towards an arched doorway. The big oak door was firmly shut, so Rhys, holding Beech's reins in one hand, leaned forward to knock. His hand smarted as the hard wood hurt his knuckles, then the door slowly moved inwards, creaking. A smiling face peered around the edge of the door; this was obviously one of the pupils, not much older than Rhys.

"I'm sorry, I thought you were one of the warriors. I couldn't see properly through the window." Rhys looked up; the few windows were small and high up, like the ones in the large stone houses that he had heard of.

"I'm Rhys of Penhal," stated Rhys, puffing out his chest.

"Penhal? I've heard of Penhal." With that the boy, now holding the door wide open revealing his long brown tunic, shouted into the darkness of the interior. "Brothers. Brothers. It's Ruthall's friend, Rhys from Penhal… come quickly."

Rhys had not expected to be known so far from home.

"Bishop Dyfrig said I could come here for schooling," said Rhys flatly; he could hear running footsteps inside. "I was told to ask for Abbot Aidan."

A host of other young pupils rushed through the doorway making Beech rear up, shaking his head angrily. Rhys soothed him and held back the inquisitive boys. They stared at Rhys intently. He was not used to being stared at like this.

"Welcome. Welcome," they all chanted together and yet again Rhys' hands were grasped. A senior monk in a dark tunic pushed through the mob to look Rhys up and down. But when he saw the bow strapped onto Beech he glowered angrily.

"I'm Father Fracan. I'll take you straight up to Abbot Aidan." This seemed to be a command. "The boys will put your horse into the stables and bring in your packs." As the boys started rushing forward once more, Rhys knew that Beech would rear up again; did they know nothing of horses?

"He won't go into a stable without me," warned Rhys, looking at Fracan. "He needs to be rubbed down and watered. Perhaps I should do that first."

"Very well, young man. Dingad, you and Govan help him; and get rid of that awful bow and arrows." Fracan was obviously in charge and one not to be offended.

Rhys turned Beech toward the stables where two old nags were looking over their doors indifferently. Beech ignored them too. Dingad and Govan, although a little older than Rhys, regarded him warily but with dawning respect. Arriving with a large stallion and a fearsome looking bow, he was an unknown quantity. They gently coaxed Beech into a large stable with clean straw and hay. The boys dipped buckets into a large water butt and followed Rhys inside as he started to rub Beech down with clean hay. Just as Rhys had expected, they asked him many questions; he was now resigned to this and realised that everybody he met would want to know everything about him.

When the saddle had been hung up and Rhys' packs put by the door, the boys looked nervously at the bow and quiver full of arrows.

"We'll have to hide these up in the loft, Rhys. Abbot Aidan would go mad if he saw them indoors." Govan scaled a ladder and Dingad handed the offensive items up to him.

"They'll be safe up here," Govan assured Rhys with a satisfied smirk.

They then entered the cold gloomy building and Rhys was led up a stone staircase – something he had never seen before – with Fracan leading the way and the two skinny young pupils struggling to carry Rhys' packs between them.

Abbot Aidan, a stout elderly man but with a full head of greying hair, sat behind a table strewn with parchments held down by pebbles. Light from the south streamed through a window behind him and through it Rhys could just glimpse the town in the distance.

Hands folded over his pot-belly, Aidan looked for any signs of rebellion; the last thing he wanted in the monastery was a troublesome young man, and boys from country farms were not always easy to discipline.

"Welcome to Saint Aaron's monastery and school, Rhys. I remember seeing you at Penhal when I accompanied the bishop to Cunval's funeral. Were you forced to come here?" Aidan was testing him out.

"No, sire. I have always wanted to come to this school. Cunval told me all about it." Rhys hoped that Aidan would not suspect his other, more real motive. "I can already do some reading and writing, and I'm quite used to rising early in the mornings."

"Good. Good. It's time for our evening refreshment, so you can join Fracan and the boys for supper before prayers." Rhys had been trying to get a better view of the town as Aidan was speaking. But that word 'prayers' gave him a jolt: it was something that probably he would have to endure every day. A younger boy entered with a tray of food for Aidan – it looked more like a feast when it was placed on the table. Rhys hoped that the pupils' food would be just as plentiful.

"After prayers in the morning," continued Aidan, "come and see me and I'll arrange a new tunic for you. You can keep your old clothes 'til then." They all stared at Rhys' homespun woollen trousers, leather jerkin, and muddy, well-worn boots. Rhys was not at all sure that he really wanted to wear a tunic.

Then Fracan and the boys led Rhys up another set of stone stairs to the dormitory. The younger boys stood up respectfully when Fracan entered and he showed Rhys to his bed – it looked quite comfortable, with woollen blankets and a soft pillow.

"You all know the rules; especially the one about not touching other pupils' belongings," said Fracan as Rhys' packs were deposited on his new bed. Rhys wondered what Fracan would say if he knew that one of the packs contained his precious dagger, inherited from his father.

Introductions were made all around. There were twenty or so boys in the dormitory. Some of them had only just joined, while others had been there for a lot longer. Rhys knew that they would have come from all over the Silurian territory for schooling – some would go on to be monks or priests and some might later want to return to their farms, or even become warriors. Ruthall had explained that the college instructed them all to become good Christians, but the final choice rested with each pupil. The system of schooling had been devised by the King who hoped for a steady supply of willing, educated soldiers for his army.

The eating area was a huge hall near the entrance of the monastery with long oak tables set on stone-slabbed floors. Wooden bowls and small jars of salt lay evenly spaced along the tables and a smell from the kitchens wafted through the air as about sixty young wolves sat down on the benches. Rhys was seated next to Dingad and Govan. Younger boys brought in cauldrons of fish stew and baskets of bread. Dingad held down Rhys' arm to show that he must wait and not start eating yet. They all rose to their feet, then Fracan and two younger monks mumbled some prayers in the Roman tongue.

Rhys bowed his head like the others, but had no idea what the chanting meant.

Prayers over, the congregation sat down and the young boys ladled out the stew.

"We can eat now," whispered Dingad eagerly "but try and save some bread for later. We won't get anything else until breakfast, and we're not allowed to talk at meals."

The stew was fairly good and Rhys was able to hide some bread in his jerkin, just like the others who all seemed to be quietly hiding bread in their tunics. A cauldron of milk appeared and an exact amount was ladled into mugs and passed around. Rhys began to find it all a bit boring; he wanted to see the town and began to wonder if he would ever be allowed out.

Finally Fracan rose and stood at the doorway.

"Quietly, now… top table first," he said. The older boys filed silently through the doorway, Rhys fitting in between his two companions who ushered him to his place.

The trek down dark corridors seemed endless, but the chapel itself was a revelation to Rhys, although he had heard it described by his friends, the priests, several times. The light, as the late afternoon sun shone through windows made of small panes of coloured glass, had a magical effect. The boys obediently squeezed onto the narrow benches and Dingad smiled as Rhys' eyes wandered around the stone walls and up to the timber-vaulted ceiling.

"See the west window behind us, Rhys. That's an image of Saint Aaron, they say he's watching over us all the time. We often come in here when the sun is setting. That's the best time to feel his presence."

Soon everybody was seated and prayers began. Rhys thought he knew what to expect, but they seemed to go on forever. Still, it was a good chance to be able to daydream – and Helena was foremost in his thoughts.

"We're off to the fields now, Rhys. You're lucky, the ploughing has all been done and now it's just the harrowing and sowing that's left."

This was going to be a long evening, thought Rhys. Would he ever be able to visit the town?

Groups of boys were sent to the various outbuildings to collect tools and Rhys grabbed the chance to check on Beech. A warm greeting from his beloved horse showed Rhys that Beech had settled in comfortably. Perhaps he even liked the company of the old mares in the neighbouring stalls. After the three boys had fussed over and stroked the horses, they collected some heavy hoes and made for the ploughed fields down by the river. Fracan was in charge of one large group and got the boys hoeing and breaking up the soil which had been well tilled. It was dry enough to break up fairly easily.

Dingad and Govan started to describe life in the monastery, causing Rhys to wonder if he had made the right decision. It all sounded very strict. Although Dingad was the same size as him, Rhys could hardly stop smiling at Govan. He was small with freckles, sandy hair and a squint. He seemed to have difficulty in lifting up the hoe. Rhys was thinking of his ambition to become a well-schooled warrior like Cynan, and his vigorous hoeing caused the other boys to gape.

Dingad shook his head and continued his explanations. "Fracan calls us early every morning, and I mean early, Rhys. Govan has a job to wake up and I have to drag him from his bed. Then it's a wash in cold water, then to prayers and later some breakfast just before we collapse." Rhys knew that Dingad was exaggerating for his benefit when Govan laughed loudly. "Then we start lessons…"

"Just a short break, boys," shouted Fracan and everybody dropped their hoes. Dingad straightened up and sighed. "Let's soothe our hands in the river. Rhys, I'll show you the pool where we go swimming." The whole work-gang ambled to the river and soaked their hot hands.

Rhys was used to hard work and brandishing weapons, so he was not bothered about getting blisters. He examined the two boys' hands.

"How long have you been here, since your skin is so tough?" he asked.

"I've been here since I was ten and now I'm sixteen," replied Dingad. "Govan's only been here for two years. Why didn't your parents send you earlier?"

"I'm not here just for schooling, you know. I'm going to train with the King's army as well. And I'm going to see the coast. Have you two ever seen the sea?"

"Of course," said Dingad surprised. "But the Abbot will never let you leave the monastery to go with the soldiers. The only day we don't work is a Sunday, and then we go for walks and have three services."

Rhys' dismay was interrupted by a shout from Fracan – it was back to work. "Now don't go too fast, Rhys," advised Dingad. "You don't want to wear yourself out."

Rhys' idea of learning on some days and doing military training on others was obviously not going to fit in with the organised monastic life. He decided he certainly wasn't going to be a monk.

"I've got a letter for Cynan, the King's captain, he'll sort things out, you'll see." The boys looked puzzled as Rhys once more attacked the soil with his hoe. He had some fast thinking to do.

***

Eventually the work was done and all the boys stripped off to bathe in the river. Normally they would all wash thoroughly in the monastery bathhouse, but if the weather was not too cold, washing in the river saved congestion indoors. With spirits high, now that the working day was over, the boys started splashing each other. The river was really only a wide stream with pools just deep enough for a short swim, but with the water still icy cold, running and jumping, then leaping out of the water was sport enough.

"We're allowed to go for a walk in the gardens and orchards before dark," enthused Dingad as they shivered and dressed. "I'm starving! It's a good job we saved these crusts, don't you think?"

Rhys agreed. "I may have a little present for you later," he added mysteriously. He had just remembered that his pack contained bread, cheese, butter and boiled eggs for his journey, not to mention honey-cakes. There had been no occasion to even unpack them during his journey.

The many aspects of the gardens were now interesting to Rhys: the high brick walls surrounding the vegetable gardens were covered with budding fruit trees and the long rows of field beans were already growing tall in the sheltered part of the garden. The senior boys had milked the cows earlier and were now carrying pails of milk to the dairy. Time was certainly not wasted in this hard-working community.

At bedtime, the whole dormitory seemed to congregate around Rhys' bed as word got around that he had a 'present'. It was getting dark and one solitary candle on a table in the centre of the room would be the only light until sunrise. Rhys opened his pack to lay out the food.

"Food," gasped all the boys together; this was indeed manna from heaven. It was left to Dingad to try and share out the various items.

"Here," said Rhys, laughing. "You'll need a knife." He drew his sharp dagger from the sheath in his pack, but the boys jumped back fearfully.

"You can't keep a knife in the monastery," pleaded Dingad. "We're not allowed to have anything like that".

"Oh, well, I'll cut everything up for you." The objections from the boys were soon overcome by the temptation of extra food, not that there was much to go around. As the rest of the pupils knelt by their bedsides to say their last prayers, Dingad and Govan tried to teach a bewildered Rhys how to pray. He was beginning to realise that there were very strict rules here and he didn't much like them.

Lying in bed, he thought over the day's events. All in all his arrival had gone very well, but now, it seemed, there were other problems to face. However, his bed was surprisingly cosy and he soon fell asleep.

CHAPTER 4

Caerllion at Last

Stiff from the long ride of the previous day, not to mention the hoeing late into the evening, when he woke, Rhys lay back and listened to the morning birdsong. It would be just the same at Penhal; he could recognise the urgent songs of the sparrows, thrushes and blackbirds and realised that Helena would be listening to exactly the same sounds at Blaeno. The rest of the boys were reluctant to wake up, and it was only when Fracan burst through the door and rang his bell that the boys groaned and stirred.

Rhys recalled what he had learnt from Dingad of the morning routine: prayers, a hurried breakfast of gruel, bread and milk, then classes. Despite this unavoidable schedule, he hoped the meeting he expected to have with Aidan would somehow give him a chance to go into Caerllion. Prayers were, once more, a complete mystery to Rhys, but Dingad assured him he would soon begin to understand the Latin words. Breakfast was just like the evening meal, with the younger boys serving their impatient elders. Nothing was wasted. Brother Fracan held Rhys back while the rest of the school went to their three separate classrooms, then he explained what Rhys' fate would be.

"You seem to be friendly with Dingad, so you can sit by him in class. Now the rest of the boys are well advanced in their studies, therefore I will give you special attention so you can catch up, and Dingad will also teach you while you are doing farm work. I expect you to work very hard indeed."

Rhys could only nod; this new life was going to be extremely painful.

"When can I see Abbot Aidan?" pleaded Rhys. "I have an important letter for Cynan."

He knew that letters must always be handed over personally – Aidan would never risk taking the letter from Rhys and showing any disrespect for one of the King's captains.

Fracan sniffed. "I'll send word to him and he'll call for you later."

Rhys was led into the classroom and found himself sitting between Dingad and Govan.

"Now, this morning," commenced Fracan looking directly at Rhys, "I will tell you the exciting story of how Christians were thrown to the lions in Rome." The boys all looked at each other smiling; this meant that they would not have to endure the endless chanting of the psalms until they had memorised every word. "Then afterwards, you can all write down the story in your best Latin." Dingad groaned quietly.

Fracan was well aware that some stories would always keep the boys' attention and when a new pupil such as Rhys arrived, it was important to see that they were not bored in their first days.

"Now, you've all heard of the Emperor Diocletian. If you were captured by his guards and put in chains, how would you escape being eaten alive by the hungry beasts in the arena?"

Rhys looked around as a bright lad, who Dingad had told him was untrustworthy, jumped to his feet.

"You would have to deny that you were a Christian and offer to sacrifice a chicken to the gods, then you would have to say that Christians cooked and ate their own babies."

"Well, ah. Yes, something like that. The point is you would be placed in a position where your faith would be tested to the full. However, to escape imprisonment and torture you would have to betray your fellow Christians in hiding. Now, young man, what would you do?"

"I really don't know, father," the boy admitted and meekly sat down.

"The truth is, I don't know what I would do either," Fracan had to admit. "None of us had to face death. I just use this situation as an example of what the early Christians had to endure during many years of persecution. What we do know is that some men, and women, in those early days, decided that they would rather die than deny their faith in Jesus. And all this was nearly five hundred years ago. Ordinary people who were poor, even slaves, would walk towards the lions."

Rhys had heard some of these stories from Cunval; he wondered if he would ever see any real lions. They sounded terrifying. It also brought into his mind the day, three years earlier, when he had witnessed his grandfather killing two Saxon raiders on the bridge at Penhal. The Saxons had appeared suddenly whilst the estate warriors were away and his grandfather, alone except for his oldest retainer, had saved the day. It was so brutal that Rhys, watching from the Penhal barricade, had been petrified with fear. He often wondered if he would be brave enough in battle when faced with death, but the thought of his dead father and uncle made him grit his teeth angrily.

"So, there you are, boys; this is something that you should always meditate on." Fracan continued with the stories of various martyrs who had been rounded up from all over the empire, just to entertain the emperor and the mobs in Rome. The time went by quickly until Rhys was summoned by one of the younger monks to see Abbot Aidan. They entered the office ceremoniously.

"Sit there, Rhys. Now, this is my scribe, Brother Felix. We are all hoping that he will become a full monk here soon." Rhys nodded to Felix, who was not much older than himself – he looked frail and too timid to be a teacher. "We have to go to Bishop Dyfrig's house in town this morning and I've decided to take you with us. The bishop will want to see you again and he will be able to arrange for you to deliver your letter personally to Cynan. But first, you must be made to look like a normal pupil. Felix will trim your hair, and here I have a tunic that will, no doubt, fit you." Aidan then looked down at Rhys' dirty boots and sniffed. "And some sandals will look much better. You have your bowl of soap-water and your razor, Felix?"

"Yes, Abbot. Now, Rhys, please take off your outer garments and then come and sit over here."

Rhys had been dreading this moment, although he knew that he would have to become just like the other pupils. It was to be one of the disciplines he must suffer in exchange for the schooling that he had firmly decided to go through.

Rhys' curly locks fell to the floor one by one as Felix, humming to himself, sliced away with his razor. The sides and back were trimmed short and the fore-part of his head was shaved in a straight line from ear to ear. Felix gently mopped up the blood from several inevitable cuts, then brushed down his victim and handed over the long brown tunic. Rhys was now resigned to his fate; he even accepted woollen socks to wear with his new sandals. Rhys was glad that his old friends could not see him like this. No matter, if his looks could get him into town, then so be it.

"You can put your old clothes into your pack, Rhys," said the abbot. "No doubt you will want to change into them when you go home for the harvest."

"Will my horse, Beech, be allowed to go into one of the paddocks, Abbot? He won't be happy with people he doesn't know." Rhys hoped that Beech would be able to adjust to life at the monastery, just as his master would have to.

"We have had quite a lot of experience with animals, Rhys. The monks are quite capable of talking to him and leading him out with the other horses. And you will be allowed to see him every evening now that it's getting lighter again." Aidan had been sipping occasionally from a silver goblet and smacking his lips – Rhys supposed that it was wine he was appreciating. "I'll meet you in the yard, Felix."

Felix and Rhys went by the stone staircase to the dormitory to store Rhys' old clothes in his pack. Rhys realised that he could still smell yesterday evening's cheese as he opened the flap, but Felix chose to ignore this minor breach of discipline. Rhys tucked the letter for Cynan inside his tunic before they set off for the yard. Some boys were trying to put a halter on Beech, but the animal's snorting made them jump back and keep their distance.

"He'll settle down if I talk to him," suggested Rhys. "If we walk through the gate with you onto the open trackway, he'll be fine."

Sure enough, this went smoothly and Beech walked off with the boys knowing that his master approved and he would be going out to grass. Then Felix showed Rhys around the workshops.

"You see, Rhys, we have an iron-working forge and a carpentry shop that the monks use and one for the pupils to learn in. Now, you can put your tools next to mine. They'll be safe here until you need them." Rhys began to feel that life might not be so bad here after all.

Aidan had entered the courtyard dressed in his ceremonial robes and was obviously ready to leave. The three of them walked quickly down to the river and crossed over a stone bridge just wide enough for carts. Rhys admired the squared-stone arch of the bridge; he had heard of such a thing over smaller rivers and wondered if he might build one over his own river one day.

The slope leading up to the gateway of the town kept the buildings inside the walls out of sight, but when they passed through it, Rhys was overwhelmed with the noise and bustle.

Children were running wild in some of the ruins and elsewhere horses, carts, people and soldiers seemed to be moving along every street in endless streams. Some of the fine two storey buildings had the gates to their courtyards locked and Felix said that they were the homes of families related to the King.

Aidan and Felix became a little nervous when a group of noisy young ruffians approached. They made faces and swaggered alongside the group shouting out rude words and waving their fists right in front of Rhys' face. Rhys had been warned about this kind of behaviour and knew that under no circumstances must he show any reaction. He looked down at his tunic and winced inwardly. The leader of the troublemakers would have had a nasty shock if Rhys had tripped him up and wrestled him to the ground then grabbed his throat just as he had done in his training with Arteg. Felix urged Rhys along faster and they deftly avoided further abuse. Soon they arrived at a magnificent house with Roman columns forming a portico to the front.

An elderly, smiling deacon let them through the door and escorted them to the rear quadrangle. Rhys was surprised to see a garden in the town with bright flowers and shrubs; it was such a sharp contrast to the rubbish-strewn streets outside. They were shown to a bench in the central cobbled area where they sat down in the sunshine. Aidan looked pointedly at the deacon, who smiled and left. When he returned with a jug of wine and a goblet, Rhys supposed that this was probably the normal procedure on Abbot Aidan's visits. This wine drinking reminded him of his grandfather.

"Good morning. Good morning." Bishop Dyfrig burst through one of the doors. He looked very agile for his age, which Rhys knew to be over sixty. "And Rhys, I'm so glad that you've come to join us. I knew you would eventually. My word, you've grown since I was last at Penhal. And I hope you're not too embarrassed by your new image; a young warrior has to go through many tests, I'm afraid." They all laughed uneasily, especially Rhys, although he was encouraged by the words 'young warrior'.

"Rhys has a letter for Cynan," said Aidan. "I thought that whilst we were discussing our business, Felix might show Rhys to the officers' headquarters near the amphitheatre. I know how much he wants to see the town."

Rhys felt a surge of excitement. He had not seen Cynan for three years since he was recuperating from his battle wounds in Abermenei.

"Of course," laughed the bishop, "any letter to the King's captain must be treated with the greatest of respect. We wouldn't want Cynan to draw his sword on us, would we? But first, I must know all the news of Penhal and Abermenei, Rhys. Did you see Tidioc on your way here?"

Rhys had, by now, become well used to relating all the important events from his homeland, and with such great detail, that it seemed to surprise Aidan as he spoke easily and confidently. Aidan and Felix listened intently as Rhys spoke of Helga, whom the bishop had met. It would seem that there was more to Rhys than they had thought and the bishop nodded his approval at Rhys' eloquent narrative.

"Helga and Arteg might even get married," continued Rhys. "At least, that's what mother and grandmother think. They said it would tame Arteg a little."

"You speak fondly of your little cousin, the boy Cadaer. Now, tell me, have you learnt much of the Saxon tongue, Rhys? Your good friend Cunval was able to converse with the Saxon slaves here as you know, and we were able to give them the succour they needed." Aidan drew himself up; he was obviously more interested in his own welfare than that of mere slaves. He poured himself another goblet of wine, drawing a knowing glance from the bishop.

The formalities over, Felix led Rhys back to the busy streets and along the road towards the army barracks and parade ground. Rhys was so engrossed looking at the shops and houses that he didn't notice the same group of boys who had pestered them before waiting in ambush for them.

"Aha. The Jesus-lovers," mocked the older boy. He was about fifteen and the same size as Rhys. "I wonder what they've got under those girlish tunics. Come on. Let's have a look." The boys prodded Rhys and Felix, which caused Rhys to square up to them ready to fight. Felix grabbed him and pulled him away.

"You know the rules, Rhys, no retaliation. It would just make them worse." The mob leader jumped in front of Felix, poking his tongue out. The monk said loudly, "My friend has a letter for Cynan, and you don't want to upset Cynan, do you?"

"A letter? I don't believe you. You've got no business with soldiers." The boy backed off as Rhys called his bluff by patting the bulge in his tunic and staring him in the eye.

"Yah! They're not worth it, boys, let's go down to the river."

Felix had, no doubt, sensed that Rhys would have gladly taken on the town ruffians.

"They won't be so tough when they have to join the King's army. That'll stop their swagger," he mused, "and did you see how dirty they were?"

Rhys grinned at him, grateful for the small monk for dispelling the tension before he got himself into trouble.

The two companions rounded a high stone wall and were confronted by the soldiers' barracks, built by the Romans many years ago. The row upon row of low timber buildings, with whitewashed walls and roofed with gleaming red tiles, looked spectacular. Rhys noted the square layout of the whole military area: a levelled-off parade ground of fine gravel was filled with jousting soldiers and commanders barking their orders. It looked so magnificent with all the soldiers in full battle armour, which Rhys knew was just what the Roman troops had worn years ago. He loved every movement that the muscular fighters were making; thrusting, parrying, darting back and forth expertly and dodging from side to side.

Felix led the way to the headquarters building and knocked on the door. It opened to reveal some sprawling commanders who looked disdainfully at the brown tunics. This was the first time that Rhys had seen any of the King's commanders and he admired their thick leather jerkins and gleaming boots.

"Greetings, sire." Felix bowed slightly. "My friend here has a letter for Cynan from Penhal."

This caused one of the officers to raise his eyebrows and look closely at Rhys. "I'll give it to him," he scoffed.

"I have to give it to him personally, sire." Rhys had hesitated and had only just remembered to say 'sire' at the last moment.

The officer looked annoyed at this pert reply but knew what would be in his own best interests. He just waved Rhys away.

"Cynan's at the amphitheatre, you'll find him there."

The visitors bowed and backed away.

"Those soldiers can be a bit arrogant, Rhys," whispered Felix as he led the way outside. "It's best to act like a servant with them, you know."

Rhys nodded. The last thing he wanted was to make any enemies in the King's army.

The noise from inside the amphitheatre suggested hectic training was in session within the ruined walls. Felix led the way through the tunnel that led to the old arena; this was exactly what Rhys wanted to see. Men were fighting on foot amid the riderless horses, all mingled together in a chaotic enactment of battle. Rhys realised that this was all part of the hard training which enabled men and horses to get used to the deadly mayhem of a battle. For some time the two companions held back and watched – even Felix appeared to be excited by this rare spectacle. Some of the soldiers were getting badly bruised by the flat of the sword blades and the kicks of the soldiers who had gained the upper hand.

The terraces above the arena held a number of young men who Rhys judged to be army juniors, and also some elderly civilians some of whom were probably retired soldiers.

Eventually the battle subsided and benches and tables were rushed to the centre of the training ground by the young recruits.

Cynan stood out among the other men, he was well into his twenties now and looked strong and fearsome as he strode around helping up the fallen and moaning victims. When he noticed the two brown tunics in the shadow of the passageway, he beckoned them over, then slouched wearily against one of the tables.

"Have you come to do battle with us, you hideous scarecrows?" Felix knew Cynan's humour and laughed good-naturedly.

Rhys bowed. "I have a letter for you, sire."

Cynan leaned forward to study him.

"I don't believe it. You're Rhys, Cunval's friend. My word, you have grown. I didn't recognise you dressed up like that... and look at your hair." Rhys beamed as Cynan spoke – he was so proud that Cynan remembered him. "Don't tell me they've put you in that prison up on Aaron's hill. How long have you been there?"

"Only since yesterday," replied Rhys. "And I've got a letter for you from Arteg. Ruthall helped us to write it. I've been training with Arteg ever since I was thirteen, and I was hoping to join the King's army here later on."

Cynan took the now crumpled scroll and put it on the table.

"It will take me most of the day to get through that. Now, come and join us. We're just about to have some food."

"And drink," said an imposing, upright commander sitting at the head of the table. He toyed with a dagger and stabbed at a piece of bread. Rhys felt the blood rising up to his neck. Was this the prince? Was this Arthur Pendragon? Rhys gulped and stared.

"Now this, my friends, is Prince Arthur," laughed Cynan. "The wayward son of King Myric and the biggest boaster in Siluria."

The rest of the group, who were tucking into the meat, bread and cyder on the table, guffawed and banged the table. Rhys was amazed that Cynan could talk like this to the prince. "On our last incursion into the Tamesis Valley, he killed five hundred Saxons in one charge." The soldiers hooted with mirth and gesticulated at Cynan, who was clearly exaggerating wildly.

"You're lucky I don't carry you off into the woods on my horse, Cynan; just as you did with that Saxon woman, whilst the rest of us were chasing the enemy." The crowd laughed even louder. "The rest of us brought back booty and you brought back a screaming Saxon woman."

"She fell in love with me. Anyway, she's working in the camp kitchens now and enjoying every moment." Rhys thought this was hilarious, but Felix folded his arms tightly in distress.

"If I remember rightly," said Arthur, turning to Rhys, "Arteg and his men told me about you after our last raid. You're Brochvael's grandson, aren't you? I knew your father and uncle well. They were true warriors."

"Yes, sire," Rhys felt very honoured at being addressed by Prince Arthur. Arteg had told him all about the raid and how

Arthur was the main leader of the cavalry when the King was away. "Arteg told me all about the battle. I wish I had been there, sire."

Rhys was transfixed by Arthur's demeanour; he was muscular, tall and proud, and with well-groomed long dark hair. For a prince, he seemed to be so tolerant – and why did he allow Cynan to make such fun of him?

Arthur and Cynan laughed. "You will have to do your schooling first, young man. I had to go through it myself, when I was young and I'm glad now. Different to that ox, Cynan. He escaped before learning how to read properly." The men around laughed uneasily, which suggested to Rhys that none of them could read or write. "I'll probably have to read out that letter for Cynan to tell you the truth."

Cynan tossed the parchment over to Arthur.

"I have to admit, you're just a little quicker than me," he said. "But only because your father made you stay at the college whilst the rest of us were defending the young ladies up at Saint Albans nunnery." Once more the soldiers laughed at this good-natured banter between the two leaders.

Arteg's letter was read out somewhat haltingly by Arthur – this was, undoubtedly, a rare occasion for the soldiers. "Aha. Arteg is being a little forward here. He's asking that young Rhys should join us for training after school. It seems that he doesn't know the rules. Our friend, Abbot Aidan will not be pleased at that suggestion."

Rhys became downcast at this news; it looked as if he would be confined to the monastery forever.

"Arteg hopes you are well, Cynan," continued Arthur, "and looks forward to being called upon when the next raid is planned. That may be sooner than he thinks if our reports from the east are correct." Rhys' heart quickened as he realised that the army might well be off on an expedition soon.

"Why can't Rhys joins us for training on Saturdays? We used to do that ourselves if you remember, Arthur. You can give the order." Cynan was offering Rhys some hope.

"I'm good with the bow, sire, and I shoot at long-distance targets now." Rhys looked brightly at a smiling Arthur. "And I've got my own stallion, Beech."

Arthur was known to be a shrewd man – he had to take many decisions and a strong, confident army was his overriding priority. He knew that Rhys would want to avenge his father and uncle, and schooling, together with hard training, was just what this bright young man needed to possibly become a useful officer. The prince leaned back on the bench.

"First, we must eat. Everybody help yourselves, and you two must try our health-giving cyder." Rhys was more than willing, but poor Felix was clearly apprehensive. When Rhys was given a goblet, he drank thirstily, but with restraint; he had been allowed small quantities of wine and cyder at Penhal and knew how dangerous too much could be. Felix sipped nervously.

"You, monk…" continued Arthur, pointing at Felix with his dagger, "give a message to Aidan. Rhys is to be sent to the jousting fields after morning prayers every Saturday. He will return to the monastery in time for evening prayers."

Felix spluttered and coughed loudly, whilst Rhys had trouble containing his joy.

"Yes, sire. I will tell the Abbot who is at this very moment at the bishop's house awaiting our return." Felix continued to sip more nervously then ever from his goblet. He was worried at this turn of events, he hoped that the bishop and the abbot would not hold him responsible for it. If Rhys were to be released every Saturday, it could cause disruption to the discipline and routine of the monastery.

The soldiers all nodded at this decision but the youngsters, who had retired to the edge of the arena, whispered to each other. Who was this new boy from the monastery? Was he going to join them? Rhys glanced in their direction and hoped that he would be able to hold his own in such experienced company.

The banter continued for a while until the soldiers decided to go down to the river to check on the ships – and then visit a tavern. The boys eagerly finished off the drinks and food. Then, as Rhys expected, they questioned him closely about where he had come from.

One of the older boys seemed hostile towards Rhys and stared at him.

"It looks as if you're a favourite with Cynan. Well, I'm the one who passes on orders to this lot. We're called the colts and we'll be joining the army proper next year. You'd better remember that if you come here with such a stupid haircut…"

Felix looked alarmed. "We'd better take our leave now. The abbot will be waiting for us, thank you for your kind hospitality."

Not wishing to cause any friction, Rhys rose from the bench and made a dignified exit with Felix. As one of the colts escorted them out, he whispered, "That's Lewys; beware of him, Rhys. He's really bossy. Next year he'll be a full soldier, thank goodness." Rhys had already worked out he should be wary of Lewys. He looked tough and had probably become a favourite with the soldiers.

As they left the amphitheatre, Rhys realised that his companion may have had a little too much to drink. He smiled knowingly and caught Felix's arm once or twice to prevent him from stumbling.

On reaching the bishop's house and being led once more into the garden, Rhys found that Abbot Aidan also looked the worse for drink and the bishop and his deacon seemed to be thoroughly bored.

"Did Cynan recognise you, Rhys?" asked Bishop Dyfrig lightly.

"Yes, sire, and I can't believe it. I met Arthur as well. And the amphitheatre is such a marvellous sight. Oh, and Felix has a message for both of you from Arthur." Rhys tried to conceal his excitement.

"Well, Felix," Aidan looked at him suspiciously, "what are those soldiers up to now? They have no respect for the church."

"I'm not quite sure how to put this, Abbot…" the monk slurred a little as he spoke, which caused the bishop to raise his eyebrows. "Arthur said that Rhys should be able to join the soldiers at the jousting field on Saturdays."

Aidan slapped the wooden table in rage causing the elderly deacon to jump.

"How dare he! This will ruin the boy's discipline and the other boys will be unsettled too. Bishop Dyfrig, I think you should seek an audience with the King."

The bishop put his hands together as if in prayer.

"I think the King would probably burst out laughing, and he would never reprimand his own son on such an unimportant military matter." He also knew all about Rhys' spirit; it would be far better to have him as an educated soldier than for him to leave the monastery altogether. "I'll have to give the matter some thought. Rhys, you will have to pay special attention during your schooling if you are going to miss Saturdays. And you mustn't boast about this to the other pupils."

"Yes, bishop, but Arthur said that I need only leave after morning prayers and be back in time for evening prayers." The bishop nodded resignedly as Aidan nearly choked.

As they left, Rhys found himself walking behind a swaying Abbot and a singing monk; thankfully, the young ruffians were no longer around.

Back at the monastery he was ushered into the classroom and, in between whispering to Dingad and Govan, he tried to avert the searching looks of Fracan.

"Can you believe it? I met Arthur, he was with Cynan and the soldiers and he actually spoke to me!" His new friends gasped, their eyes wide open.

Later, supper and prayers over, the boys noisily congregated for work in the fields. Rhys took the boys to see Beech and they chatted excitedly about the coming Saturday. Rhys soothed and stroked all of the horses, almost bringing them into the conversation. Once again in the ploughed field, Rhys wielded his hoe with great gusto; he now had a purpose and laughed loudly as the other boys begged him to slow down. Another dip in the river rounded off the evening and that night Rhys dreamed of horses and battles.

CHAPTER 5

Joining the Colts

The next three days went by quickly. Rhys enthusiastically absorbed his lessons and Dingad was eager to help him with his Latin writing. The other boys looked upon Rhys with respect. If anybody could speak with Cynan and Arthur and then go to join them on Saturdays, he was surely going to be an important soldier one day. But most of the pupils were more interested in becoming monks or priests and avoiding any involvement with wars.

By the end of prayers on Saturday morning, Rhys had worked out his plans. He would dash up to the dormitory and change into his own clothes, then saddle Beech and retrieve his bow and arrows from the loft. He thought that he should leave his dagger where it was for the time being. Dingad and Govan had waited in the stable and now eagerly helped Rhys to get ready.

"Don't get hurt," whispered Govan.

His two friends waved goodbye as Rhys cantered up the hill behind the monastery in order to skirt the town and go directly to the training camp. As he was working his way through the outlying fields, some labourers looked up, bemused. They did not expect to see a young lad on a strong stallion coming from the direction of the monastery.

The open ground beyond the amphitheatre and barracks was full of cheering townspeople who were watching the soldiers as they competed in various sports; archery, mock sword play, spear throwing, wrestling and charging with horses. In a real battle both horses and men had to work together – Rhys knew this was all based on the rules of the old Roman cavalry. He gazed in awe at the spectacle, before letting Beech pick his way down through the heather and gorse.

It was difficult to know who to approach among this heaving mass of people. Some spectators looked around as the stranger approached. He certainly looked like a young warrior, with a fine stallion and a bow, and with a quiver full of arrows strapped onto his back. Lewys galloped over – it seemed to Rhys that Lewys had been watching out for him, and he looked mean.

"So. You can ride a horse, can you?" he teased. "Follow me around the outside of the field; then we'll test you on jousting to see if you're good enough to join our troop."

As Rhys wheeled Beech around, he realised that Cynan, among a group of laughing soldiers, had seen him. Cynan waved and turned away.

Lewys raced off and was soon galloping at full pace with Rhys in hot pursuit. Beech had no trouble keeping up and enjoyed the race. They approached the rest of the colts on the hillside who were outside the main centre of events and both horsemen pulled up abruptly, jumping from their mounts and scattering the other boys.

Each colt had a stout staff; this was a form of training that Rhys was quite familiar with and was designed to hone reflexes with whatever weapon could cause injury. Each opponent tried to hit the other on any part of their body, whilst at the same time parrying blows. The horses were tied up and Lewys paired off the boys according to size.

"Here, Hwyn; you spar with Rhys. Now, remember everybody, you must protect your head and arms. If this were real swordplay one bad blow would cripple you."

He threw a staff at Rhys and the whole company spread out and faced each other grimly. Hwyn, who was quite heavily built, glared as if he had been prepared for Rhys – this was obviously a plot to cut him down to size. He lost no time in swiping at Rhys, while Rhys, eyeing him carefully, backed away and side-stepped to get his measure. He could see anger in his opponent's face, so he waited until he was overstretched, then lunged forward quickly and jabbed Hwyn in the chest. As Hwyn stumbled and fell, Rhys pinned down his forearm with his foot and held the staff ready to strike a fatal blow. Hwyn was too winded to resist, and as he coughed and wheezed, Rhys stepped smartly backwards.

"You fool, Hwyn. You left yourself wide open," shouted Lewys. Hwyn scowled as he struggled to his feet. This newcomer was dangerous and the other boys, distracted for a moment, looked on apprehensively.

"Right... carry on, men." The order was given as Hwyn squared up again to Rhys. Rhys, well disciplined by Arteg, immediately went on the attack, jabbing quickly, forcing Hwyn to use all his skill just to avoid being hurt. Then, as his opponent stumbled whilst backing away, Rhys caught him with a glancing blow to the side of his head. Once again a jab to the chest finished Hwyn off.

"Change over," ordered Lewys, pushing the boys into a different order. Rhys was now with an older – and even bigger – boy. But it soon became obvious that this opponent was as slow as an ox, and after witnessing the downfall of Hwyn, he could only back away from Rhys' savage thrusting. The next battle looked more serious. Half the boys were given heavy mock axes, all made of stout oak, and the other half had round leather shields and swords made of tough, straight yew-wood. Lewys separated the boys into matching pairs.

Rhys, with an axe, soon had his opponent on the ground, much to the dismay, it seemed, of Lewys. When weapons were being changed around Rhys knew that the other boys were watching his swift side-stepping and swerving. This was just the excitement that Rhys craved, and now, pitting his wits against complete strangers, he could see the value of Arteg's constant shouting and harrying. Exhaustion soon took hold of the boys – many of them were badly bruised and some had blood running down their faces. Suddenly, Lewys threw a sword to Rhys and motioned for him to pick up a shield.

"Now," snarled Lewys. As Rhys grabbed a shield from Hwyn, he noticed that Lewys had moved uphill to take advantage and unfairly slash at Rhys. Rhys was just able to counter the blows with his shield and moved sideways, but Lewys, who was now aware of Rhys' tactics, soon had him off-balance. It was as much as Rhys could do to avoid the blows of an enraged Lewys and was soon forced downhill by his stronger opponent. Just as suddenly, Lewys stopped.

"That's the way to attack, boys," he bragged. "Break! Let's drink some water, and then we'll try some archery."

If the first part of jousting was anything to go by, then Rhys felt that he would do well with his bow. Large logs had been set up as butts at a standard distance and the boys now looked relieved that the heavy work was over – some of them sat on the grass trying to recover. Hwyn stepped forward eagerly to show that he had not been hurt.

"Six arrows each… three archers in line." Lewys obviously enjoyed his role as leader and, despite his arrogance, he was clearly the one to have on your side in a real battle. Rhys was sidelined until most of the boys had shot. They certainly needed more practice and had probably not had too much experience of hunting on the moors and hillsides as had Rhys. With his bow stretched and hitched to his satisfaction, Rhys stepped forward with just Lewys and himself as the last two.

Without hesitation, the two young warriors let fly at the butts. Out of six arrows they eventually had three hits each, the other three arrows being as close as most of the others had achieved.

"Well, you seem to be lucky, Rhys. We'd better step back six paces and try again." The other boys ran to retrieve the arrows. Both Rhys and Lewys had arrows that were easily identified and Rhys noticed that his new leader had honed and oiled his equipment carefully. Once again all of the arrows were close, but after the exertions of the mock battle, Rhys was unnerved and only scored one hit.

Some serious fighting had commenced on the main jousting field, which provided a welcome break for the novice soldiers. A full cohort of mounted warriors charged into the spacious arena and at full gallop into a solid wall of 'Saxons'. If the ensuing fray was only practice then a real battle would be terrible to behold. A sort of hatred was apparent on both sides, and it was only the discipline of the leaders that prevented real sword wounds. The crowd shrieked encouragement to the mounted men – their heroes – and the watching boys became completely carried away with this exciting battle.

"Now lads, let's get the horses and have our own attack!" Lewys, clearly worked up by the sight of all this blood-letting, decided that the young warriors would attack some spread-out bushes further up the hillside. This would be in full view of the spectators around the arena and would clearly draw their attention as the main battle was ending.

"Remember, we all shout like madmen as we charge, then swipe at the bushes with our swords. Let's give them something to cheer at."

Lewys lined up his men and called the charge. The uphill slope taxed the horses and riders and just before they got to the bushes, Rhys saw Lewys veer his mount towards him causing him to skid downhill into the other horses. There was a brief clash of saddles and reins as Beech stumbled and fell throwing

Rhys head-first to the ground. He was able to roll and bounce off the soft turf, just missing the flying hooves of other horses. He caught a glimpse of Beech staggering and just able to regain his feet – this meant, thankfully, that he had not been injured.

Most of the other warriors carried on and slashed at the bushes with their wooden swords. Rhys got to his feet.

"You did that on purpose, you dog," he shouted angrily at Lewys, furious that his mount had been put in danger. Lewys, incensed, swung his horse around and swept down on Rhys who was able to duck and roll downhill. As Lewys pulled on his reins to swing the horse around once more, Rhys sprinted and jumped at the now unsettled rider. Lewys spilled out of the saddle and landed heavily on his back. In an instant, Rhys swung his foot and kicked his enemy hard in the stomach. Then clutching at the position of where his dagger would normally be, he dived on top of Lewys with a stabbing motion. Had the dagger not been in his pack, back at the monastery, Lewys would have surely died. Rhys had never felt this angry before. He punched Lewys in the face.

"You could have maimed my horse," he shouted wildly.

Lewys, full of hate, kicked Rhys in the shin causing him to stagger away.

The other boys rode back in disbelief to help Lewys. By now, they were all aware that the spectators and the warriors below had been watching them. They were too far away to see too much detail, but they were obviously excited at this fight between two angry lads. Lewys recovered and sprang to his feet. He looked up at Rhys and decided that he could not risk any further humiliation; he was bigger, but Rhys' piercing glare looked too dangerous.

"I'll get you for this," he hissed as he recovered his mount. Beech walked over to Rhys – this was a new experience for both of them. Lewys trotted down the slope cursing and the boys felt compelled to follow him. Rhys stroked Beech knowing that he was, at least, equal to Lewys.

Two riders cantered up the hill towards Rhys; it was Cynan and another officer. "You certainly caused a stir there, Rhys, whatever started that off?" Both men gave Rhys a knowing look.

"We fell out, sire; that's all".

"The crowd enjoyed it anyway," laughed Cynan. "Now, this oaf here is Tarou, the Protector of Caerllion. He's a good friend of mine. I think he should take you down to the river and show you around. I know you're anxious to see the ships and the barges. See that he's fed and watered, Tarou. He's all yours, and make sure he's back at the monastery in good time." With that Cynan raced off to join his men.

***

Tarou was short and hairy, and built like an ox – it would be impossible to stop him if he charged. His easy smile told Rhys that here was a friendly face.

"We saw what happened, young Rhys. You're going to have trouble with Lewys, and you're on your own I'm afraid, we can't help you with any squabbles. Now, it looks as if they're all going to stop for a rest. Let's explore."

Rhys checked over Beech, collected his bow, then mounted. The two new companions set off down the slope to the river with Rhys sitting high in the saddle. Everything had happened so quickly, but he was happy that he had proved himself to be more than just a pupil at the monastery school.

The riverbank was a hive of activity; a variety of ships and boats lay motionless on the water. Some had sails flapping gently in the breeze and some had oars left carelessly hanging over the sides. Rhys had seen barges and small boats on the Gwei at Abermenei, but as they rounded a bend in the river a huge Roman merchant ship came into view. This was just as Rhys had imagined; a tall mast in the centre and a smaller mast at the bow. Ropes and rigging stretched in all directions flapping against the furled sails. This type of ocean-going ship had been described to him and now he was admiring the real thing.

Tarou smiled as Rhys studied the scene and took in all the details. They sat on their horses while Tarou described the various activities. "This is high tide at the moment, Rhys. Soon that water will turn into a river and rush down to the sea. A lot of the smaller ships will use it to get under way." Tarou swept his arm toward the hills. "I came here from the north when I was fifteen, you know, just like you. I always wanted to join the King's army and now I'm nearly thirty, I have my own family in the town and some good companions. When I'm forty, the King will give me my own small farm, then I'll leave the fighting to lads like you." He laughed at Rhys' serious expression.

"I know I have to do my schooling, Tarou. I can see the

importance of reading and writing, and I can't tell you how glad I am to get Saturdays here in the town. I'm hoping to see the sea-coast this summer. Have you been there much?"

"Oh, yes. Sometimes in the summer on a Sunday, my wife makes us all go to church and then we go downriver with the tide in one of those long, open boats. After sailing further down the coast, we land on a beach and then, when the tide turns, we get back by evening. I'll see if we can make an arrangement for you to go one day."

"I'd love to learn all about ships," sighed Rhys. "Can we get closer?"

"Better still, I know the captain of that galley; he'll show us around. Now, I think I know where to find him."

The riverside tavern was full of singing and laughing men. Dismounting, Tarou handed the reins to Rhys.

"You settle the horses in the stables over there," he said "and meet me back here at this table outside. That lot inside might start joking a bit too loudly if they see your haircut."

Rhys tied up the horses and settled them with hay and water. He then hid his bow and quiver under the straw and admired the other animals in the stable. Later, sitting on a bench at the table pointed out by Tarou, Rhys was surprised at the number of people walking by. It was so busy and everybody seemed to be carrying goods. He was quite content to listen to all of the city noises, though nobody spoke to him or even took any notice.

But he was suddenly aware of someone pointing at him – it was the youngsters who he had encountered on his first visit with Felix. The older boy laughed into his face.

"I thought I recognised your lovely hair. What are you doing in those proper clothes? Have you run away then?"

Rhys moved to the end of the bench; he wanted to avoid any trouble and hoped that Tarou would soon appear. The boys grabbed the end of the bench and tipped it skywards. Rhys held on to the table but then toppled to the hard ground. This was too much – younger boys were not going to knock about a colt warrior. He jumped to his feet and lunged forward at the lout sending him sprawling into the street. He then rounded on the next boy who seemed to be transfixed in shock and pushed him backwards over some barrels. The smaller boys all retreated as Rhys stood over the first assailant and dared him to get up. But he did not; he crawled backwards in the dirt of the street.

At that moment, Tarou walked through the tavern doorway holding two mugs. He had seen enough to know that, once more, Rhys had shown his suitability as a fighting man.

"Here, my man. Here's your ale."

The sight of a laughing soldier handing a mug to Rhys, who had just spread-eagled most of the gang, suggested they had made a big mistake; they scuttled around the nearest corner as passers-by, who had witnessed the scene, laughed and walked on.

"They had a go at me the other day. I didn't want any trouble, but I couldn't avoid it."

"Enough said. I think you deserve that ale."

Rhys, more familiar with cyder, looked into the mug.

"What's ale made from?" he asked.

"What's ale? Surely you've heard of ale… it's what the Saxons make. They brew it from grain. Taste it."

Rhys sipped at the strange concoction; it was a bit heavy. Realising that he was now quite thirsty, he took a second swig and smacked his lips.

"Not too bad," he ventured. It wasn't particularly pleasant, but he certainly did not want to admit that to Tarou.

A large jovial man dressed in a long heavy coat staggered from the tavern and slapped Tarou on the back, then smiled down at Rhys.

"Is this the boy, my friend?" he said.

"Rhys, I want you to meet Ronan, the sailor. He hails from Armorica and trades back and forth in that wreck tied up in the river." Ronan roared with laughter. "He's going to show us over his ship; well, what do you think?"

"Yes, sire, that's just what I was hoping. I can't tell you how much I've wanted to see a real ship." This was the most exciting thing that Rhys had ever known.

Ronan put his arm around Rhys.

"I'm always looking for sailors, lad. Nobody seems to like the sea around here; they all get sick!" Tarou nodded in agreement. "Now, if you get me that jug of best wine you promised, Tarou, we'll go down the back steps to my trail boat, while I can still stand!"

The tavern keeper and Tarou guided Ronan down the steps into a heavy, timber-built sailboat. A tall mast had a sail tied upwards out of the way and two oars hung loosely over the side.

"Just in time, my shipmates; the tide is starting to turn and we don't want to be rowing upriver. You sit beside me, Tarou and you can sit in the stern, lad, and hold that jug tight." Ronan set the oars into their locks either side and pushed off. Tarou had some experience with boats and after some splashing and cursing, the two oarsmen rowed unsteadily upstream. Rhys' own experience of rowing on the river Gwei was in much smaller craft; he knew that this bigger boat could face even a rough sea.

The big Roman-built galley was held fast in the deeper water in the middle of the river by strong ropes from either bank. As they approached, Rhys could see the long rudder set into the stern and when they arrived at the rope ladder hanging over the side, two sailors took a line and held the boat steady. Rhys passed up the jug to one of the sailors who grasped it with great care; they both seemed to sense that any mishap might endanger their lives.

Rhys' first visit to a real ship was something he couldn't wait to tell all his friends about. The deck was planked from stem to stern with high hatches giving access to the huge areas below and short ladders led to raised decks at both ends of the ship. Rhys looked skywards to try and work out what all the ropes were for. The large square mainsail was furled up onto its yardarm and a smaller sail above the bow was tied back to its sloping foremast.

Ronan recovered his wine flask and made his way aft.

"Here lad, he said "I'll show you the captain's cabin and you can see my charts and sailing instruments. Have you ever seen a map before?"

Tarou, who had rarely been on board one of the bigger

ships, was as interested as Rhys. They both followed Ronan around the ship as he explained how the holds had been almost emptied of the goods from Armorica.

"Wine, oil, tableware, cloth, and goblets. Some of these goods have already been unloaded at Din Tagell, the fortress on the coast of Dumnonia, and also at the island out in the big sea, Ynys Ygraine." Rhys had heard of these two garrisons which needed to be regularly supplied by the King.

Ronan pointed to barges upstream that were waiting to load up his ship with salt, hides and wool for Armorica.

"We'll be making the same two stops on our return journey to Armorica to give the garrisons salt, meat and grain; and in return we'll be given smoked fish and sea birds." This was all very interesting to Rhys and he wondered if he would ever get the chance to visit these faraway places.

Later, Rhys emerged from the dark holds, where one of the sailors had shown him the ship's timber work and the solid beams and struts. He had learned some carpentry, but he marvelled at the skilled woodwork of these big ships.

Ronan could see Rhys' interest and explained, "These ships, you know, are built in Constantinople in the Great Middle Sea, and can stand up to the storms of the big Western Ocean. The Saxon ships, open boats with many oars and one large sail, can't cope with the Western Ocean too far from land, but they're fast and usually raid with three ships and nearly a hundred warriors. Their favourite tactic is to sail into the coast overnight and suddenly attack at daybreak." Rhys whistled. "That's why we sail way out into the ocean and then turn for

Armorica on the south-westerlies. We dare not go within sight of the southern shore of Britannia. Three fast Saxon ships together would overpower us for sure."

Rhys listened intently as Ronan recounted past adventures and described dangerous ocean storms. One day he might be able to travel to these foreign lands on Ronan's ship. Tarou had great difficulty in dragging Rhys away.

It was time for Rhys to return to the monastery. They bade farewell to Ronan and were rowed by a young sailor to the steps leading up to the tavern. The river level had dropped considerably and a ladder had been lowered down to the exposed shingle on the waterline. The two companions collected their horses.

"I can't thank you enough, Tarou," said Rhys when they were mounted. "I won't mind the schooling now, if I know that I can escape on Saturdays!"

Tarou laughed and squeezed Rhys' shoulder. "Build up those muscles, Rhys, you're going to need them, I can see."

CHAPTER 6

Danger from the East

It seemed safer to walk Beech through the busy streets to the main gateway of the town, but once outside, Rhys mounted up and made his way down to the stream. When he arrived at the monastery stables, he found that the pupils and monks were returning from their various activities, so after cleaning his boots and safely storing his bow, he scuttled up to the dormitory to change.

"You're back," shouted Dingad and Govan together as they entered the dormitory. Dingad sat wide-eyed on the bed beside Rhys. "Well, tell us all about it. Did you see the cavalry charging? We saw them once, you know."

"It was better than I ever thought," replied Rhys with a satisfied grin. "But the best part was, the captain of the big Roman ship showed us around… that is, Tarou as well, my new friend. He's a top commander. And I had some ale to drink." Dingad could only sigh as Govan squinted and blinked in amazement.

The rest of the boys surrounded Rhys as he continued his story. He was careful not to mention his feud with Lewys – that was a problem that was going to fester for some time. They pressed Rhys for every detail, and Rhys, only too ready to oblige, made the whole day sound madly exciting.

It was soon time to wash before supper and then prayers.

"On Saturday evenings," explained Dingad seriously, "we are allowed to wander around the gardens and orchards. The monks give lectures on the growing of vegetables and the proper care of all the animals, the chickens, the ducks, the bees and the fish ponds."

Rhys sighed heavily when Govan continued, "Then, a normal Sunday involves lectures in the chapel given by Bishop Dyfrig or the abbot. The subject is always on the history of the church after the time of Jesus."

On his first Sunday at the monastery, Rhys found the stories most interesting. In the morning Abbot Aidan talked about the Old Testament and in the afternoon Bishop Dyfrig arrived to talk about the Egyptian deserts and the first hermits and monks. The boys were fascinated by the tales of these faraway lands; the bishop knew that he could hold their attention by including the tales of the Roman persecutions and the hardships of the first Christians. The gruesome events of the history of the old Roman Empire were always a good talking point in the dormitories.

***

Rhys found that the next week flew by. The friendship of his new companions and the helpfulness of the monks, blended in with the glorious spring weather, were enough to convince him that he had made the right decision. By Saturday, and his next meeting with Lewys, Rhys was a little apprehensive, but eager to see more of the army.

With morning prayers over and Beech saddled up, he followed the stream down to the Isca River to find that Ronan's ship had left. The tide was out and people were working on the various craft that lay beached along the riverside. Some fishermen were netting for any salmon that might be drifting down-stream and children were happily splashing around in the pools. Rhys was sad to see that the ship – his ship – had left for the high seas.

Walking Beech through the streets, he came to the amphitheatre and the barracks. There was much activity and shouting; orders were barked out all around him and horses were galloping around the training fields. Rhys mounted up once more; this was the life that he yearned for and he knew exactly what he wanted from Caerllion.

Head high and back straight, Rhys trotted into the jousting fields. The soldiers were sword fighting with the colts and, despite the difference in size and muscles, the boys were desperately trying to land a blow on their counterparts. Tarou waved casually across to Rhys after the colt who opposed him rolled on the grass clutching his stomach. As Rhys tied up Beech on the long hitching rope, a shout from Cynan indicated that Rhys should take him on. The lad who had been sparring with Cynan gratefully handed over his shield and wooden sword and Cynan moved in swiftly before Rhys was prepared. The ensuing blow to Rhys' shield caused him to fall backwards, and as he tried to roll out of harm's way, Cynan pounced and held his own sword up ready to strike. Rhys would have been unable to escape certain death.

"One to me!" shouted the powerful warrior as the other boys laughed.

Cynan stood back and pointed his sword menacingly as Rhys struggled to his feet. It was now up to Rhys to make an impression, but he knew that a frontal charge might leave him open to a quick sidestep. He circled to the right, jabbing with his sword and causing Cynan to parry, but at the same time, covering his left side with his shield. Rhys made several attacks, smartly stepping backwards before Cynan could counter, then changed his tactics by circling to his left.

The eye contact was intense, then Rhys saw a slight flicker in Cynan's eyes as he lunged forward under Rhys' shield. The young combatant was able to push down Cynan's strike and thrust his sword against his forearm. A real blade would have cut deeply into the flesh. Rhys charged forward striking his shield against the side of Cynan's sword and then, spinning right around, he lashed out at Cynan's back with a hard swipe. The shock showed up on Cynan's face as he tried to regain his balance, but Rhys relentlessly swept forward with blow after blow against Cynan's raised shield.

Cynan was able to jump backward, giving himself enough

time to regain his stance and move sideways. As the other combatants looked on in disbelief, the battle continued.

"Die, you swine," shouted Rhys much to everyone's amusement. A colt being so bold with a King's captain caused Tarou to cheer him on boisterously. This in turn made Cynan laugh as he swiped at Rhys' shield with a constant stream of blows, forcing him backwards and scattering the watching crowd. Rhys knew that there were several moments when Cynan could have made a hit, but he was more concerned to wear Rhys down. Eventually Rhys, despite his fitness, was showing signs of tiredness.

"Keep going, you little suckling pig," laughed Cynan. "You have to stay alert despite your weariness. In a real battle, the first to be worn down is a dead soldier." Eventually Rhys had to hold up his sword in surrender gasping for breath.

Tarou clapped his hands.

"You did very well, captain. I'll report back to Arthur that you knocked out Rhys without having to stop for a rest." This was just the sort of banter that the fighters enjoyed, although without looking round, Rhys sensed that Lewys kept his facial expression set hard.

"That's enough rest for you lot. Now pair up again and let's fight," shouted Cynan.

Rhys found himself facing Lewys.

It seemed that Lewys had been saving his energy as he launched a fierce attack on Rhys. Rhys could only move backwards and sideways to avoid the sword blows – but he knew that Lewys would soon use up his own energy with such a forceful drive. Staring into his opponent's eyes, Rhys saw the moment to counter attack. Feinting to the right, and then, once more, to the left, Rhys was able to swipe his sword downwards onto Lewys' drooping shield. Then pushing forward, Rhys thrust forward to jab him in the stomach with the rounded swordpoint. This hurt Lewys' pride as much as the sharp pain that doubled him up. But as Rhys held his sword up to inflict a downward swipe, Lewys jabbed under Rhys' shield to pierce him in the thigh.

Cynan and Tarou had been watching this display with great interest – they were well used to animosity between colts and covertly encouraged it.

"Well done lads, keep it up," said the captain. "Never mind how tired you are, remember, it's all about staying alive!"

Within a short period of time, both Rhys and Lewys had battled almost to a standstill; it seemed that there would be no clear winner at this encounter.

"Time to exercise the horses, my men." Cynan next showed the colts how to rescue a fallen comrade whilst on the move. They all practised picking up a dismounted rider in an arm lock and swinging him up on to the back of a horse without stopping. "Now, sometimes, one of your comrades will be on the ground wounded. Lewys, you and Tarou back off up the hill; and you, Rhys, lie down on the grass half-dead."

Rhys' two rescuers galloped down to him and Tarou jumped off his horse, while Lewys grabbed the reins. Tarou lifted Rhys and threw him over the horse in front of Lewys. In an instant, Tarou mounted again and both horses galloped off.

The boys clapped; this was exciting horsemanship. Rhys jumped to the ground glad to be on his feet again. He guessed that Cynan had set up this contact with Lewys; in a real battle they would have to look after each other.

"Take it in turns, now. I'm off to the amphitheatre. Tarou, you stay here and knock them into shape. They need to practice twenty times this morning." The boys groaned, this would surely kill them all off.

"Then they can practice archery before joining us at the amphitheatre."

The physical exertion was extreme for the boys. Tarou shouted encouragement and just at the point of collapse, they were allowed to rest before archery practice. It wasn't surprising that they were all wide of the targets and even Lewys gave an exasperated laugh at their poor efforts.

"That's enough. It's time for some food. Ale for me and milk for you lot," declared Tarou.

The battle-weary troop had lost their appetite for humour and led their horses across the fields to enter the amphitheatre where the colts had only enough energy to slump on the benches.

The arena mysteriously started to fill up and many soldiers and officers gathered as Arthur stood on a table to speak. Rhys sensed that something important was happening; he had felt this atmosphere when the warriors of Penhal had been called to arms. Did this mean that the Saxons were invading again?

Arthur towered above the men, hands on hips.

"I've received several reports that West Saxon warbands are

raiding into our territory and some villages have been attacked. This may be a trap to draw us to the east while they attack somewhere else... perhaps well to the north, or even down into Dumnonia and the coast. Whatever the situation, we will need a large force on horseback. We'll cross the Havren at Black Rock, then follow the hills to the headwaters of the Tamesis. Our comrades there are in a good defensive position, so we'll join with them and send out scouting parties far and wide. We'll need plenty of provisions. We may be away for some time. I'll not rest until we sweep clean the whole of their forward territory and kill every Saxon swine in sight. Remember, we don't kill women and children. We'll bring back enemy slaves and any loot, and everything else must be destroyed. King Myric, as you know, is at Caer Taf and has now given me the authority to do whatever is necessary. Messengers will soon be off to gather all the clans and the Cornovians will be guarding our northern borderlands. Your officers will be giving you further orders. Now, eat as much as you can and then see to your weapons."

The colts all looked at each other. Rhys felt that on the one hand they wanted to join the soldiers, but on the other hand were glad to be too young. Then the food from the barracks' kitchens arrived together with large quantities of cyder and ale. The colts helped to distribute the platters and cauldrons to the tables that were ringed around the edge of the arena. There was much boasting and swaggering – the officers said that with such a large force, there would be little chance of heavy casualties.

Lewys arranged for the boys to have some space to eat and drink.

"Cynan wants to see us afterwards. He's got an important job for us while the army's away."

Rhys could see that Lewys was delighted to be such an important part of the plans; but when he, himself, returned to the monastery, he realised he would be completely out of touch. As Arthur and his officers talked earnestly around their own table, Lewys stood upright awaiting orders.

After a while the officers dispersed and Cynan, followed by Tarou, approached the colts.

"Half of the army," he said "will be staying to defend Caerllion, with Tarou in charge. Most of the men will be on guard around the town and along the coast. Arthur is worried that if a diversion is being planned to the east, then the South Saxons might amass a large sea force and attack our homeland somewhere on this coast. They've never dared anything like that before, but we cannot take chances. They could attack anywhere, and they've been building up their numbers quietly for some years."

Everybody nodded.

"Where do you want me to station my men, Cynan?" asked Lewys, boldly. He was determined to be an officer one day, thought Rhys.

"You move your troop into the King's palace near Saint Albans nunnery, there are only a few servants there, now that the King's away. Rest during the day and patrol the outskirts at night. If the Saxons were to come in during darkness on a fast tide, they would attack at daybreak. That's the dangerous time. If the outlying guards warn you, get the nuns and helpers into the stone buildings around the cloisters. You'll be safe there for a while until help arrives. See to the defences and put extra timbers on the doors. And store plenty of water in case of fires. Any questions?"

"If they try to break in, we'll have our swords ready, Cynan." Lewys looked grim. Cynan nodded and thought for a while. "And set up some vantage points on the roofs for your bows, just in case. You can help the soldiers now, Lewys. But not you, Rhys, Tarou has a job for you."

Lewys led the boys away, shooting an inquisitive glance at Tarou as he spoke with Rhys.

"Well, Rhys, Cynan tells me that you speak the Saxon language. That's good, because we've got to tell the slaves downstream that they're confined to their village for a few weeks."

Tarou and Rhys mounted up and crossed the fields to the river. It was a short distance to the cluster of huts on the riverbank, and as the two riders approached, an older man in Saxon dress stopped his work and stood meekly in the open yard. Others came from the huts and workshops to join him, mostly older people. Tarou stopped in front of them and signalled with a sweep of his arm, at which they all stood in line.

"They need to be counted now and again. One, two, three..." Tarou raised himself in his saddle and counted off the forlorn looking group, "there you are, Rhys; twelve men and seven women... oh, and four children. Mind you, there are Saxon women married to some of the soldiers as well, but they're not allowed to mix with this lot. Now, tell them their orders."

Rhys could not help feeling sorry for them. He knew that Saxon invaders had enslaved many of the Britons and he dare not think of their plight, but it just didn't seem right for anybody to be captive for life.

The leader had been glancing at Rhys' hair and gave a faint smile as they were being addressed.

"I have some news for you," said Rhys haltingly. "Some of the soldiers have to leave for a short while, so you're not allowed to leave your village."

The group looked up at Rhys, surprised at his knowledge of their language.

"Anyone caught outside their farm will be executed in front of the rest. You are to carry on with your work and someone will come here to collect the ale, soap and skins."

Tarou nodded as Rhys finished.

"Let's have a look around, Rhys. They're not allowed to have a smithy in case they make weapons."

Rhys did not think that they would dare risk any disobedience. One man took their horses as the village elder accompanied them into the timber-built houses and outbuildings. Rhys was intrigued by the timber-work of the buildings and the large-scale working of the farm – it was not at all what he had expected. He noted large stone-built vats for making ale for the town, with clean water coming through a stone duct from a spring up the hill. A nearby stream was utilised for the tannery ponds which gave off a putrid stench and a lime kiln fire was still burning on the hillside.

As Rhys asked the Saxon leader about their activities, Tarou laughed at his interest in every detail.

"Let's mount our horses, my friend, I have something else to show you. Something that will make even you turn your nose up."

Rhys bade farewell to the Saxon, who, by now, had become enthusiastic at explaining to Rhys how they lived and worked. The fields around the village were well tended and there was no shortage of pigs, fowl and cattle – all for supply to the army. Tarou led the way further downstream and the smell soon made it obvious what Tarou had been laughing at. They came to a huge cesspit which was fed by a large underground culvert taking all the sewage from the town.

"I knew that your enquiring mind would enjoy this one, Rhys. When the tide turns, twice a day, the slaves let out the sewage into the fast-flowing current, then it goes out to sea. It was all built by the Romans, you know."

This seemed sensible to Rhys. He wondered what Caerllion had been like when the Romans ruled the town.

"It's time to think about getting you back to the monastery, but first, we'll go up to the old fort on the hill. You can just see the estuary from there, and I know that's what you are longing for." Tarou spurred his horse and they both galloped up the hillside. Rhys, once again, rode high in his saddle. He would remember this glorious day for ever.

The old hillfort was a high earthen rampart that surrounded the entire top of the hill. Rhys and his companion could stand on top of the rampart and look out over the estuary and the nearby hilltops.

"Further down the coast, Rhys, there are islands in the estuary where we go sometimes in the summer. When I was a young colt, the sailors used to take us way down on the tide to visit. You wouldn't believe how fast we would travel if the wind was right."

Rhys whistled in wonderment.

"I can't wait to finish at the monastery and do things like that. Where do you think Ronan and his ship are now, Tarou?"

"Oh, he's probably at Ynys Ygraine by now, loading or unloading. The island is the best place for looking out to the ocean. If a Saxon sail is spotted, they send a fast ship to the mainland to warn everybody on the coast. Mind you, we haven't seen any Saxons for a few years now. They've taken a good beating on this coast, especially since the King moved part of the army down to Caer Taf."

"So, is King Myric going to move everything to Caer Taf? I hear he's got lots of new ships down there." Rhys wanted to know all about the King's ships.

"I doubt it. Caerllion is such a good place for the army and for ships to get to safely. Arthur can soon get word to the north if there's any danger and, as you know, everybody can get to Black Rock to cross the Havren at the safest place. Anyway, we have to protect the monastery and the girls at the nunnery." Tarou laughed once more as Rhys screwed up his face.

"And you have to protect the tavern, of course!"

"Of course."

They mounted up once more as Rhys continued to ask Tarou questions. He wished he were older and part of the army.

"We'll skirt around the outlying farms so I can tell them all what's happening. The farmers will have to set up lookouts on every hilltop all along the coast, so that a horseman can get word to Caerllion if they spot any danger."

Rhys was pleased to meet so many people from the countryside. He tried to remember all their names and studied the farming activities. He sat upright and the younger boys admired him on his horse accompanying a senior officer. When, finally, they were approaching the monastery, Tarou bade him farewell.

"After the main troop leaves in the morning, Rhys, I'll be busy organising the town's defences. No doubt, we'll be seeing you next Saturday."

Rhys soon arrived at the stables and rubbed Beech down vigorously in his stall. Beech had enjoyed the day with his master and nudged him contentedly.

The monks were returning from the fields and had already heard news of the army's imminent expedition.

"We will be offering special prayers until the soldiers return safely," said Fracan gravely.

Rhys wondered if he would ever understand the prayers correctly; he decided to ask Dingad to translate any words he could not guess. It suddenly seemed ages since he had left Penhal, but, at night, he took comfort in picturing Helena's smile and lovely hair. And the kiss.

CHAPTER 7

Learning to Sail

After the evening meal and prayers, Rhys had time to relate his adventures. The questions continued in the dormitory until well after dark when Rhys was glad to fall asleep. Sunday had the usual history lessons and Rhys did his best to concentrate on the old Roman language; he wasn't quite sure about God and Jesus, but for the moment he would pray, just as all his friends around him did.

The next few days went quickly by and the only news from the town was that the cohorts and their pack animals had successfully crossed the Havren and would send back reports to Tarou as soon as there was news. King Myric had sent word from Caer Taf to reassure the population that all able men along the southern coast were on standby in case of a surprise attack.

During the course of the week, the pupils had been helping with some of the monastery activities and the young monk Felix and Rhys had now become good companions.

One evening, Felix offered to take Rhys for a walk in the gardens – he seemed to have something on his mind.

"You know, Rhys, I had an older brother who was killed in a battle against the Saxons, just like your father. I thought you should know. Then when I came to the monastery, I gradually lost my hatred of the enemy."

Rhys could see tears in the young monk's eyes.

"I know how you feel, Rhys," he continued "Anyway, you'll always have a friend in me."

Rhys was silent for a while. "I can never stop hating, Felix. I'll never rest until I've avenged my kinfolk. What worries me most is that if I'm killed, my family will be devastated: mother, grandfather, Helena, all the children. I just cannot fail them, Felix. That's why I have to train hard and become stronger than the enemy. Do you understand that?"

Felix nodded and turned away.

***

After prayers one Saturday, Rhys was called to the abbot's room.

"I suppose you'll be off to the town again this morning, Rhys. Well, I have to admit you have been very well behaved during lessons and I'm told that you work hard on the farm. I hope you intend to continue as you've started."

"Yes, Abbot," replied Rhys. He was very pleased to hear the abbot's praises; this was all part of his plan. "I'm very happy here, and I've made some good friends."

"Good. Now I have a message for you to take to the bishop. I'm sure he wants you to call. You can give him some preserves that I promised and pass on my best regards."

"Yes, Abbot." Rhys wondered what was in store for him.

In no time at all he was mounted and on his way to the bishop's house. The town was still as busy as ever and showed no apparent sign of alarm; but he hoped there might still be some news from the east.

After tying up Beech in the bishop's stable yard, Rhys carefully took down Aidan's pack and handed it to the deacon. "This way, Rhys, the bishop is expecting you."

Rhys was shown into the office where Bishop Dyfrig was sitting back in his chair with his arms folded.

"Your father and your uncle would have been proud of you, Rhys. You seem to have settled into monastic life quite well. I take an interest in all the pupils, you know. Now, I have a message for you from Tarou. He's down on the coast checking defences most of the time and trying to get Caer Gwent ready for action if there is an attack. So there are only a few soldiers left in the barracks here and Lewys and his troop stay awake all night up at the King's palace. Therefore Tarou has found a job for you."

Rhys shuffled his feet; this sounded promising.

"As part of your training today, you will be joining one of the sailors on an estuary boat." Rhys' eyes lit up. "These boats go off on every tide to check the shoreline and islands, just in case any Saxons have landed during the night and are in hiding. So, there is another adventure for you."

"I couldn't have wished for anything better, Bishop. And to think that I was hesitant about coming to Caerllion just a few weeks ago."

"I can't stand the water myself; it unnerves me. I went across the estuary to consecrate a church a few years ago and I was terribly sick. I only hope you don't get that dreaded seasickness, Rhys. Here, I've got an old coat you can have, it can get a lot colder out at sea. The tide will soon be on the turn and there's something I want to show you on the way down to the river."

The bishop and Rhys set off together and soon came to the town basilica.

"There – I doubt you've ever seen a proper church before."

The old Roman basilica was one of the few ancient buildings still intact in the town and had wooden scaffolding poles along one side where workmen were repairing the tiled roof. They went inside and Rhys noticed how quiet it was compared to the noisy streets outside. The walls were thick and some of the plaster was peeling but the stone pillars and the timber-work of the roof were magnificent. The bishop showed Rhys around.

"I have several young priests who stay here until they're ready to go out and take on their own parishes. This is exactly how your old friend, Cunval, started off, you know."

Rhys' thoughts turned to Penhal. He knew that Arteg and his troop would have joined up with Cynan's army far away to the east. They might even be fighting at that very moment. In the quiet of the church he had fleeting images of Helena. He could only pray that she had meant what she said about them being together one day.

"Cunval would have been very pleased to see me here, Bishop."

"Quite right, Rhys. We can only accomplish little while we are down here, on earth. You must realise I myself have only a few more years to go; and also Aidan, of course; not to mention the King. And then a new generation will take over. We all have our place in the scheme of things and sooner or later you'll be called upon to take great responsibilities. That's where the monastery and myself can help you."

"I think I understand, Bishop." Rhys felt a little nervous when presented with such far-off plans. It was best not to think ahead too much.

"Anyway, that's enough serious talk for one day. Let's find your boat!" said the Bishop.

The water level on the slipway between the buildings showed that the tide was high. The quayside was busy with sailors fitting out boats of all sizes, but there were no really big ships in the river. Ronan's galley was not due back for many weeks.

A shout from the riverside caused the bishop to wave in acknowledgement. An elderly sailor and his mate in a trail-boat were unfurling their sail and making ready for sea.

"Jump on the ferry, lad, we'll pick you up," shouted the old sailor.

"That's Bran," explained Bishop Dyfrig. "He's your captain. You may be back late, so I'll get a message to Aidan at the monastery. Good luck, Rhys."

A flat ferry, with a line looped onto a huge rope strung across the river, rested on the slipway and two soldiers were trying to manoeuvre their nervous horses between the side rails. Rhys immediately ran down to help and soothed the horses by patting their necks and coaxing them forward gently. The soldiers grinned at this bright young man with the monastery tonsure, but they appreciated his skill with horses. Rhys had time to wave to the bishop as two strong boatmen heaved on the line. The ferry edged across the still water and Rhys leaned over the upstream rail.

"Slack off," called Bran as his young mate eased their mooring rope. This allowed the trail-boat to glide downstream toward the ferry. "Get ready to jump aboard. I'll tell you when."

This was no problem for Rhys; he clambered over the rail and, when Bran gave the signal, stepped deftly onto the rear of the trail-boat.

"Sit down beside my mate, Rhys; this is Canna. You two can row together. Have you rowed before?"

"Yes, sire; but only on the River Gwei," Rhys shook hands with Canna and couldn't help noticing an ugly wound on the side of his head.

"Canna was wounded in a skirmish. He was only a young soldier and hasn't been the same since. He doesn't talk very well, but he's a good sailor."

Canna grinned and nodded at Rhys who took an immediate liking to him.

"Now then, we ought to have some food before we set off. Could you get it, Canna?"

Bran settled on the rear transom and rested his arm on the steering oar. He smoothed his hand over his white beard as he studied Rhys.

"Tarou is an old friend of mine and a good friend at that. He's told me all about you, Rhys. It seems you're interested in the sea."

"Well, to tell you the truth, I've never really seen the sea, sir. But I'd like to." Rhys looked up at the sail and the rigging. "I've done some sailing on the river, but only in a small boat."

"This trip will cure you one way or another. I'll explain the ropes to you when we leave the estuary. One thing we must avoid at all costs is to finish up in the water. See those blown-up water bags stored in the bow; they would keep us afloat for a short while if we turned over." Rhys grimaced while Canna merely laughed.

"Yes, sire. But I can swim quite well." However, Rhys wasn't too happy at the thought of trying to swim in the cold water of the estuary.

"Half the bread and cheese now and half before we start back with the tide… unless we catch a fish, of course."

They ate noisily and then carefully wrapped up the remainder.

"One more thing before we set off;" said Bran. "A little ale to give you boys strength."

Canna reached under the fore-deck to retrieve a jug and unplugged the stopper. He poured some ale into a large bowl and handed it to Rhys; this was much better than boring lessons.

When Canna hauled in their bow-line the boat started to drift downstream with the gathering current. Bran checked the rudder and the mainstays of the mast while Rhys set his oar. Then he and Canna turned the boat to face downstream with the sail, still furled, hanging loosely in the calm air. The muddy edges of the river were overhung with trees and, after some steady rowing, they eventually left the Isca river to enter the wide Havren estuary. The breeze became cooler and they buckled up their heavy coats. Rhys breathed in deeply to smell the sea at last and gazed across the wide estuary to see the coast far away in the distance.

"You can lash the oars aboard now, lads. Canna, you give Rhys the sail ropes and show him how you unfurl and set the sail." Canna reached up to unfurl the sail and haul it up the mast. Rhys watched every move as Canna braced the main ropes and showed him how to haul in the sail lines.

A sudden gust caused the boat almost to keel over as Bran turned the bow into the wind. Canna automatically moved across to sit behind Rhys and balance the boat up. Then the square sail filled and the boat moved swiftly forward away from the shore. As all three sailors leaned over, Rhys glanced back at the foaming wake. This looked like good fun, but he was a bit nervous.

Bran shouted to Rhys above the noise of the wind, "We're going to cross the estuary to the far shore and sail down with the tide. If we keep close inshore, we can see if there's anything unusual. Our neighbours on the far territory will have lookouts on each high point, but our main concern is the islands. It's too dangerous to keep men there overnight, so we have to check for invaders daily. Well, what do think, Rhys?"

"I like it, sire. I can't believe how far we've travelled already, but there looks to be some big waves further out."

"Yes, the wind is blowing up the channel and over the tide. It will get a bit choppy in the middle.

Canna, I think we need our caps now." Canna pulled three light woolly caps from under the fore-deck and they all donned them against the cold breeze. Rhys, by now, was elated with this new experience; he definitely wanted to be a sailor.

As they sailed into the rougher water, occasional spray spurted up from the bow. The two youngsters laughed together. Suddenly some shiny black sea-creatures leapt up from the water near the bow. Rhys felt his heart jump, but Canna laughed.

"Porpoise," shouted Bran. "We don't hurt them; they're supposed to be the souls of long dead sailors."

Rhys watched in awe as the porpoise dived and played in front of the bow; it seemed as if they had been waiting to join the boat. Breathing in the salt-air deeply, Rhys, once more, felt that he had made the right decision. This was the life.

In no time at all they were approaching the far shore; the boat felt stable and strong as the wind blew hard on the sail, and the tide was now running swiftly out to sea. Rhys looked around and could hardly see their home shore. He now realised how the larger Saxon ships with many oars and a sail could approach a shoreline at night so swiftly. It seemed that the Saxons were the masters of the sea and the Britons had no ships to take them on. He wondered if he should try and pray for the army who were still somewhere far to the east.

"We'll make straight for that low hill over there," pointed Bran. "There should be someone about to signal to us that all's well." The boat left the rougher water and glided smoothly towards the shore away from the fast tide. As they turned alongside, a now exposed beach, Bran slackened off the sail lines and allowed the boat to drift. A figure appeared on the distant hillside and waved slowly with his arms over his head. This was the signal that they had been looking for. The three sailors waved back and drifted slowly down the coast.

"We don't want to go too far just yet, Rhys. We need to get to the islands at low tide. First we'll drift on down to Sandy Point and rest on the beach."

Rhys was in wonder of the coastline and he had never seen so many birds. There were seabirds of all colours and sizes wading in the shallows or landing on the newly exposed rocks. After checking along the muddy shore, they rounded Sandy Point and the breeze allowed them to sail onto a shallow beach.

"You can stretch your legs now, lads," said Bran. "There are some rock pools all along the bay, Rhys. If you haven't seen the seashore before, Canna will show you the crabs and the small fish."

Canna was glad to show Rhys around the sandbars and rocks. Rhys had indeed never seen seaweed before and the smell of the sea was wonderful. Canna hardly spoke, but he eagerly pointed to all the things that would interest his new friend.

Bran kept the boat away from the receding waterline as the boys explored. When the tide started to run quickly, he now judged it time to leave. His crew jumped aboard and they set off once more along the coastline.

"See the islands, Rhys; that flat one is called Ynys Echni and the big one is Ynys Brenin. We'll pull in behind the big hill at Brenin Point over there on our left and meet the local clan. Then we'll wait until the tide is right to cross over to the islands." Rhys was shown how to cross the sail to the opposite tack and the boat moved out into the stronger current. There was now one thing that Rhys wanted more than anything; and that was to learn how to sail a boat.

"It will be some time before the tide turns, Rhys. I want to be ready to ride the current with the wind behind us to get back home. You'll be surprised how quickly we'll get back to the Isca."

Eventually, they approached Brenin Point and Bran expertly sailed the boat around the point and onto a steep shingle beach. Several fishing boats were lying well above the water line and a group of men and boys, smelling strongly of fish, left their fire to greet them. They were obviously old friends.

After introductions had been made, the men invited the visitors to share their fire. Three large fish were cooking on skewers over the fire and a pile of washed-up logs made comfortable benches. Rhys had not tasted such fine fish before; it was all very different from his life on the Menei.

"Here, Rhys," said one of the men. "You'll want to see our fishing lines and hooks." He held up some strong animal gut attached to a line of leather, and a metal hook which was the biggest Rhys had ever seen. "And here's a sea eel for you to take back with you." Rhys looked down into the fishing boat and there, still moving, was a huge, black sea eel. They all laughed as Rhys gasped. He had never seen an eel so big and with ugly-looking teeth.

"I hope you've got a sack to put it in," laughed Bran. "I don't want that thing trying to take my foot off!"

After exploring the steep hillside and the long pebble beach with Canna, it was time to set sail again. Rhys could hardly carry the heavy wet sack with the eel inside; he had made sure that the top was tightly tied. The fishermen bade them farewell and pushed the visitors' boat off the beach. With the sail hauled in tight, Bran set course for Ynys Brenin. The sea in the main channel was still choppy and Rhys was now glad of his heavy coat against the sea breeze and the spray. It took some time to cross to the island, which loomed high above them. The noise of the sea-birds was deafening as Canna pointed out the nests on the cliff face.

Bran steered the boat along the rocky cliffs, then turned out of the current behind the island to make for a small inlet. "We collect a lot of eggs early in the season; then later, when the young birds start to fly, people come from both sides of the channel to hunt them. They pluck them and smoke them here on the island. See all the driftwood, Rhys?" Rhys nodded – he had heard of such things.

They pulled the boat a little way up on to the shingle. "There's nowhere for any Saxons to hide their ships on this island, so I'll stay here, Canna, while you show Rhys the top of the island. Then you can look around with your sharp eyesight. This island is where the Silurian Kings used to be buried, you know, Rhys. At one time it was a very sacred place. That was before you Christians took over of course."

They all laughed at this jest as Bran pointed to a steep pathway and the boys set off.

"This is the steepest pathway I've ever seen," gasped Rhys as they emerged onto the plateau and surveyed the mass of heather, gorse and flowers. "It's no wonder the old Kings wanted to finish up here, Canna. You can see the whole country in every direction."

Canna led the way along a worn path overlooking the sea. They came to a high point and Rhys stared across the channel to the flatter island – Ynys Echni.

"I can't see any movement, Canna. I suppose if a Saxon ship came in on the tide, they would try to land on the far side of the island out of the strong current." Canna nodded in agreement. The boys then crossed to the middle of the island, where Canna pointed out the remains of an old Roman temple. There was also a group of mounds; the graves of the ancient Silurian Kings, mimed Canna. At this point, angry sea birds swooped down on the boys making them duck – were the spirits of the dead objecting to this intrusion?

"I wonder what gods they worshipped," said Rhys. Canna shrugged his shoulders. Rhys thought his grandfather, Brochvael, who scoffed at the Christians, would be most interested in this island; he would tell him all about it. They trotted back to the cliff edge and carefully picked their way back down to the water where Bran was relaxing in the boat.

"Here we are, boys, the last of the bread and cheese. But only water to drink, I'm afraid. I had to finish off the ale before it got too stale. Well, it's nearly low water, Rhys, see the bare rocks and seaweed?"

This was all most enjoyable, thought Rhys, as he hungrily finished off some crumbs. The tide coming in and out was all very strange and, as Bran pointed out, a man wouldn't survive very long in the cold, swirling water out of his boat.

With the sails once more filled by the breeze, Bran steered out into the now abated current.

"We'll sail round the rest of the island just to check and then make for Ynys Echni. I bet you've never seen so many birds, Rhys."

Rhys could only agree. The slack water between the islands was calm enough as Bran offered Rhys the helm. Under Bran's guidance, they tacked back and forth in the light breeze and Rhys soon got the measure of changing direction and sailing as close to the wind as the sail would allow. This was good sport indeed and they soon approached the low island of Echni.

"We'll skirt right around the island. Now, there you are… see the goats?" Bran asked. Bran pulled into the shore and the boys held the boat on some rocks. Canna pulled a bag from under the foredeck and threw lumps of stale bread and old vegetables onto the foreshore. The goats pounced noisily on this welcome food as Rhys looked on in amazement.

"You see, Rhys – there are six goats altogether. If there were Saxons hiding on this island, they would surely have killed one of them for food; especially after being at sea for a few days, so I think we can relax now." Bran laughed at Rhys, who could only nod his head at this clever plan.

They pushed off once more and sailed just offshore around the whole island. The goats followed them, jumping ditches and bleating for more food.

"You see, Rhys, we would soon know if there was anyone hiding there." Rhys nodded once more.

The new incoming tide was starting to swirl around the rocks and the southerly wind was getting stronger.

"We'll make for home now, boys; you'd better hang on."

The boat picked up speed and sliced through the water. In no time they were off the coast near Caer Taf and waving to figures on the higher ground.

"If we hadn't appeared with the tide, they would report to their commander; it might mean that we had been cut to pieces by the sea-devils."

Bran and Canna laughed at Rhys' wide-eyed expression.

"I should have brought my bow and dagger," countered Rhys.

"Here you are, take the helm again, Rhys. You can sail us right into the mouth of the Isca while I rest." Bran swapped places with his new apprentice and Rhys sat proudly in the captain's place – this was quite something to tell the boys back at the monastery.

Eventually they arrived at the shoreline that Rhys recognised. The wind was blowing up the river towards Caerllion and Bran allowed Rhys to continue up the centre of the Isca on the fast-running tide. They hit the jetty with a jolt and, after a quick lowering of the sail, Canna jumped ashore and tied up the bow and stern. All was secure.

"I can't thank you enough, Bran; and you Canna. That was the best day I've ever had." Rhys stretched his legs and was reluctant to leave his new companions.

"I'm always looking for sailors, Rhys. If Tarou can spare you, we'll see you again soon. Now, you'd better get back to your schooling. It's a pity you can't join us in the tavern!"

Rhys pretended to be very disappointed.

***

Back at the bishop's house, Rhys excitedly related the day's events to Bishop Dyfrig and his deacon who gasped at the sight of the sea eel. They were glad for him and more than pleased that he was concerned about getting back to the monastery in time for evening prayers.

Beech was excited to be out again and joyfully cantered along the trackway to the monastery. Rhys let him into one of the paddocks to graze and carried his saddle back to the stable block. He was now aching all over but glad to be back in familiar surroundings.

The abbot and Felix were apprehensive about the gift of the sea eel. It would be a welcome dish for Sunday, but there was some concern over who would kill the still squirming monster.

"That will be no problem, sire," said Rhys, quietly laughing to himself at their distaste at killing any living creature. "If Govan and Dingad will help me to hold it, I'll cut off its head and it will be ready for cooking first thing in the morning."

A sharp knife was brought from the kitchen as Rhys emptied

the contents of the sack into a large trough in which he could later wash down the remains. Everybody had gathered around but promptly scattered at the sight of such a large ugly fish. Govan and Dingad were eventually coaxed closer as Rhys put the sack over the eel's head and held it down with two hands.

"You see, it's easy; now you two hold him like this and I'll cut his head off."

The assembled crowd saw Rhys in a new light as he deftly dispatched and gutted the eel. Not everybody enjoyed their supper that evening.

CHAPTER 8

The Army Returns

The evening instruction by the monks in the gardens gave Rhys the chance to tell his friends all about his adventurous day. Felix joined the group when they were out of sight of the other monks, for he was intrigued by Rhys' new status with the soldiers. He gasped as much as the pupils when Rhys told them of the porpoise and explained how the goats played their part in detecting any intruders on Ynys Echni.

"I could really feel the presence of the old pagan gods on Ynys Brenin, you know. I'm sure the Kings' spirits are still there wandering around…" Rhys glanced round as Felix and the pupils looked aghast at this heathen notion.

"You can't mean…" Felix cut short his outrage as he saw a wicked smile appear on Rhys' face. "You're having me on…" he started to say as the boys all laughed and pointed at him.

Crawling into bed later, Rhys dreamed happily of ships and long journeys to faraway lands, but later in the night he woke with a start thinking about the soldiers in the east. Surely, there would soon be word to say that they were all safe.

Eastertide was soon upon them and Good Friday was a day of rest and prayer. The whole of the monastery left for the morning service in the basilica and Rhys was surprised to see how many townsfolk were in attendance – there were obviously many Christians in Caerllion and the huge church was packed as Bishop Dyfrig led the prayers. The previous evening, word had arrived that, thankfully, the army had pushed back the Saxons after some fierce fighting and were due to return soon. The town was in a festive mood – it certainly was a good Friday.

***

On Saturday morning Rhys was desperate to find out more news. With Beech saddled up, he galloped from the monastery and around the town to the barracks. On arrival Rhys could see many horses ready to move out. Tarou and his officers were clearly making arrangements for an important trip. Rhys dismounted and surveyed the scene with interest as he waited to be called.

"You can store your bow in the barracks, Rhys, then go to the kitchens and help load up the food packs. I'll explain later." Tarou continued giving orders as Rhys went to the kitchens where he was surprised to find Lewys and the colts.

"About time," said a disgruntled Lewys. "Here, carry some of these packs."

"Where are we off to? Is the army coming back today?" Rhys was anxious to know what was going on.

"We're taking these fresh horses up to Black Rock. Arthur and the army are hoping to cross on the next low tide. They'll need plenty of food and ale."

"How are they? Are there many wounded?" Rhys dared not ask if any were killed.

"They cleared out the Saxons but lost many men. There are a lot of wounded; that's why two surgeons are coming with us. The tide is just starting to turn, so we need to be at Black Rock before low tide for the crossing." Lewys was making sure that everybody in his troop, and that included Rhys, knew just who was in command.

When the boys were loading up the horses, Tarou came across to them rubbing his hands.

"Well, lads, it sounds as if Arthur and Cynan have had a good foray. The rest of us have to stay here, so you have an important job to do. Now, if there are ten of you altogether, you should be able to manage three horses apiece on long reins besides your own. You may even have to walk back to Caerllion if your own horses are needed… but that's good training, don't you think, Lewys?"

"Yes, sire," said Lewys inwardly groaning. "Good training, sire."

Rhys could see that the colts were looking a little pale from their night-time duties up on Saint Albans hill. They had probably found it difficult to get much sleep in the daytime before keeping watch all night. He wondered if they had time to meet any of the girls at the nunnery – they all knew how strict the abbess was.

Soon, the arrangements were complete and two ferries and various rowing boats got everybody across the Isca intact. Lewys led the way and one by one the procession started off along the old Roman road eastwards. The inland road overlooking the wide estuary eventually led downhill to the Havren and Black Rock. When the troop stopped to rest on the hillside, Rhys looked across the wide expanse of swirling water and the now-emerging rocks; he could clearly see Arthur's army gathered on the far shore, most men just slumped on the ground. This was a place that he had wanted to see, for he knew that his father and his uncle had both crossed the Havren here on their own expeditions with the army.

Rhys' main concern was the Abermenei warriors led by Arteg; until the army started to cross, there was nobody he could ask. He prayed quietly.

There was a small garrison and village overlooking Black Rock and the elderly commander approached Lewys to ascertain his mission. As they talked, Rhys turned to one of the surgeons who looked worried.

"I hope there aren't too many casualties, sire. Have you seen many battles with the Saxons?" asked Rhys.

"Yes," sighed the surgeon. "I used to be a soldier so I saw many of my friends die unnecessarily from their wounds and decided that I wanted to be a surgeon. I have quite enough work to do after they've all been training at Caerllion. I just don't have the stomach to fight wars any more."

A large crowd from the village and many families from the area had gathered on the shore, all watching intently as the tide receded. Luckily, the weather was fine. There were many boats gathered on the far shore and several ferries were being kept in the slack water behind the rocks. A shout went up as a long rowing boat pulled away from the other side and oarsmen frantically rowed across the current to make for the near shore. The boat was carried a little way upstream and then made its way to the muddy landing stage. Lewys urged his troop forward to the bank as the boat pulled into shore and a group of soldiers climbed onto the jetty including Arthur and two officers. Rhys was relieved to see that they were in a jovial mood.

"Good news, everybody," shouted Arthur as the crowd cheered. "We hunted down Saxons way over to the east and burned down their villages. They had encroached on our territory and paid the price. You can be sure they'll stay away for a very long time. We also rescued some captives and reunited them with their families. They don't have very pleasant stories to tell." Arthur surveyed his subjects. "The wounded will be here by low water and they'll need help to cross. Are the surgeons here?"

Lewys ran forward. "Yes, sire, and I've got the colts and fresh horses – and food and ale."

"Well done, Lewys. I dare say my men here would appreciate some ale. Lead us to it!"

Tables and benches had been prepared and tents erected to tend to the wounded. Arthur spoke with the surgeons and gave them orders to do everything possible for the wounded men; then he and his officers drank thirstily before recounting details of the battles.

"We only lost twenty four men and most of the wounded are not too bad. Lewys, you and your men help the surgeons when they get back across and then find some carts to get the wounded up to the village. They've had enough travelling, so find them rooms with the commander where they can be comfortable. Then you can take your orders from Cynan, he'll want the wounded horses and the equipment belonging to the dead brought back to Caerllion tomorrow."

Rhys heaved a sigh of relief to know that Cynan was all right. He desperately wanted to ask about Arteg, but knew that he must wait.

"Yes, sire," said Lewys smartly. "You can rely on us."

Arthur surprisingly turned to Rhys.

"We have a number of captives, Rhys. Your job is to question them. We can't understand a word they're saying; they seem to think they're going to be killed the way they're bleating. Do it your own way, but I want any information they can give us; the plans of their leaders; how many soldiers are moving west. And most important, what they're up to on the south coast."

Rhys was pleased that he should be given such an important job and couldn't help noticing that Lewys looked annoyed.

"Yes, sire. I'll question them separately. May I ask, sire, is Arteg safe?"

"Yes, indeed, and all the men from the north. Now, we'll need three good horses to get us back to Caerllion." Arthur rose as Lewys quickly arranged for fresh horses.

One of Arthur's captains called Rhys over and spoke to him gruffly.

"When the Saxon captives get here you'll see a good looking woman with a young boy. She belongs to me. See that she gets a horse and when you get them all back to the barracks, bring her to me."

"Yes, sire, of course." Rhys felt that he had better not make any mistakes with this officer; he looked mean and hard.

Lewys arranged with the garrison commander to set out more benches and to bring baskets of bread from the village to feed the hundreds of hungry soldiers. Sheep, pigs and sides of beef were already roasting on spits nearby. Rhys thought out his plan of action with the captives; he knew that he would have to be subtle to get them to talk.

Eventually, the tide had gone out enough to reveal a trackway down to the waterline and the remnants of the army appeared on the far shore. Rowing boats had strung lines from shore to shore on the rocks to enable the ferries to cross straight away and bring back the wounded. The soldiers crossed over to Black Rock in a large fleet of rowing boats, as their horses were packed onto the ferries and quickly hauled across the slackening river current. There was much shouting and jesting as the weary soldiers struggled up the bank and tucked into the feast before them; they were certainly in the mood for celebrating.

Eventually, Cynan stepped from one of the boats, issuing orders and looking pleased with the proceedings. He called Rhys over.

"You know about the captives, I dare say. We need information. You'll be glad to know that Arteg and the men of Abermenei are at the rear; they'll probably want to set off home soon after they've eaten." He could see that Rhys was a little perplexed by all this activity. "If you do a good job, you'll be wanted in the army next year."

Rhys nodded and tried not to look too pleased as Cynan made for the benches. Everything was happening so quickly, but at least Arteg and his troop were safe.

The colts scuttled around trying to please the rowdy mob as Rhys kept an eye on the ferries. Soon a bedraggled and exhausted group of Saxons landed on the jetty with two guards who, on learning of Rhys' orders, were now glad to put them in his charge. The captives were in no condition to be of any danger; the ankles of the men were tied with just enough rope to enable them to walk. Rhys immediately recognised the Saxon woman and her child and knew they must be cared for. This reminded him of Helga back at Penhal for she, also, had once been the Saxon captive of his uncle. He counted seven men, most of them older and some of them with bruises and wounds, and three young women besides the mother and boy.

"I'm here to look after you," stated Rhys in the Saxon tongue. They looked up in surprise at this young warrior who spoke to them in their own tongue. "I know that you're tired; well, you can rest here and have some food, then we must move off downstream."

Rhys looked for any sign of resentment in their faces, but there was none. He then waved them off the ferry and led them up a pathway, away from the soldiers. Without thinking, he picked up the exhausted boy and carried him in his arms to a grassy bank. The group slumped to the ground as Rhys sought out Lewys.

"They need some food and water and then they must rest, Lewys…" Rhys was annoyed when Lewys cut him short and said they were just prisoners with no special rights.

The garrison commander, having already got the measure of Lewys, could see the difficulty and called both boys to one side.

"I think we must interpret Arthur's orders carefully, Lewys. He told Rhys to interrogate the prisoners his way, and he wouldn't be pleased if any of them collapsed or died."

Lewys could sense the danger of getting blamed for making a wrong decision, and shrugged his shoulders resignedly before walking away.

"I'll help you to feed them, Rhys," said the commander. "It will be a while before all the baggage is across."

Rhys knew enough of the Saxon language to gain their confidence and make them feel at ease. They gratefully accepted the food and water. None of them seemed to be warriors and he tried to explain that if they told him the truth, they might be allowed to join the other Saxons in the village near Caerllion – but if they lied, or tried to escape, then he might not be able to save them from terrible torture and execution in front of the others.

Rhys next sought out Cynan and explained his strategy.

"There is one thing, Cynan; I'd like to take the ankle ropes off the men. Their sores could turn nasty and I'm sure they haven't got the strength to try and escape."

Cynan thought for a moment.

"Yes, Rhys, I think you're right. It might boost their respect for you and encourage them to talk. Dismiss."

"Yes, sire." Rhys grinned. Arteg's advice at Penhal had been to always think matters out carefully before making an important decision – bad decisions could prove costly.

Just then, a cheer from the tables greeted Arteg and his men who had crossed with the baggage. Rhys could not help himself and pushed through the crowd to the ferry to grip a surprised Arteg by the hand. The band from Penhal together with the men of Abermenei, some of them with wounds, were all pleased to see Rhys; they rubbed their grubby hands into his new monastic haircut, which caused him to threaten them all with drowning. This was indeed a good meeting. While the helpers took charge of the unloading and led the men to the tables, Rhys gave Arteg the details of his orders from Arthur.

"I'll bring my food and drink over and join you, Rhys. Now, you see that Saxon there on his own; well, I've been watching him and I don't trust him. I think he's one of the Saxon equerries. We caught him escaping through the woods after a battle. I suggest you should question him now while he's still a bit confused; otherwise, he might use his position to threaten the others and upset your plans." Rhys nodded.

They all ate in silence as Arteg glared at the lone Saxon. Rhys spoke first.

"I know, I'll ask him why he didn't fight alongside the others… and I'll tell him that you'll strangle him if he lies."

"What's your name?" asked Rhys gruffly as he and Arteg led the Saxon away from the rest of the group and out of earshot.

"Athelgar... I'm just a farmer. I haven't harmed anybody."

"Let me see your hands." The Saxon's hands were certainly not those of a farm worker; he looked about thirty years of age and was well groomed. Rhys then observed the inside of his breeches. "You're a horseman judging from your breeches. They're worn." Rhys made himself look angry and signalled to Arteg.

"I'll cut your throat, you dog," shouted Arteg drawing his dagger. The other Saxons looked on, cringing with fear. Rhys held Arteg back as Athelgar croaked and tried to crawl away.

"You're a spy, aren't you?" shouted Rhys. "Where were you going when our men caught you? I'm the only one who can save you now."

"Don't kill me... I only obey orders. I don't know anything."

Although he was genuinely angry with the Saxon, Rhys felt a new spirit welling up inside himself. He was not Rhys the boy any more – he was part of the King's army and was going to act like a soldier. He had discovered a new inner strength.

Arteg called one of his men to fetch a rope and pretended to get ready for a hanging. At this point, the Saxon broke down completely and begged Rhys to spare his life.

In a whispered conversation with the distraught Saxon, Rhys said his life would only be spared if he told them everything. At the same time he pointed out that, when he questioned the others, they would expose him if he tried to cover up any lies.

"What will happen to me if I talk?" bleated Athelgar.

"You'll go to the King's prison camp at Caer Taf. We only kill Saxons if they don't behave. Think about it this way; if you escaped and got back to your own clan, they would probably kill you after questioning you anyway."

Rhys felt that he had guessed right when Athelgar decided to resign himself to his fate. After a long discussion which Rhys had to interrupt occasionally in order to fully understand his dialect, Athelgar was led dejectedly well away from the others. Rhys did not want any further contact between Athelgar and the other Saxons.

As Athelgar sat hunched on the bank with his head resting on his knees, Rhys had one more question for him.

"What do you know of a Saxon with long white hair?" he asked quietly.

Athelgar looked up inquisitively.

"Cenwulf? You've heard of him?"

Rhys nodded, noting the name Cenwulf.

"Well, he's the leader of three keels and a mighty warrior. You'll never get the better of him."

"Was he at a big battle about ten years ago?"

"Yes, that's where he got his wounded leg – so he took up commanding long-boats."

Rhys turned away, angry, but relieved that he knew more of this hated Saxon. The blood surged to his head as memories of his father came flooding back. Breathing in heavily, he walked away and made for Cynan and Arteg.

Regaining his composure he joined the group and, when

they were all huddled around a table, proudly summarised his information.

"You were right, Arteg. He was an important messenger and when you ambushed his war party and killed them all, he was trying to get back to his headquarters in the east. His masters will probably think he was killed with the rest. Anyway, the West Saxons are planning to raise a huge army, drive northwest to the coast of the Summer Land and capture the three rivers. Then they'll build a stronghold on the Maendibyn Hills and use it as a secure base for controlling the Havren estuary. At the same time, the South Saxons will send a fleet of ships along the south coast to raid inland just east of South Isca and eventually join up with them. In that way, the whole of Dumnonia will be isolated."

The soldiers gasped in anger and disbelief and Cynan thumped his fist on the table.

"Arthur knew they were planning something big. We must get reinforcements down from the north. Well done, Rhys, and you, Arteg. Now, men, we must keep this to ourselves. Don't say a word to anybody. We'll take that Saxon back with us to Caerllion, but the King will want him in Caer Taf for further questioning. When are they planning to attack, Rhys?"

"It's planned for midsummer, Cynan. I'm pretty sure Athelgar's telling the truth. He's no warrior and he wants to live."

As the group broke up, Rhys noticed that Lewys was nearby, trying to overhear the whispered conversation. Cynan called him over and gave his next orders.

"Lewys… you're doing a good job. Tell Hwyn and one other colt to join Rhys and get the captives back to Caerllion. He's going to question them to get information and they need to be back before nightfall. I'm setting off later with my two officers and that Saxon over there… we'll need four fresh horses. Your job is to help the wounded and then stay with them overnight. Any who can travel tomorrow you can bring back together with the wounded horses."

"Yes, sire," replied Lewys squinting his eyes suspiciously at Rhys.

Handing Athelgar over to Lewys, Rhys assured him that he wouldn't be harmed – he was too important. It was time to set off, so Rhys went to say goodbye to Arteg and his troop. He tried to disguise any sign of anxiety for he and Arteg were the only ones present to know that a big battle was planned for midsummer.

The Saxon woman and her son were hoisted onto Beech and the other captives struggled to their feet for the long journey. Hwyn and the other colt mounted their own horses and the group set off for Caerllion.

With Rhys well in front and his companions keeping the other captives out of earshot, it was time to question the woman. She was more at ease when Rhys tried to comfort her and her exhausted son, but she bowed her head on learning that she and her son were to join the officer.

"I'm sure you'll be well cared for," offered Rhys sympathetically, at the same time smiling at the nervous boy. He was well aware of his responsible position and was now so glad of Helga's help in learning to speak the Saxon language.

The woman, in many ways, resembled Helga, but her fair plaits were ragged and dirty and her shoulders were rounded in dejection. He hoped that the officer would not treat her too harshly.

The other captives, he explained, would probably be sent to the Saxon village to work and none of them would be harmed. She would be well aware that the Saxons leaders always sacrificed one tenth of their Celtic war captives to their god, Woden.

It appeared that the woman's small village had been destroyed in a surprise attack by Arthur's army and the defenders all killed. The captives were mostly from her area, but she had never seen Athelgar before. What she did know was that one of the young men from her own village had been training with the Saxon army and had been boasting of breaking through the defences of the Britons to capture the coast somewhere to the west. Her own husband had been killed in the battle and she was now only concerned for her young son's safety. Rhys could only pity them.

Satisfied that her story confirmed Athelgar's account, Rhys separated and questioned all of the others in turn. The whole company kept moving and occasional rest stops at springs gave Rhys the opportunity to gain their confidence. They were all so weary that they answered Rhys' questions without hesitation. The other two colts were impressed by Rhys' command of the situation and looked on respectfully.

Just as Rhys had hoped, Cynan had settled all his business at Black Rock and now caught up with them.

"What else have you found out, Rhys? These Saxons are going to be late getting back to Caerllion by the state they're in."

"I'm sure that Athelgar was telling the truth, sire. The Saxon woman with the boy knows about a plan for a Saxon push to the coast somewhere in the west and some of the others have heard of it. But they're all farmers and labourers, and I'm sure none of them know any more."

"Good. We'd all of us best get back to Arthur. You jump on that horse with Athelgar, then we'll lead the woman on your horse and I'll have the boy in front of me." Cynan then motioned to his two officers to help out. "Hwyn, you're now in charge of the rest of the prisoners. Make sure you get them all back in one piece. They can see your daggers and I doubt they'll get any ideas."

"Yes, sire." Hwyn's eyes lit up on receiving such an important order from Cynan.

Rhys was hoisted onto the spare horse behind a dejected Athelgar and they all cantered off to Caerllion. After an uncomfortable journey they arrived back at the barracks just before the sun set.

The senior officer, who had given Rhys the order to escort his captive woman, appeared on the parade ground a little drunk. Rhys thankfully slipped to the ground and handed Athelgar over to a waiting soldier. He then comforted the frightened little boy and led Beech and the woman to the waiting officer.

"They're both very weary, sire... they need food and water." Rhys was well aware of the woman's fate and felt sorry for her, but he shuddered to think of the number of captive women who had been taken by the Saxons and forced into slavery.

The officer grunted and helped the woman down from Beech.

"I'll take great care of this one, don't you worry. And the boy will find in me a second father."

Rhys noticed that the woman straightened up and took her son's hand – she now seemed to accept her fate and had regained her dignity.

As the officer led his new family to his quarters, Cynan beckoned Rhys.

"Get your bow, Rhys and follow me to Arthur's quarters; he will want to know everything you found out."

***

On the edge of the town and with a garden that backed onto the barracks, lay Arthur's extensive town villa; Rhys knew that a large room was used for military planning with the senior officers, but he never dreamt that he would be involved in such high-level discussions.

Rhys found Arthur reclining on a divan sipping wine, and an important-looking older man who Rhys had not seen before stood at a table with a large rolled-out map on it. Some pretty girls were laying a table and arranging the furniture as they chattered and giggled. Rhys watched intently when they lit oil lamps which showed off the old wall paintings. It all looked very gracious and Rhys thought how well the Romans used to live.

Cynan and his men greeted the new arrival with a salute then, teased the girls. Arthur waved them from the room and everyone assembled round the table.

"I think we have some important news for you, Arthur. Young Rhys here has been questioning the captives and one of them turned out to be an important equerry."

Arthur jumped to his feet and called Rhys forward.

"This is my dear uncle, Geraint; he's the high King of Dumnonia and without him and his men, we would have lost the whole of the south-west by now."

Geraint's tunic was salt-stained; Rhys supposed he must have arrived by ship as he bowed instinctively to the King.

"So, what can you tell us, Rhys?"

The King looked into Rhys' eyes, obviously disconcerted that one so young should be in their company. He was very much the nobleman; clean shaven and with neat clothes under a gold rimmed green cape.

Rhys nervously related every detail of his questioning of the captives while the commanders listened carefully and studied the map. Rhys swallowed hard as Arthur stroked his stubbled chin and cursed.

"What do you think, Geraint? You know how the Saxon mind works. If they gathered an army at their base at Caer Sallog, they could advance along the old Roman road and get to the Maendibyn Hills in two days."

"It makes sense, gentlemen; it's just a question of numbers. The Saxons can strike where and when they like, and if they have enough men and supplies, a push to the coast at the three rivers would leave us completely outmanoeuvred. If they managed to set up a defensive base at this point on the coast, they would have a safe port for their ships and be able to cut off the whole of the Havren Channel. With defences on the Maendibyn heights and Brenin Point and with supplies coming from the sea, they could forage at will and our villages and farms would be at their mercy."

Geraint, older than the rest, looked stern and tough, and he was obviously worried at the possibility of just such a move by the Saxons.

Arthur slowly moved his finger over the map.

"If they made a sudden thrust into these two positions and dug in, we would have the devil's own job to attack them; then, with the enemy threatening the narrowest part of the peninsular from the south, we'd be in a hopeless situation."

Cynan stepped forward.

"It seems to me that these recent incursions were meant to test us, Arthur. They knew how we would react to their setting up villages in our eastern territory, and they were quite prepared to lose a few men. I'm pretty sure they think their equerry has been killed, because we put all the bodies into the houses and burned them down. I doubt if they suspect we know anything of their plans."

Geraint thought this made sense and the rest of the men seemed to agree, turning to each other and nodding.

"Cynan, you arrange for this Saxon equerry to be taken to King Myric in Caer Taf. He has people there who can make sure he's telling the truth. If an attack is planned for midsummer just before the harvest, they know they would then capture enough supplies to last them the winter. Geraint, you should have your army ready in the south and with our army marching down from the north, we must catch them in open country before they can get to the hills. The Cornovians from the north will be eager to join us with their cavalry." Arthur smiled down at Rhys. "You mustn't breathe a word of this, my boy… you know the penalty for treason!" The men all laughed as Arthur patted his dagger meaningfully.

Rhys nodded vigorously.

"Yes, sire, I won't even tell God." The men thought this was very amusing, coming as it did from a pupil of the monastery.

"Oh, yes, I daresay you're anxious to get back to your abbot and explain why you're late. I know, take a flask of wine for him as a gift from me." Arthur said and grinned.

Rhys was then dismissed and felt as if he was floating on air as he rode back wearily to the monastery. He was more than pleased with the way the day's events had turned out and the abbot was more than pleased with his wine.

CHAPTER 9

Battle Plans

Easter Sunday found the monastery in a festive mood. The Abbot had graciously dismissed Rhys' late return of the previous evening on receipt of the flask of wine from Arthur and had called in the senior monks for a brief summary of Rhys' story. Secretly, Rhys felt that the abbot was glad to be in touch with all the latest news from the army and the city.

The pupils too wanted to know everything about the campaign and Rhys held his audience spellbound, but again made no mention of the ominous Saxon plans.

After prayers and breakfast, during which some muted chattering was allowed, Fracan outlined the plans for attending the bishop's Easter morning service in the basilica.

On arrival at the grand basilica, Rhys was surprised to see such a large crowd stood outside. The church itself was full and the pupils were marched down the centre aisle to the front. They were ushered into rows facing the congregation; their duty was to lead the singing in the Roman language. Rhys was unable to avert his eyes from his fellow colts, who, apart from Lewys, all smiled at him. Tarou and his family warmly acknowledged Rhys. The front row was made up of a bored-looking Arthur, Cynan and the senior officers. A buzz of whispered conversation filled the huge hall.

A small rear door creaked open as Bishop Dyfrig and his three priests entered to stand on the raised dais in the rear apse and solemnly commence prayers. The congregation then fell silent as the Bishop made his Easter address, but Rhys was much more interested in the vaulted timber roof of the basilica which amply relayed the bishop's words to all parts of the building. He also wondered at the intricate wall paintings.

The chanting of the psalms was led by Abbot Aidan and the effects of the well-practised singing of the choir seemed to impress even the soldiers, most of whom had only attended to please their superiors. Rhys quite enjoyed the service, held in such distinguished company, but after returning to the gloomy monastery, he found the rest of the day boring.

Part of the Easter celebration, devised many years ago by Bishop Dyfrig, was to invite all of the townspeople to the monastery, where food and wine were laid on after a tour of the orchards and farmland. Rhys suspected that the bishop hoped to convert the largely indifferent townsfolk to Christianity and convince them to give up the ancient festival of Beltane.

Arthur had declared the festival a day of rest and he himself was going to visit the monastery and enjoy their hospitality. Unknown to the army and the townspeople, he had been sending King Myric's equerries to Caer Baddon and Caer Gloyw to instruct the commanders in the secret build-up against the imminent Saxon threat. King Geraint and his

Dumnonian army to the south had also been planning military manoeuvres. It was imperative that the Saxons had no knowledge of the Britons' movements: if they suspected that their plans had been discovered, then they could strike elsewhere and cause havoc with their battle-ready force.

The day of the festival was the Saturday following Easter, and after morning prayers, the monks and pupils rushed to set up tables and benches in the orchard. The trees were in full blossom and the bees and insects were hard at work in the morning sunshine. The loud buzzing was music to the ears of the monks; it would be a good harvest with an abundance of honey. Every spare cask had been sent to the Saxon village for filling with fresh ale; and horses and carts trundled back and forth with firewood, pots of stew, baskets of cakes and bread, not to mention fresh fish from the ponds. Several fires had been started early in the morning and mutton, pork and beef roasted slowly on spits.

"I hope we get chance to try out the ale," said Rhys to Dingad, hopefully.

"If it's anything like last year, Aidan will get as drunk as the rest of them; then we can sample a small beaker ourselves." Dingad was certainly getting into the spirit of the occasion.

Pails of water were ready for the symbolic washing of feet as the first guests arrived. It was the duty of the pupils to offer each arrival a seat so that they could have their feet washed and salved.

"It is an ancient custom," explained Dingad, "and many of the townsfolk are glad of such attention as their feet are often bruised or cut."

Lewys was well aware of this tradition and deliberately sought out Rhys. Followed by the other colts, he strode to the bench where Rhys was waiting and stood with his hands on his hips, smiling slyly. Before the church service, Rhys' fellow colts had never seen him in his tunic and sandals, and with the front part of his head newly shaved he looked nothing like the young warrior they were used to.

Rhys had anticipated this situation and smiled warmly.

"Please, sire, take a seat and allow me to wash your feet." He well knew that this act was a part of his monastic schooling in humility and he tried not to show any discomfort, although he felt it.

Lewys stepped forward and sat on the bench smiling.

"Welcome, sire, allow me," said Rhys kneeling in front of his colleague.

He pulled off Lewys' boots and, humming to himself, lathered his hands and lovingly washed his master's feet. Lewys, himself, became embarrassed as his companions stared down at him. As soon as Rhys had soothed in some sweet-smelling ointment, he smartly pulled on his boots and declared himself ready for some meat.

"Perhaps I'll get something to eat as well," said Hwyn, not wishing to offend Rhys by this ritual that he found merely silly.

"No, Hwyn, please, I insist. You'll feel much better for this ointment, and all the rest of you." Rhys firmly took Hwyn's hand and led him to the bench.

One by one, and ignoring the smelly odours, Rhys attended to his duty and each of his fellow colts agreed that they were well pleased and glad to see him. They chatted happily about the day's feasting and promised Rhys that they would let him drink from their mugs when no one was looking.

"I have some good friends here, you know. Later on I'd like you to meet them and we can show you around the farm. Abbott Aidan has asked us to show you around the monastery as well, if you like."

Hwyn pulled a long face and said jestingly, "I hope you're not trying to lock us up in this prison, Rhys. I think we may have to fight our way out, boys." He laughed loudly, clutching at the hilt of his dagger.

The orchard was soon crowded with soldiers, townsfolk and screaming children. It was as much as the pupils could do to keep everybody satisfied and at the same time control the children who had decided to run all over the farm. Rhys had been looking out for the young ruffians he had encountered near the tavern and eventually saw them grouped around some soldiers listening to stories of battles.

"Good morning, sires," said Rhys, cheerfully. "I hope we're going to see you amongst the colts next year. Army discipline is a wonderful thing!"

The boy who had felt the brunt of Rhys' reaction when he had stupidly tried to bully him coughed nervously, nodding his head in agreement. The soldiers, who knew Rhys well from the training fields, smiled knowingly. Rhys had learnt much about human nature and felt that this approach to a potential enemy could serve him well in future.

When the festive group seemed to be settled, Rhys, with Govan and Dingad, sought out the colts.

"Lads," said Rhys with good humour, "these are Govan and Dingad, my good friends. Would you like us to show you around our school and the gardens?"

Lewys looked sullen, as usual, in the presence of Rhys and declared, "I don't think we really care to."

The other colts gave a disappointed sigh, so Rhys good-naturedly thought he would have to try another tack. Just then Arthur walked through the crowd, mug in hand, and greeted the boys.

"Lewys and Rhys. I want you to both come and see me at my villa in the morning. We have some important plans to discuss. Well, I hope you're all enjoying Beltane… or perhaps I'd better call it the Bishop's Blessed Festival."

They all laughed at Arthur's irreverent jest.

"I was just going to show them around the monastery, sire. I know the boys would love to see the chapel." Rhys smiled at Lewys who sighed and gave in.

Arthur sensed the humour.

"Well, Lewys, with a bit of luck, you'll be able to join the pupils here next year. I'll put in a good word for you with the abbot." As Arthur turned away, he added, "perhaps I'll even mention it to the King." Lewys was not amused.

As Rhys ushered the boys into the monastery building, they were certainly impressed with the coloured glass window in the chapel as it gleamed in the morning sunlight. Rhys felt quite proud explaining life in the monastery and the boys even showed some interest as they all trooped around the dormitories, stables and workshops.

"We'll show you the vineyards next," offered Rhys, then explained how the grape-juice was fermented and stored. All in all, Rhys felt that his friends were now glad to have been shown around the grounds and the farm.

Rhys drew Lewys to one side.

"Lewys, I'll meet you in the morning. It sounds like we'll have another big job to do soon."

Lewys shrugged, as if now forced to accept Rhys as his equal.

The clearing up was carried out in high spirits and the pupils took advantage of the abundance of good leftovers. Dingad was particularly happy.

"I must say, Rhys, your friends were very pleasant and not a bit like fierce warriors. They were certainly generous with the ale."

"Yes, Dingad, and who knows, one day, we may all have to fight together in battle. Perhaps we'll all die." Rhys chuckled as a look of horror swept over the faces of his friends. "Anyway, I have to tell the abbot that I'm off again tomorrow. I bet he'll groan."

***

The morning gallop to the villa was bracing and Rhys met up with Lewys as they waited to be summoned. Each wondered what was about to happen; lately the Saturday training sessions had taken on a new urgency and Arthur and his officers were driving the men hard. The colts, led by Lewys, were given many tasks including the handling of boats under sail. Bran and Canna's instruction proved a great help and, gradually, Lewys had become more tolerant of Rhys – but only when it came to sailing boats. Eventually, some officers departed and Tarou called them into Arthur's presence. Rhys was surprised to see Bran there.

"Now, gentlemen, let's gather around these charts." Arthur looked serious. "Lewys, I hope you won't feel offended, but you're the only one here who isn't aware of the huge danger that faces us. As you know, Rhys was able to question the Saxon prisoners and one of them turned out to be an important messenger. The King at Caer Taf has questioned him further and there's no doubt; the Saxons are planning a big push before midsummer. We've had to keep this a close secret, so Lewys, you must keep this strictly to yourself. We don't want to spread alarm in the town."

Lewys kept a straight face as he glanced at Rhys.

"Yes, sire. I knew something was up when Cynan took off last week with his troop. But I didn't mention it to anyone." Arthur nodded and Lewys felt that his pride was restored.

"Let me show you all." Arthur waved his hand over the table. "This is a map of the whole area: you see, the Havren, the islands, Brenin Point and most importantly the Maendibyn Hills and the marshes beyond. Now, the Saxon plan is to move quickly up the old Roman road from Caer Sallog and take the Maendibyn Hills. From there they can strike at Brenin Point and then take the whole coast between the River Asc, the Bru and the Pared. Once established in forts, we will have no chance of beating them without suffering horrific losses. They can get supplies from the sea and as you know, we dare not tackle their longships at sea. Eventually, the whole of the south-west would be isolated."

Rhys felt a little scared, but also excited at this coming battle. Would he and Lewys be expected to fight? He wondered how Lewys felt.

Arthur pointed to the map.

"Geraint has scouts in the east. He's sent word that Saxon warriors are trickling into Caer Sallog and their army could number over three thousand already. They won't have many horses, but if they take a day's march to the forests below Maendibyn and rest overnight, then they can strike uphill at any point at daybreak. They will undoubtedly form into a Roman tortoise if we charge them in the open and that will counter any of our cavalry tactics. We will only be able to use spears and arrows if they bunch up and then we would have to try and wear them down. My plan is to keep clear of them until they strike uphill. They will probably be thinking they're going to have a clear run. We'll trap all of the roads and approaches with fallen trees, which will make them split up and then we can charge downhill when it suits us. Now, I'm telling you all this because I'll be in charge of our army at Aqua Sulis and ready to move south when the Saxons set out. Geraint with his army already in the south will be ready to move up through the marshes at the same time and Cynan will be on Maendibyn coordinating the cavalry and foot soldiers. The King's army at Caer Taf are using every available boat to cross to the beach south of Brenin Point and are, indeed, starting the build-up as we speak."

Arthur looked up at the solemn faces.

"It's imperative he continued, "that the enemy doesn't suspect any of our movements or they may change their plans. If they had word that we were in great numbers on the Maendibyn Hills before they got to the forest, then they could turn south through the marshes and ravage everything all the way back to their base. Now then, boys, this is where you come in. Tarou will be in charge of a garrison at Brenin Point and the colts from Caerllion and from Caer Taf will be manning the boats for their crossing. You've been practising your sailing and a fleet of new larger boats is almost ready." Bran shuffled his feet and coughed. "Bran will be giving you intensive training in the channel over the next few weeks. When it comes to the big crossing, each of you will have a boatload of soldiers from the northern valleys. It will take several trips. Tarou will set up defences on the hill and all the boats will be moored in nearby Ascmouth harbour."

Once again Arthur looked up.

"Well, boys, why do you think we need defences on Brenin Hill?"

Lewys looked a little perplexed; surely the Saxons would not be able to break through the armies and get to Brenin Hill! But Rhys had been following the plans with interest and thought he knew the answer.

"The Saxons might send a fleet of ships up the channel to

take Brenin, sire. They know we couldn't tackle them at sea and they could come in on a tide and sweep up the hill ready for their main army to join them."

"Exactly, Rhys. And they would then command the whole coast. We could never sail on the channel again if they had longships on the loose in our heartland. They must be stopped…" Arthur looked at each of them in turn, "even if we have to fight to the last man."

Tarou nodded in approval at Arthur's command of details. He had been half smiling at the two young colts.

"If we're needed in battle on Brenin, your troop will be archers in the first line of defence. Needless to say, we'll have to take hundreds of arrows with us."

"It won't come to that," reassured Arthur. "I don't intend the Saxons to even get onto the hills in the first place." Rhys noticed that some of Arthur's hair was falling over his forehead as he studied the map. He sensed that with such responsible decisions, Arthur was a very worried man.

"Tomorrow morning, we must act as if nothing is amiss, so we need to start our preparations quietly."

With that, Arthur left the room.

"Phew!" breathed Bran. "I'm glad the fighting will be up to you, youngsters."

This relieved the tense atmosphere somewhat.

"Never you mind, Bran – you leave the hard stuff to me and the boys," smiled Tarou.

***

Once on the streets of Caerllion, Tarou, Bran and the boys made their way to the river.

Sunday was largely a day of rest and the townsfolk were strolling about rather than doing their usual rushing back and forth. Tarou arranged for ale to be brought to a bench on the riverbank and they chatted furtively about events to come.

"You'll have to get back to the monastery by midday, Rhys," said Tarou apologetically. "Bishop Dyfrig knows all about the situation and I'll get him to release you full time when the new boats arrive. I dare say he'll find a suitable excuse for Abbot Aidan without actually telling him the truth."

Rhys had mixed feelings; he knew that he must carry on as if everything was normal, but at the same time he didn't want to miss any of the preparations. He was beginning to relish the thought of being near a battle with the Saxons and there was no question that the enemy would be defeated. There was only one nagging doubt – if it came to it, would he be brave enough in a real battle? Would he be badly wounded – or worse?

With a new sense of comradeship with Lewys, Rhys knew that they might find their lives in each other's hands. They laughed together uneasily and sipped their ale.

***

Next Saturday after prayers, Rhys galloped to the training fields. All was normal except for one thing – Lewys did not show his usual hostility. Rhys felt assured that their commander, Tarou, was going to be the one to save them if there was trouble on Brenin Hill. He was a family man and got on well with the young colts – they all looked up to him and now, thankfully, he would be spending more time with them and their mock battles.

"King Myric in Caer Taf is sending us some new estuary boats soon," explained Tarou as he gathered the troop around him. "No doubt, he wants you lot to enjoy yourselves." The troop cheered as Lewys and Rhys glanced at each other knowingly.

CHAPTER 10

The New Boats

One Saturday in the middle of May was a day that Rhys would always remember. After morning prayers and as he was about to change into his warrior clothing, Felix informed him that Abbot Aidan wished to see him.

On arriving at Aidan's office Rhys was surprised to see Bishop Dyfrig looking out of the small open window. He turned to give Rhys a knowing smile. Aidan did not look at all happy.

"I've just been talking to your abbot, Rhys. It seems that the army wants the pleasure of your expertise in sailing boats. Arthur has asked that you be released from your studies for a few weeks to train in the new boats due here from Caer Taf."

"Have they arrived already? I can't wait to see them." Rhys was elated; his heart thumped at the prospect of soldiering full time. He would probably be out in the channel every day battling with the fast tides. He put the thought of any danger to the back of his mind.

"It seems that the boats will be arriving on the midday tide. The colts from Caer Taf will be bringing them in and then staying at the barracks with you. Well, that's all. Good luck, Rhys."

Dyfrig turned away, but Rhys had noticed the bishop's eyes moistening – no doubt, he had had to deal with many war casualties previously and had known many young men who had not returned from battle. Rhys suspected that the bishop and the abbot would soon be praying for them all.

"Yes, father," said Rhys solemnly. Then turning to Abbot Aidan, he asked, "may I say goodbye to my friends, Abbot?" Aidan nodded wearily. He did not appreciate yet another disruption to his strict regime as he listened to Rhys race noisily up the stone stairs.

Collecting his backpack from the dormitory with his spare clothes freshly laundered and his sparse belongings neatly packed, Rhys rushed back down the stairs. He was not surprised to find Felix waiting with Dingad and Govan; they followed him to the stables and eagerly helped him with his saddle.

"I'm needed to train on some new boats," explained Rhys before his friends could question him. "I'll be gone for a few weeks and Arthur has excused me from the monastery."

His companions looked worried; what did this mean?

"Well, who's going to pass down my bow and arrows?"

The boys scrambled up into the loft as Rhys slipped into the adjoining workshop.

"I just need a few bits and pieces from my bag." Rhys delved into the bottom of his carpentry toolbag and retrieved his dagger and sheath. Quietly hiding his beloved weapon in his jacket, he returned to the stable and led Beech out to the courtyard.

"God bless you, Rhys. Be careful," his three friends shouted as Rhys cantered out onto the trackway. They obviously suspected that there was more to his departure than just training. He looked back and waved.

On the way to the barracks, Rhys strapped his dagger onto his leather belt and patted it lightly.

"If I get the chance, dear father," he whispered to himself, "I'll use it."

Brochvael had given the dagger to him when he had proved himself whilst training with Arteg and soon, perhaps, this weapon was going to be used against the Saxons once again. He wondered if he would really be called upon to fight – as Arteg had explained to him, once a battle started, anything could happen.

Arriving at the barracks, he found that all thoughts of the monastery had vanished – he was now a soldier in the King's army. Tarou directed the troop to the lower end of the fields near the river for archery practice, explaining that when the new boats sailed in, they would be on hand to greet them.

"Firstly," said Tarou, "you will collect defence bows from the armoury. As you know, they're longer and stiffer and with thicker arrows. We must also practice defence tactics."

Rhys and Lewys glanced at each other and nodded knowingly; training so far had been with their lighter cavalry bows.

Beech and the other horses were left to graze together. They all knew each other and were well trained to come when called. After all, a shout from their masters could mean a mad gallop around the training ground.

Lewys suggested that they should set up a whole variety of targets including tree trunk defences up on the hillside at the old fort. Tarou was due to accompany Arthur up into the valleys and mountains to speak with the various leaders, so Lewys was left in charge to make arrangements as he thought fit.

"I think we should shoot at the long-range targets, lads. That means all of us firing off our arrows together." Lewys had obviously been thinking ahead. "If the enemy was approaching in a tight formation with their shields over their heads, they could fend off individual arrows; so we all fire together when I give the signal."

"What about charging an enemy downhill?" suggested Rhys.

"Good idea," replied Lewys, "and with swords drawn. When Tarou gets back, I'll ask him if we can get rid of those stupid practice swords. What do you think, boys?"

"Yes!" they all shouted together. "We want real swords."

***

Later in the morning, the tide started to come in and the boys looked expectantly downstream. They decided to stack their weapons and walk on down to the Saxon village to make sure everything there was in order. As they approached, the elderman greeted Rhys and offered him some ale. Rhys declined; it would not be right for warriors on duty. He explained this to Lewys, which made him laugh as he sauntered into the courtyard. Looking around, Lewys arrogantly kicked at a half-open door to peer inside. The headman, knowing Lewys' temperament, invited him to go through the door; he knew his place and stood back.

Just then, Hwyn shouted from the riverbank.

"Here they come, boys. They're just coming round the bend."

The colts watched as the new boats, under full sail, sped toward them on the fast running tide. A tall young man, with long black hair making him look like a wild animal, stood upright in the leading boat; he was obviously their leader and Lewys shouted to him.

"Welcome. We'll meet you at the jetty."

With that, the colts had to break into a trot to keep up with the speeding fleet of six boats. On a word of command the sails were lowered and the oars put out at the ready. As Lewys and Rhys jumped onto the jetty ready to throw the mooring lines, the boats were expertly pulled into the slack water to be tied up.

The leader jumped ashore and he and Lewys clasped hands and smiled looking intently into each other's eyes. They both knew that they would have to respect each other, for they could well be comrades in arms for a long time to come.

"My name's Garwyn and you're Lewys, so I'm told. Well, what do you think of the boats? We had boat builders up from the west coast to help our own people. They were trained by the Romans in Armorica. See, four oars and plenty of space for cargo... or soldiers."

Garwyn gave a sly smile and led Lewys and Rhys up the steps away from the others. Rhys, following behind and admiring their demeanour, could understand why the two new acquaintances were sure to be army leaders in time.

"Don't worry, Lewys, I've been told all about Arthur's plans. The rest of the boys only know that we all have to get familiar with the new boats and the channel. I was told to report to Bran the boatman." Garwyn then looked around at the riverside activities and admired the buildings that were clustered on either bank.

"You've not been here before then, Garwyn," said Lewys. "We'll show you and the boys around later. We've got a barracks all to ourselves, and plenty of food. Tarou, our commander, says we'll be training all night sometimes. I think he's going to drive us into the ground." Garwyn laughed; he and Lewys were going to get along. The rest of the colts were happily chatting together and looking over the rigging and sails.

"These boats are so strong," enthused Hwyn. "I can't wait to get out into the estuary."

A loud cough caused them to turn around and see Bran striding towards them.

"Welcome Garwyn. You did a good job getting those boats up to Caerllion; they're bigger than I thought. Let me have a closer look."

With that Bran stepped nimbly down onto the jetty and jumped into the leading boat. The boys all gathered round as Bran inspected the planking, the rigging and the covered front area. Each nod of his head was accompanied by a quiet grunt.

"Good, the rudder paddles are strong, that's most

important. Well, they certainly look seaworthy. Tomorrow, Garwyn, you can show us how they handle. I do believe the wind will be up in the channel." Bran then stood up on the foredeck and caressed the mast with both hands. The boys looked at each other and smiled.

Lewys realised that he should introduce Rhys and the rest of his troop. "Garwyn, I'd like you to meet Rhys. He's had the most experience of us lot with boats." Lewys stepped back to allow Rhys to grasp Garwyn's hands. Rhys almost flinched at Garwyn's grip and couldn't help feeling intimidated at his piercing dark eyes and determined smile.

Before Rhys could speak, Garwyn burst out laughing at his shaven head.

"Oh, no, not you too! My poor younger brother is imprisoned down at Illtyd's school. How did you manage to escape?"

Rhys and the others laughed at Garwyn's teasing. Rhys could see that Garwyn was full of confidence and bravado and was going to be a good ally.

"You should see him with a cavalry bow!" laughed Hwyn. "Not to mention a thick staff."

Garwyn nodded knowingly.

"Well, I suppose I'd better pass on Tarou's orders, now," smiled Bran, joining in with the humour. "As part of your training, he wants you all to sit on the riverbank while I order some food and ale... not too much, mind you!" The boys all whooped at this unexpected pleasure.

As the young warriors ravenously grabbed at the baskets of

meat, bread and cheese and carefully shared out the jugs of ale, Bran turned to the two leaders.

"I suggest that Lewys shows you your quarters and the workshops, and then you can test each other with archery. This evening, you can explore the town and be sure to get an early night."

Bran then outlined Tarou's orders for the next week or so.

"We sail out into the channel every day. Don't forget you'll need heavy coats and fresh water flasks. At low tide you go onto the training fields, and sometimes at night!"

Lewys and Garwyn nodded eagerly – it sounded as if they were going to be stretched to the limit.

***

Later, Lewys led the whole contingent to the fields to collect their bows and show Garwyn the targets. The amphitheatre was of great interest and as expected some of the soldiers jeered at them and invited them into a battle. The boys retorted that they wanted some bigger, tougher enemies and after giving as good as they got, they hurried on their way. The rest of the day was hectic as the Caer Taf colts explored.

Lewys' troop had previously slept at their respective homes, but now they were all to stay in the barracks and act like soldiers. Rhys wondered if he would ever sleep at the monastery again.

The early morning awakening was too soon for the sleepy colts, but trotting around the parade ground with packs soon woke them up. Breakfast was substantial – eggs, salt pork, field beans and bread; they should not expect to eat again until evening apart from some bread stored in their packs. Soon, it was time to rig the boats and prepare for the next ebb tide.

Garwyn thought it would be best if he paired off the boys, two to each boat – he knew the capabilities of his own sailors and was well aware of the dangers of the open sea.

Bran gave his approval.

"Canna and I will lead the way in our trail boat. If we were ferrying equipment across the channel we would need to set out well before high tide. If that means getting swept upstream as we cross, then don't worry. We may well need to make two crossings before the ebb tide runs too swiftly below the islands."

Then, with only two oars per boat, they struggled to row down to the mouth of the estuary.

As Bran had predicted, the first leg of the journey took the fleet upstream, but by tacking close to the wind on the far shore, they were able to reach Brenin Point in good time. The new boats were a little sluggish, but safe. After a short break and a good-humoured chat with the Brenin fishermen, the steersmen all changed places for the dash to the two islands. The wind from the south was in their favour and after passing Ynys Brenin with its usual unbearable bird noise, they glided past Ynys Echni with its goats safely counted.

They sailed in line up the middle of the turbulent channel, then Bran gathered them at the mouth of the Isca.

"We'll pull into the old jetty on Ebyr Point. There's no need to go on upriver. If we ever had to make a second crossing with stores, we would load up here and go straight back."

The sails were lowered and the oars took them into the muddy bank. Ropes were thrown in order to pull the fleet together and tie up on the old jetty. Ebyr was the point where a smaller river joined the mouth of the Isca and soon a group of small children ran across from the nearby farm. They stood a little way off nervously watching these strange visitors until Rhys waved them over to see the boats.

"Here you are, children," said Bran, smiling at their nervousness. "Come on board and man the oars, then you can tell your parents you're going to be sailors."

Rhys thought that this was a nice gesture and was glad to help the children to board.

"Stretch your legs, lads," ordered Bran. Anything to do with boats and the channel meant that he was in charge. He inspected the jetty and the steps cut into the bank above it. "With the next rough weather when we can't get out into the channel, we'll row down to this old jetty and make it safe. We'll need some tree trunks and lashings. Now then, a little light meal. I've got some boiled eggs."

The eggs to go with their bread were very welcome and a brisk walk soon warmed up the shivering sailors.

"That's it, lads. Off we go again, the tide is turning and our crossing will be quicker this time." Bran was determined that the boys should be able to do two crossings on a tide when the time came.

***

When they returned to the mouth of the River Ebyr for the second time the boys were exhausted.

"We may as well rest here awhile," ordered Bran. "When the running tide abates, we'll row on up to Caerllion and have a jug of ale before it gets dark. With a bit of luck the kitchens will have saved you some supper."

The oarsmen were all glad of a rest and later, with the boats secured for the night, they settled gratefully on the riverbank to quench their thirst. Hunger was their next problem and staggering wearily to their feet and saying their goodbyes to Bran and Canna, they set off for the barracks in the gathering dusk.

"I hope everyday is not going to be like this," said Garwyn, but somehow he knew that it was likely. If they were going to face danger at Brenin, then they would have to be at their peak of readiness.

Lewys was the first to look into the kitchens and ask for food. A fat cook welcomed them in.

"Here, boys, take a bowl each and I'll ladle out your beef stew. Then you can go to the tables. There's plenty of salt and bread."

The smell of the cauldron full of stew was almost too much to bear. If this was what the army lived on in the barracks, then it was all going to be worthwhile. A group of soldiers were finishing off their meal and greeted the boys with the usual banter.

Rhys took up the challenge.

"We've crossed the channel twice today. I dare say you lot have all been in the tavern!"

Mock outrage from the soldiers gave way to a lively

conversation. The soldiers were due to go off on night manoeuvres, which they were not looking forward to. An older man spat on the floor.

"I think something must be up, our troop is due to go out every night for the foreseeable future. I hope we don't have to go east again after that last battle."

Lewys and his companions shrugged their shoulders. Just then, the cook offered them more stew, which started an undignified scramble. It was soon time to settle in their bunks by lamplight and after a few groans about the next morning's hard work, they all slept soundly.

Next morning, Bran and Canna greeted the boys and gave them some ointment for their blisters. This time the fleet, after following Bran to Brenin Point, sailed a little way up the Asc River and into the old Roman harbour.

"It's silted up compared with what it was in the old days, but it's still usable." Rhys realised the significance of Bran's remarks. This would be a safe storage place when they had to camp on Brenin Hill.

There were some fishing boats beached in the harbour and a group of men walked along the wooden jetty to greet them. A large, bearded man recognised Bran.

"And to what do we owe the honour of this visit by the whole of the King's fleet?" he jested.

"Morning, Micho. We're trying out these new boats from Caer Taf; well, what do you think?" Bran and the boys threw ropes up to the gathering crowd on the jetty and hauled themselves alongside.

"I heard you were all out in the channel yesterday, Bran; frightened us a bit, with those large boats and big sails. We thought you were Saxons on the loose. Yes, they look good… and four oars, eh!"

The colts all climbed onto the jetty to stretch their legs and look around the harbour. Rhys and the two leaders glanced at each other knowingly; they could see that Brenin Hill overlooked the mouth of the Asc.

The sailors then noticed some girls mending clothes near the houses. When they shouted wildly, the girls scampered indoors laughing. Hwyn surprised everybody by running across to the house and after coaxing them out, started chatting easily with one of the girls. Lewys turned to the other colts in amazement. This was not like Hwyn at all.

"Time to go," shouted Bran, causing a loud moan.

The boys had to row against the rising tide once more.

"I don't want to ruin your hands, or your backsides, men," said Bran. "So we'll cross to the islands and you can explore. Then we'll get back to Isca before the tide runs out." Bran had realised that the boys' blisters could be a problem if they got too bad. There was a thankful muttering among the young sailors.

With the tide still flowing, they were soon able to beach in line on Ynys Echni. The goats soon spotted them and came running through the heather and long grass.

"I've got an idea," shouted Bran. "A training run, off you all go, then. This is a race. Run to the far end of the island and back and the winner gets extra ale."

Suddenly there was excitement in the air. Most of their

training was to compete with each other and they jostled for position. Rhys had always enjoyed long runs at Penhal and knew that it was foolish to race off into the lead. A headstrong Lewys did not seem to be aware of pacing himself and set off with Garwyn in hot pursuit.

There was some higher ground over to their left and Rhys made for it. He felt that he would be able to better see over the terrain and spot a way through the undergrowth. Hwyn thought it better to follow Rhys and soon they were on a rise looking down on a trackway that had been worn down by the goats. Hwyn grunted as Rhys took off again down the slope and trotted easily along the track toward the far point.

Bran and Canna had gained a vantage point to watch the race and laughed as they saw the boys strung out all over the island with the goats joining in this glorious game. The sky was filled with sea-birds, screeching and diving at the intruders. Lewys and Garwyn got to the far point and rested their hands on their knees, gasping for breath. They spotted Rhys on the trackway and waited for him to join them before setting off once more. They were soon onto the higher ground with Rhys and Hwyn not far behind, but it was obvious that they had used up their reserves. The rest of the troop trailed behind the leaders in a long line.

Bran and Canna made their way back to the starting point in time to see Rhys and Hwyn overtake the stumbling leaders. The pair collapsed together onto the grass of the shoreline and rolled over to gaze at the sky and get their breath back.

"A tie. Can we have that ale now, please Bran?" gasped Hwyn.

"All in good time, young Hwyn, how about some refreshing water, instead?"

Bran was glad to be working with the boys. As an older man and with experience of battles in the old days, he knew that his duty was to prepare the troop so that they would have the best chances in any future battles.

Lewys and Garwyn, having now realised their impetuous mistake, trotted in briskly to avoid being overtaken by the rest of the troop. "Well done, Rhys and Hwyn," congratulated Garwyn. "I think we all need more practice; what do you say, Lewys?"

"I'm sticking to horses," groaned Lewys, sinking to all fours.

"One more race!" ordered Bran. "Now, stand in line."

The whole troop groaned as they thought they would have to do more running. They obediently stood in line.

"Turn around," continued Bran. "When I give the word, you run to your boats and set sail for Caerllion. It's near high tide and there's a good breeze upstream. Now we'll see if you've learnt anything."

When Bran gave the signal, the boys excitedly rushed to their respective boats and hoisted the sails. There was some confusion as oars were used to push the boats out into the current, but soon the race was on. Bran and Canna's trail boat was faster in the wind than the new boats, which were built for safety rather than speed.

The six boats were soon spread out, each one trying to keep their sails at maximum stretch, while Bran held back just in case of accidents. He said a little prayer knowing that if anything went wrong, he would be to blame. The centre of the channel was relatively smooth, but they all knew to be beware of a sudden breeze.

Rhys and Hwyn thoroughly enjoyed this new experience – perhaps the training every day was not going to be so boring after all. It was difficult to say who was in the lead, but as they approached Ebyr Point, Garwyn and Lewys edged their way into the Isca and sailed up the centre of the river. Rhys knew that he would not catch the more experienced Garwyn, but was grateful to see that he had a long lead over the others.

"Well, I'm glad I was in the same boat with you, Rhys," said Hwyn as he sat back swigging some water. Rhys gave a satisfied smile.

Eventually, the leaders tied up at the Caerllion jetty, then, with a crowd of young children joining in, they ran down the bank to shout encouragement to the others. With all boats safely moored and sails furled, it was time for a little ale.

While they rested, Bran gave the boys their next assignment.

"Tarou and Arthur are due back later. After your break you can collect some axes and ropes at the stores and ride out past the old fort to the forest. You'll find some felled oak trees near the trackway that you can haul up to the fort. It will be good practice for you and your horses."

"To the fort?" queried Lewys. Rhys nudged him and winked. Of course, Bran was thinking ahead of making a barricade on Brenin Hill.

"Now," continued Bran, "what if we made up some practice

defences on the hillside? You could use the logs to set up a barricade downhill of the fort's ramparts."

"That's a good idea, Bran." Lewys jumped up ready to go. "I'll tell you all about it as we ride, Garwyn." This sounded like another adventure.

CHAPTER 11

Training for War

After a brisk walk to the barracks to arrange horses and saddles, the colts were soon ready to set out. Rhys was glad to be riding Beech once more and moved up to the front with the two leaders. They quietly discussed the log defences that they would set up on Brenin when the time came.

Lewys had it all worked out.

"As Arthur said on Sunday, if the enemy have to climb any defences, that's when they will be vulnerable to our arrows. I just hope the trees we're collecting are not too big for the horses."

They paused at the old fort on the hilltop trying to imagine what Brenin Hill would be like. Lewys knew there were forests below Brenin with plenty of stout trees.

"We must remember to take the big axes with us when the time comes," he whispered to Rhys and Garwyn. His companions agreed.

When they arrived at the felled oaks, there was a sigh of relief. The half-grown oak trees had been cut down in the winter and their branches left untrimmed to keep them off the ground.

Garwyn could see the possibilities – he was well aware that any soldiers charging uphill would not want to climb over obstacles.

"If we leave part of the branches on, we can drive them into the ground so that they're about waist height."

"Good idea," conceded Lewys.

The horses grazed peacefully as their masters set to with their axes. Soon it was time to harness the trunks to the bewildered horses and trudge up the slope to the old fort.

Luckily the grass had been grazed down by sheep and cattle and eventually the tree trunks were rolled into position. The stub ends of the branches were pointed with the axes and with everybody jumping on the trunks together, the newly pointed ends sank deeply into the earth. This was looking good.

"There's somebody coming from behind us," shouted Hwyn who had gone back to retrieve the ropes.

They all turned to see Arthur and Tarou with a small troop coming over the brow towards them.

"Greetings," shouted Arthur. "I'm glad to see you all so busy, and Garwyn, it's good to see you again. How is my father?"

"The King is well, sire. He's recovered from his winter chill and is hunting again."

"Good. Now, this barricade looks impressive. How about some sport? You, boys, go downhill and get ready to charge us, after all you outnumber us two to one. We promise not to fire arrows."

Tarou and the men laughed as the boys scrambled over the barricade and lined up further down the slope. Arthur said it would be good practice for the colts to experience a charge from the enemy's point of view.

Lewys gave the signal and with much shouting the uphill charge commenced. As they scrambled over the barricade, Rhys realised that an enemy would probably lower their protective shields for a moment and lay themselves open to the archers.

"Charge, men!" shouted Arthur to his own troop.

The boys found this a bit frightening – the look on the soldiers' faces showed that they meant business. Soon, a wrestling match was in progress. Tarou with two of his companions threw Lewys and Garwyn to one side – they were especially targeted, and Arthur kicked two of the other boys in their knees to send them tumbling downhill. Rhys had sidestepped and was able to dive at the ankle of one of the attackers and send him sprawling. Other boys jumped on the attacker pretending to stab him to death. Arthur then turned on Rhys, who had now gained the higher ground, but Rhys, knowing that speed was essential, charged Arthur, butting him in the thigh. As the mighty prince tumbled down the slope, Tarou and the rest of the soldiers automatically rushed to protect their commander. This, in turn, enabled Lewys and Garwyn to jump on their backs causing them all to fall and, soon, there was a jumble of arms and legs with the whole contingent wedged up against the barricade. The shouts and threats soon turned to laughter as the men disentangled themselves and regained their composure.

"Well," laughed Arthur, "I wouldn't want to tangle with you

lot in the dark. Now, that reminds me, it's about time you went on some night manoeuvres. What do you suggest, Tarou?"

"There's a half moon tonight, sire. If the boys get those wooden dummies up here from the stores, they can fix them onto the barricades. Then we'll see how well they fire their arrows in the dark."

Tarou looked pleased with himself. He also knew that any night attack by the Saxons could be deadly if the defenders were unprepared.

"I'll leave you to it, Tarou, I must get back to the barracks." With that Arthur and his men gathered their horses and cantered down to the town laughing and joking.

Tarou rubbed his hands together.

"Gather your equipment, lads, and let's go." The troop eagerly jumped on their horses and rode down to the barracks.

The dummy Saxons from the armoury were strongly made and covered with realistic leather tunics – they had often been the subject of target practice and had been roped together and repaired many times. They were hoisted onto the horses and the colts set off once more for the old fort.

"I'm starving," grumbled Garwyn. "I hope we're not going to stay up here without any food!" Tarou, realising that it was now past the normal mealtime, assured the boys that they would soon get back.

On arriving at the barricade, the dummies were fixed in various positions with stakes and ropes.

"That's it for now, men, we'll come back after dark."

Back at the kitchens, the colts devoured everything they could get their hands on while Tarou explained the next move.

"Collect your bows and put them by your bunks ready and don't forget, your arrows must all be individually marked. You're free this evening, but get an early night."

Trying not to grumble, the colts finished their meals and bathed in the old Roman bathhouse near the barracks. With their equipment prepared it was time to show Garwyn and his troop around the town.

On the way to the tavern, Lewys made sure that the twelve young warriors passed a certain house with an open courtyard at the side. There were smiles all round as a group of women and girls could be seen lounging among the trees and shrubs in the evening sunshine. A small group of older soldiers, comfortably seated and with wine goblets raised, insulted the colts and made rude remarks about their youth.

"If I give the order..." shouted Lewys, hands on hips defiantly, "these men will come in there and cut off your manhood."

The soldiers and women burst into laughter and continued with further ribald insults. However, Rhys knew that Lewys was familiar with this place and, much to Garwyn's delight, Lewys strolled into the garden area and beckoned two of the younger women.

"I wish I could go in there," whispered Hwyn to Rhys. "Lewys said he'd take me one day."

Rhys felt embarrassed, but strangely excited at the sight of Lewys and Garwyn talking and laughing with the two women.

His thoughts turned to Helena; he would never betray her at such a place.

The rest of the troop looked on with interest until their two leaders returned and started a race to the tavern.

With most of the garrison away, the boys found room in the tavern and settled around a large oak table with benches.

"Only two jugs of ale each, boys, then we get an early night. Oh, and Garwyn and I will be back sometime later."

Garwyn smiled wickedly and idly tapped the table with his fingers.

Later in the barracks, and after the return of a smiling Lewys and Garwyn, bows and quivers were put safely at the ready, it was time to sleep. Several oil lamps gave a faint glow inside the small barrack block that had been allocated to the troop. With many of the soldiers away with Cynan, it was quiet enough to sleep and dream. The boys decided to take off only their boots in anticipation of a rude awakening.

***

Rhys was dreaming of Ronan's Roman galley and the wide open sea when loud shouting startled him. He sat up in his bunk in complete confusion to hear Tarou barking orders in the darkness. It was time to go. Some of the boys found it difficult to wake up and others couldn't find their bows and quivers.

"If I were a Saxon, I'd have killed most of you by now," swore Tarou.

He was quite frightening in the darkness. Eventually the

troop was assembled outside and with their eyes slowly becoming accustomed to the fading moonlight they could begin to make out the familiar landscape and the fort on the hill.

Tarou mounted.

"I'll follow on. Don't lag behind or my horse may trample you. Go!"

The run up to the ramparts left them aching. They hadn't expected such hard work with these new manoeuvres, but the leaders knew that Tarou was thinking of Brenin Hill. They had to be ready for anything.

"Hitch up your bow strings and get in line," ordered Tarou, as the troop panted and puffed. "Sling your quivers around your waists, ten arrows apiece."

The shuffling in the dark led to an eerie silence as the boys peered downhill at the barely-discernible dummies. When the order came they were ready. Rhys was able to see well enough to concentrate on one of the dummies that he knew was securely fixed. In no time at all the deadly strike was over and once more there was silence.

"Back down the hill," ordered Tarou. "We'll return at first light to count up. Run all the way and no stopping." With that he cantered off and left the boys to follow.

Rhys found that it was not easy to get back to sleep, but he realised that the next morning would see the start of another hectic and arduous day.

It was full daylight when Tarou once more shouted at the bottom of each bunk. The boys stretched their aching legs to try and get moving and once more collected their bows.

"You'll need a sword each, lads. Now, off to the armoury." This sounded like more hard battling and soon the troop was lined up for the run uphill.

The arrows were strewn all over the mock battlefield, and as they approached, Rhys was glad to see that many were stuck into the Saxon dummies. In the morning light, it looked like the gruesome aftermath of a real battle. Tarou strode down to the barricade.

"Now, count your arrows, then line up."

Rhys was disappointed to see that he had scored only two hits whilst Lewys and Garwyn had three each.

"Put your arrows away, it's time for a downhill charge. Remember, you must be all abreast as you reach the enemy. The force of a charge is important. If you can't swing your sword, then you must knock your enemy down. Once down, a soldier is at his most vulnerable."

The boys lined up on the rampart stamping their feet. Tarou, in the centre gave the command and, shouting wildly, the troop descended onto their enemy with slashing swords. The Saxon dummies were soon slaughtered.

"Well done, men, time for breakfast. I think you've learnt enough about defence." Tarou looked pleased. "Next year, some of you will be joining the army full time. By then, I want you to be as hard as those dummies." A tired smile crossed the faces of the colts as they trotted once more down the hill.

***

The next few days were a blur for the colts. With hard practice at the barricades and blustery sailing on the channel, there was little time for any fun. Sleep was their main concern.

One evening, as the troop was drying off from a rough crossing of the estuary in driving rain, there was an eruption of excitement in the barracks. The rest of the Caerllion garrison was to move out on the morrow and cross the Havren at Black Rock. There was no word of a coming battle – it was probably going to be another skirmish. Lewys, Garwyn and Rhys glanced at each other. Rhys' stomach became knotted with fear and seeing the reaction of Lewys and Garwyn, he thought they must be feeling the same way too.

"Garwyn," shouted Tarou as he entered the bathhouse. "You'll be glad to know that the rest of your boats are ready down at Caer Taf. The Caerllion boys will be sailing you down to your homes tomorrow and, well, it's been nice knowing you." Tarou could hardly say that they would meet again soon.

So this was it. Preparations would soon be in hand for the big battle. Rhys had noticed odd sailing boats crossing the channel to Caer Taf and reasoned that it was news from King Geraint.

After a late supper it was time for some relaxation. As they all walked around the town together, there was laughter tinged with a little sadness at the parting of such close friends. The boys were allowed a little ale at the back of the tavern while noisy soldiers celebrated their last night and boasted of their chance to do some fighting and looting.

After their longest sleep for some time, it was the job of all the colts to help the soldiers pack and load their baggage. Arthur and a small force crossed the Isca and cantered off towards Black Rock. The townsfolk, wives and children often with tears running down their faces, were all expected to help with the preparations. On crossing the river, a long trail of horse-soldiers streamed up the hillside past the King's villa and on to the old Roman road. Tarou waved them off, then turned to the boys with a smile.

"You've got just enough time to collect your packs and weapons. Bran has a job for you."

"Yes, sire," said Lewys smartly. "Follow me, men."

The tide was now rushing in as the Caer Taf colts collected their belongings for their last journey down the Isca. There would be a hard row against the current.

Bran pointed to some carts loaded with salt-meat and flour.

"I forgot to mention boys, we've got a big load for Brenin Point, they'll need some stores over there after we take Garwyn's troop to Caer Taf."

The troop looked suspiciously at this cargo as a group of women carried some newly stitched leather sacks down to the jetty. Bran smiled at the boys' consternation.

"The sacks are waterproof. Let's get them loaded."

As soon as the tide started to slacken, the hard rowing commenced and it took some time to reach the mouth of the estuary. Rhys was glad when they reached the old jetty and set the sails. It was time to sail down to Caer Taf and drop off Garwyn and his men.

The journey was swift as the sailors competently utilised

the light breeze. At the mouth of their home river a jetty enabled Garwyn and his troop to disembark. This made Bran look away as they all clasped hands and wished each other good luck.

There was no time to lose and the sailors, now two to each boat, kept close together.

Beaching at Brenin Point the fishermen helped them to unload their cargo and Bran asked them to store the sacks in their dry huts.

"We'll just manage to get back home if we hurry, men," shouted Bran. After a fast crossing, the final row up the Isca river to their jetty left them, once more, exhausted.

"That's enough for one day," said Bran. "Make the boats safe and then you can go to supper. Be ready at first light for the early morning tide. We've got to repair the Ebyr jetty, then get more stores across to Brenin."

The troop was glad to get back to the barracks, but a serious-looking Tarou later arrived to explain the real reason for the hard training.

"It's about time I told you of the plan." Lewys and Rhys were the only ones not to gasp as Tarou explained the war plans – the other colts looked a bit shocked. "Tomorrow, a contingent of foot soldiers will be arriving from the northern valleys. Then, on the next day's early morning tide, you colts will be ferrying everybody across the channel to Brenin. It will have to be two trips per high tide. Then we prepare defences on the summit and wait until the Saxons get to the Maendibyn Hills. The Caer Taf colts will be doing the same thing and joining you, and the King's army will be crossing from the Taf to the beaches down-stream of Brenin on the two trading galleys. Any questions?"

Rhys had been listening intently.

"Sire, do you think the Saxons will send a fleet of longships from the sea up to Brenin to join their main army?"

"That could be their plan, Rhys," said Tarou. "And that's why the King's army will be hidden back from the beaches. It's the only place enemy ships could land safely. I don't need to explain your role on Brenin Hill. If a Saxon force-broke through our defences on the Maendibyn Hills, they could attack us from any direction."

An early night was welcome as the troop curled up under their blankets lost in their thoughts and with disturbing dreams. This could turn into a real battle and possibly close-quarter fighting.

***

The shouting at first light meant preparation for loading the boats with axes and ropes.

Rowing down to the Ebyr jetty was now routine and with Bran's knowledge and guidance timbers had been trimmed and rammed into the muddy bank. Leather thongs were used to repair the walkway and make it safe for tramping soldiers to embark.

As the fleet rowed back up the Isca, it became apparent that a large crowd was waiting on the bank. Bran waved to Tarou who was on the jetty with a tall stranger.

"The foot soldiers have arrived from the north, lads. Tomorrow you'll have to get them all safely across the channel."

The boys realised that they were in for a long day. When the boats were tied up, Tarou introduced the leader of the northern foot soldiers.

"We start at first light, so the first batch can load up their baggage now and get used to the boats. Then the second lot will march down to Ebyr Point for the next trip. What do you think, Bran… five men to a boat?"

"They're going to be squeezed tight, Tarou, but let's get some practice."

It took some time for the boats to be loaded – five shouting soldiers and their packs eventually filled Rhys' boat and left it very low in the water. Each of the loaded boats was then hauled out to the middle of the ebbing river along the ferry line. This was to accustom the men to the oars and, after the initial chaos of rowing together against the current, some sense of order was achieved. The cheering townsfolk turned the proceedings into a festive occasion but Rhys noticed that the older townsfolk were looking on nervously at the laden boats.

Each batch of soldiers had a turn at rowing – it looked as if the boats could get everybody across in three trips, including Tarou and his own small Caerllion troop. The colts whispered amongst themselves, fully aware that they were now very important. Their training had come to fruition.

"That's it, everybody," shouted Tarou. "Food is ready at the kitchens. We assemble at first light. Get plenty of rest." He knew that the soldiers would fill the taverns at the first opportunity and had given instructions for the doors to be closed soon after dark.

After supper, Rhys reflected on the few months since leaving Penhal. He could never have imagined that he would learn so much. As he strolled down to the river with his friends to gaze over the now quiet river and to admire their very own boats beached on the shingle, he tried not to think of home. His family would be extremely worried if they knew his present circumstances, but a warm feeling came over him as he imagined Helena walking beside him. One day, he was determined, he would show her Caerllion and they might even set up home together.

After preparing their own packs and weapons, the boys were glad to retire to their bunks. There was little chatter.

CHAPTER 12

Preparations at Brenin

After easing the stiffness in their limbs and eating a breakfast of meat, eggs and fresh bread, it was time to collect their packs complete with their bows, bundles of arrows and, at last, a sharp gleaming sword for everybody. Their packs each contained a sleeping-blanket. The old retired soldiers who ran the armoury wished them all well.

The incoming tide had helped to float the boats alongside the jetty and the soldiers in the first troop arrived for embarkation. They wore their heavy battle tunics and leather helmets reinforced with steel strips. Apart from their packs, they each carried two spears, a dagger and a sword. With much jostling and cursing to add to the excitement, the soldiers on the bank waved to their comrades and wished them good luck in case they never saw them again. Rude signals were exchanged.

Bran and Canna, both in smaller trail boats, were able to take three passengers each.

Bran whispered to Rhys, "Can you pray that the water in the channel won't be choppy?" Rhys laughed, shook his head and gazed upwards as if to apologise.

Few of the foot soldiers had ever seen a boat and as they rowed out into the estuary to face the wide-open expanse of the channel, Rhys could see that his soldiers were decidedly nervous. Stowing the oars and setting sail forced them upstream and well away from land, but a young soldier in the bow, who had volunteered to handle the sail ropes under Rhys' supervision, delighted in the cold spray, thrown up by the surging bow.

"Porpoise!" shouted Rhys as a school of the leaping sea creatures discovered the boats.

The soldiers had never seen such a thing and ducked for cover as the porpoise played happily around them. Once reassured that the darting animals were harmless, they looked on with mouths agape.

Sailing back down the far shore was now routine to Rhys and the other young boat captains. With a shout from Bran in the lead boat, Rhys could now see the Caer Taf fleet sailing out from between the islands to take advantage of the tide. They were also loaded with soldiers and equipment and rounded Brenin Point well ahead of them. After a smoother journey out of the current, Bran's fleet beached next to Garwyn. The relieved footsoldiers treated each other like long lost friends after the dangers of the sea, but then had to start carrying weapons and stores up to the summit.

Bran was also much relieved to have suffered no mishaps and started on the return journey without delay. The last of the incoming tide took them swiftly to Ebyr jetty where Tarou and the rest of the contingent were resting on the bank. Tarou counted out thirty or so of the soldiers and sent them off to make themselves useful at the nearby farm until the next tide in the afternoon. This meant that Tarou, with his older troops and some equipment could embark immediately and get underway. He was anxious to inspect the defences at Brenin.

"I thought you would want to use this faster trip, Tarou," joked Rhys, as they sped out into the channel.

"With this much weight aboard, I couldn't afford to risk the first crossing," replied Tarou with a wicked grin. Rhys wasn't sure if he meant it.

Once past the islands the two galleys from Caer Taf came into view. They were anchored off the coast below Brenin Point and trail boats and the Brenin fishing boats were offloading soldiers onto the beaches. This was part of the King's army and the colts felt secure knowing that there was such a large force at the ready, no matter what attack the Saxons may be planning.

Meeting up once more with Garwyn and his fleet on the beach, it was now too late to think of another crossing, so the colts were put to work on the long trek up to the summit.

After dumping the baggage and weapons on the grass inside the ramparts of the old Brenin fort, there was time to admire the view. They could see well down the channel that ran out to the open sea, which meant that in daylight, any approaching Saxon fleet would be easily seen. In the clear air and bright sunshine, the boys marvelled at their view of the islands and the whole of the Silurian coastline.

Tarou, with the leader of the foot-soldiers, shouted for everyone to pay attention.

"Well, men, over there to the east you can see the Maendibyn Hills, that's where the Saxons are making for. But don't worry, they won't get as far as Brenin." The hills looked ominous as dark clouds started to fill the sky. Rhys shuddered at the thought of a Saxon horde breaking through Arthur's lines.

The boys carried on with their duties.

"I'd love to sail out to the big ocean," said Rhys, sweeping his arm across the sky. "Perhaps we could all go to Armorica, one day."

Garwyn took up the mood.

"When this is all over, I'm going to sail my parents way down to Ynys Piro. They say that the water is as clear as glass down there and you can see the floor of the sea, miles down." The other boys listened with interest – the dangers of the moment forgotten.

"Axes and ropes," shouted Tarou. "We'll start off making the barricades."

The lower slopes of the hill were covered with ash, alder and willow trees. Suitable trunks were selected and stakes were cut and bundled. It was hard work dragging the timber up the hill, but with over fifty soldiers and the colts together, the job was soon done. Tarou watched for low water and shortly after midday sent the boys back down to the beach to prepare for their last crossing. It was now clouding over and Bran said they should keep close together in case of a squall. The running tide once more took them swiftly across the channel and, as the last batch of soldiers at Ebyr scrambled on board, a heavy drizzle began to obscure the far coastline.

"We'll wait here until the tide turns, men," ordered Bran. "Take down your sails and spread them over the boats, it will keep some of the rain off us."

As they all huddled gratefully under the sails, the boys were beginning to experience what the older soldiers had described as the worst part of any campaign – waiting around. But for Rhys, this was a good chance to share the army's humour with the tough foot soldiers and he was able to ask them questions about their homes and families. One thing was apparent – they had not been needed on any recent campaigns, mainly because they were not horsemen, but this time they were hoping to get into a pitched battle with the hated Saxon axe-men and make a name for themselves.

It was some time before Bran gave the order to cast off. The mist and drizzle developed into a squall, which meant that they were out of sight until they became aware of the noise of the sea birds around the islands. Soon they were gliding safely beside the cliffs of Ynys Brenin. The soldiers looked on with wonder. They had always been able to see the islands in the channel from their mountain homeland and now, for the first time, they were right alongside the towering cliffs of the island.

"Not far, now," shouted Rhys. "We should have just enough wind to beat the tide."

When the beach came into view, the soldiers cheered as they could see their comrades frantically waving to them from the hillside.

The boats were now dragged well up the shingle for the night and the sails, once more, were taken down to provide shelters. It seemed strange waving to Bran and Canna as their two friends set off homewards for Caerllion – the young helmsmen were now on their own.

"We're going to be soaked, boys!" protested Garwyn. "We'd better get up to the top and join the rest of the men. I bet they'll be glad to see us with these sails.

Struggling up wet grass onto the hill was difficult enough, but making up tents and shelters with the poles and stakes left them all drained. They gratefully crawled under cover with their packs; the colts sharing one tent and the soldiers huddled under the rest. They soon found that they had to dig small trenches around the tents to take the rainwater away from their precious grassy floors. That evening they ate dried meat and bread, washed down with rainwater collected from the sagging sails.

As darkness fell, the boys noticed how quiet it was on the hill. Periodically, two colts were called upon to take turns for sentry duty and by dawn, their humour was wearing thin. Rhys was thankful it was summertime and wondered how they would cope in a cold wind. Thankfully, by daybreak, the rain had given way to white clouds and the promise of some blue sky.

Tarou and his companion, the leader of the foot soldiers, called everybody to a meeting and the orders of the day were to collect more trunks for the barricades. Rhys counted over a hundred defenders. After a rest at mid-day there would be training to assess the defensive positions.

"Can we collect some willow sticks and bracken for inside

the tents, sire?" asked Lewys hesitantly. He was not looking forward to another damp night.

"Of course," replied Tarou. "And we'll need plenty of dry firewood. We'll try and keep a fire going in the middle here to dry out our clothes."

A withy bed down by the Asc river gave an ample supply of flooring for the tents and a generous spread of bracken was laid out to dry in the sun that was now growing warm. Timber was piled up to give an oval shaped barricade below the summit of the hill.

"This is only a precaution," said Tarou. "There's little chance of any attack getting past Arthur and Cynan. You can stop now for breakfast."

Glancing at the rations and the number of men, Rhys thought there might be enough food for several days. No doubt the fishermen would also keep them supplied.

At midday, the commander of the King's army on the beaches rode up the hill with some of his officers to meet Tarou. They were old friends and campaigners and spoke warmly together. The whole company gathered around the mounted commander.

"There's no word from Cynan or Geraint, I suspect we'll hear nothing for a few days. You'll need to make more shelters to keep yourselves dry. We don't want any fevers. My men will be covering the beaches and the marshes to the south and you may well see us on manoeuvres along the hillsides and through the valleys below you. We will be prepared for whatever may come."

Building up the defences and practising battle continued through the day until the afternoon tide started to flow around the point. Tarou called the colts together.

"It's time to get the boats round to Asc harbour. Micho will get you back across the river and you can climb back up here before supper."

This was a welcome relief from timber hauling and, soon, the sliding and tumbling down to the beach became a mad race.

The village at Asc welcomed the sailors with the offer of cakes and broth. The girls got to know all the boys by name, especially Hwyn, and welcomed their flirtatious attentions. After discussing the defensive situation on the hill with Lewys and Garwyn, Micho arranged for the supply of some spare sails for making extra shelters.

The girls had collected fresh bread and spare food bundled up in sacks, which were gratefully received by the boys, and soon the fishing boats were ferrying them across the small river to the bottom of the hill.

"If any Saxons decide to storm this hill," joked Garwyn, "they'll be exhausted by the time they get to the top." After battling their way up through the woodland, the whole troop collapsed on the grassy rampart.

Tarou, hands on hips, looked around.

"We'd better make up more shelters with those sails. I've got a feeling that we could be here for some time, and there's no telling if the Saxons will attack at all. Mind you, if they do, they'll never get this far."

***

The next few days were spent in training, with mock attacks and archery practice. Every soldier on the hill glanced unthinkingly down the channel with each running tide as if expecting to see a fleet of Saxon longships in the distance. There was an abundance of fresh fish and salmon from the estuary and bread was made daily from the diminishing sacks of flour. After a week, supplies were starting to run low, but some relief was given by the villagers at Asc harbour, which was itself being well supplied by the outlying farms. Fresh water was brought up from a spring just down the slope and Tarou insisted that everybody washed thoroughly.

The weather was sometimes overcast and damp, which depressed the whole company after a hard day's work; but the nights, thankfully, were not cold. One evening, the sun shone warmly as it settled in the western sky and the colts were allowed to go for a walk along the cliffs at the extreme end of the point. They chatted happily as they looked out over the channel toward their homes – any thoughts of war forgotten for the moment.

Rhys pointed.

"You know," he said "if I were a sea bird I would be able to fly due north over the rooftops of Caerllion, wave to my friends at the monastery, then follow the road to Abermenei and Penhal. Finally, I would wing my way on to Blaeno and land at the feet of Helena."

***

Rhys' friends laughed and suggested he was starting to have hallucinations, but he found it was much easier to get to sleep at night if he thought of Helena.

Then, quite unexpectedly one morning, horns were heard in the distance and the King's commander, who had regularly inspected the defences, rode up the hill with a grim smile on his face.

"A huge Saxon army is marching up the Roman road from Caer Sallog, they'll get to the forest at the other end of Maendibyn by nightfall and probably prepare to attack tomorrow morning. They obviously have no idea that we're well prepared and they certainly won't be expecting two armies to close in behind them; Arthur from Aqua Sulis, and Geraint from Lindinis. If there's no sign of longships on the early morning tide, I'm going to send half of my men up onto Maendibyn to back up Cynan. Don't worry, the enemy won't get as far as Brenin Hill."

Rhys and the colts now felt their first pangs of fear, but the foot soldiers were angry at being stuck on the hill away from the battle. Tarou tried to keep everybody busy, but the waiting during the rest of the day and through the night was frustrating. The early morning tide brought no sign of danger from the sea and occasional troop movements could be seen on the far slopes of the Maendibyn Hills.

By noon, riders could be seen in the distance and the King's commander once more galloped up to see Tarou.

"Good news, men. The enemy fell into the trap and have suffered heavy losses. But so have we. They're now trying to get away through the marshes to the south. They know that our cavalry can't fight in the wetlands, so Geraint is turning south to cut them off."

The foot-soldiers and the colts all cheered together.

"Better keep your position here..." continued the commander, "but you may be needed elsewhere tomorrow."

"After all that hard work," shouted Garwyn as he waved his fist at the distant hills. "Can't we go over there and help to finish them off, Tarou?"

Tarou and the leader of the foot soldiers laughed at Garwyn's brave jesting, but the foot soldiers themselves were disappointed at missing the action once again.

"Well, it looks as if Arthur has won the day, men," said Tarou. "Unless, of course, there's a counter-attack. You can all rest now, but we'll keep our positions until the next high tide. Then, I dare say we'll be getting further orders."

Rhys whispered a little prayer for the warriors of Penhal and Abermenei. They had undoubtedly been part of Arthur's army attacking the Saxon flank. A constant watch was kept on the sea approaches – was a Saxon fleet going to appear?

The afternoon was warm and spirits were high as the men lazing on the grassy ramparts idly looked down the channel. Rhys spotted a hare near the barricade overlooking Asc village and nudged Hwyn, who was dozing next to him.

"Let's see if we can shoot that hare, Hwyn, we could do with some fresh meat."

Rhys, followed by Hwyn, slid over the rampart and crawled down to the barricade to get a clear shot.

The other boys watched with interest as Rhys rose to his knees and prepared to fire an arrow. Just then a movement down the hill caught Rhys' eye. He peered over one of the trunks to see several men moving through the gorse bushes and long grass at the bottom of the hill. The hair stood up on the back of his neck.

"Get down, Hwyn," hissed Rhys. "I think I saw Saxons down there. I can't believe it." Ducking down and racing back up to the rampart, his heart was thumping as the rest of the troop realised that something was wrong. "Get Tarou, get Tarou," urged Rhys, as loud as he dare. "We're under attack. Keep down, don't make any noise."

As Tarou crept up to peer over the rampart, Rhys explained what he had seen – he was sure that the Saxons hadn't seen him.

Tarou raised himself above the screen of a gorse bush to look intently down the hill. He then made signals that the soldiers immediately understood. They lay behind the rampart facing the threat as Tarou moved along the line explaining his plan. A messenger was sent down the other side of the hill to warn the King's commander who was now urgently needed – there was no telling how many enemy were creeping up on them. Where had they sprung from?

Everybody kept out of sight as Tarou watched the Saxons move steadily up the slope toward the barricade – Rhys could see that they numbered nearly a hundred and they were obviously unaware that they had been spotted. As the first enemy soldiers slid over the barricade and lined up in a long row to make their charge, Tarou gave the signal. Horns blew loudly and the foot soldiers jumped over the rampart. They took two paces and hurled their heavy spears with all their might. The Saxons reeled backwards as the missiles smashed into their shields and howled as other spears pierced their bodies.

"And again!" shouted Tarou, at the same time signalling the colts to stand on the ramparts with their bows at the ready.

The foot soldiers unleashed their second volley of spears as the next row of Saxons scrambled over the tree trunks. Shields became useless as the spears weighed them down. Once again they were checked by this unexpected counter-attack. Tarou's foot soldiers now drew their swords and ducked down as the colts were given the order to fire. Arrow after arrow hissed through the air and found targets in arms, legs and unprotected bodies. The enemy tried to shelter behind the barricade, but they were completely immobilised, preventing the others from making any headway.

At just the right moment, Tarou gave the order to charge and the foot soldiers, like howling wolves, sprung down upon the confused enemy. Tarou then sent his own troop to start their charge and soon the cursing and shouting combatants were in a frenzy of slashing and killing. At that point Lewys, who could not contain himself, drew his sword and rushed down into the fray. Garwyn shouted "No!" but then knew that he, himself, would have to charge with Lewys. Tarou screamed at them to get back, but they were already slashing wildly with their swords. The other colts looked on in horror at the desperate battle – they were glad to obey orders and stay with Tarou. Rhys winced as wounded men screamed out in agony.

A small group of Saxons broke away on the right flank and fought their way uphill. Tarou and the two soldiers with him rushed downhill and, with sheer fury, cut them to pieces. The boys, unable to fire at any clear target, looked on as Tarou hurled himself into the Saxon shields like a wild bull, then worked his way downhill lunging with his sword. It was now obvious that the enemy were in complete disarray.

The remaining Saxons turned and fled for the trees below, leaving many dead and wounded. Tarou signalled the recall and shouted for prisoners to be taken. Two of the younger Saxons, stunned and wounded, were hauled back up to the rampart, as the colts looked on horrified at the next phase of this battle. Some of the foot soldiers' comrades had been killed or badly wounded and now, in revenge, they stabbed and killed any wounded enemy, their screams echoing around the hillside.

Tarou was more concerned at reprimanding Lewys and Garwyn for joining the charge – they had disobeyed orders and as a result two of Tarou's troop had been wounded.

Just then, the King's commander and his troop rode up the hill from the south; he had clearly been shaken by this unexpected encounter. After speaking with Tarou, he ordered a full cohort of men to pursue and surround the escaping Saxon soldiers. Every last one of them must be sought out.

"Where on earth did they come from?" he ranted. "They must have travelled by night and hidden up in the day." Looking down at the wounded men, he turned to one of his officers. "Fetch our surgeons, immediately. Then go on to Cynan and Arthur and tell them what's happened. There may be other Saxon bands on the loose."

The colts were still in a state of shock as Tarou congratulated everybody on a good fight and the soldiers, in turn, clasped the hands of the colts. The reality of soldiering was now apparent as the spears and arrows were collected from the battlefield. The enemy bodies were looted for anything valuable and their weapons collected. Cleaning off the blood was not a pleasant job. The soldiers collected their dead and carefully attended to their wounded, but it was obvious that some of them would not survive. A deep grave was commenced on the inside bank of the rampart for their eight dead comrades. Their talismans and personal belongings were then packed up for their families according to tradition.

"Stack the Saxon bodies below the barricade, men," ordered Tarou. "The locals will strip them later and then make up a pyre out of the timbers."

Rhys tried not to look at the faces of the enemy corpses as he and the other colts helped to lay them out, gagging at the foul smell. With his hands covered in blood, Rhys swallowed hard as it brought back memories of finding the body of his friend Cunval at Penhal years earlier. Rhys now wondered if he had actually killed any Saxons with his arrows. Hwyn gleefully counted the enemy dead and shouted, "Forty-four dead!"

"Cover up their heads," ordered Tarou. "We don't want the ravens to peck their eyes out. Well, you've experienced your first battle, you're blooded now."

Rhys noticed that Lewys performed his duty with great vigour; he had seemingly enjoyed the whole experience and pulling arrows from the dead Saxons made him smile.

Tarou then took Rhys to one side.

"You'd better start questioning those two prisoners in their own tongue. You did a good job last time, I'll leave you to do it your own way, then we must get them back to Caer Taf."

The two young Saxons had been roughly bandaged and tied together; they were clearly terrified and ready to talk rather than be executed. Rhys greeted them in the Saxon language and eased their ropes, then sat them on the top of the rampart looking down at the scene of the battle. They tried to avert their eyes from the piles of bodies.

"I'm going to do everything I can to save you," whispered Rhys. "The rest of them want to cut your throats, but the commander said that if you tell us everything you know, then you'll be sent to the King's farm as slaves. You may as well know, your army on the other side of the hills has been wiped out. We knew they were coming, so they can't help you, but I can." They both looked Rhys desperately in the eye, hoping that he was telling the truth about sparing their lives. They were certainly willing to talk – after all, they were only junior soldiers, and probably didn't know much anyway. It was better to be a slave than a corpse.

"Now, let's start with Caer Sallog. Tell me the whole story, and don't forget, we'll be questioning other prisoners, so if you tell lies, you're as good as dead."

The young prisoners nodded eagerly as Rhys called over

two of the wounded foot soldiers who were resting nearby and were clearly impressed at Rhys' knowledge of the Saxon tongue.

"If you can guard this one, please, I need to question them separately."

They grinned fiendishly at their charge as Rhys led the other nervous captive down to the barricade and sat with him on a tree trunk.

"Now. Don't forget, everything!"

The young prisoner told Rhys about his village and family and how he had been trained as a warrior from an early age. He was now seventeen. Without stopping for breath, he related the whole story of the planned attack. Rhys nodded and rubbed his chin, which he suddenly realised, was now starting to grow stubble.

Just as Arthur had surmised after the questioning of Athelgar, the captive at Black Rock, the Saxons had been trying to gauge the strength of the Britons in readiness for this bold mass attack on the Maendibyn Hills and Brenin Point. The build-up of an army at Caer Sallog had taken weeks to achieve and they were all sure of victory in the capture and occupation of the hills and adjoining coast. A fleet of South Saxon longships was due to arrive on the second day with provisions and to prevent any chance of reinforcements crossing the channel. Their reward was going to be plunder and slaves, and then be sure of a permanent base on the islands.

Rhys tried not to wince at these revelations.

"But how did your troop manage to get here without being detected?" he asked.

"Our scouts knew the terrain, they had been planning for weeks. Our troop was to travel at night along the river and take this hill before nightfall on the day of the main attack. We didn't expect to meet any resistance." The prisoner averted his eyes from the dead soldiers who had only a short time before been his friends.

"So it seems," said Rhys quietly.

Rhys went over the story once more, then changed over the prisoners. It was obvious that their will to live was stronger than any desire to be brave and the second captive gave Rhys exactly the same details.

Tarou slapped Rhys on the back as the revelations of the secretive Saxon attack unfolded.

"You did well to spot the enemy when you did, Rhys. I fear Arthur will be having words with me for not having a proper lookout on duty. All we have to do now is stand guard and wait for further orders, but we can't take any more chances."

Later in the afternoon with the tide flowing swiftly up the channel, all eyes were looking south hoping not to see sails on the horizon. Lookout posts along the coast of the Summer Land would light beacons to give plenty of warning if any sails were spotted. Rhys wondered if the Saxons had spies somewhere on the coast to give signals to their fleet.

Extra rations were handed out and the whole company stretched out on the grassy ramparts to relax. The warm sun lifted the spirits of the soldiers and, although there was sadness at the loss of comrades, they knew that they had been part of the biggest battle ever with the Saxons.

When they later returned to their families alive and well, the questions would, as usual, be endless. Rhys knew that he would have to return to the tranquillity and boredom of the monastery, then soon it would be harvest time and he would be able to compare stories with Arteg and the warriors of Penhal. He just prayed that none of them had been killed. But would Helena be horrified to learn of this terrible battle?

CHAPTER 13

The Breakdown

The quiet reflections of the defenders were interrupted by the sound of horns from the river valley below. This was not an alarm call but a royal salute. A group of horsemen appeared at the foot of the hill as soldiers of the King's army made an avenue leading up the hillside. Loud cheers broke out as Arthur, the victorious Pendragon, and his leaders cantered up the hillside where Tarou's garrison, in turn, yelled at the top of their voices. Arthur looked every inch a noble prince as he rode upright on his magnificent stallion. His officers carried the banners of the cavalry – long-tailed red dragons spilling out in the breeze behind them. Rhys and the colts had never known such a proud moment. To think that, at their young age, they had helped to save their homeland.

Arthur jumped from his horse and clasped hands with Tarou and the jubilant soldiers who had gathered around him. Then, striding onto the highest part of the rampart, he looked around at his cheering warriors. "I've already heard of your magnificent defence of this hill, and first and foremost I honour your fallen comrades. A stone monument will be erected at this spot and a small garrison will always be stationed here." Arthur lowered his eyes to the ground for a few moments and the whole company did likewise. "As you know, the enemy has been routed and will never dare attack us again. We've lost hundreds of men, but the enemy has lost many more. If we hadn't surprised them, we could have all perished. Geraint is in pursuit of the Saxons who escaped into the wetlands and the army from Aqua Sulis are clearing the battlefields and burying the dead. Cynan is taking my army back up to Black Rock. The King's army and yourselves will remain here to guard the coast against any attack from the sea, but soon you'll be going home." Arthur waited for the cheering to die down. "I must now get across to Caer Taf and report to King Myric. Good luck."

Arthur called all the commanders together for a meeting – high tide was approaching and with no sign of enemy ships, a crossing of the channel had to be commenced swiftly. As the colts looked on with great interest and speculation, a messenger was sent scurrying down the hillside to the riverbank to signal across to Asc village. Some of the colts' boats would soon be needed.

Tarou beckoned Lewys, Garwyn and Rhys.

"You three are wanted to sail Arthur and his party across to Caer Taf, and the King will want those two prisoners. Stand by."

Arthur concluded his meeting with the rest of the commanders and with a shout, strode down the hill towards the Asc river. The three colts and the Saxon prisoners quickly followed, together with a group of officers. When they had reached the river bank, Micho and his men were delivering three of the sailboats to a shingle beach from where they could immediately pick up the wind.

"Rhys, I'll go with you and one prisoner," ordered Arthur, "and we'll take two officers. The rest of you divide yourselves up to suit."

Arthur did not waste words – he stepped into the boat and sat the confused prisoner next to him. The officers moved to the forward seat and commenced rowing out into the channel as Rhys prepared the sail. The other two boats quickly joined them and, with an ideal wind and swirling current, they were soon approaching the islands.

Rhys had been waiting his chance to enquire about Arteg.

"Sire, are the Abermenei troop all right?"

Arthur laughed. "Just a few scratches I believe, young man." He then lowered his head. "However, a few Caerllion soldiers died. Now, ask the prisoner to tell us his story again and tell him not to worry, we don't sacrifice our prisoners of war." Arthur listened carefully as the aborted Saxon plans were outlined to him and soon they crossed the estuary and sailed up the Taf river to the King's fort.

A cheering crowd and dancing children greeted the three boats as they came alongside the jetty. Arthur and his officers took the prisoners to the King's villa and instructed the colts to wait for further orders.

Lewys turned to Rhys.

"Did you know some of our Caerllion soldiers were killed? I don't know who…" Rhys nodded and swallowed hard.

Quickly changing the subject, Rhys looked around at the

bustling port and the high stone walls of the former Roman City. "Look at those two galleys, I bet they were built in the Middle Sea. See the mass of ropes and pulleys. I'd love to sail the oceans in one of those."

Lewys agreed, but he was more interested in seeing the army headquarters and the training grounds. Garwyn offered to show them around the town if they had the chance. "There are some good taverns I know of," he boasted.

As they chatted to the children, a messenger asked them to report to the King's quarters.

They followed the messenger through the wide streets to a palatial villa that had been restored to its former Roman glory. The boys admired the wall paintings and mosaic floors as they heard laughter coming from the King's chamber. Rhys admired the vaulted ceilings and glass roof dome. Presently, they were ushered into the King's presence, where Rhys was surprised to see Bishop Dyfrig with his elderly deacon and a sheepish looking Felix. Arthur and his group had retired to a dining annex and were enjoying themselves at a table full of food and wine. They were all in high spirits.

"Garwyn I know well," the smiling King greeted them. He had obviously been drinking and looked much older than Rhys had imagined. His hair was white and thinning and he had a stoop. "You, Lewys, I know your family, and it seems you're as fierce as your dear father. Now, it seems you both disobeyed Tarou's orders and charged the enemy without shields. We'll forget it this time, but I want you to dwell on what the outcome might have been, had things gone wrong.

You could have lost the day." The King looked sternly at the two young leaders who, in turn, stared at the floor. "Now, young Rhys, your grandfather, Brochvael, is an old friend of mine; and I understand you were a good friend of Cunval, Cynan's dead brother. Your knowledge of the Saxon tongue has been of great assistance and it seems you'll make a fine officer one day. Don't give up your studies at the monastery whatever happens, we need people who can read and write and who are not priests." Bishop Dyfrig shuffled his feet uneasily as the King mocked him. "I've already sent messengers to all the towns and I dare say Brochvael and your family will be glad to know that you're safe. Well done, men, now help yourself to the food." With that, the King shuffled off to his quarters.

Felix clasped Rhys' hands warmly – he was obviously relieved that the battle was over. Bishop Dyfrig looked deeply into Rhys' eyes as if to read his mind, but Rhys felt quite blank after the whirlwind of events.

"We weren't in too much danger, bishop. Tarou and the foot soldiers did the fighting."

Dyfrig nodded, but he didn't seem to be really listening.

"Rhys, my deacon and I are moving to Caer Taf to set up a new church for the King. He's now going to base his headquarters here permanently where it's better suited to protect his Kingdom. Arthur will be taking over the King's palace at Saint Albans and my senior priest, Cadoc, will be taking over my duties in Caerllion." The bishop paused. "I'm telling you all this with Lewys so that you can both explain to the town councillors. You will all be in my thoughts and prayers."

Garwyn then led the way to Arthur, who motioned them to the far corner away from the noisy officers.

"Eat up, lads, and I dare say you'll be glad of some wine. Lewys and Garwyn, the ebb tide will be running later, so cross back over to Brenin with more stores and I'll get another sailor to take Rhys' boat with you. Rhys, you can go back to Caerllion with Felix and return to the safety of the monastery." Arthur laughed, as the three colts looked surprised. "That's the King's orders. Well, good luck. I hope to see you all back at Caerllion within the week."

"Will you look after my bow and sword when you get back, please Lewys? I wish I was going with you," said Rhys, shrugging his shoulders.

"Of course," said Lewys. "Anyway, I doubt if we'll be involved with any more action. Tarou said that even if six ships attacked the far coast, there would only be about two hundred Saxons, and they wouldn't get farther than the beach."

As the boys laughed, Bishop Dyfrig raised his eyes to the ceiling and said a prayer.

"You'll have to share Felix' old mare, Rhys. When you get back to the monastery, I'm sure you will feel a bit unsettled. Remember, you can always talk to Aidan and Fracan if you feel troubled… you can trust in them."

"Yes, Bishop," replied Rhys, a little embarrassed in front of his two friends. The bishop and his deacon left the hall, which allowed the three young warriors to indulge in what was a feast compared to their previous fare. Felix also took advantage of the wine.

"You'll finish up as drunk as Abbot Aidan," joked Rhys as Felix downed his second goblet of wine. "I'll have to tie you to your horse!"

Garwyn, in the spirit of the moment, drew his dagger.

"Come on, Lewys, Rhys' hair needs cutting. Look how long it's grown. He'll be kicked out of the monastery."

Felix giggled loudly, which caused the nearby officers to cheer and gesticulate. There was no doubt that the hardships and anxieties of the previous week were now alleviated by a little wine. Eventually, Arthur suggested that Lewys and Garwyn should set off and so, with fond farewells, the boys departed, boasting that their feast at the King's table would now give them high status with their lesser comrades.

Rhys had never travelled the road from Caer Taf before and Felix couldn't remember the way, so with directions from passers-by, Rhys walked briskly leading the old mare with an unstable Felix loosely mounted on her.

The evening was dull and as they approached a village a group of children ran out to tease them. The sight of a young monk on an old mare led by his assistant was too good a joke to miss. Although he was wearing his leather tunic, Rhys' heavy coat was on the boat and his pack and weapons over at Brenin. He realised that he was in for more than a mocking and sighed with worldly resignation.

Felix giggled as his mount broke into a trot under a hail of small stones. Rhys ran quickly through the village, whilst bemused adults did little to help the beleaguered pair. After a battle with the Saxons, he was not going to lose his temper with a bunch of children – even if they could throw stones with some force.

As the pair scuttled on their way, Rhys knew that he had changed dramatically since the time of his youth at Penhal. As it was, after experiencing the Battle of Brenin Hill and drinking wine at the King's table, he now proudly considered himself to be one of Arthur's warriors. And, it seemed, the King knew all about him – this was good.

Thoughts of Helena at Blaeno softened the rest of the journey home, and arriving at the monastery from the north meant avoiding the town. It was obvious from the loud celebrations that Caerllion was going wild. It would be some time before the casualty list was known and several families would be nervously staying in their homes waiting for news. The townspeople now knew the true story of the Saxon advance and such a huge battle could have meant some deaths; with more dying later from their injuries.

As the sun lowered over the western horizon, Rhys helped Felix to dismount and they walked cautiously into the rear courtyard of the monastery. Shouts and greetings rang throughout the buildings and pupils and monks scrambled up from the fields. Rhys was soon surrounded and although everybody was shouting at once, the same question rang in his ears: "Tell us all about it!"

The last thing that Rhys wanted was to relive the battle. He sighed.

"All right, all right, I'll tell you all about it after I've had a hot bath. But first, I must report to Abbot Aidan."

Fracan pushed through the crowd and removed a sobbing Dingad's arm from around Rhys' shoulder. He escorted Rhys to the abbot's rooms and knocked firmly on the door – this was turning out to be one ordeal after another.

"We're so glad you're safe, Rhys. We were all shocked when we got news of such a big battle. Were you hurt at all?"

Once again Rhys felt one of his seniors staring into his eyes.

"No, no, father. I'm fine," replied Rhys, "just exhausted."

Abbot Aidan looked as stern as ever – Rhys realised that his presence in the monastery was a blot on Aidan's strict routine and a pupil being involved in a battle was just too ungodly for words.

"Sit down, Rhys. The first thing I want to know is how are the Caerllion colts? Is anybody hurt? And how about Tarou's men?" Aidan was sipping wine as usual.

"The colts are all safe, Abbot. Two of Tarou's men were wounded, but the surgeon says they'll recover…" At this point Rhys started to choke – words would not come as he stared at the stone floor. He buried his head in his hands as a flood of tears and a sudden dejection consumed him. Rhys had never felt like this before. He sobbed quietly.

"It's all right, Rhys," comforted Aidan. "What you're going through is quite normal. You've been through so much and now it's all ended, your natural feelings are taking over. Fracan, give him some wine. He'll be staying in my guest room tonight. The last thing he wants is a lot of foolish questions from our brethren. Tell them that Rhys has a fever and must rest tonight, and when you bring up my supper include plenty of good food for Rhys." Aidan, for once, fussed around like a mother hen.

When Rhys had recovered a little, Aidan insisted on his drinking some wine. It was good and soon Fracan arrived to place a tray of food on Aidan's desk. Then, gently squeezing Rhys' shoulder, he left.

"You must eat, Rhys," said Aidan – himself tucking in with relish. Rhys nibbled at some meat and cheese; he was grateful that he was not now going to face his brothers until the next day. "Now then, tell me all about Brenin Hill, you'll find it easier to talk with someone older."

Rhys thought about Bishop Dyfrig's advice at the King's palace "…remember, you can always confide in Abbot Aidan if you feel troubled." He dried his eyes and wiped his nose on his sleeve.

"There's been so much going on at once, Abbot. I really wanted to kill Saxons after they killed my father and uncle…"

At this point the abbot stopped eating. "Yes, that was terrible, Rhys, you've had much sadness for one so young. Tell me, did you kill any Saxons in the battle?"

"I don't know, Abbot. I was just firing arrows at the enemy, I couldn't aim straight, I was so nervous. I must have hit some of them, they were all bunched up on the barricade. The worst part was after they ran away, the foot soldiers kicked them down and hacked them to death. The screams were terrible. I'm sure the other colts felt as shocked as I was. But, of course, nobody is allowed to show any weakness."

Aidan knew that his charge would feel better for talking of his terrible experience.

"I'll speak with Tarou and voice my concerns about the

other young colts. Do you still feel that you want to kill Saxons, Rhys?"

"I'm not sure. I don't think I could kill a wounded soldier lying on the ground, but I'm glad to have been able to get it off my mind by talking to you, Abbot. Do you think it will help if I pray to God?"

"Of course it will," offered Aidan. "If you tell him everything just as you've told me, he will surely understand you. After that, how you behave during the rest of your life is up to your own conscience, nobody else's."

There were several moments of silence as both the abbot and his pupil reflected. Rhys felt drained – he needed to cover himself up under some blankets and escape from the world.

"Drink some more wine, Rhys, it will help you to sleep. I'm going down to the chapel where we will all be praying for the bereaved families. No doubt, the brethren will be praying for you as well. You go into my guest room when you're ready, and don't bother rising until you feel up to it. You can bathe in the morning."

Rhys was soon hunched up in the soft bed. For a while he could not sleep – he tried desperately to stop thinking about the events of the past week. After forcing himself to think only of home and Helena, his exhausted body eventually gave in to a deep slumber.

CHAPTER 14

Unexpected Events

"I have a letter for you to deliver to the abbess, Rhys."

For a moment Rhys could not focus – why was the abbot speaking to him? What time of the day was it?

"You've slept well, I'm glad to say. How are you feeling this morning?" the abbot asked him.

Memories of the previous day came flooding back into Rhys' mind. He remembered drinking the abbot's wine and waking in the middle of the night with bad dreams.

"I'm much better now, sire. Am I late for prayers?"

"Very, Rhys, classes have long since started, but cook is expecting you down in the kitchen and he will have some hot water for you to have a good bath. Then you must change into your habit and get Beech ready to go up to the nunnery. I expect you'll want to talk with Bran while you're down at the river. You can meet with your brethren later and tell them all about the victory, but don't dwell on any killing!"

"Yes sire, thank you for letting me rest." Rhys was still half asleep as he changed into his school tunic and sandals. But why a letter for the abbess?

Cook, an elderly monk, was always very kind to Rhys and did all that he could to help.

After a meal and a bath, and being reunited with Beech, Rhys was in a happy mood. The canter down the hillside in the warm sunshine helped him to escape thoughts of the previous week. Not wishing to ride through the busy town, he turned upriver, dismounted and then strolled down the river bank to the ferry. Bran and Canna were busy repairing sails as he approached.

"Hail, young hero," laughed Bran. "You escaped from Brenin Hill, and have you escaped the monastery yet again?" Bran grasped Rhys by the hands. "I'm so glad none of the colts were hurt. Their parents have all been down here asking us questions. When is Tarou due back?"

Rhys briefly related the story of Brenin Hill as his old friends listened intently.

"I'm off to the nunnery now to deliver a letter from Abbot Aidan. Perhaps I can call in and see you on the way back. I won't be long. I hope!"

Safely across the river, it was a short ride up the hill to Saint Albans and into the sombre courtyard of the nunnery. Lewys and the other colts, having previously guarded the nunnery while the army was away in the spring and disrupting her well-ordered regime, the abbess was suspicious of any male visitors. Eventually, the big entrance door opened and, after announcing the purpose of his intrusion, Rhys was ushered in to the office of the abbess, a grim-faced portly lady of indeterminate age, her looks partly obscured under a large black headscarf.

"A letter from Aidan? That's very unusual, he generally tries to ignore me." The abbess looked Rhys up and down and snorted. "At least you're not one of those insolent young colt-soldiers. Now let me read it before you go."

Rhys suppressed a smile.

As she read the letter, the abbess once again looked up at Rhys. He got the impression that Aidan was telling her all about the battle and the victory. She snorted again.

"Why men need to fight, I don't know. I wondered what all the noise was about down in the town last night. Hmm, it seems I have to expect two more girls from an officer's family. No doubt they'll be spoilt brats."

After being questioned about the King and Prince Arthur, who was now officially to take over the King's villa nearby, Rhys was curtly dismissed.

Smiling to himself as he led Beech from the courtyard and down the trackway, he became aware of someone beckoning him from the trees. As he stopped and peered into the shadows, he realised that two young girl novices wanted to speak with him – this looked very dangerous indeed.

"Are you Rhys?" whispered the taller girl. Despite her partly hidden face, Rhys could see that she was very attractive. He nodded.

"My name is Ria, I must speak with Lewys. Will you be seeing him? Can you give him a message for me?"

"Well, he's over at Brenin Point. I dare say he'll be there for a few days yet. Did you hear about the battle with the Saxons? I only got back yesterday." Rhys realised that the nunnery was closed-off from the rest of Caerllion. He felt very sorry for the girls.

"No, we don't get much news here, but Lewys told me all about you when he was here in the spring. I know I can trust you. Can you tell him to come and see me behind the garden after dark when he gets back? He knows the place where we usually meet."

"Yes, of course," replied Rhys in confusion.

What on earth had Lewys been up to? However, there was complete trust among the colts and it was his duty to help a comrade, whatever the circumstances. "I'll tell him the moment I see him."

The girls disappeared into the shaded woodland leaving Rhys chuckling at Lewys' little secret. This visit to the nunnery had turned out to be more interesting than he had expected.

***

The next few days at the monastery allowed Rhys to settle back into an orderly life. This, in some ways, was comforting; at least he didn't have time to dwell too much on the recent events.

On Friday morning, Cadoc, now in charge of the church of Caerllion, arrived at the monastery with the news that the foot soldiers and colts were on their way back, together with the wounded men from the Caerllion garrison. There was to be a service for the war dead on Sunday at the basilica.

"Cynan is leading the bulk of the army back to Black Rock and they will be home later on Saturday."

This was a great relief for the brethren and after prayers in the chapel Cadoc called Rhys to one side.

"Rhys, you will be attending the barracks as usual tomorrow, I presume. Well, the officer Merryn, who got back this morning from Caer Taf, wants to see you. He says you will know him, he's the one who took the Saxon woman and her young son."

"Yes, father, I'll report to him first thing." This was very strange – Rhys usually took orders from Lewys or Tarou. Perhaps it was just some translation wanted. He hoped the Saxon woman and her son were all right. Merryn was among the most unpopular of the officers.

After Saturday prayers and breakfast, and dressed once more as a warrior, Rhys cantered down to the barracks to the officers' quarters. Merryn, who had previously shown only indifference towards the colts, came to his door and unexpectedly smiled at Rhys. The reason may have been that his shoulder was strapped up from a wound and he appeared to be in some discomfort.

"Come in Rhys, you'll be glad to know that all the boats are back safely and the wounded are settled in the hospital. There's no training today, of course, but you can join your troop later, they're going to sort out the equipment and the captured weapons."

"When is Tarou coming back, sire?" enquired Rhys. "Did they get the rest of the Saxons who attacked Brenin?"

"Yes, they didn't get far, some were captured and sent to Caer Taf. The rest are ashes blowing in the wind. As for Tarou, he and his men will be collected tomorrow if the weather is right." The officer led the way to his rear courtyard where the Saxon woman was clearing a table. Rhys greeted her with a wave of his hand and she smiled back with an expectant look. Merryn motioned for her to sit down.

"She's unhappy, Rhys. I can't make out what she's saying exactly, but it seems her son is poorly and can't go near the town without children spitting at him."

Rhys nodded and could see that the woman understood what was being said. She was in her twenties and very attractive, and reminded Rhys of Helga at Penhal; she had the same long blond hair tied in braids and he had the impression that Merryn had probably fallen in love with her.

"Perhaps you could speak with her and the boy and arrange to take him out into the countryside now and again. Well, what do you think?" Merryn asked.

"Well, yes, sire. I'll do whatever I can." Rhys had visions of escaping the monastery in addition to his Saturday training. "Where is the boy, sire?"

"Sceaf…" called the woman and a forlorn little boy shuffled into the courtyard. He brightened at the sight of Rhys who he recognised as a friend after their ride from Black Rock back to Caerllion.

"So your name's Sceaf. I remember you," said Rhys soothingly in the Saxon language. "Come over here, how old are you?" Rhys took him by the shoulder and squeezed him close.

"Nine."

"How would you like to come riding with me sometimes?

I can show you the river and the woods. There are lots of animals and birds to see."

Sceaf looked down and nodded slowly – Rhys felt that the boy had lost his spirit after becoming a captive and losing his father and family. He desperately needed a friend and Rhys felt compelled to help him. Rhys was thinking fast.

"I've just had a thought, sire. It's just a possibility, but what if he was allowed to come to the monastery school? Orphans are often taken in at the age of nine and nobody would mistreat him there."

Merryn groaned – he was completely taken aback at this suggestion. The Christians were a hindrance in his eyes and always meant trouble. "I'd have to speak with Arthur, he's the only one who could order such a thing. I dare say Aidan and Cadoc would object to having a Saxon pupil. They'd probably have a fit!"

"Shall I ask your wife what she thinks, sire?"

"She's not my wife…" snapped Merryn. "I wouldn't let a priest marry me to anyone!"

"Sorry, sire." Rhys could see from Merryn's fast-blinking eyes that he could envisage a lot of merit in Rhys' proposal.

"Well, ask her anyway."

Rhys spoke quietly with the woman. His knowledge of her language was not perfect, but her eyes lit up at the thought of Sceaf being under Rhys' control and mixing with other boys of his own age. She said she knew nothing of the new religion, but had found that the priests she had seen in the town were kindly enough.

"Of course, the boys can see their parents every Sunday after church, and there are other days when the monastery is host to the townspeople." Rhys felt very pleased with himself seeing her transformed from her undoubted misery; and Merryn could sense a complete change in her mood too.

"I'm so grateful to you, Rhys," said the smiling woman, "it's terrible that innocent peasants have to become slaves. I'm not too badly off myself considering the way some of the Celtic slaves are treated by my own people. It's a pity that slaves cannot be traded and allowed to go home."

This sounded like a good suggestion and Rhys wondered if the two sides could ever talk to each other and arrange a peace. Perhaps when he was older…

Merryn could see that his woman was happy with this possibility.

"Tell her that Arthur will be coming from Caer Taf later and I'll speak with him. You can join Lewys now and call back here later."

"Yes, sire," replied Rhys – he remembered that he must tell Lewys about the message from Ria.

***

The reunion with his friends was as boisterous as expected, and after catching up on all the week's events at Brenin, the day's work was to prepare the barracks for Tarou and the returning soldiers. Food and drink were brought from every available source ready for an evening feast, especially ale from the Saxon village. It appeared that Arthur was coming to Caerllion to meet with Cynan and the army from Black Rock, and then celebrations would commence. Rhys was almost glad that he would be sheltering back at the monastery.

As the boys busied themselves, Rhys took Lewys to one side and relayed the message from Ria at the nunnery. Lewys raised his eyebrows and shrugged, but said nothing. It seemed the other boys knew that Lewys had been visiting the nunnery at night, but it was never discussed in Lewys' presence. Talk of Ria caused Rhys to think of harvest time and home – it seemed a long way off yet.

Later in the afternoon, word arrived that Arthur and a large retinue would shortly arrive and soon the whole town had gathered together. Arthur rode into the amphitheatre accompanied by a beautiful lady on a pure white mare. Rhys was aware of a whispering – 'that's Cenedlon'. All eyes were on them as a tumultuous cheer broke out – their prince was back.

Arthur raised his arm for silence and made a moving speech praising their fallen comrades and the many wounded. But now it was time for victory celebrations. His servants escorted the lady Cenedlon to the villa at Saint Albans, while Arthur called a meeting with his officers at the barracks. Later, Rhys was called for and as he entered the prince's house in the barracks, Arthur beckoned him to the refreshment table where Merryn and another important-looking officer were drinking.

"I have a job for you, Rhys. This is the King's commander

and his wife from Caer Taf and this young man is Patheu." A small boy was pulled from behind his mother's skirt and for the second time that day Rhys was confronted with a nine year old boy. "He's going to the monastery and I want you to look after him. His mother and father are going to the garrison on Ynys Ygraine and he's now old enough for schooling. I've called for Cadoc. His mother and the baggage will be going with you to meet Aidan and I want you to see that he has some new friends."

Just then, Merryn coughed politely. "Sire, this is very strange, it must be the work of the gods. My woman also wants her boy, Sceaf, to go to the monastery for schooling. It needs your approval and I've spoken with Rhys about it…"

Arthur burst into laughter and slapped his thigh.

"A Saxon boy at the monastery. I can't wait to see the face of that pompous ass, Cadoc, and Aidan will need some strong wine." Arthur shook his head in disbelief. "Well then, fetch the boy, Merryn… let's all meet him."

Just as Merryn returned from his nearby house with Sceaf, Cadoc arrived and bowed dutifully to his smiling prince. Arthur picked up the two boys and stood them on the table for all to see. He explained the situation to all present, then when all eyes turned toward him, Cadoc stared at the floor and coughed awkwardly.

Arthur, once more, burst out laughing and gripped the two trembling boys by their arms.

"Now, you two, this is a moment you'll never forget. You are both going to be true friends and don't be afraid of the monastery, it's a good place. Now turn and shake hands. Explain to the Saxon boy, Rhys."

Patheu's mother was obviously upset at her son's initiation to a future without her, but appeared to be consoled somewhat by the presence of Sceaf, even if he was a Saxon boy. At least they would have each other to lean on and with tears in her eyes, she held both their hands.

"Well, I'm off to my villa, gentlemen. Cynan and his men will be back well before dark, so I'll see you at the amphitheatre." With that Arthur strode out and left the company to make their arrangements.

Patheu's mother offered to meet Sceaf's mother, which Rhys thought was generous, as she was really considered to be just a slave. Returning to Merryn's house, Rhys helped them to converse by translating for them and soon the concerns of motherhood overcame any notion of being enemies. The circumstances created by men at war were out of their control.

The two boys were hoisted onto Beech with Cadoc leading the way to the monastery. As predicted, Aidan was most perplexed, but Fracan rose to the occasion and with a fussing Felix, the boys were settled into the junior dormitory before attending prayers and supper. Rhys felt that, once again, events had turned out quite satisfactorily, although he had not been allowed to join the evening feast with the army.

***

The next week drifted by and Rhys decided to pursue his

studies vigorously. He felt that the sooner he was in command of the Latin language, then the sooner he could become a full-time soldier. One of the things he most wanted to do, was to travel across the sea to foreign lands – there was so much to look forward to.

The two boys had settled into the routine of the monastery and Sceaf, particularly, seemed anxious to please his new masters. Despite his limited knowledge of the Celtic language, he was learning new words every day.

The following Saturday arrived and Rhys looked forward to meeting Tarou, who he had not seen since leaving Brenin Hill. The whole of the Caerllion garrison had returned and had spent the week carousing. Everybody was in high spirits and jousting had been arranged as much for fun as for the training. Arthur was travelling around his territory meeting with the various outlying commanders and enjoyed hunting with his close friends.

Rhys sought out Lewys to quietly ask about Ria. Lewys, looking serious, took Rhys to the riverside.

"I've got a big problem and I haven't told anyone else. Ria is going to have a baby."

Rhys gasped – he had no idea that Lewys and Ria had been going that far. She would surely be expelled from the nunnery in disgrace when the abbess found out.

"Ria has agreed to come and live with me and my mother, she hates the nunnery anyway. I've spoken with mother and she wants to help, but there's another problem."

"Goodness, Lewys. Of course, you know you've got the rest of us on your side."

"Well, Ria's parents are important people in Caer Gwent and they know the King well. I'm in big trouble and I don't know what to do for the best."

Rhys was thinking quickly – Arthur was the only one who could smooth things over. It might be that Ria's parents would not accept Lewys and would want her back home with them.

"I think you should tell Tarou all about it, Lewys. He has a family and he might be able to speak with Arthur. I'm sure it can all be sorted out."

"You'll have to come with me, Rhys. I'll try and get him alone when we stop for our midday meal. We'd better do some work now."

Lewys certainly seemed a changed man – Rhys wondered what it would be like to be a father.

Tarou was eventually cornered and Rhys had to do most of the talking. Lewys was the bravest of warriors in a fight, but dealing with such a delicate matter left him almost stuttering. Tarou soon got the message and chuckled loudly.

"I don't mean to laugh, Lewys, but I had heard rumours of you going up to the nunnery at night. You'd make a good army spy if you can fool the abbess and her lot so well. Do you love the girl?"

"I'm not sure, sire… I like her very much."

"So it seems. Well, there's only one thing I can do, I'll speak with Arthur when he gets back tomorrow. Carry on."

That evening in the chapel, Rhys prayed for Lewys. It wasn't a convincing prayer, but it was all out of his hands anyway. Despite his friends asking him why he was so quiet, he was sworn to secrecy.

UNEXPECTED EVENTS

All of the brethren were due to go to the basilica for morning service on the Sunday and as Arthur was in attendance, Rhys hoped that Tarou had been able to arrange a sensible outcome. After the service, he had occasion to take Sceaf to one side to meet his mother and was then able to approach Tarou and his family.

"Arthur never ceases to amaze me, Rhys. He got hold of the situation straight away and after his usual bout of laughter, he's charged Cadoc and myself to ride with Lewys to Caer Gwent soon to see the girl's parents. I've got to be there in case her father tries to kill Lewys in a rage and to also vouch for his good character. Lewys, if he gets the chance, is to say that he's very much in love with the girl and wants to spend the rest of his life with her. Arthur told him to sound completely genuine. Let's face it, Lewys is too important to the army to have any outside distractions, he'll be a full soldier next year." Tarou folded his arms and smiled at a wide-eyed Rhys. "Keep your fingers crossed."

It was two days later that Cadoc visited the monastery and with everybody in the fields for the afternoon, Aidan made a rare visit out of doors. It was hot and sunny as he called for Fracan, Felix and Rhys to join him and Cadoc in the garden.

"Cadoc has been telling me all about that wicked colt, Lewys, and although I believe Rhys is aware of the situation, I'll relate the story from the start." Aidan jerkily informed his monks of Lewys' indiscretion with the young novice and Cadoc's recent mission to Caer Gwent with Tarou as bodyguard. "It seems that the girl's mother is anxious that her daughter and Lewys get married in the church at Caer Gwent next Saturday."

"Lewys wants Rhys and the colts to attend with him," interrupted Cadoc. "We were lucky that our visit to the girl's parents didn't end up becoming violent."

Rhys had to bite his lip to stop smiling.

"To continue…" said the abbot, " her parents are waiting for Cadoc and myself at Arthur's villa and we are to take Ria's mother to the nunnery. It seems that her father in Caer Gwent is still suffering from shock and they're giving him plenty of strong wine. Now, it appears that the abbess has no idea what's been going on, and, as the nunnery comes under my jurisdiction, it's my sad duty to break the news to her as gently as possible." The abbot raised his eyes to the heavens and whispered a little prayer.

Rhys could hardly keep a straight face as he glanced at Felix and Fracan. They looked horrified.

"The girl will then be placed under Cadoc's care in the bishop's house with the other priests until next Saturday. No doubt they will be instructing her in suitable prayers and penitence." The abbot looked soberly at Cadoc. "I would suggest, Cadoc, that whilst we are with the girl's mother at the nunnery, your colleagues visit Lewys' mother, I believe she has quite a large house. And make sure that the interior has a good Christian atmosphere. I understand that she attends church every Sunday, which is the only good news I've heard today."

"Be sure I will make the necessary arrangements, Abbot."

Rhys was a little annoyed that everybody was referring to Ria as 'the girl'.

"Ria is a good Christian, sire," he offered brightly. "She's been at the nunnery for several years now."

"But not for much longer," replied the abbot.

When Aidan and Cadoc finally left for Saint Albans hill, Felix questioned Rhys, "You knew all about this, why didn't you tell us?"

"It was my duty to be discreet, Felix. As you know personal confessions must not be disclosed," replied Rhys with a slight smirk.

***

An early start was necessary on the following Saturday and Rhys, dressed in his cleanest clothes, rode smartly down to the bishop's house to meet with the troop. They were in high spirits and Lewys confirmed to Rhys that his mother and Ria's mother had chatted away like old friends. Suitable horses were assembled and the first call was to collect Lewys' mother for the journey east.

Shortly after midday, the entourage entered the western gate of Caer Gwent where a large crowd had gathered. Refreshments had been arranged at the parents' house – they were obviously of high rank – and after a few tears from the bride's mother and a little huffing from the father, it was time to set out for the marriage ceremony at the church. The colts glanced at each other awkwardly.

The resident priest officiated and all went well until the couple were pronounced man and wife. Then Ria's elder brother staggered down the aisle cursing. Lewys had only a moment to turn and duck as the brother lunged at him with a dagger and when Rhys stepped forward he was promptly punched in the forehead by one of the other brothers and sent reeling. There was soon a confused battle, but Lewys, with greater strength, was able to wrest the dagger from his new brother-in-law and cradle Ria in his arms protectively. The colts soon calmed the situation by sheer numbers and, despite the screaming women and shouting men, the offended brothers were hustled outside and guided to the nearby tavern.

Rhys tried not to wince at the painful bruise on his forehead and gradually his friends soothed the brothers into a drunken acceptance of their sister's new husband, assuring them that Lewys would be an ideal father.

Returning to the monastery later in the evening, Rhys felt that another chapter of his life was now closed. It was time to try and return to normal, but, of course, everybody would want to question him about his throbbing bruise.

CHAPTER 15

Homeward at Last

The month of August finally arrived and most of the boys were to go home for the harvest. Some had completed their schooling and intended to stay at home and two had decided to return and train as monks. There was a certain sadness as everybody packed, despite the hardships and discipline they had suffered, and, as Rhys, the warrior, rode across the ridgeway and away from the monastery, he knew that he was no longer Rhys the pupil and colt. He had said his goodbyes to his fellow colts on the previous Saturday – it was now time to retrace his steps back to Penhal and Helena. The old Roman road made the going easy for Beech who could sense that he, too, was going home.

Arriving at Abermenei late in the afternoon, the children, led by his old friend Conmael, rushed across the meadow to greet him. They escorted him into the town and Rhys was glad to find that Tidioc was already at the governor's house. This would save a trip upriver to Tidioc's sombre cemetery and meant that he could now relate all the news just once.

"It's good to see you, Rhys! We've heard all about your exploits. You've certainly grown up." Pedur called Conmael to his table. "Conmael has been anxious to see you, he apparently wants to go to Caerllion to be a colt. But Tidioc has suggested he goes to the monastery with you." Even Tidioc chuckled at this possibility.

Conmael grimaced. "Will you take me back with you after the harvest, Rhys?" he asked excitedly.

"Of course." Rhys knew that the army would never want any boy who had been pushed into joining the colts. A young man must really want a soldier's life.

Pedur and Tidioc now seemed to be treating him as an equal, although he had only been away for half a year. After a little wine, Rhys was anxious to move on – he was eager to be back in his own river valley. He decided to go up onto the moor and visit the priest Ruthall before approaching the hall across the river. It was a strange feeling to come home and see everything just as he had left it.

"Hail, Ruthall, are you asleep? It's not that late," boomed Rhys as he approached the cemetery enclosure. Ruthall dashed from his hut beaming, clearly delighted to see Rhys back safe and sound.

Rhys dismounted and the priest clasped him tightly.

"I've prayed for you so many times, young Rhys. Goodness me, you're a full grown man. Look at that chest, and those muscles. Let's go down to the hall."

As they expected, Rhys and Ruthall had only walked halfway down the track before the children spotted them. Rhys mounted Beech again to cross the river, whilst Ruthall took the bridge. On reaching the training field, he jumped off to let Beech go charging across the field toward the warriors and their horses, who were way up on the hillside. The Penhal dogs were the first to assail Rhys, jumping up and barking furiously. His own dog, Hawk, whined uncontrollably. The children mobbed him as he picked them up one at a time, then gripping his sister, Olwen, by the shoulders, he half-shouted, "Well aren't you going to kiss me?" which caused her to cry with emotion. They embraced as Rhys was led towards the gateway. By the time his mother and grandparents had greeted him, the warriors, led by Arteg, had galloped down the hill to find them all tearful. Even his old friends, the farm labourers, had to wipe their eyes.

"Welcome, warrior," laughed Arteg. "Have you come back to train us properly?"

The following hours were a dream. He spoke with all of his family and friends in turn – Helga's young son jumped all over Rhys and laughed at his shaven head.

"You're a big bully, Cadaer," scolded Rhys in the Saxon tongue. Then turning to Helga, Rhys smiled.

"Helga you're looking as beautiful as ever." This caused Helga to blush and Arteg to wag his finger threateningly.

After some refreshing cyder and wine, Brochvael and the warriors walked with Rhys along the riverbank. It was time for many recollections. Arteg had a scar above his eye from the battle where he and his men had joined Cynan on the Maendibyn Hills and it was now that Rhys learned the full facts of the Saxon defeat. The battle, at one stage, could have gone either way and much of the fighting had been hand-to-hand. It sounded pretty gruesome and Rhys was glad that the colts had not been there.

Arteg described the battle, Brochvael nodded.

"Now, tell us all about your travels since we last saw you, Rhys. Did you meet Prince Arthur and my old friend, the King?" Brochvael looked a little older and slower – his gruffness had partly abated.

The full story and constant questioning went on for an age, so it was with some relief when they all returned for the evening feast.

Without the restrictions of Caerllion and with the encouragement of the warriors, Rhys drank a little more than he was used to, then boasted and staggered about as much as the warriors, before falling into his bed where he slept deeply.

The children wanted Rhys up early the next day to play in the river and after a fuzzy start he eagerly joined in with the boating and swimming. The water was low for the time of the year, but delightfully warm, and after some freshly caught fish for breakfast, Rhys needed some time to recover by the hall fire. Soon it would be time to call Beech and ride upriver.

"When are you going up to Blaeno?" asked Olwen. "I bet she's waiting for you."

Rhys growled at her mockingly.

"I think I'll give Beech some exercise!" He swaggered from the hall and whistled loudly.

***

On approaching Blaeno, Rhys thought he would skirt the hill overlooking the settlement and gather his thoughts. For some reason his heart was thumping. This was foolish. He stopped on the ridgeway and glanced across to the gateway where he had kissed Helena goodbye all those months ago. Blaeno was quiet apart from the children playing in the river. Marc was the first to spot a proud warrior sat on a magnificent horse high up on the hillside. Rhys did not know that Helena, when called, had dropped her dish in shock and run back into the house.

By the time Rhys had ridden down to the open yard followed by some curious cattle, the children and the whole settlement were running to greet him – he had been expected.

"Hail, Rhys," smiled Marc." We're so glad that you're safe. We never expected for a moment that you would be involved in a battle. Arteg told us all about the campaign. My goodness, you're looking well."

Rhys nodded and looked expectantly toward the doorway. Helena's mother emerged.

"Welcome, Rhys, Helena won't be a moment."

Rhys dismounted. "Here you are boys, you can take Beech up to the field to see the other horses. I know he's fond of Marc's mare." Marc smiled and led Rhys to the riverside table and benches. The river was full of life and Rhys realised that he had sorely missed the precious sound of the water running over the stones. He was so glad to be home again.

Milk and honey-cakes preceded the inevitable questions. Thankfully Marc only wanted the children to know all about the monastery with its farming and animals. Rhys was so involved with his story that he hardly noticed Helena walking towards them. Her long hair was newly combed and her eyes looked more beautiful than ever he had imagined. He rose and tried to smile, but felt so overcome with his longing to see her again that he could only say, 'Hail'. This sounded a bit silly, but her parents understood.

"Come and sit here, Helena," said Marc. "The children will tell you all about the monastery and Rhys' school." This was a welcome respite as the children, oblivious to Rhys' flushing cheeks, all spoke at once. Rhys and Helena laughed uneasily – they hardly dared to look at each other, trying to appear normal.

"Well, I dare say you two will want to go for a walk. Helena has lots of things to show you around the fields, Rhys, and the children have some work to do in the stables," Marc said pointedly to the groaning youngsters.

Helena's mother looked away as the couple walked quickly up to the orchard. It seemed natural that they should make for the gateway.

"I'm so glad you weren't hurt in the battle, Rhys. Tell me all about your friends, are they all right?" asked Helena. "You must have been very busy…"

"Yes, it all seems a blur since I last saw you. Every week has gone by so quickly… mind you, I've learnt so much. I can almost read and write in the Roman language now. My teachers say that it's spoken throughout the old empire and once you've mastered it, you will be able to speak with other people all over the world. I hope to travel to other countries one day." Helena looked hurt as Rhys laughed. "But I wouldn't go without taking you, Helena."

They suddenly felt at ease, just as Rhys remembered when they last met.

"I have to tell you, Helena, when I was camped out on the hilltop at Brenin, it was difficult to sleep. But every time I started thinking of you and home I was able to drift into pleasant dreams and fall fast asleep."

Helena smiled.

"I've thought of you so many times, my dear Rhys. It always gives me a warm feeling to know you're not too far away."

"I hope we're not going to fall hopelessly in love," Rhys joked. "My older friends in the army have families and have warned me against such weakness." They laughed together.

"Well, I am in love with you, Rhys, so you'll have to tell them that it's too late."

Rhys felt happier than he had ever known – it was such a relief to know that Helena had been waiting for him to return. They would always be together, even though he knew that he would have to return to Caerllion.

Then they embraced and Rhys could smell the fragrance of her hair and her delicate skin. This was a feeling he had never experienced before and with their arms around each other, they each cried with the release of such powerful pent-up emotions. It was only natural to kiss; this was the first time that Rhys had kissed Helena so passionately and he sensed her willing response.

It was a little while before they could part and look each other in the eyes. Rhys wondered if their mumbled conversation was the same for every boy and girl who had fallen in love. It didn't really matter what was said – they just wanted to be together.

"Perhaps we should walk for a while, Rhys. Would you like to climb the hill? We can look out over our domain."

"Our Kingdom," corrected Rhys laughing. "Remember, one day I'll be yarl of the whole valley and I'll need a bossy woman to help me rule."

"Of course, good sire. Oh, and I'll need lots of servants."

The view from the hilltop was more lovely than they could remember ever seeing it before. The sun shone warmly and the peaceful scene left them feeling relaxed and in tune with nature all around them.

"Did you kill any Saxons, Rhys?" asked Helena, suddenly. This was not a question that Rhys wanted to answer.

"I don't think so, we fired lots of arrows when they attacked. If we hadn't, they would surely have killed us. The older soldiers charged them after that and the ones who were not killed ran away. Anyway it serves them right for trying to conquer our land." Helena nodded in solemn agreement. "Anyway, let's go for a ride upstream, Helena. It's ages since I saw the pools with all the overhanging trees."

"Very well."

Helena ran swiftly down the hill to the horses. They clasped hands to steady their precipitous dash in the long grass and bracken and soon arrived laughing and panting at the Blaeno fields. In no time, Beech and Helena's pony were bridled and, without the need for saddles, they set off at a canter along the riverbank.

Eventually the horses were steered down the bank and into a shallow pool. Ducks and moorhens scattered at this intrusion. It was pleasant just to sit quietly on their mounts.

"Let's throw stones across the pool and see who can skim the farthest, Helena," suggested Rhys. They dismounted and shrieked with pleasure at each good throw. They decided to try and cross the shallow stretch below the pool on large stones just above the water.

Inevitably a headstrong Rhys slipped and fell to his knees in the water. Helena in a fit of laughter didn't see Rhys grab at her ankle until it was too late and she finished up flat on top of him. As Rhys rolled and lay on top of her, their arms automatically clasped each other and they lay entwined in each other's arms, partly laughing and partly awed at such beautiful feelings. The warm river water splashed around them as they rolled on the pebbles in a mock wrestling match, their clothes thoroughly soaked.

"My mother will be furious," laughed Helena, as she tried to cool the situation and scramble from the river. "I'll tell her that you pushed me in!"

"It's your own fault for picking a fight with a warrior. And I'll tell your mother that you tried to seduce me."

"Oooh…" screamed Helena, kicking water into Rhys' face and causing him to fall back into the river. They looked down at their clothes and burst out laughing once again. Helena felt it was surely time to mount up and return home.

Marc raised an eyebrow good-naturedly whilst his wife clucked like a hen as the two lovers squelched into the courtyard.

"Fetch some clothes for Rhys, Marc," ordered Helena's mother as she ushered a giggling Helena into the house.

The children looked on with great interest.

"How did you get so wet, Rhys?" they clamoured, laughing as he went to the barn to change. Rhys just shrugged his shoulders.

Helena's mother and the other women had been preparing a big evening meal in Rhys' honour and, while they busied themselves, Marc and Rhys wandered down the riverbank chatting like old friends. Rhys was now a man and having noticed his daughter's obvious concern and occasional melancholy whilst Rhys was away, Marc hoped that things would work out favourably in the fullness of time.

It was decided that Rhys would stop another night and then he and Helena would travel to Penhal to help with the harvest there. Rhys wanted his mother and the whole estate to know that he was in love with Helena.

Next evening the young lovers rode downstream, chatting away like an old married couple.

Rhys' mother was delighted to see Helena – it was soon apparent that the two mothers had spoken at length of a possible match and Rhys' grandmother was also pleased.

"Well... we'd better help with the farm work," said Rhys. "Times must be busy... look, even those lazy warriors are working today!"

Rhys and Helena worked alongside Ruthall in the fields,

which allowed them to talk at length of the monastery and the grand basilica. "I can't wait to see Caerllion for myself," sighed Helena.

Helena stayed in Helga's room at night, with Rhys having his own corner in the hall, away from the children. As the days went by, the pressure of work eased off and Rhys spent some time training with the warriors. Now that he was stronger, he was a match for most of the men and thoroughly enjoyed the competition and good humour.

Rhys was able to take Helena on long rides around the territory; she particularly enjoyed the open moors and the intoxicating freedom they both felt on the high hills. A visit to Abermenei enabled Helena to meet Pedur and Rhys was not surprised when Pedur's wife fussed over Helena and took her into her kitchen for the latest urgent gossip. There was much talk of the victory, and Pedur very much enjoyed recounting his own battles in the company of Brochvael and the King in the old days. Eventually, Pedur suggested that he and Rhys should stroll up the riverbank to visit Tidioc.

"I thought you were never going to call and see me, Rhys," grumbled Tidioc good-naturedly. "I particularly wanted to test you on your Latin grammar and see how much ancient history you've learned." Pedur groaned as Tidioc winked at Rhys.

"Well, Tidioc, I dare say you'll want to know all the latest news from Caerllion," laughed Rhys. "Anyway, I think you should know that Bishop Dyfrig is now based at the old church on the River Taf and Cadoc has been left in charge of Caerllion, but he doesn't seem to be too happy about it."

"He probably doesn't like the hard work," said Tidioc unkindly.

Pedur suffered the conversation politely for a while until he suggested that they all walk on upriver and cross at the ford to give himself a change of scenery.

"There's an old Roman villa up on the slope, I've been wondering about collecting some of the stone for my house in town. Shall we go on up and take a look?" Pedur led the way through the gorse and bracken to the ruin. Rhys had heard of the old villa and was very interested to see how much it resembled the buildings in Caerllion with its straight lines of masonry and upright corners.

"The Romans were certainly good at building," he mused. "If I ever retire to Penhal, I'm going to build a villa like this. Perhaps I could have some of your stone from Abermenei, Pedur."

They all laughed.

"You'd be welcome, Rhys. But don't you think you're looking a bit far ahead, unless, of course, you're thinking of getting married and having lots of children?" Rhys spread out his arms as much as to say 'of course'.

All three had a pleasant stroll back to the ford and were glad to wash in the warm river water which was now at its lowest during the summer. Once they felt presentable, it was time to join the ladies again at the hall.

At the end of their visit, Pedur escorted Rhys and Helena to their mounts. "It's been good to see you, Rhys. Give my regards to Brochvael, and call to see me when you return to Caerllion."

***

The end of August was approaching and it was time for Rhys to prepare for his return to Caerllion. He spent the last few days with Helena at Blaeno but eventually had to wrench himself away from his loved one. He tried to compose himself on mounting his horse and knew that Marc would forgive the tearful farewell.

His last night at Penhal added to his sadness and early the next morning, Rhys wanted to set off with the minimum of goodbyes. He was given some cyder and venison for Pedur and some messages from Brochvael.

Conmael and a friend galloped up as Rhys approached the town.

"You must take us both with you, Rhys, we want to join the army at Caerllion. Our parents have agreed as long as we can go with you. You ask Pedur."

The boys were both fifteen and would have to pass some rigorous testing under Lewys in order to be accepted. Rhys could hardly refuse them the chance if Pedur was in agreement.

"They've been worrying me for weeks," Pedur sighed. "I'll be glad to see the back of them and I dare say the town warriors will be too. Anyway, I must visit Brochvael before the autumn." This sounded like a dismissal and the boys were jubilant.

"Wow! Look at that!" Rhys had led them over the ridgeway to the monastery, so that the boys would get their first view of Caerllion from the top of the rise. Conmael was fascinated by such a sight, and his friend was too dumbfounded to speak. They eventually rode into the courtyard of the monastery and Rhys sought out Fracan to explain the situation.

"Well, you'd better take those boys on into town and get them settled. I'll expect you back here for prayers," Fracan said sternly.

"Yes, father," said Rhys. "But could I just introduce my friends to Dingad and Govan?" Fracan sighed and left.

Just then, the two nine-year-old pupils, Patheu and Sceaf, rushed into the courtyard to clutch at Rhys. "Well... you two look happy enough, and here come Dingad and Govan." Rhys' two friends from Abermenei could only stand and gape – they had never seen so many new faces at once. Rhys made hurried introductions before escaping to the trackway.

The first thing was to find Lewys, who looked genuinely pleased to see Rhys. Perhaps family life had mellowed him.

"I hope Ria is well, Lewys." Lewys shrugged and looked suspiciously at the two nervous boys. "I'd like you to meet two keen young men from Abermenei. They want to join you and the colts."

"I'll have to speak with Tarou, and I suppose they'll want accommodation." Lewys sounded grudging, but Rhys could tell that underneath he was pleased to have some new recruits.

Rhys tried to smooth over the initial shock that he knew his friends would be experiencing and, after finding Tarou who slapped them on the back and nearly sent them sprawling, Hwyn was assigned to find them suitable living quarters with willing families.

Rhys could do no more – they were now on their own.

Mounting Beech he prepared himself for the drudgery of monastic life and to wait patiently for the next Saturday.

With everything back to normal, and a busy time of the year in the orchards, the first week flew by. Rhys was glad to see his young friends settling in at the barracks and Hwyn agreed that they would make good colts. Two others from Caerllion had also joined – Rhys' old nemesis from the town, and a boy from a nearby farm. Next year Lewys would be joining the main army for further training as an officer and it looked as if Hwyn would become the troop's new leader.

One morning during lessons, Rhys discovered that Fracan had a quick temper. His thoughts had wandered to Ronan and his galley and as he was whispering to Dingad, Fracan suddenly stopped in front of their bench.

"Pay attention, you two," shouted Fracan, swiping them both on the head with his long willow stick. "What are you hiding, Rhys?"

Rhys had tried to cover up his parchment with his arm. "So. You're making drawings instead of learning your Latin. Get to the front, both of you."

Rhys had drawn a sketch of Ronan's galley on his parchment and didn't have time to wipe it clean with his damp rag.

Both boys knew what was coming – they held out their hands, palms upward and winced at the stinging blows. Fracan's temper only eased after each hand had received one vicious swipe with his stick. Rhys noticed the alarm on the faces of the rest of the class. It was rare for anyone to misbehave –Fracan's caning was extremely painful.

When they took their seats, Rhys noticed tears in Dingad's eyes, but he wasn't able to apologise to his friend for getting them both into trouble. The lesson resumed in deathly silence with the other pupils occasionally glancing at the two culprits.

For the next two days the weals on Rhys' palms were painful and humiliating. He knew he must accept his fate without complaining, but events the following Saturday soon banished thoughts of his punishment from his mind.

CHAPTER 16

Off to Sea

Training, once more, was in full swing and as Rhys was engaged in a wrestling match with the larger-bodied Hwyn, he did not at first hear the shout from a galloping horseman. All eyes turned to the lone rider who charged down the hillside towards them. It was obviously a messenger. Tarou and his officers strode forward to take the reins of the snorting horse.

"A galley is coming in fast on the tide," reported the soldier who had ridden from the sea fort on the estuary. "I dare say he's loaded with fresh wine!"

The assembled soldiers cheered and Rhys was elated to know that Captain Ronan was returning. He would be able to ask him about his summer voyage to Armorica – had he seen any Saxon longships? What places had he visited? How rough had the sea been?

"Back to work, men," shouted Tarou. "It will be some time before they tie up in the river. We won't stop for refreshment now, but later we can help them offload the wine." Another cheer went up and the whole garrison continued their training with renewed vigour. The thought of a boisterous evening in the taverns with the sailors was very pleasing – especially as the next day, Sunday, meant only light duties.

The colts resumed their combat and threw each other about with relish. Rhys felt well pleased with himself – both physically and mentally, he was much tougher than in his youth at Penhal. Nobody dared make fun of his tonsured haircut and his knowledge of other languages nowadays.

Eventually, when the tall mast of the galley appeared above the riverbank, Rhys and the whole company turned to Tarou expectantly.

"Finish!" shouted Tarou, waving his sword in the air. "Weapons and equipment back to the armoury."

There was a mad dash to clear up and get down to the riverside.

When the colts had finally finished their work, they ran down to the jetty. Lines were being thrown from the ship to pay out the mooring ropes and, once they were secured on both shores, the large galley was slowly brought to a halt in mid-river. Tarou signalled for Lewys and Rhys to row him out in one of the harbour boats and soon they drew up alongside the ship.

Ronan, the jovial galley's captain, finished giving his orders and helped them on board. They all clasped hands.

"Good to see you, my friends! I can't tell you what a relief it is to finally be moored. Tarou, my friend, and young Rhys, welcome aboard. Now who is this other ruffian? I don't think we've met."

"This is Lewys, Ronan. He's captain of the young soldiers

at Caerllion, and a veteran of the battle at Brenin Point. Oh, ah, and he's also happily married!"

Tarou and Ronan laughed loudly, while Lewys tried not to look embarrassed. Rhys tried his hardest to stop grinning.

"Now, you men are the talk of the coast, as soon as I got back to Din Tagell they told me all about the battle. Come into my cabin and tell me the full story." Ronan led the way and soon, they were all settled with a goblet of fine wine in front of them.

Ronan questioned each of them in turn.

"You may know that I also saw action as a young man during the Saxon advance along the south coast, and I well know the horrors of battle."

The two boys smiled as he boasted of his prowess, but they were proud to be part of such a high-ranking discussion.

All too soon, it was time for Rhys to return to the monastery and undergo yet another change of character.

"We expect to be off again next Saturday," said Ronan looking at Rhys affectionately. "I hope to see you before we set sail."

After prayers and breakfast on Sunday morning, it was time for stories from Fracan and Aidan. Fracan, without any reference to the caning, held the attention of the boys as he spoke about the Egyptian deserts. Rhys and his friends had secretly spoken about travelling to Rome and even Alexandria in Egypt. One day, perhaps!

Later, while walking in the gardens a flustered-looking Cadoc arrived from the town.

He strode down the pathway with a sweating Aidan and walked up to Rhys.

"Cynan has just arrived from Caer Taf and he wants to see you at the bishop's house. You'd better come straight away just as you are and bring your horse."

As Cadoc spoke, Rhys felt a surge of excitement. Why bring Beech? It was surely quicker to run down into the town. And why not change into his warrior clothing and boots? With his mind racing and his friends helping him to saddle up, he turned Beech sharply across the courtyard and down the hill.

Cadoc had already returned and led the way into the bishop's house. Cynan and Tarou were comfortably seated in the open garden and two young girls were playing with the water in the fountain. They all looked up as Rhys entered – he was aware that Cynan had rarely seen him before in his monastic tunic and sandals. He looked down as the captain's eyes scanned him and smiled.

"Good morning Rhys, I hope you have forgiven the King for sending you back to your studies at the monastery, there is good reason as you are aware."

Rhys was dying to know the reason for his summons.

"You will recall young Patheu's father, the commander who went to Ynys Ygraine to bolster the garrison there? Well, let me introduce you to his two daughters."

Rhys remembered Patheu mentioning his two sisters. They bowed to Rhys and he bowed back – the older girl, about fourteen, was dangerously attractive and looked as if she was full of fun. The younger girl scowled and looked rebellious.

"I have an important job for you, Rhys," continued Cynan. "Patheu and his sisters are going to Ynys Ygraine to join their parents for the winter. Their mother misses them, and she has connections with the King, so, you are to accompany them on the galley with Ronan. The priest on the island will continue their schooling."

Rhys' heart leapt – what a wonderful chance to go out into the big sea in a galley and visit a famous island. This was unbelievable luck.

Cadoc raised his eyes to the heavens. Yet again there would be disruption at the monastery – Aidan would be livid.

Rhys stared at Tarou who had been looking very smug. "You may be wondering why you should be chosen, Rhys. Well, after the ship has offloaded stores and fuel at Ygraine, you are to carry on with Ronan to the fortress at Din Tagell. King Geraint has a wounded Saxon prisoner there who needs to be questioned in his own language. He's quite fearless and expects to die. Geraint is hoping that you, a mere boy, can trick him into giving information. His own man can't get him to speak a word."

"I'll try my best, sire," replied Rhys trying not to sound too pleased. "Will Ronan be setting sail next Saturday as planned?"

"Indeed," laughed Cynan. "And when you've finished at Din Tagell, Geraint will arrange for you to come back on a coastal trader. I'll meet you back at Caer Taf. Now, your first job is to take these two girls up to the abbess, they'll be staying at the nunnery until Saturday, and may well be going there to study next spring if all goes to plan. They have their own ponies with their luggage, and Tarou, I think you had better escort them all across the ferry, just in case of bad behaviour by the peasants. Now, I have to get back."

"Yes, Cynan. Well, Cadoc, I'll leave you to explain to the abbot. Let's go, Rhys." Tarou beckoned to the girls and they all made for the stables.

"Rhys…" Cadoc seemed to be almost pleading, "please don't boast of this with the pupils." It was obvious that Cadoc wished he could avoid Abbot Aidan, who was not going to be pleased at this latest piece of news.

It was only a short distance to the ferry and Rhys was able to wave across to Ronan and his crew as they were pulled past the galley by the ferryman. On the way to Saint Albans, Rhys now realised why Cynan had not wanted him to change from his monastic habit. Cynan was good at planning everything in advance and he had obviously thought of every detail.

The abbess looked as haughty as ever and gasped to the heavens when Rhys explained the plan – all as instructed by the King, of course. The two girls looked horrified on realising their fate; they began to feel that this so-called school was going to be a big shock after their previous luxurious existence.

Milk and cakes were called for, which both surprised and pleased Rhys. The reason soon became apparent. The abbess, starved of news from the outside world, wanted to know all about the latest goings-on in the area. How was the harvest at Penhal and Abermenei? What about Arteg and Helga? And the young Cadaer? Was Brochvael still as grumpy? Rhys felt that his extreme politeness with the abbess was cultivating a friendship that might well be useful; he found that after a while, she smiled and laughed at his humour. Perhaps she was not such a grim taskmaster after all.

Back at the monastery though, his good mood faded at the thought of waiting a full week. Dingad and Govan demanded to know the latest news.

"First, I have to call Fracan and Patheu," said Rhys tantalisingly. "Then I can tell you all about the sea voyage." The boys gasped. Sea voyage? What was Rhys up to now?

Patheu came running at Rhys' command and they all strode into the orchard to find the senior monk. Fracan had received the news of the voyage from Cadoc and eyed Rhys with resignation.

"Oh dear," he sighed bitterly. "The abbot nearly had a seizure last time. The Lord knows how he will react to this!"

The week dragged by, but early on the next Saturday morning Rhys had his weapons and some spare clothing all ready to board. Patheu was excited at the prospect of seeing his sisters again and was dying to tell them of his new Saxon friend and his schooling at the monastery. On collecting the two sisters, the abbess fussed over their luggage – Rhys felt she was relieved to be getting rid of them.

High tide had brought many of the townsfolk and the soldiers to see the big ship off on its voyage and the crew were all ready with their oars to steer the galley down the centre of the Isca and out into the channel. It was time for the passengers and their luggage to board and to slip the moorings.

With the galley under way and Ronan anxiously directing

the oarsmen while they negotiated the Isca, Rhys watched every move. Soon the sailors unfurled the huge square mainsail followed by the foresail, and the ship surged forward in the sharp breeze that was blowing down the estuary. As Rhys watched the trail boat skimming over the water behind them he could feel the power of the galley, now free from the slacker water of the shore. Ronan handed over the ropes of the rudder to a crew-member and approached Rhys and the girls.

"It's going to be a bit chilly now, Rhys, so the girls and the young boy had better go below to my cabin. The weather looks good, but we'll have to check the sea condition as we pass the coast of the Summer Land."

Rhys watched carefully as the crew struggled with the rigging and sails. Ronan advised him of the various points on the shore and how to make the best of the fast-running tide and the wind. When Rhys looked back, he was amazed at the distance they had already travelled; the islands that he had come to know so well were fast disappearing astern. The ship started to pitch fore and aft in the heavier swell and the coastline on either side of them became misty.

"We're approaching Saint Illtyd's coast on the right shore and there are some old Roman signal stations on the shore of the Summer Land," explained Ronan. "If there's any sighting of Saxon ships, they'll light beacons. We'll keep to the left shore and if everything is all right we'll sail straight across to Ynys Ygraine whilst the tide is still running. The sea looks a bit choppy and we'll have to tack quite a few times, but we should get there before nightfall."

Rhys asked many questions – he was eager to learn as much as he could under Ronan's tuition, and Ronan, as jolly as ever, was glad to find a young man so enthusiastic. Rhys was allowed to help on the helm which taxed his every muscle and soon he was able to anticipate the movement of the ship – the worst thing that could happen was to sail too close to the wind and lose headway altogether. Ronan and the crew took it in turns to go below for food, but when Rhys retired to Ronan's cabin, he found that the girls were feeling ill. He had to admit the motion of the ship was making him feel a bit queasy himself and the thought of food did not seem very appetising. Surprisingly, Patheu felt fine and was thoroughly enjoying the experience.

"You'll get used to it after a while, ladies," sympathised Ronan, who was well aware that he should make the children of a commander as comfortable as possible.

By late afternoon it was time to sail from the coast of the Summer Land to the island, and with a moderate breeze and gentle swell, Ronan ordered all sails to be set for the first leg of the crossing.

"I'm not happy with the visibility, Rhys, we can't see the island yet, and it's a bit misty in the distance." Ronan ordered two men up into the highest rigging – if there was any sighting of Saxon sails in the distance they would immediately turn for the coast.

After making good headway, a shout from the main mast indicated that the island was now in sight.

"We'll stay on this tack for a while, and then turn to the left of the island. The wind is steady from the south west and we're more than halfway." Ronan sounded cheerful.

Patheu and his sisters now came on deck for some fresh air and to see the first glimpse of their new home – soon they would all be safe with their parents.

"Only a few miles to go, ladies," laughed Ronan. "I dare say…" his sentence was cut short by a shout from the rigging. The lookout was pointing to the island, where a small beacon was apparent on the cliff top. As the fire started to grow in intensity, the lookouts and all the crew stared intently to the south. There was nothing in sight.

"Oh, no," shouted Ronan. "Look! There are sails behind us to the north." Panic swept the ship as three dark sails could just be discerned in the distance. Ronan gauged the tide and the wind and cursed. "We'll have to stay on this tack, it's too late to make for the Summer Land. Those devils are faster than us… our only chance is to make straight for the island."

Rhys felt a terrible chill as he squinted to make out the three sails, which were undoubtedly Saxon. They must have sailed near to the Demetian coastline, well away from the island, to scout the channel on the off-chance of prey. No wonder the sailors called them sea-wolves.

Ronan ordered the children into his cabin and went from man to man making sure that every rope was giving the ship best advantage in the wind. He called Rhys to the aft deck and leaned on the rail, staring at the horizon. He patted the rope that secured the trail boat.

"You see, Rhys, the sail on the trail boat is ready for rigging. Now here is what you must do if they get too close to us. We'll bring the trail boat alongside and the three children will be lowered down. You'd be in charge and you'll be on your own. We won't be able to help you, the trail boat is much faster than us and you should be able to outrun them and get to the island. They'll be more concerned with capturing my ship, but I'll scuttle her first rather than let them capture us."

Rhys could not believe what he was hearing – scuttle the ship? Sail off with the children? Surely the galley could get to the island before the Saxons reached them.

"See, they're getting closer, Rhys, those longships are faster than us, and they'll be able to use their oars to gain more speed. Our only chance is if the sea gets rougher, that'll slow them up."

"We're getting closer to the island," asserted Rhys bravely. The warning beacon was blazing on the cliff top and it would be obvious to the islanders that a dire situation was unfolding before them. Ynys Ygraine only had trading boats and they would be cut to pieces if they were foolhardy enough to face the Saxon longships.

The three sails gradually grew larger. It seemed as if time was standing still as all eyes fixed on the ominous shapes to the rear of the galley. It soon dawned on Rhys that the Saxons might well be able to overhaul them. Ronan called for all spears and bows to be brought on deck. Their duty was to kill as many Saxons as possible – their three keels would contain nearly a hundred howling warriors. The Saxons would throw spears and axes at the galley sailors, most of whom were older men and unable to cast off the many grappling irons.

The Saxons could not only now be seen, but their

bloodthirsty cries echoed across the water. Rhys had wondered what a longship would look like and now, with their large sails and foam spraying up from their bows, he knew they were truly a terrifying sight.

"Fetch the children, Rhys, and get a bow." Ronan looked grim as he signalled for the trail boat to be hauled alongside the galley. He ordered a younger sailor into the boat to unfurl the sail as Rhys helped to lower the children. Ronan shouted down to the sailor. "You'd better go as well, Alan, the boat needs more weight in this sea."

Rhys and his new companion pushed off and hauled in the ropes to set the sail as close to the wind as possible. They quickly veered away from the galley. The children cowered in the foredeck and as the boat started to buck in the choppy sea, they pulled the spare sail over themselves. Rhys couldn't bear to think of them all being captured. He checked on his dagger and pushed his quiver of arrows safely under the seat as the boat heeled over and sped away from the galley towards the island. At this level, closer to the surface of the sea, they could not see the longships, which was only a little comforting. Rhys checked every rope to get maximum speed from the sail as Alan leaned into the wind.

"They're getting close to the galley," cried Alan. "The sailors will kill them as they try to board, you watch." It just didn't seem real to have to watch a desperate sea battle. Rhys and his companions were well away from the galley as the crewmen burst into their own war cries – they were brave and angry, but despite their bravado, they were badly outnumbered.

Two of the longships approached the galley from either side as the third one swung wide to get to the bow. Rhys then realised that the third longship was, in fact, heading for them. The Saxons threw out their oars and started rowing to increase their speed, but thankfully the swell left them rowing out of unison.

"We're well away," shouted Alan with a hollow laugh. "They'll never catch us, well done, Rhys."

Rhys wasn't so sure; he could see that his boat was heading up to the wind better than the longship, but it was gradually getting between them and the island. They obviously had no intention of letting this small prize get away. Rhys asked Alan to take the helm while he strung his bow and propped the quiver against the seat. If the longship got close enough, he would try and shoot at them.

"We're shipping too much water from the spray," warned Alan, as he baled out furiously.

In the distance Rhys could see that the other two longships had drawn alongside the galley and a noisy battle was in progress; he felt sick to his stomach when he thought of it. Just then the pursuing longship changed tack and after stalling for a moment, started to surge past them to their rear.

"Good," thought Rhys. If they did that and moved farther out to sea, then he could change tack also and move close to the island. Rhys waited for the right moment, then suddenly tacked. The longship did the same and again lost a little headway, but its speed was once more bringing it close to Rhys' stern. He stood up and carefully tried to balance whilst pulling back his bowstring. It was difficult with the heaving movement of the boat under him and he nearly toppled over the side. Alan held onto his belt, which gave Rhys just enough balance to draw back his first arrow. It went so wide of the mark, he decided to wait until the longship got closer. He could now see that a burly Saxon was standing in the prow, his long white hair billowing in the breeze.

"Cenwulf!" cried Rhys in complete shock. "I can't believe it."

Suddenly, all his past feelings welled up in Rhys – he thought of all the people the Saxons had killed. Now was the time for war. He angrily fired arrow after arrow at the target in the prow. Some of his arrows struck the hull and the sail, he just couldn't keep his balance long enough to get an accurate shot. The crew of the longship ducked down, but suddenly there was a howl as the Saxon leader took an arrow in the thigh and toppled backwards into his boat.

Rhys could hear orders being shouted and suddenly the longship stopped in the water and turned away from them.

Perhaps it could be that Cenwulf had been badly wounded. Perhaps they had decided that two youngsters in a small boat were not worth the effort. But, no doubt, they wanted to be sure of the galley with its prize cargo. This was a great relief.

"Look, Alan," shouted Rhys. "The galley is sinking."

"Yes, I know, Ronan would have ordered the smashing of the sea-cocks if he knew that they were doomed. He had no choice."

"Will they all die? This is terrible."

"No," said Alan, keeping his own sail taut. "Any who

surrender will probably become slaves. Any wounded will be stabbed. I know Ronan would not surrender, that's for sure."

Rhys was devastated at the thought of Ronan perhaps already dead and thrown overboard. He watched as the galley sank lower into the water and keeled over sideways. The Saxons scrambled back onto their ships with the little booty they could salvage.

The island was getting closer and closer and soon Rhys could make out figures on the cliff top descending to the beach below. He had completely forgotten about the children under the sail and scrambled forward to comfort them.

They were cold and whimpering.

"It's all right children, look, your parents will be on the beach waiting for us. We're all safe."

"I was so frightened, Rhys," Alan shuddered as they waved to the islanders. "I've never had much training with a sword. If I'd been on the galley, I think I would have been hacked to death you know."

Now that they were safe, Rhys was aware of a tightness in his chest. What would he have done if he had stayed on the galley? Would he have fought to the death?

CHAPTER 17

South to Din Tagell

The lee side of the island offered calmer water and, as Rhys manoeuvred the trail boat closer to the beach, the three children waved frantically to the silent crowd. They were soon able to pick out their father who waded into the surf to gather them up in his arms.

"Rhys saved us, father," cried Patheu. "He sailed us away from those terrible Saxons."

"Thank you, thank you, Rhys. Of course, I remember you from Caerllion." The commander had obviously been beside himself with anguish at having to watch helplessly from the high cliff. "We thought everybody was killed or taken prisoner until we saw your boat being chased by the Saxons. I'll never doubt God again."

Alan eagerly explained, "Rhys shot their leader with an arrow, that's what made them turn back. They would have caught us for sure before we got to shore."

The commander winced. "That's what we were afraid of, but all we could do was watch. It was heartbreaking to see Ronan go down with his galley."

The boat was pulled onto the shingle and the children ran for their distraught mother who hugged them tightly. Rhys collected his bow and noticed that he had only four arrows left – he dared not think what would have happened had the longship caught up with them. Would he have drawn his dagger and fought them?

A messenger ran down the steep pathway from the cliff-top.

"Sire, it looks as if the three keels are sailing south past the island. Perhaps they intend going home."

"Well, they won't dare attack the island, at least not in daylight. Keep everybody on standby tonight. There should be enough moonlight to spot them if they get anywhere near us."

"Yes, sire. Shall we haul all boats well away from the beaches?"

The commander nodded as the messenger sped away.

"Now, let's get you all into the warm." It was only at this point that Rhys realised that he was wearing just his woollen shirt. His heavy jacket had gone down with the ship. For the first time, he shivered with the chill.

As they climbed the pathway from the beach, the commander explained how helpless they were against Saxon longships.

"That's why we have such a large garrison on Ynys Ygraine," he explained. "If the Saxons captured this island, it would be very difficult to shift them again, and it would take a fleet of galleys and hundreds of men. All we have on this coast are slow supply boats built to stand up to the ocean swells."

"What happens if you spot Saxon sails? Can you warn the people on both coastlines?" asked Rhys.

"Oh, yes. We have trail boats that can sail quite fast with a good wind. That gives us plenty of time to get a warning to the mainland if we see Saxons approaching from the south, provided there is no sea fog. But today we were taken completely by surprise when they suddenly appeared through the mist from the Dyfed coast. They must have sailed just out of sight of our watch towers and just by chance, you were caught in the wrong place. Had you been closer to the Summer Land, Ronan might have been able to get back to shore in time."

"I can't believe that Ronan's dead," said Rhys dejectedly. "Do you think he might have been taken prisoner?"

"It seems doubtful. Any prisoners taken are valuable, they can trade them with their own Saxon barons, you see. I'm sure they would have killed quite a few Saxons before the ship went down, though."

The island's priest approached the morose gathering and said to the commander, "I think we should have a special service in the chapel tonight, sire. I have candles we can light and there are many of us who will pray for the lost souls." The commander acknowledged him with a wave of his hand.

When the children were settled, Rhys and Alan were shown to a small house above the cliffs. The scenery was spectacular in the setting sun and later, after the service, ample food and wine were provided for the heroes from the sea.

"We will be on alert for several days," explained the commander. "It's doubtful if the Saxons will have enough provisions for more than that. Their sails will have been seen on the far shore and you can rest assured that beacons will be lit tonight all down the Summer Land coast. So, you'll have to stay here for two days, then if the weather looks suitable, I'll get you two across the straight to Herculis Point in one of our boats, which can then take you on down to Din Tagell. You can report to Cai, the commander there, and tell him all about the loss of the galley. He'll take over and get you back to Caer Taf."

"Yes, sire," replied Rhys. "It's going to be terrible explaining to everybody what happened to the galley and the crew. I hope I can be of help at Din Tagell."

The commander sighed.

"I've a suspicion that after their defeat at Maendibyn, the Saxons are going to increase their attacks from the sea. They know that we can't take on their longships, and now that the days are getting shorter, they're going to have more cover during the long dark nights."

***

After a good night's rest, Rhys and his companion had the next day free to tour the island. Sea birds were diving and screeching everywhere. They spoke with the lookouts at various points and enjoyed the peacefulness of the cliff tops and coves.

"I can hardly believe what happened to us yesterday," said Rhys. "It's as if it was all a bad dream." Alan looked away and they sat silently for a while.

They agreed not to mention the sinking of the galley again.

This was a good chance to question Alan about his experiences as a young sailor. It turned out that Alan was only just seventeen.

"I was from a farm near Din Tagell originally," he explained. "But it was too much like hard work, and I always loved the sea. So last summer, when the galley was moored by the island, I approached Ronan and asked if I could join him. Well, as you can imagine, my poor mother was shocked, but surprisingly father said it would be a good thing for me, and so, there I was... off to Armorica."

"What luck," said Rhys. "Tell me all about Armorica, how long does it take to get across there?"

"Well, I was sick for the first two days. After that, I loved it. The crew were good to me, and most of them were from Armorica, so we had a good time between loading and unloading along the coast."

Rhys wanted to know everything about foreign places and closely questioned Alan who laughed at his eagerness.

When they reached the far side of the island, they noticed a strange craft making for a small beach and decided to climb down a pathway and investigate.

"It seems to be a fisherman," said Alan. "Perhaps we could cook some fish on the beach. It's a pity we don't have any wine."

As the small boat beached on the shingle, a smiling old man greeted them.

"I suppose you're Rhys and Alan, there's not much I don't know on this island. We all saw the galley coming on the horizon last evening and started cheering. You can imagine how we felt when our lookout spotted the Saxon sails. They came from nowhere. My guess is that they were preparing for a night attack when they spotted your galley."

Rhys took to the kindly old man straight away. "We're here for two days, but then we're off to the mainland and hopefully, the Saxons will be long gone by then."

"Ah, you need a fast currach, like mine," said the old man. Rhys noticed that he spoke with a strange accent.

"It's a bit like a long coracle," said Rhys inquisitively as he lifted one end. "Goodness me, it's very light. With that sleek sail, I bet it skims over the water in a following wind. But you wouldn't make much headway against a headwind, you'd get pushed sideways. It's just as well it's got two oars."

"Aha, you're a man with knowledge of boats I see. Now if I get these fish to my dear wife in the hut, what do you say to going for a quick sail just offshore?"

"Oh, yes, I'd love to see how she handles."

Rhys was only then aware of a hut hidden partway up the cliffside. An elderly woman struggled down the pathway.

"This is my wife, Berach, and my name's Ryan. We've been on the island for over twenty years. My job is to catch fish for the garrison and help with the sheep."

"So where did you come from originally?" asked Rhys. He was intrigued to know everything about the island and especially the skin boat.

"We're of the old Desi tribe of Erin. When our people were conquered years ago by our treacherous neighbours, many of us escaped to Dyfed and my wife and I just kept going until we arrived here. And this is where we'll stay now." The old man laughed easily. Rhys could understand why they wanted to spend their later years on such a beautiful island.

"Now, Berach you take the fish on up to the lookout post, my dear. The boys are going to have some fun. Perhaps you'll have a little refreshment for us all when we get back." He winked at her playfully, then stepped gingerly down the rocky pathway. "Jump in boys, you sit with an oar apiece and row us through the surf. I'll keep the sail slack until we get offshore."

The boys both had much experience in rowing and were surprised how quickly the skin boat reacted to their strong pulling. Soon they were into the gentle swell of the bay and Ryan set the sail to send the craft surging seaward.

"See that stronger wind out there past the headland, Rhys. When we sail into it I'll turn away from the wind, so you two get ready to trim the boat."

As Ryan turned into the swirling tide, the sail snapped against its ropes and the craft bucked up and down on the choppy swell. The boys had to dive to the left hand side as the boat heeled over and leapt forward.

"We're skimming over the waves," shouted Rhys at his laughing companion. At the same time, he realised that this was not the sort of craft to be in too far out in a strong wind. If they capsized, they would certainly be in trouble – and the water was cold, even at this time of the year.

"When we get a bit further along the island, I'll change tack and turn into the shelter of the cliff, boys. Now, get ready to cross over."

The two sailors gave a sigh of relief as the currach glided into calmer water. Making their way slowly along the shore back to the beach gave Rhys a chance to take over the stern rudder oar and get used to steering such a craft.

"A bigger skin boat like this could outrun a Saxon longship, don't you think? The trouble is, you would slide sideways." Rhys scratched his chin.

"There are bigger skin boats, Rhys," said Ryan. "They're used to cross back and fore to Erin when the weather is settled enough. But you'd need a whole fleet to be able to fight off a Saxon ship."

"I'd love to sail to Erin," enthused Rhys.

"Well, if you ever get the chance," offered Ryan, "you can see the big skin boats down on the western peninsular at the Harbour. Some of them are eight paces long. The remains of the Desi tribe are probably still making them down there. There's an old cousin of mine called Colman, if he's still alive. He's a real craftsman and spent all of his life making skin boats for the old Desi King… God rest his soul."

"Hmm, I'll definitely get down there one day. First, Alan and I have to survive the next voyage and get to Din Tagell." Alan grimaced – he admitted he was still shaking from their escape the day before.

After dragging the currach partway up the cliff path, the trio arrived at Ryan's hut to find his wife tending a fire and gutting some fish.

"First, I think we should celebrate with some cyder," said Ryan, rubbing his hands together. "Thankfully we have good orchards here to keep us going, but now with our supplies gone down with the galley, we're going to have to haul what we can from the mainland with our own supply boats before the winter."

"If you had some larger skin boats, you could transport stores from the Summer Land pretty fast without having to rely on galleys." Rhys, as usual, was thinking hard.

"You're right, of course, Rhys. But, until recent years, it has never been a problem. It was rare to see Saxons this far north, they were always afraid of the currents and tides up in the channel. And when the trading galleys bound for Armorica went way out into the big ocean to skirt around the Syllan Isles, the Saxons would never risk getting caught by the big seas out there."

The rest of the afternoon was spent pleasantly exploring the island. Ryan, who knew every little nook and cranny, led the way. Finally, the two boys arranged to meet their new friend the next morning and help with the fishing. They were going to learn how to catch crabs, lobsters and eels – and how to smoke them in Ryan's stone-built smoke-oven.

***

That evening, the pair was invited to supper with the commander and his family. Their gratitude was overwhelming as they tried not to think of the consequences, had Rhys and

Alan not rescued the children. The weather was becoming calmer and it was arranged for the pair to leave for Din Tagell early the morning after next. Two boats would cross to Herculis Point and on their return would bring back essential stores.

Patheu's elder sister made Rhys feel uncomfortable with her constant giggling – she did not seem to feel any sadness at the terrible fate of the sailors on the galley. At least, thought Rhys, come next spring, the abbess would soon teach her manners.

Next morning the boys walked eagerly down to Ryan's cove and it was not long before they were once more at sea in the precarious currach.

"You see those floats and coloured flags off the rocks, boys, that's where we'll go first. If you take the rudder, Rhys, and get me alongside where I can reach, I'll show you what we've got." Ryan had a long hooked pole and was soon hauling up the first trap. A large lobster was pulled from it, claws waving wildly.

"I've heard of those," said Rhys. "They always go to the King's table."

"Ah, you'll taste one later, boys. We get lots of them here. Can you see the way I'm holding him, his claws are dangerous. Help me to tie him up, Alan."

Lobsters and crabs soon filled the bottom of the boat and Rhys watched carefully as Ryan baited the traps with smelly fish and lowered them back to the sea bed. As it was low tide the currents were slack, so Rhys was invited to take the currach around the headland and into the south-westerly wind. This was most exciting and the boys were amazed at how manoeuvrable the currach was, compared to the heavy wooden boats they were used to.

Eventually, they beached the currach and between them carried the morning's catch up to the lookout point for collection.

"Now, a taste of lobster with a little fish broth first, boys, and perhaps something nice to drink." Ryan winked as he produced a flask from the bottom of the currach. The two boys tucked in with relish.

After such an enjoyable day, with Ryan telling the boys all about his wild youth and his many experiences, they returned to their quarters for the last night on the island.

"Well, Ryan was a most interesting old sailor," said Alan. "And I know exactly what you're thinking, Rhys. You want to see one of the big skin boats, don't you? I bet you'd like to have one back at Caerllion to show the colts!"

"We need a craft to outrun the longships," replied Rhys, deep in thought. "I wonder if I can persuade Tarou to speak with Arthur when I get back."

The boys were once again invited to supper with the commander and the priest, who both gawked as Rhys explained his connection between the monastery and the army. With ample wine, Alan had a job to stay awake, but eventually he and Rhys were able to excuse themselves.

"Get to the beach early in the morning, boys. I'm sure the Saxons are long gone, the two boats will be rigged ready." The commander winked at Rhys. "You'd better be sure you've got plenty of arrows…"

The eastern cove was already bathed in the early morning sunshine as six oarsmen and a captain to each boat eased their craft out to catch the wind. It seemed that the whole garrison had turned out to cheer Rhys and Alan on their way. They each sat proudly in the prows.

The air was clear and a stiff breeze blew from the southwest across a flat sea. This meant that the dash westwards for Herculis Point would be fast and furious, for at sea level, Rhys knew that they could not see far to the horizon. Everybody kept a wary eye on the high cliffs of the fast disappearing island for any warning signal.

Rhys and Alan were glad of the heavy coats that they had been given to counter the chilly morning breeze and it was towards noon before they could see the coast of the Summer Land. The captains confirmed that they were on the right course when they saw a lookout on Herculis Point waving a large black signal flag in greeting. They then turned south and glided into a small cove where an excited crowd had turned out to greet the visitors. The mood of the villagers soon turned to gloom as the captains related the fate of the galley three days earlier.

"We've got food and drink for you, friends," offered the headman. "I'll send a messenger on our fastest horse to spread the news and get word to Din Tagell. We've not seen any sign of longships on this coast, so as you say, they've probably gone south with their captives."

The captain of Rhys' craft explained his mission. "I'm going on down to Din Tagell with the two boys. As you know we've lost our winter stores, so if you can arrange for extra salt meat and grain to be brought here, my colleagues will get straight back to the island now the wind is favourable, and I'll get back tomorrow."

After a much appreciated meal and a little time for Rhys and Alan to explore, it was time to set off again. Despite his constant thoughts of Ronan, Rhys was quite elated with all this voyaging – he thought of his friends back in Caerllion; they would never believe his story when he got back.

The trip down the coast to their destination took the rest of the day. With a bright red skyline showing in the west, the captain turned inshore to the fortress of Din Tagell. The oars were not needed to approach the natural rock jetty and as a small contingent of soldiers helped them to tie up, the visitors scaled the steep pathway and steps to the large stone built castle.

They were immediately shown into the main hall where officers were seated at a long bench silently eating their evening meal. The commander rose and smiled weakly at the captain.

"I've heard the news. Ronan was a dear friend of mine and related to my wife. He will be sorely missed. Sit down along the bench and join us."

Rhys was aware of the commander looking into his eyes. He had expected this and stared back unflinching.

"I'm Cai, and you must be Rhys. You're very young, but I've heard that your young troop had some experience at Brenin Point. I was with Geraint's army in the south and after the Saxons broke up, we trapped a lot of them in the marshlands. Mind you, we couldn't follow with our horses, so a lot of them got away."

"Yes, sire," replied Rhys. "Perhaps they'll stay in the east, now." Cai was a large muscular man who looked fearless and also a little frightening. He reminded Rhys of Tarou. It was good to know that the army had such powerful commanders.

"I doubt it, they're greedy for war and loot. We've lost many families as captives along the south coast and now the Saxons are getting reinforcements from their homeland. My guess is that they want to wipe us all out, or better still, make us all slaves." The other officers thumped the table with their goblets and cursed the invaders. "As you can see, my men want to recruit a big army and march east, but we can't risk it. If we lost one battle, we'd leave ourselves vulnerable. And that's Arthur's opinion as well. We have to look to our defences for the time being and be ready for anything."

The officers shouted and waved their fists with much bravado. Rhys knew that after a night's drinking, they were game for a fight.

"Now, Rhys, as you know, we've got an important Saxon prisoner here. He was captured after a raid down the coast a few weeks ago. Luckily, one of our troops was able to surprise them before they all got to their boats. The prisoner is the maddest Saxon you've ever seen, but I'm sure he's got information that's useful. He won't utter a word to my man, but if you can speak with him in his own language and make him angry, I think we can learn something. He's not afraid of dying, you know."

"I'll do everything I can, sire," replied Rhys, wondering how difficult it might be to get a Saxon warrior to talk. "When do you want me to start?"

"Tomorrow will be soon enough, he's been chained up since we caught him. I'm sure if he had the chance he'd kill himself rather than be a prisoner. Let's all drink to our next victory!" Cai cheered with the soldiers and the guests happily joined in.

***

Next morning, Rhys and Alan reported to Cai. Alan was hoping for permission to visit his family at their nearby farm. The boys had already discussed Alan's future and Rhys was hoping that his new friend could return with him to Caerllion. This would mean that Rhys would avoid having to explain the disaster of Ronan's galley by himself.

"Sire," enquired Alan nervously. "I don't have a ship now, so could I go back to Caer Taf with Rhys? They might need me on the galleys there. I've got lots of experience."

"I dare say," said Cai with a wave of his hand. "Now Rhys, let me introduce you to our Saxon friend."

Stone steps led down to a dark cell with a heavy oak door. The smell was enough to make Rhys retch as the door was unlocked. Some light came through a small opening in the outside wall to reveal a scowling Saxon warrior glaring at the intruders.

Cai turned to one of his attendants.

"Get water to wash down this mess, it stinks in here. And you'd better get a stool, Rhys."

Rhys was glad to leave the cell whilst the two men sluiced down the floor and swept the dirt into a drain.

"You're on your own now," said Cai as he left.

Rhys went to the small window and was glad to see the blue sea and distant horizon. He had no idea how to approach the Saxon – was there any information that they didn't already know? He knew that he must not show any nervousness.

The Saxon had long dirty hair and looked to be about thirty. His demeanour suggested to Rhys that he had been of high rank.

Rhys gritted his teeth, moved the stool to the centre of the cell and stared intently at the Saxon. The Saxon glared back and hissed insults at this strange boy.

"Your god, Woden, has deserted you, Saxon. Where was he when you marched against us at Maendibyn?"

The Saxon looked shocked when this boy spoke to him in his own language.

"I was there and saw hundreds of your men skewered. I killed six of the scum on my own. They ran away like old women."

"Lies!" shouted the Saxon. "You dare to insult Woden. He rules the whole world!"

"He's a stupid joke," countered Rhys, goading his adversary into a rage. "He's only in your imagination. I spit on him!"

The Saxon strained at his chains, his wrists were already raw from trying to unleash himself.

Rhys continued,

"Our one great God is master of the universe, you poor

fool... you'll see when our army marches east in the spring. We're going to wipe you Saxons from the face of the earth, and drown Woden in his own vomit."

The Saxon was beside himself with anger.

"You wait until our cousins, the Angli join us. We're going to smash you in the south and occupy all the land below the Tamesis and then we're all going to move north and drive you into the western ocean. We'll have all the land and you will be our slaves. This is our destiny, our leaders have ordained it."

"It's too late, you stupid ox, we're going to take all your women as slaves and throw your children into the Tamesis to drown. Our God is ten times more powerful than Woden."

"You lying pig, you're all going to die. We're building hundreds of keels to sail up the coast and attack you. You wait and see. Mighty Cenwulf will lead our ships..." With this the Saxon broke down and put his head between his knees. He seemed to realise he was going to die.

"Cenwulf?" whispered Rhys to himself, alarmed. So Cenwulf was a now Saxon fleet commander – and Rhys had put an arrow into his leg only a few days ago. "I've heard of Cenwulf the Butcher, he cuts up dead bodies after a battle just for pleasure. He's a stinking pig and a coward."

The prisoner growled with rage.

"How would I recognise him?" shouted Rhys.

"You'll recognise him, you fool. His hair is long and white...," the Saxon checked himself abruptly; but it was enough for Rhys to realise Cenwulf was well-known among the Saxons.

He stood up and carried the stool to the doorway where the two guards had been watching the shouting match with great interest. Rhys was glad to leave the Saxon to his fate.

Cai and an officer were waiting in the hall and they listened thoughtfully as the Saxon plans were outlined to them.

"If they're building up reinforcements and joining with the Angli, they'll be able to muster a huge army by next year. And that's our biggest problem, if we don't have forewarning, we're going to be in trouble. I dare say the King was thinking the same as me, that the enemy wouldn't dare try anything again for years."

"He talked about hundreds of keels attacking our coast, sire. I think he was probably exaggerating, but it must be difficult to protect the whole coastline."

"It's impossible, Rhys, every time they've raided during a dark night, we've been taken by surprise. Well, you'd best get back to Caer Taf and make your report. Guto, my officer here will be going back with you to speak with the King, and when you get to Herculis village he'll arrange for you all to sail north with another vessel." Guto offered his hand to Rhys.

Rhys knew that he had to ask about Cenwulf.

"Have you heard of a Saxon leader called Cenwulf, sire?"

Cai's eyes flickered.

"I've heard the name, he's the leader of three keels. If he's the one who's been raiding our south coast, he's a brutal killer."

***

The two boys loved the boat trip up the coastline and were able to wave to farmers and their families on the high ground.

"They'll all be keeping an eye on the distant horizon for any danger," explained Guto. "Fast horses are always available to race to the nearest lookout points if Saxon sails are spotted. Lighted beacons are all very well in clear weather. But sometimes the fog and the darkness leave everybody very nervous."

The headman at Herculis village welcomed the returning sailors and confirmed that he had arranged for loading the extra stores bound for Ynys Ygraine. Guto inspected the sturdy fishing craft offered to him for the morrow before they sat down to the evening meal.

The Saxon threat dominated the evening festivities, with drink encouraging the usual bravado. Cai's officer was warm and friendly towards the boys who learnt a lot from him. He spoke of the southern army's experiences below the Maendibyn Hills during the summer battle and seemed to have enjoyed killing Saxons.

"Don't say you heard it from me, lads, but the battle at Maendibyn nearly went wrong. When the Saxons started their ascent up the roadway, they hesitated and spread out through the woods. Arthur and Cynan held back too long and when they gave the order to charge, the Saxons were ready. There was a bitter fight on our right flank and the army from Caer Lin suffered terrible casualties. If it wasn't for them, we might have lost the initiative."

Rhys and Alan looked at each other with concern. It seemed that there were two sides to a story when victory was declared.

CHAPTER 18

More Adventure

There was much excitement the next morning as two sailors were allocated to take the boys and the officer to up Caer Taf.

"It's a bit blowy today," observed Rhys as they sailed out to sea in order to skirt the headland. When they turned to run up the coast with the wind behind them, Rhys had to admit that he was a bit queasy as the boat pitched and yawed from the following sea. However, the passengers were able to sit back and enjoy the cliffs and the coast-line – it was a terrible thought that in time the Saxons might be strong enough to invade and take over all this beautiful country.

The water gradually changed to a muddy colour as the Silurian coast and Ynys Brenin came into view. The running tide took them swiftly to the mouth of the Taf where lookouts waved to them reassuringly, and with enough breeze to take them upriver to the jetty without need of the oars, they were soon whisked away to the King's palace.

The boys and the officer were ushered into the hall where the King and his company greeted them and offered them some wine.

"Well, Rhys, you seem to be a survivor," said the King, his eyes twinkling despite the gravity of their news. "A messenger got the news to us. You and your friend here did a good job. I dare say you can't wait to get back to your monastery for a rest."

The company laughed loudly at Rhys' pained expression.

"Losing Ronan and the galley has been a terrible shock to us all, but you can all rest assured, the Saxons are going to suffer for this." Rhys could see the barely concealed hatred and anger in the King's expression, something he had also seen in Prince Arthur's eyes. "Now, let's hear all the news from Cai."

Guto outlined the whole story of the outburst from the Saxon prisoner concerning the new build up of their joint forces. This clearly troubled the King and Rhys listened carefully as the company turned into a war council. The King said there would have to be more vigilance and better defences against sudden attacks.

After a while it was time for the evening meal and Rhys was surprised when the King and his senior sea captain called the boys over. "We'd like you to tell us all about the chase, boys, I'm sure that we have much to learn. Those accursed longships are too fast for us, we would need three galleys full of fighting men to be able to fight them off on the high seas." The King and his captain listened carefully as Rhys and Alan related the whole story.

"Sire," said Rhys hopefully, "I met an old Desi sailor on Ynys Ygraine and he was telling me all about the skin boats that are used to cross the Western Sea to Erin."

"Yes, I've seen them," said the galley captain, "and I wouldn't want to sail up the channel in one of those. They always look a bit flimsy to me."

"Well, I was thinking, sire, if we could build a large one, say eight paces long and get an extra foresail and better keels we could sail close into the wind."

The King sat back staring at Rhys and licking his lower lip thoughtfully.

"When we were being chased by the longship, sire, we just had the edge on them sailing into the wind and every time they tacked they lost way. But then they picked up speed and might have eventually caught up with our smaller trail boat. Luckily, the swell was too big for them to use their oars as well."

"We could never build ships like the Saxons," said the sea captain. "We've always had to exchange large amounts of gold for our Roman galleys from the Middle Sea. The coastal sailboats that we have now are about the best we can build, and they're not safe in a big sea."

The King was nodding his head quietly.

"If we had big skin boats, Rhys, are you saying that we could outrun longships if we were caught off the coast?"

"Yes, sire, and I would say that we could sail to places like Ynys Ygraine in rough seas in the winter as well."

The captain scoffed at Rhys' confidence, but Guto listened with interest.

Alan was reluctant to speak, but couldn't help himself.

"Sire, I've heard about these boats covered over against the spray in a heavy sea, and able to heel over without capsizing." The King smiled at Alan's enthusiasm.

"I think that will do for now, boys, I intend to visit Caerllion shortly, Rhys, so give a message to Tarou to expect me in a few days. There's a supply boat going up the channel in the morning, you can take Alan with you and explain the recent events to Arthur together. But remember, no mention of any Saxon plans to anybody else."

Dismissed from the palace, Rhys led Alan to the Caer Taf barracks where he was soon reunited with his old comrades. Garwyn was as mischievous as ever and after Rhys introduced Alan, they were welcomed into the quarters and shown spare bunks. After the inevitable recounting of their story, the boys were taken to the tavern to finish the evening. Despite being coaxed, Rhys said nothing of his meeting with the King.

The next morning Garwyn accompanied the boys to the jetty to meet the crew of the supply boat and, with the tide running swiftly up the channel, they were soon sailing up the Isca river and home. Caerllion had heard the news of Ronan's galley two days earlier and despite the terrible loss, there was jubilation at Rhys' safe return.

"You appear to have become quite famous," laughed Tarou as he helped Rhys up the slipway. "You seem to find trouble wherever you go!"

After exchanging greetings with all his friends, Rhys introduced Alan and indicated that they were to report to Arthur.

"He's at the barracks," said Tarou. "I'll come with you. I suspect he'll want to call a full meeting." Rhys wasn't sure if he liked all this attention. It was beginning to be a strain and he couldn't help thinking of poor Ronan and his crew. At least Alan had gone through the same experience and they would be able to lend each other some support.

Arthur gathered his senior officers to listen to Rhys' report and Cai's concerns about another Saxon build-up when they were least expecting it.

"My father is visiting Caer Gloyw and the north soon," confirmed Arthur. "It seems we'll have to think of part of our garrison being stationed on the other side of the Havren by next summer."

As the meeting broke up, Arthur called Tarou and the boys to one side.

"Tarou, put Alan with Lewys and the colts for the time being. We can use someone with experience."

"Thank you, sire, I've had some training in fighting at sea. And I can ride well."

Arthur smiled at Alan and slapped him on the back.

"As for you, Rhys, I think you'd better carry on at the monastery. No doubt you'll be going home for Christmas, but next year you could be busy."

Did this mean that Rhys would be joining the main army?

***

After leaving the barracks, Rhys called at the bishop's house. Cadoc was surprisingly pleased to see Rhys and escorted him back to the monastery. It was a little annoying for Rhys to be treated like a pupil again, but after quickly recounting his story he joined his incredulous friends. In some ways it was a relief to get back into a settled routine.

"We've been looking after young Sceaf," reassured Dingad. "He was lost when you took Patheu away, but he's learning our language well and the other young boys show him what to do. He's teaching us some Saxon words, you know."

By the following Saturday, Rhys was restless for more fun with his comrades. King Myric was due at Caerllion and the whole monastery was to turn out in the town to greet him. The abbess and her girls from the nunnery were to gather on the far bank of the river without entering the town and follow the King back up the hill to his old palace. Rhys slipped away after prayers to join Lewys.

"We're arranging a mock battle for the King, Rhys. Tarou's army is going to charge down the hill to attack the barracks and we're going to suddenly appear along the riverbank to take them on from the flank."

Rhys was impressed by Lewys' decisiveness and authority, as everybody swung into action. He was pleased to see that Conmael and his friend were enjoying their first weeks in the troop. Alan with his experience would also soon fit in.

By noon, the King's return to his old headquarters had been announced and after the usual tumultuous welcome the entourage retired to a suitable vantage point on the hillside to watch the battle. The townspeople and the monastery pupils apparently found the blood-curdling attack a bit frightening, but loud cheers went up when Lewys' colts charged the attackers from the flank. The confusion of battle led to frayed tempers and some of the more violent soldiers injured their supposed adversaries. Arthur felt it was time to call a truce and signalled Tarou to withdraw. King Myric was clearly impressed and gave a rallying speech from his platform. The huge crowd wildly cheered their beloved King.

Arthur then waved the company to the amphitheatre for refreshment, while the King and his retinue crossed the river to be escorted to his old villa.

Benches and tables had been arranged around the amphitheatre and cold meats, bread, cheese and suitable drinks were in ample supply. Once more, Rhys and Alan were summoned to a meeting with Arthur and Tarou – what surprise was in store this time?

"I've been speaking with the King, Rhys. It seems he's impressed with your idea of a skin boat that could outrun a Saxon longship." Arthur was speaking with his usual humour. "Personally, I think you'll need wings. Anyway, he wants you to join up with Garwyn at Caer Taf, then sail on down to the West Harbour to examine the skin boats there. If Garwyn backs up your ideas, then it's all arranged for you to bring a suitable skin boat back up to Caer Taf for further trials."

"Yes, sire," said Rhys with enthusiasm.

"There's a boat builder called Colman I've heard of. I'm sure it's all going to work out."

"You'll know soon enough, young man. Garwyn is expecting you on the next tide. And Alan goes with you, he's had experience on the open ocean I understand."

Alan clapped his hands in excitement, but Tarou shook his head in disbelief.

"I dare say Abbot Aidan would be glad to see the back of you for good," said Tarou. "Bran will have to go with you, he's the only one who knows the coast that far west, so he'll make sure a sail boat is ready with stores and some heavy coats."

"Well, what are you waiting for?" laughed Arthur. The boys grabbed some food and sped off to collect their spare clothing. Alan was billeted at the barracks and they arranged to meet at the quayside.

"Hail," greeted Bran when they arrived just in time to catch the ebbing tide. "We'll be down to Caer Taf in no time. I've seen those skin boats, you know. They can be a bit unstable in a rough sea. Well, let's cast off." Canna saw them off dejectedly as he was expected to take over Bran's duties, and there was no telling how long they would be away.

Bran gave Alan the job of steering the boat down the river and out into the channel – they both hoped he would be able to stay at Caerllion. On arrival at Caer Taf, Garwyn ran along the riverbank with his troop to greet them.

"I was hoping you would make it on the tide. Good evening, Bran, I've arranged accommodation for you tonight and we'd better be off before dawn tomorrow to catch the tide."

Garwyn was as excited as Rhys and Alan, but Bran seemed a little apprehensive.

"I've got some old friends to visit while I'm in Caer Taf, boys, so I'll leave you to enjoy yourselves this evening."

Once again Rhys and Alan joined Garwyn and his troop at the taverns, but were sensible enough to get to bed early.

It seemed to be the middle of the night when the boys were woken by Bran and ushered to the jetty. Rhys and Alan were allocated oars while Garwyn lazed in the bow. It was deathly quiet and moonless, but the sound of their oars alerted a lookout at the mouth of the river. As they were challenged and their password acknowledged, Rhys realised that an enemy attack in the darkness of night could cause complete confusion. Once they were well out into the channel, with dawn showing in the eastern sky, the thick morning mist over the swirling tide gave Rhys an eerie feeling. The sail was not picking up any wind as they were swept along unable to keep the bow into the tide.

"We can't see any land," said Alan. "You can imagine what it's like when you're caught in a sea fog in a slow-moving galley and you know you're not far from a rocky coast. Ronan would always stay well away from shore if he could."

Rhys agreed – he hoped they were well offshore, but not too close to Ynys Echni. Gradually the mist cleared and they found themselves just down the channel from the two islands.

"At this rate we might get to the Harbour before dark," said Bran encouragingly. "If the tide turns and the weather doesn't look too good, we'll pull into a cove for the night. I do believe it's going to rain, so you'd better get the spare sail ready to cover yourselves, it's not good to get wet when you're out at sea."

The boys enjoyed the view of the coast and tried to

memorise all the various landmarks for future reference. They had to tack occasionally when the breeze veered from the west, but as they passed Illtyd's Point, Bran was able to head further north and pick up speed under a full sail.

***

By noon, Bran judged that the tide was against them, so they sailed further inshore to calmer water and enjoyed their food whilst taking it in turns to steer and trim the boat. On the last leg across the Bay of Caer Myrddyn, a squall blew up and threatened to obscure any sight of land.

"I can just see Ynys Piro in the distance, boys, we'll stop there for the night and get away early in the morning." Bran turned to Rhys. "You've no doubt heard of the monastery there. I dare say they'll have some good food for us."

"Yes, I've heard all about it, and I have to say, it will be a real blessing for me to stop there and meet the monks. I'll be able to tell Abbot Aidan and Cadoc all about the island when we get back. Perhaps then, they won't think so badly of me."

His friends mocked Rhys and suggested that he stay at the Piro monastery while they went on to the Harbour and tested the skin boats. They could call and collect him on the way back.

"When we meet Colman, the boat builder," countered Rhys, "and I'm sure he won't be expecting us, I'll mention to him that you're just beginners."

Their humour and banter continued until they saw a group of monks on the island waving madly. The boys had to admit to feeling a bit queasy as the sea had become choppy, so landfall was a relief. The monks welcomed them like long-lost friends and led Rhys off to the abbot to explain the object of their journey.

Bran, Garwyn and Alan were glad to explore and leave their companion to the abbot. It took a while for Rhys to explain his position at Caerllion, which left the abbot a little confused, however, it was not for the church to question the orders of the King. In fact, the abbot had a clear duty to help the travellers on their way and he was obviously glad of the chance to get some recent outside news.

Rhys was eventually worn out by the endless conversation and was glad when everybody gathered for evening prayers in the chapel. He tricked his companions into attending by insisting that they would get no supper unless they joined wholeheartedly in the singing.

Supper was plentiful and the accommodation provided was warm and comfortable. The monks and novices alike fussed over them and relished this rare opportunity to talk with visitors. The visitors were surprised at the comfort of the bunks and were fast asleep in no time.

CHAPTER 19

The Skin Boat

After prayers attended by Rhys, whilst his companions prepared the boat, a breakfast of smoked fish and eggs was followed by a clear run along the coast and into the Harbour. Bran wasn't sure which village they needed to find, so they rowed to the nearest beach where some fisherman were repairing their nets. They looked up in surprise at this unexpected visit. Greetings were exchanged by both sides as the boat neared the beach. Rhys was pleasantly surprised to see such clear water and clean sand rather than pebbles. There was no surf inside the Harbour and it looked a good place for children to have fun and learn to swim.

More people scurried down the beach to see the visitors.

"Good morning," smiled Bran as the boys jumped knee-deep into the water and pulled the boat a little way up onto the sand. He introduced his companions. "We're looking for Colman, do you know him?"

"Yes, indeed," replied one of the fisherman. "He's an old friend of mine. But he's way upriver at Lake Village. The best thing you can do is wait a short while 'til the tide starts to turn;

there are a few rocks you need to avoid. I dare say you could do with some broth, please join us and then I can tell you about the landmarks and shoals."

This seemed like a good idea – the boys were always hungry. Bran noted the directions given for the journey to Colman's village. The tide was running fiercely as they bade their farewells and glided along the smooth surface of the estuary. Eventually they reached the village and, as usual, a crowd soon gathered. A rope was thrown to them and they tied up against a wooden jetty. Rhys could see why it was called Lake Village – the river here broadened to form a beautiful natural lake bounded by woods and hillsides.

"You'd better do the talking, Rhys," said Bran as an older sailor came to the fore and introduced himself.

"I'm Colman. Tell me how is that old seadog, Ryan of Ynys Ygraine?"

"Ryan and his wife are both in good health," replied Rhys, surprised at Colman's knowledge of their visit. He thought it better not to ask. "My friend Alan and myself enjoyed two good days with him and learnt so much. He told us a lot about you as well. Anyway, let me introduce the others."

Colman shook hands with the visitors.

"We heard that a galley was lost to the Saxons, but we haven't seen them off this coast at all. They're wary of our big ocean swell I dare say."

Rhys had to explain the whole story of the Ynys Ygraine disaster and related King Myric's desire to know if a large skin boat could offer any advantages against the fast longships.

"Come with me and I'll show you what we've got." Colman led them to a small sheltered beach. Rhys and his friends all took a sharp breath as they saw two magnificent curved skin boats lying on the soft sand with their masts and rigging pointing majestically to the sky. The stays fitted to the top of the mast were humming in the breeze.

"They're at least six paces long," said Rhys excitedly. He ran his hand over the smooth skin hull, which curved over the top-side with stout leather stitching. He could see that, as with Ryan's currach, the framework of the hull was criss-crossed with curved ash and there was room enough for four oarsmen and stores. Polished oak seating was fixed to two main runners that ran the whole length of the boat. It looked strong and yet very light.

"I see that the mast can be dismantled," observed Rhys, examining the various stays that were fixed to the masthead. The bow and stern of the boat had lighter leather stretched over a central spar that ran from stem to stern at head height above the rowers. This gave plenty of shelter at both ends of the craft for the crew and Colman explained how necessary this was in a stormy sea.

"I've many times had to throw out a long rope as a sea anchor in rough seas and sit out a storm head into the wind. It's a bit frightening, but with plenty of ballast these craft won't capsize." Colman seemed pleased with the visitors' admiration of his boats. "See these large flat stones, we tie them down in the bottom of the boat to hold her down and to walk on. And as you say, Rhys, I can take down the masts in the worst of the winter and turn the boats upside down on the beach. Mind you, we have to grease the hulls and the rigging constantly."

"They must be over two paces wide," said Bran. "They could carry a lot of stores... how many men do you think they would take?"

"As many as you could fit in," laughed Colman. "If the weight is evenly spread, you'd be surprised how much they carry."

Rhys wanted to know every detail. The rigging and sails were made of strong flax and the stitching of the leather hides was made waterproof with wool grease. The tough thongs gave a stiff but flexible hull that would withstand shingle and even rocks.

"I dare say you'll want to go for a trial, my friends. The river is wide and deep here and there's enough wind to try out a few manoeuvres. If we get one of the boats onto the water, I'll show you how to rig up the rudder paddle and the side boards."

The large boat danced on the water despite its weight and once Colman had settled everybody in place they drifted out into the current. The large square sail was hoisted and Colman turned the craft into the breeze to show his crew how well she would point into the wind. Rhys and his comrades hauled in the sail ropes as tight as they dared.

"She skims over the water very well," observed Bran.

"You're right, Bran. Tomorrow we can all go to sea and have some fun, I do believe a gale is blowing up specially for you."

Rhys watched every move that Colman made as they sailed up and down the wide lake. There was no doubt that this skin boat was very manageable and quick to turn – he was already confident that she could outmanoeuvre a longship in open water.

"Take the helm, Rhys," said Colman. "See how it compares with Ryan's currach."

After making a few small mistakes Rhys knew that he could quickly get used to such a craft and longed to sail well out into a wild ocean.

They glided back to the jetty, all very satisfied. Only Bran seemed a little nervous of the morrow.

"Come into my workshop and I'll show you how they are made." Colman led them to a large thatched boathouse, which was big enough to hold a long bench with cradles. Carpentry tools hung on the walls and ropes of different thickness hung everywhere. The smell of wool grease was terrible, but nobody mentioned it.

Rhys and the boys asked so many questions that by supper-time, poor Colman was quite exhausted. They talked long into the night and boasted of attacking Saxon longships at sea; hardly a wise move.

***

Next morning, as predicted, the skies confirmed that there was stormy weather out at sea, so Colman ordered extra ballast and more crew to give the craft stability. Two young fishermen from the village introduced themselves and clambered aboard as Colman made sure that everybody had a heavy leather coat and a woollen cap.

"The tide is running strong, so are we all ready?"

Rhys was certainly ready. But as there was a stiff breeze blowing upriver, Colman decided to row down with the tide, which gave the boys their first experience of using the long oars. The total crew now numbered seven and Rhys noted that there was still enough space for more men or stores. As they reached the mouth of the Harbour, the oars were lashed to the centre spar leaving enough room to duck underneath them when scrambling from one side to the other. The side dagger boards were lowered and lashed down tightly helping to stop the craft from sliding across the wind. The first large waves crashing into the Havren made the craft buck and screw round quite unexpectedly. Colman laughed at the newcomers' alarm as the sail was hoisted.

Rhys and Garwyn looked at each other and chuckled as the sail filled and the craft heeled to one side. Bran tried to keep a straight face. They all automatically scrambled to the weather side and hung on firmly to the rail. The boat skimmed and bucked over the ever increasing waves as they headed out to sea and it soon became clear that the spray would have soaked them if they had not been wearing their sea-coats.

As the shoreline disappeared rapidly, Colman eased off the helm to put the wind abeam.

"You'll see that I will have to spill wind from the sail when she heels over too far," shouted Colman. "But you'll then see how fast she goes." The bow crashed into each wave making the craft shudder each time, but the smooth hull gave them some feeling of confidence as the craft seemed to pivot on the waves. The mast itself bent sideways under the strain.

"Get ready," shouted Colman once more. "We'll go onto the other tack and see how far she can point into the wind."

As the bow swung around and the sail flapped wildly, the crew scrambled to the other side of the boat and hauled in the lines.

Rhys could see that, with the dagger boards holding well as they cut into the water, they were making much better headway than the ordinary sailboats that the colts were used to.

"Throw out the sea anchor," ordered Colman and one of his young crew pulled out a large bundle of cloth and leather tied to a long rope. It was thrown over the bow as Colman headed directly into the wind and this allowed the sail to flap amidships. The rope was fed out as the craft slid backwards with the swell, but the boat stayed head-on into the wind. As they hung on, the colts watched every move closely.

"There," said Colman. "As you can see, if we were caught in a bad storm the sea-anchor would hold us steady and we could ride it out. If things got really bad, by bailing out, these boats would still be able to tackle the worst of storms. Those low-sided Saxon longships would be swamped."

In such heavy seas and with the shoreline now well behind them, Colman decided it was time to return. He asked for the sail to be lowered and reefed, whilst the sea anchor was hauled in. He turned the bow away and after some wild bucking they found themselves athwart of the waves for a while. With that dangerous manoeuvre over and with the wind behind them they surfed over the crest of each wave towards the shore. The boys laughed as they watched their wake foaming behind them.

When they reached the safety of the Harbour, Bran admitted that he had probably been the most nervous – he couldn't bear to think of the danger of capsizing.

Colman laughed at Bran's confession and discomfort.

"We'll call in at the village for a little refreshment. Then you boys can try to take us on upriver against the tide and we will see how you cope."

Rhys noted how shallow the draught of the boat was as they beached her. After drying themselves by a fire under the cliffs well out of the wind, hot broth was served with bread and cheese. The boys all loved the feeling of this rocky coast – the smells, the birds, the wild countryside.

When they eventually arrived back upriver, Colman suggested that the three boys drop the rest of them off at the jetty and then carry on upriver to get even more experience. This was just what the colts had been hoping for and they eventually re-appeared at dusk on the last of the ebbing tide. They agreed that it had been a very exciting day. It was only during the bustle of getting supper ready that Rhys and Alan noticed the absence of Garwyn. After looking vainly for him they finally saw him on the jetty talking with the sister of one of the young fishermen. He obviously wasn't wasting any time.

"Would you believe it, Rhys, we've only been here a day or so and that Garwyn is already looking out for a bride," The boys laughed loudly and shouted out to Garwyn to beware of seductive mermaids. He ignored them.

Next morning the weather was calmer and it was agreed that the four visitors and Colman could go once more out to sea and around Ynys Piro. Colman wanted the more experienced Bran to gain complete knowledge of his boat, so that he would be able to report back to Arthur and give his honest opinion. If there were anything he could do to combat the Saxon menace, then Colman would be proud to help.

"I hope we're not too late for prayers, Rhys," joked Garwyn as they neared the island.

When it was Garwyn's turn to take the helm, they decided to sail around the island close inshore and then tack way out to sea to return to the Harbour with a following wind. As expected, the monks ran to the high ground and waved to them excitedly.

"I wouldn't normally sail this close to a weather shore," said Colman. "But I want you to get used to all possible situations."

The boys were now quite familiar with their new craft and after an exciting outing that lasted till dusk they were glad to be running back up the Harbour. On the return journey Colman had insisted that they take it in turns to rest under cover of the fore and aft covers.

"It's not wise to stay out in a cold wind if you can avoid it. And if it's really cold, you must wear leather gloves."

After supper it was agreed that Bran and Alan would return to Caerllion next day, while Rhys and Garwyn would stay on to make sure they had mastered the handling of a skin boat before delivering it to Arthur.

"Well anyway, I was due to make another boat soon," sighed Colman. "Perhaps I should start on it while you two are still here, then you can say you're experts at building and sailing the fastest boats on the coast."

"We'd be only too glad to help," said Rhys smugly. "I need a break from the monastery at Caerllion and I know that Garwyn will be only too happy to stay away from the Caer Taf taverns!"

Garwyn, they knew, had other reasons for wanting to linger at Lake Village.

***

Autumn seemed to be setting in as Bran and Alan prepared their trail-boat the next morning. It seemed strange to Rhys and Garwyn to watch their friends disappear downriver with just a brief wave. However, it was time to get to work and soon they were off with Colman and the other two sailors to prepare the correct sizes of ash and oak.

Both boys had some experience of making coracles and Colman appreciated their assistance as they prepared the framework of the boat. The smelly ox-hide skins had been steeped in a large vat with oak bark and lime to soften and cure them. Flaxen rope was prepared, with pitch, tannin and grease. Over the next few days and when the weather allowed, Colman encouraged the boys to take one of the village skin boats out to sea to gain more experience. Nobody took much notice when Garwyn walked along the beach with his new girlfriend each evening – she loved to laugh and she was certainly pretty, thought Rhys. His own thoughts, as usual, turned to Penhal and Helena. Home was such a long way away and his family and the warriors there would never believe all his experiences. He knew that, by now, they would have heard of the galley disaster and how he had returned safely, but still Helena was sure to be worried.

"I've been thinking," said Rhys one day. "These boats still slide too much when beating against the wind. When Garwyn and I fix the dagger boards to the side they are often half out of the water. Could a deeper keel not be fitted with even more weight?"

"You would not be able to beach them then, Rhys, and you cannot leave these boats lying on their side. It would distort their shape."

There was silence for a while as Rhys ran his hand over the framework of the new boat that was now upside-down on its cradle.

"What if a centre dagger-board in a slot was fitted, capable of sliding down into the water when you needed to point into the wind, and afterwards it could be pulled up?" Rhys rubbed his chin and mused. "Well perhaps not… "

Colman laughed at Rhys' enthusiasm, "It's a wonderful idea, Rhys, I only wish it were practical. I'm afraid it would weaken the design of the whole hull. Mind you, if you wanted to point close to the wind, I've heard about boats in Erin where the sailors have rigged up a smaller sail on the bow, that seems to work well."

"Just like a foresail on the galleys. That sounds marvellous.

You see, Colman, when we were being chased by that longship, we had the edge on them in the wind because we were narrower and lighter. If any boat is only a little bit better pointing into the wind, it can escape a longship easily."

"Well, I suppose we could rig up a foresail on the boat you're practising in. If we set to work straight away, you can try it out tomorrow." A suitable oak spar was fashioned so that it could be fixed to the bottom of the mast, then lie across the forward housing and finally out past the bow. An extra stay was then taken from the tip of the spar to the top of the mast.

"I'll need to cut and sew another sail that can slide up the new stay," said Colman, now enthusiastic himself. "I know it will work."

Supper that evening was later than usual as the boatmakers slumped down after their hard labours. However, morning could not be too soon for Rhys and Garwyn.

***

After a hurried breakfast, they found there was enough breeze to launch their craft and set up the new sail for its first test on the river. Colman and both young fishermen wanted to join in, and they all rowed smartly downriver with the tide. It was surprisingly quick to rig up the new foresail and turn it expectantly into a stiff breeze.

"It's working well," shouted Colman. His experience told him that his boat was behaving just as he had hoped – it was sailing even closer into the wind than before.

After sailing back to the village for some refreshment, the two fishermen took the boys exploring. They climbed up to a promontory overlooking the glorious coastline and gazed in awe way out across the western ocean.

"It's getting colder by the day," said Rhys shivering. "I doubt if even the Saxons would want to be out at sea during the winter months."

"You should see the waves during a winter storm," offered one of the young fishermen. "Not even a Saxon longship would survive out there."

When the boys raced back to the village, they noticed that Colman was smiling, but seemed distracted. He bade farewell to his friends and they set off once more upriver on a fast-moving tide.

"I started thinking about your idea of a keel, Rhys," said Colman finally, "and I've been talking it over with my old friend. He thinks it would work well, but only if we could stitch leather up into a long socket that would be waterproof. Then a heavy iron keel could be slotted down through it when you're away from shallow water."

The four boys listened intently and Rhys clapped his hands.

"Well, can we fit a keel into the new boat you're building? How long do you think it would take?"

"You'll have to wait, I'm afraid," laughed Colman. "It will take weeks and weeks to finish the boat and I would have to arrange for the King's smith to make a keel, if he agrees, that is. Anyway, you're due to go back to Caer Taf tomorrow. Perhaps I can send word to you if it all goes well."

Having to return was a bit disappointing, but they would have their skin boat to show the King and Arthur; and they hoped to be allowed to return when the new boat was ready.

They continued their conversation over supper and next morning got ready to leave. Once more it was a sad farewell as the whole village came to the jetty to see them off. The women handed them some food and milk for the journey and Garwyn, who seemed to have become besotted with his new girlfriend, looked especially sad.

"Never mind. We'll soon be back here, Garwyn, you'll see," said Rhys.

The breeze was favourable so they thought they would make for Ynys Piro as their first landmark.

By noon, they passed close to the island and signalled to the waving monks. They were expecting to reach the mouth of the river Taf before dark and settled down to enjoy the views of the coastline and indulge in a leisurely meal.

"I've been thinking, Garwyn…"

"Not again!" groaned Garwyn. "What is it this time?"

"Well, if we had six of these skinboats, and, say about fifty warriors, do you think we could take on a longship? Imagine it, if we attacked them with heavy spears and arrows from several directions. We'd be too quick for them if they tried to board us."

Garwyn thought carefully, and said "You might be right, Rhys, we'd be in terrible trouble in our old sailboats, but in the open sea, I'd be more confident in these new leather boats. Anyway, the Saxon longships always sail in threes, so I don't think we'd ever get the chance."

"Unless we attacked them on their own coast."

"Attack them! You must be dreaming. I think the salt water is affecting you."

The mouth of the Taf came into view and they waved at the surprised lookouts who had never seen such a strange craft. After sailing upriver with the last of the tide everybody on land wanted to examine this strange skin boat with its forward spar and bow sail. The boys had to answer many questions.

As the King was not back from the north yet, it was decided that Rhys would stay the night and seek orders in the morning. A messenger on horseback was sent to Caerllion to report to Arthur while the boys were ordered to visit the King's galley captain. He offered them supper and listened intently as Rhys and Garwyn told him all about their trip to the Harbour.

"I'll come out with you in the morning to see for myself, and bring some of my senior crew. The other colts can sail in their own craft, so we can make comparisons. The King will surely want my opinion." It seemed as if the captain was hoping things would all go wrong for Rhys and Garwyn, but they grinned at each other confidently.

***

The atmosphere next morning was almost like a tournament and word got around that there was going to be a race. A crowd made their way down to the river mouth, while many others on horseback made for the high cliff across the bay.

From there they would be able to see the whole channel. The galley captain had three companions, which filled the skin boat without overcrowding it.

It was almost high tide when the fleet rowed downstream to the open sea and set their sails. On the skin boat, the Captain's men helped to fit the side dagger boards, while Garwyn set up the foresail. From the start, it was obvious that Rhys and Garwyn had the faster boat and it was decided to make straight for the far shore with the wind on their beam. The middle of the channel was choppy and the crew clung to the weather rail, looking tense.

"If we drop back a bit and let the others catch up, we'll show you how she heads into the wind," said Rhys. "Garwyn had better take the helm now, he's got a fine touch."

The galley captain kept glancing to the rear as the other boats struggled to keep into the wind. When they were near the islands, Garwyn made for a small beach on Ynys Echni where he hoped to beach the boat and show how quickly they could get back to sea again. As the island's goats ran to greet them, the captain and his men stepped out onto dry shingle without getting their feet wet.

"Hmm, I have to admit, she handles well, but I can't say I'd want to be in a storm with this flat bottom." The captain examined the hull and took a good look at the bowsail.

Rhys was quick to respond.

"We're hoping to make a new craft with a heavy iron keel, sire, one that can be drawn up in shallow water. And the other day, this one handled perfectly with a sea anchor in rough seas."

The captain looked skywards as Rhys tried to explain the construction of the keel. His crew did not look too impressed either.

"How would you like to take the helm, sire?" offered Garwyn. "The others are nearly here now."

Rhys and Garwyn rubbed their hands in triumph as the Caer Taf colts struggled ashore and looked on with envy. They all wanted a chance to sail this new craft.

The captain expertly put the skin boat through every possible manoeuvre on their voyage around the islands and the boys knew instinctively that he was becoming more and more impressed. By the time they set sail for Caer Taf, the captain and his comrades were obviously enjoying this new fast boat. They constantly looked back at their wake and the other boats. On arriving at the mouth of the Taf river, a lookout beckoned them.

"The messenger from Caerllion says Rhys and Garwyn are to report there to Arthur with the new boat, and the King will be at Caerllion later today."

"Well, off you go then, boys. You can run up on the tide. I'll join the other colts when they get back."

"Yes, sire. And what do you think of our boat?"

"Could be useful, I suppose... apart from the dreadful smell of that wool-grease."

CHAPTER 20

A Daring Plan

It was only to be expected that the Caerllion colts and officers would be curious about the new boat sailing up their river. There were cheers when Rhys and Garwyn tied up at the jetty and, of course, everybody wanted to inspect the new boat.

Tarou pushed through the crowd.

"There's no time to waste, come with me up to Arthur's villa. I have some horses ready."

The three riders galloped up the hill and handed their horses to a waiting stable boy.

"Arthur's in a foul mood," said Tarou nervously as they entered the villa. "There's been another attack on the south coast. It appears that those devil Saxons made a night raid near South Isca, killed many villagers, and took captives and grain."

Rhys shuddered to think about a sudden enemy raid in the middle of the night.

Tarou pointed down the table. "See that officer with Arthur? That's Erc, King Geraint's sea captain. He's just ridden up from the south coast with a change of horses."

With his senior officers around him, Arthur was studying a map and occasionally thumping the table.

"So Geraint wants us to send another army down to his fort at Caer Lind to join him and march on Caer Sallog next spring. Well, I think it's a trap. The Saxons have lost much of their western army, but if they spend the winter building up reinforcements with the Angli and others, we could find ourselves overstretched in a country that suits them more than us. We need more information about their plans."

"A young slave escaped from the old village of Saint Brigits a few weeks ago, sire, and somehow got back to our stronghold at South Isca," explained Erc. "He said there were two Saxon keels on Saint Brigits' river, and he's sure they would have been the attackers." Tarou whispered to the boys that St. Brigit's was due east of South Isca.

Rhys took an immediate liking to Erc. He stood bold and upright, with quick movements and alert eyes. Rhys whispered to Garwyn.

"He must have had lots of experience of the sea."

Another officer stepped forward.

"They know they can't march on a strong position inland, sire. My guess is that they're testing us further and further along our south coast while at their eastern base of Caer Durno they're building up new defences. If they manage to keep us away from the coast, they could eventually make a surprise attack on South Isca and we would never know when."

"That makes sense," said Arthur. "If they sent an army along the coast at night and combined it with a large fleet of longships landing by river at the same time, can you imagine the confusion in South Isca?"

The officers coughed and shuffled their feet.

"If Isca fell, then Caer Lin would be isolated," continued Arthur. "We must persuade the King to muster a large army and drive south next summer at the latest. That would entail huge numbers of soldiers coming down from the north to join us."

Rhys knew nothing of these places but listened intently trying to imagine the south coast. A messenger entered the room.

"The King is expected for supper, sire, he's on the way from Caer Gwent."

"Good," replied Arthur. "I hope our propositions don't upset his appetite too much." There was an uneasy laugh among the officers. "Carry on with your duties, men. Tarou, let's take a walk in the rose garden."

Rhys and Garwyn were signalled to follow Arthur and Erc into the garden that overlooked the river.

"Bran has told me all about your new skin boat, Garwyn, it is indeed fortuitous that Erc here arrived today. You see, we need better ships to combat the Saxons at sea. I don't mean that we should fight them at sea, but we must have a better warning system, and these skin boats may be of help." Everybody agreed. "Erc knows the south coast well, and tomorrow he can inspect your boat and advise us of a long-term plan. Did our galley captain examine the boat, Garwyn?"

"Yes, sire, I think he was quite well impressed." Erc grew even more interested when Garwyn described the skin boat and the race across the estuary.

"Rhys and I helped with the boat building at the Harbour and Colman is going to fit a new type of keel to his next boat."

Arthur motioned for Rhys to continue the story of the new keel and the new foresail. Rhys was now so used to relating stories and making reports that he made everything sound important. His audience listened with interest. Erc was studying Rhys closely as he spoke.

"Well, there you have it, Erc. You can work out a plan tomorrow and then report back to Geraint." With that Arthur turned to leave. "I'll see you all at supper tonight, the King may want to ask some questions."

Tarou decided that they should return to the river and speak with Bran and the garrison officers. Rhys was dispatched to the bishop's house to talk to Cadoc and explain that his absence was due to the wish of the King.

"I believe that Abbot Aidan is getting resigned to your comings and goings," said Cadoc with a shrug. "He will certainly be glad to hear of your visit to Ynys Piro, so perhaps your travels will have some merit in his eyes."

Rhys did his best to avoid smiling at Cadoc's pompous demeanour.

"I suspect Arthur will want me to return to the monastery after the King leaves for Caer Taf. By the way, I hear that Bishop Dyfrig is now starting a small college at Llan Taf. Will you be visiting him before the winter? I'm sure he'd be glad to see you."

Cadoc's spirits lifted as he thought of a brief escape from Caerllion.

"Hmm, yes. Perhaps I'll take Fracan with me. One of the

junior priests can look after Caerllion for a while." Rhys felt he had been quite clever to have mentioned such a visit, he knew how necessary it was to keep in favour with Cadoc now that Dyfrig was getting older.

***

Rhys had time to spend the rest of the day with his friends. The new skin boat was incorporated into the Caerllion fleet and everybody wanted to sail her out in the estuary. Tarou suspected that Garwyn would be needed back at Caer Taf, so he suggested that the next morning the whole fleet should go on a training exercise and drop Garwyn off at his home port.

The King's arrival at his Saint Albans villa meant the presence of all senior officers would be required so that the King would be able discuss his visit north and outline his orders for the winter. When Tarou led Rhys and Garwyn into the main banqueting hall, the boys could see why it was sometimes referred to as the King's palace. The old Roman wall paintings and ornaments were lit up by a host of large oil lamps which gave an air of overwhelming splendour.

Arthur explained, once again, the possible dangers on the south coast and the need to strike at the enemy next summer. The officers, who had been drinking wine, heartily agreed and cursed the Saxon invaders. The King smiled knowingly – he had recently discussed the various options with his commanders in the north and asked Erc to relate the recent events on the south coast.

"As you all say," the King declared. "We need more information on any movements they make. We were lucky at the battle of Maendibyn, but next time we may not be so prepared. Now, my old friend Brochvael's grandson, Rhys, isn't it? I've heard reports of your new leather boats, and you say they can outrun a longship?"

Tarou nudged Rhys to get to his feet.

"Yes, sire, Garwyn and I have been testing the new boat with your galley captain, and there is an even better boat being built by Colman down at the Harbour. I think that if we had a fleet of six we could sail into Saint Brigits' river at night and sink the longships there. We would be back out to sea in no time."

The hall erupted into raucous laughter, but Rhys stuck his chest out defiantly. Even Tarou looked a little embarrassed, but Garwyn knew it could be done. He and his troop had tasted battle at Brenin Point and they regarded beating back the Saxons as their destiny.

The King was the only person not to laugh – he rubbed his chin and looked intently at Rhys.

"How many warriors could we get into Saint Brigits?" asked the King. "I know the harbour and the beach well and I'm told that these Saxon enclaves have about fifty warriors and their families."

"We could land about sixty, sire," stammered Rhys, a little flustered at such a quick response. "We would need bigger boats to be made, at least six, and with three oars either side and two sails."

The assembly looked in disbelief from Rhys back to the King. The soft light from the candles masked his hardened eyes and gritted teeth.

"Erc, when you've discussed matters with my galley-captain tomorrow, proceed immediately back to King Geraint at South Isca and discuss this possibility with him. Tell Geraint that I'll see him in Caer Taf when he's ready to make plans. We have much to discuss with him and all of the commanders. And bring that young escaped captive with you."

The assembly murmured amongst themselves at such a daring plan. It seemed that talk of war was now over for the evening as the King boasted of his latest hunting expeditions.

Tarou turned to the boys.

"Are you mad, Rhys? Sailing into a Saxon stronghold would be suicide."

"Not if we landed unsuspectingly before dawn," explained Garwyn, anticipating Rhys' answer. "Let's face it, they surprise our villages even when they're a long way upstream, so with Saint Brigits right on the coast they would never expect to see us come in on the tide during darkness. We could smash up their ships and attack their houses before they could pick up any weapons."

"And we'd be a long way out to sea before the alarm was raised," added Rhys waving his arms grandly. "We could rescue any of our own captives there, then set fire to the Saxon houses. They deserve worse."

Tarou shook his head slowly. He felt that such a daring raid might work, but he hated the thought of losing any of his men

– and if things went wrong, the whole attack could turn into a disaster.

"We'll have to wait and see what King Geraint says, it may be possible to work out something together with a land attack. I have to admit, King Myric seemed to like the idea."

***

As planned, the Caerllion fleet was to sail on the morning tide down to Caer Taf so that Erc could talk to the King's galley captain. Rhys and Garwyn, with a full crew including Lewys, would show Erc how well the skin boat sailed and allow him to become familiar with her handling. When the fleet hoisted their sails on reaching the breezy estuary, there were whoops of excitement as the skin boat sped away from the rest. On the calm high tide the new boat just skimmed over the surface.

Erc took control of the helm and was reluctant to give it up until they reached the lookout post at the mouth of the Taf river. He strode off to meet the King's captain and by the time the other boats rowed up to the jetty, he had returned. Rhys knew instinctively that Erc was deeply impressed with the new leather-clad boat.

"I need to get over to Brenin Point straight away, boys. No doubt I'll be back with Geraint in a few days. The King's galley captain nearly fainted when I told him of the possible raid on Saint Brigits. Now, I suggest that all the boats cross together, then you can go straight back upstream on the next tide."

This seemed like a good idea, and as Garwyn waved

goodbye from the jetty, Lewys, firmly in charge, sailed the fleet swiftly across the water and onto the beach at Brenin Point. In no time, Erc was mounted and on his way south to report to his King. The newer colts were glad of the chance to join their troop on this important crossing and welcomed the attention of the fishermen.

Lewys decided to show the new colts the Brenin battleground and soon the whole troop were racing and scrambling up the hill. This was a good chance to pay their respects to their dead comrades and true to his word, Arthur had already erected a stone monument near the spot where his soldiers had died.

After some fun and wrestling, the boys got into their boats for the return and Lewys allowed the crews to alternate with the new boat. The King was due to stay for a few days at Caerllion with his senior officers to formulate a plan for the next spring and Lewys, commanding the colts, was determined to show the King how efficient his young troop was in their training and discipline.

It would be some time before Colman had the new boat ready for trials and it would be up to Garwyn and his troop to visit The Havren when summoned. Rhys was confined, once more, to the monastery where time passed much too slowly through the autumn months.

***

It was usual for the pupils to be allowed to take a three week break over the Christmas celebration and so, once more, Rhys' thoughts turned to home and Helena. He was indeed lucky to have such a long break at Penhal and constantly dreamed of having Helena in his arms.

The first frosts had arrived and the evenings became darker. Rhys decided to work hard at his studies, at the back of his mind was the hope that next year he would be able to leave the monastery and join the army. If the King and his advisers decided to mount a summer attack down the south coast, he wanted to be ready, and if there was going to be a sea raid on Saint Brigits, then there would have to be special training with the new boats.

One Saturday morning in late November, Rhys, as usual, rode down to the barracks to join in the training and mock battles. It was now usual for the various troops to hike all day and sometimes at night with heavy packs. Tents and poles were transported by packhorse in order that quick encampments could be prepared and dismantled, even in the dark. It was all hard work, but good food and good humour ensured their loyalty and respect for their leader, Prince Arthur.

Tarou and Lewys had finished breakfast and were waiting for riders to arrive from Caer Taf. A trumpet signal had been sounded from the old hillfort a short while earlier. This was the result of Arthur's orders to set up a better signal system in his district. All eyes turned towards the hilltop as riders galloped down to the Caerllion fields.

"It's Cynan," shouted Lewys. "I'd know his riding style anywhere."

As Cynan and his officers pulled up their horses next to the amphitheatre, Arthur and his men strode from the barracks.

"We're on our way north," announced Cynan, jumping down from his horse to shake hands with his prince. "Geraint and King Myric have plans for a big attack next summer. The details are secret, but every district is expected to prepare half of their army before Beltane. This will mean amassing stores for two weeks and ensuring that every horse is made available."

Rhys sensed that Arthur was offended that these plans had already been made without consulting him – especially as such a push south had been his idea in the first place. Cynan had, no doubt, anticipated such a reaction from his old friend.

"The King has placed you in complete control, Arthur, everything will hinge on Caerllion and the starting point at Maendibyn. My job is to inform all the commanders to the north to expect your orders next spring."

Arthur realised that Cynan had been teasing him and grunted.

"I'd better put you in charge of the baggage in the rear, Cynan, or perhaps you'd rather go by boat!"

As the assembled officers roared with laughter at their two leaders sparring, Cynan motioned for Tarou, Rhys and Lewys to join him and Arthur.

"Well, now that you mention boats, my prince, there is more news. Garwyn has been testing the new skin boat at the Harbour and it seems that the King and his galley captain have agreed on making a surprise attack on Old Saint Brigits. This will be a few days before the main attack from the north and, we hope, it will draw the Saxons down to the coast. Six new leather boats will be built by Easter and Erc will be put in command as he knows the south coast well. Garwyn and Lewys will pick two helmsmen for each boat from their troops and the soldiers will be handpicked by Erc. After training they will start off from Ynys Ygraine without landfall to avoid any enemy spies."

"You make it all sound so simple, Cynan," retorted Arthur. "But where will you be whilst all this is going on?"

"The King has assigned me and my cohort to be your personal bodyguard, Arthur. It seems that your father values your life after all! Anyway, I have no time to chat. I'm on the King's business." With that Cynan mockingly rallied his troop and they quickly mounted to continue their journey.

Tarou whispered to the boys, "Not a word to anybody." The boys looked at each other with some concern – it looked as if the raid may well be on.

During the day's training, Lewys and Rhys quietly discussed their plans for the coming spring – it seemed such a long way off, but they both knew that their futures in the King's army depended on a successful raid. They must practice for every possible eventuality to make sure there was no chance of overlooking any details and making obvious mistakes.

***

By the following week, the weather had improved and the colts with all their boats set out for Caer Taf to meet Garwyn and his troop. The new boat with the flexible iron keel was just as good as Rhys had imagined and the new design caused great excitement among Lewys' troop as they joined Garwyn to test the boat out in the estuary.

Arthur gathered the officers and colts on the jetty.

"Colman has agreed that the boats should be built here in Caer Taf. We are better placed to supply the ox leather and timber. Colman and his men will arrive here soon and there are other skilled boat builders coming from the west coast. Our smiths can cast the new iron keels, so we'll need masses of charcoal."

It was going to be a huge job building the boats over the winter and the decisive way that Arthur spoke made Rhys feel a little nervous. It seemed that the sea-raid was now definite and Rhys began to wonder if his idea was a good one after all.

"Beach training with Erc will start in the early spring," continued Arthur. "Lewys and Garwyn will have until then to train their helmsmen and look for any weaknesses in the craft."

There was subdued excitement on the way back to Caerllion. The prospect of charging the Saxons and fighting with swords sounded dangerous. There would be twelve colts to steer the six new boats and, no doubt, Erc would pick the best fighters to embark as soldiers – even so, the colts would be called upon to fight as well.

***

Back at the monastery, there was much talk of the Christmas festival, and this helped Rhys to ease his thoughts of the coming spring. Young Sceaf, as usual, wanted to stay near Rhys and speak his own Saxon language.

"I've been thinking," said Rhys haltingly, searching for the right words. "Conmael and his friend will be riding back to Abermenei with me for Christmas. What if you came with us, Sceaf? I could ask your mother tomorrow after church. You see, my young cousin is half-Saxon and I'm sure his mother, Helga, would be glad to meet you."

Sceaf whooped with delight – Rhys was his hero and he wanted to see new places, especially if it meant riding a pony. After the Sunday service in the basilica, Rhys was able to confirm the Christmas arrangement with Sceaf's mother. There was a happy mood in the town; for there would surely be no battles over the winter months and the harvests had been good.

***

On the Saturday before Christmas, Rhys was able to wish his army colleagues a happy festival and on the following Monday morning the three boys, with young Sceaf on a pony, set off for home. By late afternoon, the children of Abermenei, who had long been looking out for their returning heroes, rushed across the frosty fields towards them.

With the smaller children packed onto the horses, the whole contingent charged past the gathering townsfolk to

Pedur's house. Pedur and his wife, as usual, made Rhys feel very welcome and, when Sceaf was introduced to them, they could hardly conceal their astonishment.

"First, you must eat and drink, boys." Pedur's wife had taken charge of a slightly bewildered Sceaf, who helped her to bring in meat, cakes and milk from the kitchen.

The three boys now realised how hungry they were and noisily tucked in.

Tidioc, who had rushed downriver, entered and clasped Rhys' hands, at the same time reciting a prayer. When the Abermenei warriors came in to greet Rhys it was time to tell them of his travels in full. There was no doubt that his standing in the community had now been elevated to that of warrior. Although he would not yet become seventeen until late winter, he was strong and confident and enjoying his new status.

The assembled company listened attentively as he spoke and as the warriors left, Pedur called Rhys and Tidioc to one side.

"We have some bad news, Rhys. That menace Durwas has been seen of late skulking around," whispered Pedur gravely.

"But he's been missing for a couple of years," said Rhys, stroking his chin. "We all thought he was dead. When Ruthall and the warriors expelled him, he just disappeared. He was a horrible thief and a danger to the children of Penhal. I suppose he must be about twenty now."

"Well, I definitely saw him just a few weeks ago," said Tidioc. "I was walking beside the river one evening and he was netting on the river bank. He saw me and dashed into the woods."

Pedur groaned.

"Some outlying farms have had goods stolen; not too much, but enough to worry them. The warriors have all been told to capture him on sight."

"Ah, well, he knows better than to come near any of our settlements," sighed Rhys. "Anyway, we must be off. Thank you for your hospitality, Pedur."

Rhys wanted to ride upriver before dark and Tidioc offered to join them and visit his friend Ruthall. The north wind was now blowing cold and an overnight frost beckoned, so Tidioc was able to borrow a horse for the journey. When they arrived at the main gateway of Penhal, Brochvael was just leaving the hall. He was very surprised at the unlikely trio.

"This is Sceaf, grandfather," smiled Rhys wickedly. "He's a Saxon boy."

Brochvael choked on his greetings – the very word Saxon made his face go red.

"I dare say you have a good reason for filling my hall with Saxons."

The older people came from their houses to welcome Rhys and the estate warriors put down their drinking vessels to shake him warmly by the hand. The hall was well lit as Sceaf nervously followed Rhys inside. Rhys' mother and sister Olwen hugged him affectionately with tears in their eyes. After a while this became a little annoying for Rhys the warrior as he gently extricated himself. They had all heard of the sinking of the galley and Rhys' lucky escape; it seemed as if everyone wanted to touch him.

"Helga, it's nice to see you again," said Rhys as his uncle's widow came from her room with her young son. "And Cadaer, look how you've grown. I have a surprise for you both. This is my friend Sceaf, he's nine and goes to the monastery school." Brochvael growled a little as greetings were exchanged in the Saxon language. Rhys turned to Arteg the war-leader. "Don't worry, Arteg, Sceaf doesn't want to be a Saxon warlord when he grows up, just a monk!"

The warriors laughed uneasily – this unusual mixture was very confusing.

Just then Ruthall entered, puffing and panting.

"Welcome home, Rhys! I saw your horses from the moor when I was putting the cattle away. Welcome Tidioc, I'm so glad to see you. My goodness, Rhys, you've grown even taller."

The warriors returned to their drinking whilst Rhys made further introductions, then Brochvael called Rhys to the fire to hear about his latest escapades. He explained that Cynan had passed through a few weeks earlier to outline the battle plans for next spring and Rhys was careful not to mention the proposed sea-raid.

Brochvael sighed. "This is just as things were forty years ago when the King and I were young men. The Saxons would accept a treaty and promised they would stay behind the borders agreed on, but we should have settled for an all-out war then and finished them off. They'll never rest until they take over the whole country."

"Don't worry grandfather, we'll stop them," said Rhys defiantly.

The warriors cheered, but Arteg was surprised at Rhys' outburst – he could see the same spark in his eyes that he had known so well in his dead leader, Catvael. Rhys had learned so much in such a short time and Arteg knew full well from his last meeting with Cynan that Rhys was destined to become a valued officer in Prince Arthur's army.

The end of that evening's celebration found everybody sprawled out on all the available beds or sleeping on the floor on cow-hides until the dawn smell of hot broth gradually woke them. Rhys needed the bathhouse and a good wash to wake himself up. His mother had clean clothes ready for him, for she knew that he would soon be setting out for Blaeno. She heard him whistle for Beech.

Looking back at Penhal, Rhys smiled at the trail Beech had left in the frosty grass. Arteg would notice this lone imprint across the field and know exactly where it led. Rhys was glad that Arteg had, himself, found love with Helga. As he cantered along the riverside, Rhys thought of Lewys and his wife Ria – both only seventeen – and then of Garwyn and his girlfriend at Lake Village. There were times when a man must expel all thoughts of war and killing. Whatever the outcome of the war with the Saxons, life must go on; like the four seasons; or like night and day. New babies were being born every day somewhere.

Halfway to Blaeno, Rhys pulled Beech up on a rise to admire the wintry riverside. He was unaware of a rider in the distance until Beech whinnied, but why was the horseman riding so fast? As he trotted down the slope towards him, Rhys could see that the rider was one of the labourers from Blaeno; and he was in a panic.

"Rhys! Thank God you're here. Helena's been captured. It

was that young shaman, Durwas from the mountains. She was out with the children in the orchard when he grabbed her and took her on his horse."

"Grabbed Helena – that's impossible – this can't be true," shouted Rhys, aghast. He stared into the face of the frightened labourer.

"Marc's chased after them. He's taken his bow, but Durwas must be well ahead of him…"

"Get to Penhal and tell Arteg," ordered Rhys as he dug his heels into Beech and galloped down the trackway. Durwas couldn't be that far ahead and would be surely making for the hills. He prayed that Helena wasn't hurt – how could even evil Durwas do such a thing? As he sped toward Blaeno, he recalled how Durwas had been a student of Brochvael's shaman some years earlier, but after his master's death alongside Catvael, he had disappeared to the mountains and joined a group of renegades. He had been spotted occasionally over the years and must have been watching Blaeno secretly. Rhys shuddered to think that he and Helena might have been spied upon by this wicked intruder. If only he had got back a day earlier.

Galloping into the settlement, Rhys found Helena's mother and the children huddled in the hall doorway. They jumped up and down at Rhys' arrival and pointed across the fields where Helena's father, Marc, had sped off a little while earlier.

"Don't worry, we'll get her back," growled Rhys grabbing a spear from one of the boys who had stepped forward. Beech snorted, as his master, once more, kicked him forward. Galloping along the riverside trackway, Rhys knew that he would come to the northern forest and then the foothills leading up to a bluff. He prayed there would be enough tracks for him to follow – if Durwas managed to get onto the bluff, the rocky terrain would leave no marks and they could then take any route north.

Slowing up at the forest, Rhys could make out the churned-up tracks left by two horses – Durwas' horse with Helena, and Marc's tracks in pursuit. If Durwas had a sturdy horse, it would take Marc all morning to catch up – and then what? Could Marc take on a vicious Durwas in combat? Rhys dare not think of such a tragedy – all he knew was that Beech would gradually overhaul them both given sufficient time, but he must be able to follow their tracks.

Emerging from the forest onto the foothills, Rhys guessed that Arteg, following on later, would be able to see their route, but as the ground hardened and left few marks, he realised that he must leave a trail. Snapping off branches from trees as he rode uphill, he threw them on the ground for Arteg to see. There was one more valley to cross and Rhys slowed Beech as much as he dared to avoid any falls.

Rhys knew that he must now be gaining on his quarry and coming to a gap in the trees he was glad to see the tracks of two horses in a wet patch of ground. He was surely getting closer. Durwas would have no idea that Rhys was on his trail, but he would be certain that Marc was close behind. What if Durwas laid an ambush for him with his bow? Just then Rhys came to a hillside spring and found fresh footprints. This meant that Durwas had stopped for water. He gasped when he noticed Helena's kerchief wedged in a bush – she must have known how necessary it was to leave a sign. This meant that she wasn't hurt, but there was no doubt that her hands were tied and would be fearful of trying to escape if Durwas had threatened her with a dagger.

Brought down to a trot by the now rocky surface, Rhys was aware of a movement higher up the hill to his left. A rider was picking his way through the boulders and it soon became apparent that it was Marc. But why had there been two sets of hoofmarks at the spring? This could only mean that Durwas had a companion – Rhys cursed at not having considered that possibility. He screeched a buzzard-call to attract Marc and hoped that Durwas would not hear and realise that he was being closely followed.

Just as Rhys signalled to Marc to work his way downhill to meet him, he heard the faint sound of a falling stone in the distance. Walking Beech as quietly as possible, a thicket came into view – they were surely hiding there and watching. Mad at the thought of Helena being a prisoner or worse, Rhys tied up Beech and crept forward with just his spear – he didn't even have his dagger.

With enough scrub and dead bracken to hide his approach, he crawled silently towards the thicket wondering if Marc was aware of the danger. A muffled cry came from the thicket – it was surely Helena struggling. Rhys rose and charged, ready to kill. He was hardly aware of an arrow piercing his side as he tumbled to the ground in pain. He couldn't believe he had been hit, but staggering forward he then found himself crashing through the bushes into a leather-clad figure. In an instant his adversary, sprawled on the ground and as shocked as Rhys, became the target for a quick thrust with Rhys' spear. There was a blur as Rhys found himself kicked in the leg from behind and falling backwards he finished up staring into the eyes of Durwas who had his arm around Helena's neck. In an instant Durwas leapt forward at Rhys with his dagger drawn. Helena, incensed and screaming, tripped Durwas up allowing Rhys to roll to one side. Then just as Durwas was about to spring for the kill, an arrow thudded into his back. He toppled forward, arms raised in pain.

As Rhys slumped to his knees clutching the broken arrow in his side, Marc dashed into the small clearing and gathered up a sobbing Helena. Rhys crawled towards them unable to raise his hands – he could only stare at a bruise on Helena's cheek-bone.

"Am I glad to see you, Marc," croaked Rhys painfully. "I'm only wounded. Helena... my love..."

As Helena helped Rhys to a sitting position, they both stared dispassionately at Durwas lying flat on his face with only his head shaking violently. His companion, still with Rhys' spear hanging from his shoulder, was trying to crawl backwards from an advancing Marc.

"No, Marc, don't kill him," cried Rhys. "Arteg will want to question him. I think you've done for Durwas though, your arrow's gone deep into his spine."

"You're safe," cried Helena cradling Rhys.

"Me! It's you we were worried about. Your father saved my

life." Helena felt so good against his cheek. Rhys could not understand why his eyesight should be so misty. Marc shrugged and glared at the wounded renegade.

"Tie up his feet," suggested Rhys. "I'm sure Arteg will get here soon."

Then the shock of his wound overcame him and he knew no more.

***

It was after noon when they heard the sound of galloping horses and Marc ran towards them waving his arms in reassurance. Rhys, who had only just regained consciousness, tried without success to prop himself up on one elbow. Arteg, panting, strode into the clearing and quickly sized up the situation.

Kneeling to inspect Rhys' wound, he sighed with relief.

"I'll see if I can get the arrow-point out. Luckily your jerkin took most of the force. If we let it bleed a little, I'll bind it tightly with your belt. Ruthall will have some ointment when we get back."

Arteg turned to see the cringing prisoner. Marc had managed to remove the spear from the wounded renegade and used Durwas' clothing to bind up his shoulder.

"Who's this? Wait, I know you. You deserted the army in Caerllion. Arthur will be very pleased to see you."

The prisoner groaned at the thought of his fate. He would have to tell his captors everything about his comrades in the mountains in exchange for a quick death.

CHAPTER 21

Secret Preparations

One of Arteg's men rode off to get news to Blaeno, whilst the slow-moving procession picked its way through the gathering dusk. It would be some time before they all got back, but luckily there would be enough moonlight. Helena rode on Beech behind Rhys and held him tightly as he pressed on his wound to staunch the bleeding. Helena prayed that there would be no infection.

Both Rhys and the prisoner were beginning to be affected by the cold air when Arteg's messenger galloped back towards them.

"Half of Penhal are waiting for you at Blaeno, sire. The two priests are ready to treat the wounded."

It was well into the night when Arteg led the first of the tired horses into Blaeno. He had been questioning the prisoner and led him to the barn to try and recover. Durwas' body, strapped across his horse, was left on view. The priests rushed to Rhys and gently helped him into the warm hall. His wound was cleaned with hot water and treated with ointment before being bound up. He tried not to groan at the piercing pain in his side and gratefully gulped at some wine before Helena fed him stew. The children sat in a corner looking forlorn.

Before curling up near the fire, with Helena kneeling beside him, Rhys whispered to Ruthall and Tidioc, "Tend to the prisoner, he's badly hurt. He needs your help."

Rhys had woken up in pain during the night, but later slept through daybreak while Arteg took everybody back downstream. Ruthall was to stay with Rhys until he could see there was no infection and it would be some days before Rhys could walk any distance.

After a few days, there was no sign of infection. Helena and Rhys were sheltering in the barn as a light dusting of snow covered the fields when Helena took his hand and smiled. "I spoke with your mother and Helga when I was last in Penhal and they said that if it was all right with you I could join you for the winter festival. Well, what do you think?"

"Of course," laughed Rhys. "I was hoping we would be together, but I was too nervous to mention it."

"That's just silly! That wound must have affected your mind!" They laughed together.

After six days, Rhys was just able to hoist himself from a platform onto Beech and ride quietly around the farmyard. He sorely wanted to get back to Penhal for the festival.

Marc's wife fussed when the time came for the young couple to ride slowly downriver.

"You look so grown up setting off together," sobbed Helena's mother. "It seems like only yesterday that you were just children."

"For goodness sake, mother. I'm only going for a few days, and Ruthall will be coming back with me."

Rhys laughed quietly – mothers were always the same; and probably always had been.

***

Rhys had to suffer the close attention of the women of Penhal, but the mood leading up to mid-winter's day and Christmas was a joyful time. The farm labourers were on light duties and well out of the winter weather, whilst the Penhal warriors, apart from hunting, spent the dark evenings around the hall fire, drinking and telling stories.

Brochvael had become surprisingly amenable, keeping the children interested by his description of past battles and the hunting down of far-away giants and dragons. Holding hands, Rhys and Helena laughed and sat close. The pain in Rhys' side was at last abating.

When the ten days of festivity came to a close, Rhys announced his intention to return to Caerllion with young Sceaf. Conmael and his friend, as arranged, had ridden upriver to join the Penhal warriors for some archery practice and on the last night almost all the available drink was finished off.

"We must be off now the weather is fine, Helena." Rhys took her in his arms in the darkness of the hall. "When we meet again in the summer, I'll have some important things to say to you. After I leave the monastery at Easter I will have much work to do with Prince Arthur's army. We're testing the new boats on a long voyage."

Helena was downcast at this inevitable parting and Rhys had to look away to hide his emotion. The sea-raid in the summer, he thought, must be successful at all costs.

***

After a boisterous farewell with Arteg and his men, Rhys' party took most of the day to retrace their steps to Caerllion where Rhys had to relate the story of his arrow wound and near-death several times. The next three months at the monastery dragged by with much of the studying being done by candle-light.

Saturday training, as usual, was a great relief, but nearing Easter the six Caerllion colts, including Rhys, were stationed temporarily at Caer Taf where all the training revolved around a sea-borne raid. Rhys felt that, whatever the outcome of the raid, he would not be returning to the monastery. The young captive who had escaped from Saint Brigits had been helping Erc, the commander, to reconstruct the layout of the village. This was set up near Caer Taf with the beaches, complete with huts, laid out to resemble the Saxon village – when the time came, Erc wanted his men to be in an unassailable position, even if the Saxons had a lookout posted during the night.

Arthur came to observe a practice raid one Saturday and then called all the soldiers around him. Apart from the six pairs of colts who would be handling the boats, Erc had selected sixty of the toughest soldiers from all parts, some of whom Rhys recognised from the battle at Brenin. Erc had brought many of his own men, most of whom had good reason to seek revenge, and Arthur had selected the rest from his own army including several experienced young officers. During these practice attacks, the men had been changed around and become sometimes attackers, and at other times defenders. Erc sometimes had trouble stopping the opposing soldiers from injuring each other when they got carried away. The raw violence sometimes made the colts wince, but wisely, Erc had included a surgeon amongst the band; the one who the boys had previously met at Black Rock.

"As I see it, men," boomed Arthur, "the best time to attack would be before dawn on a high tide and with the moon in the northern sky so you can't be seen offshore. When the raiding party comes in from the sea there must be silence, and let's hope the wind will be a favourable south westerly and the sea not too rough. With four boats on the right hand beach behind the sand dunes, the other two boats will stand off ready for the signal to move upstream towards the longships. There will probably be Saxons sleeping on board. When Erc and his men are in position and he gives the signal, then the charge into the village and the smashing of the longships must begin at exactly the same time. The charge will be in one wave only, but don't worry… the enemy doesn't stand a chance."

A huge cheer went up from the soldiers but the colts glanced at each other and smiled nervously. Rhys was glad that Lewys and Garwyn would be there.

Arthur continued, "If all goes to plan, the colts will spread out with their bows on the right flank and then move behind the village to pick off any Saxons making a run for it. Now remember, don't hurt women and children, they will just want to run inland. You may think I'm being soft, but if we kill women and children, they'll take it out on our own people who are captives elsewhere. Now, you know where the Saxon thane's house is…" Arthur waved to the mock village behind him, "he's the prime target. Once he's killed, the rest will panic. The slaves will probably be locked up in the barn, so get them back to the beach unless they want to join in the fight. Erc will want to speak with any of them who may have important information. The thane's house can be looted and probably every house will have the embers of their cooking fires, so smash in the thatched roofs and set fire to everything. Throw their weapons well out into the river. Any questions?"

A large soldier with a long black beard stepped forward. "After I've killed them all, sire, can I drink their ale?" A mighty roar went up which relieved the tension.

"I won't be able to stop you, you ox… but not all of it, bring some back for me!" Spirits were high in this newly formed troop of sea-raiders.

Arthur then asked Erc to continue with details of the battle plans.

"Any wounded must be helped back to the boats and any dead must be buried at sea." Erc coughed and cleared his throat. "When we get back out to sea, the boats should try to stick together for the journey home which will take two days and two nights at least. We must sail south of the Syllan Isles and keep well out into the big ocean… just in case other longships are near the coast. If the weather is against us and we get split up, we can pull into our own shore and hope to find refuge. But under no circumstances must any of our boats fall into Saxon hands. Remember, we'll be on our own."

A murmur among the soldiers signalled their approval of the plans and Arthur stepped forward again. "The new skin boats will be ready soon. When they have been thoroughly tested, you will all move to the west coast where the seas are rougher. Another mock village will be set up, but most of your time will be spent far out on the ocean testing yourselves and the boats." With that Arthur swung up onto his horse and galloped off.

Satisfied that his small army was now taking shape, Erc decided that the colts could go back to their own barracks for Eastertide and return when the new boats were ready for them. Lewys led his troop back to Caerllion, thankful for a break after so much hard training.

***

It was Easter morning when Rhys called in at the monastery to make arrangements for his final departure and to say his farewells.

"Well, Rhys…" Aidan leaned back in his chair as Rhys entered his office for the last time, "I must admit, you've worked hard and achieved much with your schooling. I've seen you listening intently at lessons and I can only hope that some of it has rubbed off on you. I've never known so much disruption as you have caused here at Saint Aarons, but now that you're going, I dare say we'll find life a little boring."

"I have to say, abbot, you and Fracan and Felix have done so much for me, you'll be with me wherever I go. I know that my friends, Dingad and Govan, will make good priests one day and I will come often to visit them. Sceaf and Patheu will make you proud, I know. They have such good natures and are most willing to please." Rhys could feel a lump gathering in his throat and tried to swallow.

"God be with you, Rhys," said Aidan.

After being hoisted onto Beech by his chattering friends, it was time for Rhys to ride through the gateway for the last time. He had been allowed to grow his hair again and now felt like a true warrior. "You can have my carpenter's tools, Felix," he shouted as Beech trotted down the track-way to the town. "See you in church later."

Rhys then reported to Merryn as he had been ordered to.

"Sceaf is doing well, sire. He will make a good priest in time." Merryn glowered and scoffed as Sceaf's mother thanked Rhys for all he had done. "I don't think he wants to join the King's army, sire."

Merryn growled at the very thought of a Saxon boy joining his army. Rhys' joke had worked. If there was one thing he had learned from his contact with senior officers, it was that it could be useful to add a little humour to a tense situation.

After settling into his new quarters and exchanging insults and greetings with the older soldiers, it was time to join the other colts before preparing for the big Easter service at the basilica. Most of the soldiers and the townsfolk were expected to attend, with the main councillors and officers having bench space within the basilica itself.

"After the service, let's go down to the Saxon village," enthused Lewys as they were strolling to the basilica. "I hear there are some pretty young girls growing up."

The group sniggered, but Rhys felt uneasy. Alan, together with Conmael and his friend had never been to the Saxon village and Rhys did not like the idea of them witnessing some of Lewys' arrogant behaviour.

The colts were shown to their own pew and shortly afterwards Aidan and his monks ushered in their pupils. They all glanced at Rhys and smiled, which seemed to annoy Lewys – perhaps he was put out at Rhys' new billet in the barracks. Arthur and his party were shown to their seats with suitable dignity. Rhys caught Tarou's eye and nodded – he was with his wife and children and looked much too smart to be a soldier. As the church filled up it was time for Cadoc and his priests to make their grand entrance and after some Latin prayers, Cadoc turned to deliver his sermon. As acting bishop he seemed to revel in his new position.

"We understand that the army will be moving off in the near future and I want you to know that the whole of the town will be praying for you. The church is powerless to intervene in such matters and the King has assured me that the victory will be so enormous that the Saxons will never dare attack our shores again." There was a murmur of approval from the congregation. "We can only hope that there will be peace in the future." Cadoc then quoted some episodes from the bible and finished with more Latin prayers.

Lewys heaved a deep sigh of relief when the service ended.

There was much laughter and jovial greeting as the district councillors mingled and jostled for position close to Arthur outside the basilica. Hundreds of soldiers drifted off to the taverns and after Rhys and the boys had paid their respects to Tarou's wife and family, it was time to stroll downriver to the Saxon village.

The lingering smell of the sewage outfall down river from the village was unpleasant as they approached the village green where a table was occupied by the older Saxon men. They stood up quickly as the troop approached.

"Ale," shouted Lewys as he commandeered the now-vacant bench and banged on the table. The village elder glanced anxiously at Rhys, who he knew could speak his language and would hopefully be able to spare the villagers any trouble.

Some women brought jugs of ale to the table and the colts quaffed liberally at this generous gift.

"Everybody out of the huts to be counted," demanded Lewys. "I want to make sure that nobody's escaped." His troop felt obliged to laugh, albeit uneasily.

Rhys translated and assured the elder that they would come to no harm. The children looked frightened as their mothers coaxed them onto the green to confront a glaring Lewys.

"Line up. Line up." Lewys' eyes lit up as two girls about fourteen years of age were led into the line, one girl particularly catching his eye. Rhys felt a little disgusted at

Lewys – he was newly married with a baby due, and was now behaving like a drunken warrior.

Lewys ambled along the line counting and lingered in front of the girl who was clutching her mother's hand. As he reached out to caress her long golden braids, she recoiled into her mother's arms. When Lewys laughed and once more moved forward to reach out, the village elder begged him to stop. Lewys turned and viciously punched him to the ground. The rest of the troop tried to reason with their leader as Rhys and Alan helped the old man to his feet.

"Let's sit down, Lewys, we don't want to get into trouble with Tarou. We're not supposed to take their ale, anyway." Rhys helped the old man to rejoin the women, then whispered to them all to disperse.

Lewys turned on Rhys, and said, "I'm the leader round here, just you remember that!" He then grunted as the women quickly ushered their families into the houses. The elder called for more ale and soon Lewys was joking with his men and taking deep draughts of ale. Rhys said nothing.

"Anyway, it stinks here, let's take a jug or two of ale up to the old fort and look at the scenery. We need to make plans for when we leave." Lewys staggered a little as the troop made off uphill clutching two jugs of ale. Rhys thanked the elder, who was grateful that nobody had been badly hurt.

It was a long climb up to the old fort and they were glad to sit down on the high rampart and admire the view. "I've been thinking, men," said Lewys to the whole contingent. "When we go to Caer Taf, there'll be myself, Hwyn, Rhys, Alan and the two brothers. There'll be nobody left in charge of the other colts except for Tarou. We could be gone for some time, what with training down on the west coast, so I'll ask Bran to carry on training the rest of you in the wooden boats."

Rhys glanced around. There were seven younger boys left including Conmael and his friend. "I dare say Tarou can give you some hard training as well, so you won't really miss us." The young boys laughed and said they preferred to join Lewys. They were quite unaware of the real reason for training at Caer Taf.

"Tomorrow, we'll make a list of all the things we need to take with us. Water bags, dried food, axes, heavy coats and weather caps, hides and gloves." Lewys nodded as his men made other suggestions.

"I've been thinking, Lewys," whispered Rhys. This was a chance to bring up an idea that had been on his mind for some time. "When a Saxon longship is under sail in a fairly calm sea, they can go much faster if they have twenty oarsmen rowing as well. But, if it's too rough, of course, they can't row properly, but then, neither can we."

"We bunch up our boats and take them on all together!" Lewys shook his fist.

"Well, there could be times when we're split up. Anyway, when I was shooting arrows at the longship that chased us, some of my arrows went through their sail and just hung there. It's very difficult to take aim in a rough sea, but if we had heavy arrows with a wedge-shaped cutting edge that ripped their sails open, they'd be left wallowing."

Lewys looked thoughtful.

"What are their sails made of? Ours are of light leather and would take any amount of arrows…"

"I'm pretty sure they're made of flax and wool. Why don't we get the blacksmith at the barracks to make us a few heavy arrows and then we can practice on some of our old flaxen sails."

"I'll ask Tarou, tomorrow, but first we have to share out this ale carefully, one jug for me and one jug for the rest of you."

A wrestling match ensued, which led to much rolling downhill trying not to spill the precious ale.

***

Lewys was now keeping his helmsmen apart from the younger colts and during training the next morning, Tarou listened patiently as Rhys explained his thoughts about the wedge-shaped arrows. Rhys' previous ideas had usually worked and, although this seemed a bit far-fetched, it would be good for morale and help to create some interest while the troop was waiting for orders from Caer Taf.

"Let's go and see the blacksmith, boys, but he'll probably laugh at me."

On the contrary, the old blacksmith welcomed a change from his usual boring work, and in any case, Rhys could see that it made him feel important.

"I'll have some ready for you later today, but you'll need to speak with the fletcher if you want heavier shafts and flights. I presume you'll be taking attack bows."

Rhys smiled at Tarou's resigned expression.

"Back to work, Rhys, you can practice with some old-fashioned arrows for now."

Spear throwing, swordplay and archery were the order of the day. Fast runs up to the old fort before dawn were meant to get the colts used to what was to come. Later in the day they were curious to see what the blacksmith had made and they were joined by the army fletcher who had already heard of their strange request.

"I've honed theses blades and given them a slightly wedged shape… you see?" The boys all leaned forward to inspect the new arrowheads.

The fletcher was obviously interested and carefully felt the sharp edges.

"We'll need some thicker shafts, that's for sure, but you won't have a very long range, even with our stiffest bows."

"They don't need a long range," said Rhys. "If we have to use them at all, it will be at the last minute." Alan shuddered as he recalled the last time they had fired at a longship.

The fletcher seemed keen to help.

"Come and see me later tomorrow."

"Well, Lewys, what do you think?"

"We need to test them, Rhys. Let's go down to see Bran and Canna and get a spare sail. We can set it up tomorrow and get some practice."

Tarou allowed the boys to spend the evening in the tavern. He was getting increasingly worried about his young troop, for they would soon be off to finish their sea training and then embark on a very dangerous mission. If things went wrong, he might never see them again.

The Caerllion army and the surrounding warrior bands would eventually be moving off to get to Maendibyn in time for Beltane, when they were to meet up with the northern army. That would leave Tarou in Caerllion with the older reserve soldiers and it would be a long, painful wait before the King's messenger got back to Caer Taf to report on the battle.

The next evening saw the colts setting up an old flaxen sail on the hillside. It was tightly stretched between two posts and luckily a stiff breeze filled it fully.

"You fire first, Rhys, it was your idea," ordered Lewys. Tarou and Bran had joined the excited troop, together with the blacksmith and the fletcher. They all raised their eyebrows as Rhys paced out an appropriate distance.

There was a hush while Rhys took his stance and drew back his bow. "It's certainly heavy... here goes." With an unusual-sounding whoosh the arrow cut through the sail, leaving a gash in the flax. Then the wind noisily tore the sail from top to bottom along a seam. There was a gasp as the two parts of the sail flapped wildly and the throng stared in disbelief.

"It doesn't look as if we need any more arrows, men" joked Tarou. "Mind you we don't know if it would rip open a Saxon sail. Either way, these blades would cut through and cause a lot of damage." Even Lewys nodded approvingly.

Tarou had received a hint that the call to Caer Taf was imminent, so he agreed that the batch of arrows could later be shown to Erc as he was their commander. The evening became festive after Tarou had praised the troop for their hard work in training.

***

It was luxury for the boys to be able to sleep through the dawn and only woken up for the call to breakfast. As expected, by mid-morning a messenger from Erc had arrived to summon them immediately to Caer Taf, so Tarou arranged for Bran to sail the troop down on the tide. The mood was subdued as the six chosen colts loaded their packs and the Caerllion boats pushed off. The trip down to the River Taf was strangely quiet.

Garwyn and his troop greeted their colleagues and led them to the six new skin boats, which lay in line down the centre of the river, tied to moorings in the swirling tide. Colman and his workmen smiled with satisfaction as the boys marvelled at the sight. Rhys suddenly felt more confident than of late – he had been having doubts when thinking of all the things that could go wrong.

Erc stepped up to give his orders.

"All twelve helmsmen will now get together and check their equipment. Tomorrow we start sea trials out in the estuary, with all the soldiers aboard and under full sail. Landing practice on the beach will be six boats abreast, this is essential. In a few days, we'll all sail down the coast to take on the western ocean. That will be the big test."

CHAPTER 22

The Fleet Sails South

After a boisterous night in the taverns, the twelve young helmsmen and the soldiers were anxious to try out the new boats. Erc joined Garwyn's boat, which led the fleet out into the estuary. A stiff wind was blowing from the east which made the going difficult. The helmsmen gave warning before each tack and the soldiers scrambled to balance their craft as each manoeuvre was carried out. Rhys wondered if the boats could all stay together when in the open ocean with a fierce swell running.

Colman had personally tested each boat as it was completed, but even so, some of the ropes and thongs parted under the constant pressure. There were adjustments and mishaps, but the main benefit for Rhys was that the iron keels made closer sailing into the wind possible. The new craft were certainly robust and remained manoeuvrable even when heavily loaded.

At the end of the second day, the fleet glided up the River Taf to the jetty. Rhys was surprised to see Tarou and Bran waiting for them. Erc jumped from the lead boat and shook hands with Tarou. They walked off to the town engrossed in serious conversation as Bran called the colts together.

"Here are your special arrows, lads, all bundled in waterproof bags to keep them sharp." The Caer Taf helmsmen and the soldiers examined the new wedge-shaped arrows and hoped that they would never be needed.

"Where's Tarou gone, Bran?" asked Lewys, puzzled.

"To see the King," shrugged Bran. "I think I'll go up to the tavern to see some friends." This left the boys perplexed.

It was some time before Erc and Tarou returned from their meeting with the King, and Tarou was all smiles.

"I'm joining you, lads, I couldn't stand the thought of you beginners going off without me, so I persuaded the King to let me go. He wasn't very happy, but…"

The boys cheered, and especially Rhys, when it was apparent that Tarou would be on his and Alan's boat. Erc well knew of Tarou's reputation as a fighter and this was a welcome boost to the expedition.

"Who's going to help me with my pack?" joked Tarou. "I'm not as strong as you lot after all your training."

It was to be their last evening in Caer Taf. Erc had decided that they would sail out at dusk the next day and travel in the darkness down the coast to the Harbour and the new practice area. Their last night in the Caer Taf taverns was hectic, but emotional, as the raiders tried not to think about casualties. Two of the soldiers on Rhys' boat had fought alongside Tarou on Brenin Hill and were glad to know that he would be with them in the main charge against the Saxons.

***

The next morning commenced with the usual mock attacks. Each batch of four men had taken turns in lying down under the covered areas of the boats to acclimatise themselves to sleeping while out at sea. Sacks of straw and hides made up their makeshift beds. If the weather was against them on the raid they could be at sea for four days and nights and enough fresh water had to be stored. If it rained, the spare sail could be spread to catch rainwater.

The fleet was ready before dusk and the signal was given to start rowing out into the estuary. The King's army had already left Caer Taf to join the other cohorts at Black Rock and a group of old soldiers and townsfolk had gathered at the mouth of the river to wave farewell.

The fleet would have to get used to being silent when near the coast – Erc pointed out that sound travelled much further over water. The journey overnight to the Harbour was eerie and much colder than the men expected for the month of April. Everybody was ordered to wear their leather helmets to avoid any cold spray soaking their hair, and occasional fires on the shore under a cloudy sky gave the only clue as to their position off the coast. The soldiers took it in turns to try and sleep under the bow cover and every man had to eat a little bread and cheese during the night.

"Here, Alan, it's your turn on the helm. Don't let the rest of the boats get out of your sight. When they tack, shake the shoulder of the man in front of you. I'm going to talk with Tarou." Rhys knelt behind Tarou, who, like the rest of the soldiers, was hunched against his nearest companion.

"Were your wife and children upset when you said you were going with us, Tarou?"

"Very much so, but my wife knew that I could never live with myself if I stayed in Caerllion and things went wrong at Saint Brigits. Arthur forbade me at first, but then allowed me to ask the King for his permission." Tarou chuckled. "Arthur knew that he wouldn't take the blame if I didn't come back!"

"I know it's going to be all right, Tarou. I heard Erc say that if the weather was too rough for the landing, we would stay out at sea for as long as necessary. Let's face it, even if the Saxons are alerted, they don't stand a chance against this lot."

"You're right, of course, Rhys."

With the first glimmer of dawn, the fleet was in sight of the mouth of the Harbour and Erc signalled the boats to gather as close as they dare. They were to storm the practice beach all in line as soon as the sky was light enough to see the sand dunes. All thoughts of tiredness evaporated as they approached the shore, drawing up the iron keels. The oars were locked into place as the foresails took them slowly onto the beach. A wave of determined raiders moved swiftly but silently up onto the sand dunes to peer inland. With a signal from Erc in the half-light, the raiders spread out and prepared for the charge.

When Erc waved everybody over the grassy dunes, there was an ear-splitting shouting and screaming from the furious soldiers. The colts at the rear moved to the right flank and drew their bows in readiness. Rhys was surprised how quickly the soldiers rampaged through the gorse bushes, chasing along the shore after an imaginary enemy.

"That's enough, men," shouted Erc. "Back to the dunes. Remember, in the real raid at Saint Brigits we assume that the Saxons will be asleep, which will give us huge advantage. If the doors of the houses are barred, then each group with a heavy axe will have to smash through the walls before the enemy can get organised."

After a noisy mock fight Erc gathered the men together once more. Pushing the boats off, oars were put out and rowing through the surf commenced. This was not easy to start with, but after their earlier training, all six boats were soon clear of the surf and rowing in unison out to sea. The eastern sky was now brightening and a steady drizzle suggested a miserable day. Erc summoned the fleet together in the heaving swell.

"Further out to sea, men," Erc shouted his orders once more. The sea soon became too choppy to continue rowing and the sails were set. This was a welcome break for the soldiers but by noon, with the boats crashing up and down into the waves, some of them were feeling very sick. Erc had anticipated this and said that by the time they had finished their training they would have become used to the constant motion.

They were now almost out of sight of land and the order was given to sail back again with the wind behind them. The sick men recovered a little and everybody was glad when the calmer sea closer to shore gave them some respite.

"Right, everybody, lower sails and throw out your sea anchors." Rhys signalled for the bundles of cloth and leather on their long stout ropes to be cast from the bows and suddenly all seemed calm.

"See that your water bags are only half full. Pour some out if necessary." The men murmured, somewhat confused, but Rhys and Alan knew what was coming.

All eyes were on Erc, standing in the lead boat.

"Hang on tightly to your water bags and jump overboard… two at a time."

Tarou grimaced.

"Did you know about this, Rhys? You know I can't swim!"

"I didn't get the chance to mention it, but don't worry, Tarou. When it's your turn, the bag will keep you up, and I'll hold out an oar for you as well." Although, Rhys, as helmsman, was in charge of the boat, he looked away as his superior glared at him. Tarou jumped into the waves and came up spluttering, but then smiled up at Rhys as he was hoisted aboard.

Few of the soldiers could swim, but they knew that they had to experience being afloat in the open sea. Two at a time they jumped and quickly surfaced, gasping from the cold water. Each man was pulled smartly aboard and soon everybody, including the helmsmen had experienced a ducking.

"Well done, men, but you don't expect me to go in as well, do you?" Erc laughed out loud and gave a rude sign as the men all shouted "Yes!" Rhys felt this was the first time that Erc had smiled naturally.

With the sails set once more, it was time to spread out and adjust their speed for another landing, despite their sodden clothing and squelching boots. Running in soft sand had to be practised.

"That will do for now, men, make up some wind breaks and start a fire. Dry your clothes and get some sleep before midnight." Even Erc seemed relieved as he collected his pack from the lead-boat and slumped against a dune out of the cool breeze.

***

The night sky was clear when Erc called the helmsmen to a meeting.

"This is the first clear sky with a half moon, see how dark the sea is to the south? That's the direction we'll be approaching Saint Brigits. Some of you already have some knowledge of the stars and they'll be just the same off the south coast. But there's one star you can always rely on… see, up there? The north star."

Everybody concentrated on Erc's instructions – he had had great experience of sailing off the south coast before the Saxons had pushed so far west.

Getting the boats together in the dark was not easy, but the war-band had now practised so thoroughly that everybody knew their place. Rowing in a heavy sea in the dark was more difficult than anticipated and the rigging and sails creaked under the wind pressure, but after two more days and nights of practice it was time to leave.

"I think that's about as far as we can go charging about on this beach, we'll go around to the village for some fresh food and then sail overnight to Ynys Ygraine. The weather looks settled for a few days, so we may just be lucky."

The villagers at the mouth of the Harbour recognised the boys as they beached onto the soft sand. Erc asked for shelter and some food until the departure at dusk, and this was readily given. A little ale was allowed as the men rested and tried to sleep.

That evening, once the fleet was sailing in line, well off the shore, Erc pointed to the stars. The moon gave enough light for his signals to be seen, each boat repeating the order to change direction in the heavy swell. Some of the soldiers were, once more, suffering from sickness, but gritted their teeth.

Rhys and Alan, like the men, took it in turns to rest under the bow cover, but nobody could remember actually sleeping. The night wore on and after sailing due south, they finally saw dawn breaking in the eastern sky. They all cheered. By standing on the spar next to the mast, Alan eventually shouted that he could see the island. The southerly wind had held them up, but by noon the islanders were waving them onto the beach.

There were many introductions to be made as the commander and his wife greeted Rhys and Alan and asked after their children at Caerllion. He then led Erc and all the helmsmen to his house for a conference – once they set sail each helmsmen would be responsible for his own boat.

"I've been given the plans for your trip, Erc and I've got food ready for you. It's Beltane tomorrow and, as I see it, the whole army at Maendibyn will be on the move within two days to meet up with Geraint. If your raid is successful, some of the Saxons should be drawn down to the coast in complete confusion. Either way, Arthur's main attack on Caer Durno will be unstoppable."

"Don't worry, sire, we can't fail with the warband we've got. Our only worry is that a bad storm might blow up. With your permission, we'll rest until dusk and then set off. My plan is to sail west tonight and south tomorrow, then go between the peninsula and the Syllan Isles overnight and sail south east until darkness the following night. Much will then depend on the sea conditions, but I've worked out that it will be high tide just before dawn."

"When they realise what's happened, the Saxons will signal for every longship on their coast to hunt you," said the commander.

"That's for sure. After the raid, we must sail well to the south and hopefully, the Saxons will be sailing west along the coast expecting us to pull into our own territory."

Erc looked happy and confident as he told the men to rest. He then asked his host to prepare some fire-torches.

Tarou said to the boys, somewhat sourly, "If the raid goes well, Erc will surely become a hero among all the Britons."

***

Rhys and Alan wanted Tarou to meet their old friend Ryan, and, as they strolled along the cliff edge, the smiling old sailor appeared and grasped their hands.

"Good luck, boys, my wife and I will be joining the priest in his chapel while you're away. We'll all be praying for you."

"This is Tarou, Ryan. He's going to save us if we get into trouble!" Rhys laughed as Ryan took Tarou's hand and looked into his eyes.

"I know all about Tarou, boys, that's all we have to do here on the island, you know. We question every visitor and spend all our time gossiping."

They decided to sit behind some gorse bushes out of the breeze as Ryan continued.

"I've already inspected your boats, you know, they're quite beautiful. Colman has excelled himself."

As they discussed the merits of the new leather boats, two garrison soldiers strolled by, unaware of the group behind the bushes.

The boys heard one of them say "… and I doubt we'll ever see them again. That Erc is quite mad, you know…"

The group shrugged as they overheard this part of the soldiers' conversation and Ryan quickly carried on the conversation.

Later that evening, Erc called the war-band together for a thorough check of food, water, and weapons, then some fresh meat was loaded onto each boat for breakfast the next morning at sea. After that they would be on smoked meat and fish, cheese and hard-boiled eggs. Bread and oat cakes were sealed into watertight skin bags.

"Cast off," Erc shouted when everything had been made safe. "We'll sail west, then turn south before the stars disappear at dawn."

***

As soon as the fleet had left the shelter of the island, the chill wind and the choppy sea made the men don their helmets and tighten up their fleece-lined coats. The direction of the wind was favourable for them to stay on the same tack most of the night and everybody had a chance to rest under cover. Crashing into each ocean wave made the boats shudder and the men seemed to withdraw into their own thoughts. Rhys admitted to Alan that he was now a little frightened of what was to come – it had all seemed so simple at the planning stage.

"I'm just as frightened as you, Rhys, but every time I think of Ronan and my friends on that sinking galley, I know that I must get my revenge or give up and go home to the farm."

"Whenever I think of home, this voyage all seems like a bad dream," replied Rhys.

If the wind held in the same direction, they would be able to sail south with only a few changes of direction. There was no sign of land when the sun rose, so everything depended on Erc's skill to get them past the tip of the peninsula before nightfall. However, the sky to the west looked dull, grey and unpromising.

The soldiers' seasickness was now beginning to wear off and

the sea gradually settled. Most of the men hungrily consumed the last of the fresh food and measured out their drinking water.

"I hope we haven't forgotten anything," joked Rhys to relieve the tension.

Alan laughed, "I'll just check, ah, yes… we've remembered our bows and swords."

The soldiers smiled at the two youngsters, but well knew that they were both concentrating hard on keeping their boat in good trim. Rhys felt that the wake of the six boats spread out over the ocean was somehow reassuring. Occasionally, they would spot dolphins racing towards them to play around the boats and, always, there seemed to be seabirds following them. However, Rhys could feel a strange loneliness.

The passage of the sun in the sky gave them a good notion of their position and by dusk there was a slight outline of land to their east. This was the tip of their own territory and, luckily, there was no sign of enemy sails.

After darkness had fallen, a half-moon in the northern sky enabled them to see each other, then Erc signalled for a change of direction to the south east. He intended to sail between the land and the islands, then continue on the same course until daybreak. During the night they made good progress and by dawn the next day they were once more out of sight of land. It was now time to sail east and, before darkness closed in, Erc tried to get a glimpse of the coast to find out exactly where he was before the overnight run-in.

The men were now getting nervous and talked in whispers.

"It's strange," said Rhys to Alan and Tarou. "There are all

those other soldiers around us and we're not close enough to speak to each other."

"There's nothing much to say," mused Tarou. "If I know these men, they won't want to talk much tonight, they just want to get ashore and get it over with."

Erc continued to lead the fleet eastwards with almost a following sea. Everybody was now in great discomfort and the order was given to eat and sleep as much as possible. By evening, Erc had turned the lead boat north and the helmsmen watched as he was hoisted up the mast to try and get a sight of land. He waved the boats on further north-eastward and eventually gave the signal that he had recognised the coastline. The mainsails were lowered and the fleet held its position. It was essential to keep out of sight of land until sunset.

Because they were making very little headway, Erc was able to call the boats together in the now calmer sea.

"We're just off the headland and there's no sign of any longship sails. As soon as it's dark we'll sail in quietly until we can clearly see the headland which will be over to our right. Thank goodness there's no sea-mist. Try and sleep. When I've gauged the wind and the tide, we'll go in under full sail and straight onto the beach. And don't forget to raise your keels when I give the signal. Any questions?"

Everybody glanced at each other and shrugged – it was too late for questions.

"I'll see if I can get some sleep, Alan," said Rhys. "I want to be on the helm when we get to the shore."

"That means I'll be first to jump on the beach," laughed Alan. "What if there's a dozen Saxons waiting for me?"

"You'll be on your own, Alan," replied Tarou keeping a straight face. "The rest of us will be off back to sea!" The soldiers guffawed at this ribbing of the young helmsman. Alan gave a forced smile.

***

When the moon rose in the north-east, each boat could make out the distant high landmark that gave their position. As the night wore on, with everybody trying to doze, Erc suddenly gave the signal to raise the mainsails. Rhys looked at Alan and grimaced. He tried to concentrate on keeping his boat trimmed as it heeled over in the westerly breeze. If the wind held, their escape out to sea before the alarm went up would be made easier. Rhys hoped that, when they had smashed the longships at Saint Brigits, there would be no other Saxon boats on the nearby coast to give them chase.

On and on sailed the fleet; the eastern sky showed a faint glow of light as the coastline now showed up clearly in front of them. Glancing behind him, Rhys could see only the blackness of the horizon – this meant that even if the Saxons had lookouts, they would not spot them coming in from the south, just as Erc had said. Both Rhys and Alan were breathing deeply. Their throats were surprisingly dry and their foreheads were sweaty under their helmets.

Tarou turned and nodded to them reassuringly as he patted

the hilt of his sword. It wasn't long before they could make out the sand dunes. The higher ground over to their left meant that they were close to the mouth of the river and calm water.

Garwyn's boat and another moved slightly to the left and slowed down. They were to wait for a signal to sail quietly into the river and seek out the moored longships, but if there was trouble, they would immediately join the others on the beach. Rhys prayed that the Saxons would not wake until the sun was fully up. He thought of the monastery and the quiet, orderly life there – why did he now feel such weakness in his limbs?

All eyes were fixed on the beach. There was no movement on shore and Rhys was almost startled when the signal to raise the keels came – he would surely have forgotten as his thoughts had been concentrated on the land. He rubbed his watering eyes and blinked as he kept the bow head-on to the beach until suddenly a gentle scraping on the sand stopped them. There was an eerie silence as the soldiers slid into the surf and crept in a straight line up the beach to the dunes. Rhys noted with satisfaction that it was high tide. As the helmsmen knelt behind the soldiers with bows at the ready, Erc had been peering over the first dune and slid back to whisper.

"It's all quiet in the village and I can see two longships. Give the signal to Garwyn's boats to go into the river."

A soldier ran into the surf and waved frantically with his sword to Garwyn. Their oars dipped quietly into the water and the boats pulled around the rocky headland into the calm river.

"We've done it, men… get ready to move closer." Erc crept along the line to reassure his men with a wicked grin, then settled himself in the centre ready for the next move. It was almost dawn.

CHAPTER 23

The Raid

Erc watched intently as Garwyn's raiders edged upriver toward the Saxon longships. He stood up and silently waved his arm forward. Each man rose, spear and sword ready. As the warband walked down the first dune into softer sand, the colts fanned out on the right flank. They each drew an arrow from their quivers and Rhys, out of the corner of his eye, could just see Garwyn's two boats gliding toward the longships in the mist. Just as expected, a wooden jetty was close by and a smoking fire glowed near the water's edge.

Erc held up the advance until he could see Garwyn's soldiers jump deftly aboard the two longships. A muffled cry was heard as the Saxon crewmen were, no doubt, hacked to pieces and this in turn caused the village dogs to start barking furiously.

It was hardly necessary to signal the charge as a line of howling sea-raiders rushed toward the houses. It was now light enough to see clearly, some of the soldiers charging shoulder-first into the wattle walls and others bursting through the doorways. The screams of the women and the shouts of the Saxon men horrified the young colts as they saw the enemy being hacked down – some with their weapons in their hands but most of them unarmed.

"Over there," shouted Lewys as three Saxons from the nearest house fled in panic and tried to make a run for it. "Shoot them!"

A hail of arrows thudded into the fleeing men – the Saxons were still in their underclothes and were barefoot. Rhys could see people running in all directions between the houses, and women could be seen dragging children away in an effort to escape the village.

"Follow me," ordered Lewys as he led his troop behind the houses. Approaching the three wounded enemy writhing on the ground, he and Hwyn drew their swords and hacked them to death. Rhys was almost choking with shock as he drew his bow and shot twice more at other fleeing Saxons.

"Rhys... Alan." Once more Lewys showed his complete self-control. "Go to the fire and then start burning the roofs."

As they untied the fire torches from their belts, Rhys could see Garwyn's boat rowing furiously for the riverside jetty. The soldiers of Garwyn's second boat were wielding their heavy axes and smashing up the bottom planking and rigging of the two longships. As he plunged his torch into the embers of the fire and shook it into flame, Rhys could see Garwyn and his troop running along the jetty or jumping into the shallows to join the fray. He gave Rhys a frenzied smile before running wild-eyed into the village, sword in hand.

When they raced back to the first house, Rhys and Alan had to jump over dead Saxons – some of the bodies seemed to have their arms hacked off and there was blood soaking into the sand. Dead dogs lay with their tongues hanging out. The screaming and shouting intensified as Rhys ran from house to house and set fire to the thatched roofs.

"Over here, Alan. Let's get to the big barn." Rhys could see a last battle being fought beyond the village, but otherwise the enemy were completely overwhelmed. They had never expected to be attacked on their own shoreline and those who did put up a fight soon realised it was futile. A stream of women and children ran inland as Lewys and his men shot arrows at any clear target among the Saxon men; it was obvious that some of the women were being wounded as well. A small group of dazed, elderly Saxons were huddling by the water's edge; too old to fight and begging for mercy. They were ignored by the raiders.

Tarou and his men emerged from what Rhys knew to be the thane's house. They dragged the bodies of the thane and his sons to the doorway and spat on them. Seeing that the battle was won and the men were looting all the houses, Tarou joined Rhys to help try and open the doors to the barn – they hoped that the captive Britons inside were still alive and well enough to be rescued.

"Watch out!" cried Alan. Rhys swung around to see two Saxons charging them from behind the barn. Rhys held up his torch instinctively to ward off the strike from the younger man and ducked as the sword sliced through the air just above his head. He lunged back at his enemy, drawing his dagger at the same time, and landed on top of the young Saxon grabbing at his throat. With dagger raised for the plunge, Rhys was aware of Tarou kneeling over the other Saxon with his sword in his chest.

"Kill him," screamed Tarou. "What are you waiting for?"

Rhys was not aware that he had hesitated; he was looking into the terror-struck eyes of a boy his own age. His dagger plunged into the Saxon's chest and blood spurted everywhere. Gasping and gurgling, the boy went limp.

"Well done, Rhys," shouted Alan, helping his comrade to his feet.

Rhys felt a terrible dizziness as he watched Tarou wrenching open the barn doors.

"Everybody come out, you're safe now." As the doors swung open to let in some light, cowering figures with frightened eyes stared at them in silence. "It's all right, you're free. We're taking you home. Come on, get to the boats." Tarou stepped inside to usher the bewildered slaves into the open air. The smell inside was foul.

Rhys and Alan carried on setting fire to the houses and the barn. Alan was in high spirits, but Rhys could only picture the young wide-eyed Saxon as he carried out his orders. He thought he would never be able to tell Helena that he had stabbed a man to death.

Tarou had managed to get one of the slaves to talk and he had some useful information. Rhys heard him say that there were no other Saxon villages on this stretch of coast – just a few farms inland which was where the women would have fled to. It would be some time before the Saxon commanders were aware of what had happened.

The old folk huddled at the river had been spared.

"You filthy Saxon scum," shouted Rhys, throwing his torch at them. "This is what you do to our villages, but never again. Woden is beaten!"

The soldiers laughed at Rhys; they were now in a state of elation.

"What did you say to them?"

"I cursed them," shouted Rhys. "I cursed them." He was just about to turn away when a thought occurred to him. He pulled out his dagger in front of the terrified Saxons and drew the shape of a galley in the sand. "Tell Cenwulf, he'll know what it means!"

Erc gathered everybody near the jetty. There were twelve rescued men, women and children and he shared them out between the boats.

"Throw the enemy bodies into the fires, men. The Saxon swords are yours, but gather the other weapons and tools and put them onto Garwyn's boats, he'll drop them overboard in deep water." Erc waved to the river and Rhys could see that the remains of the smashed longships were sinking. "When the tide turns, what's left of those ships will be swept out to sea. Well done everybody, now dress the wounded quickly and let's get back to sea."

Rhys was glad to know that the victory was so overwhelming that none of the warband had been killed. The surgeon asked for the wounded to be helped to the two boats on the jetty.

Rhys and Alan collected their discarded bows and as they

cleared the sand dune leading to the beach, Rhys looked back at the burning village. Huge tongues of orange flame spiraled into the sky and the black smoke would soon be seen for miles around. It was a very satisfying feeling that it was all over; but the killing could never be forgotten.

As they pushed their boat off the sand, Alan sensed Rhys' mood and put his arm around his friend's shoulder. "Remember what they did to your family, Rhys. You had no choice, he would have killed you, you know." Rhys quietly shook his head and looked back at the flames.

The surf was settled enough for the men to turn the boats and start rowing. As they got to open water, Erc gave the order to raise the mainsails and speed due south with the wind abeam. It was now essential to get out of sight before nightfall. The helmsmen could not help glancing shoreward during the course of the morning and by noon, with the coast far away, it was time to eat. Spirits were high but Rhys smiled coldly as the men boasted of their prowess and killings. He was surprised that they had managed to loot some meat and ale. When the coastline was completely out of sight, Erc ordered a change of tack to the south-west; it was soon to be the direction home.

Rhys began to shiver with the cold. The men pulled their helmets down tight and covered themselves with the spare sail and hides. The sea and the sky had merged into a dull grey.

"Look," said Tarou raising himself up. "Erc's dropping sail, they're pushing something over the side." They then realised that a soldier's body was being jettisoned by Erc. "I think one of our wounded must have died."

Rhys felt numb; but there was no time for grief. As he whispered a prayer, he realised that death didn't frighten him any more.

Rhys' boat had three of the rescued captives huddled under the bow: an older man and two young girls. Emaciated and with sores from bad food and treatment, they had gladly accepted some food from the soldiers and now were gnawing gratefully on dried meat. Tarou assured them that they would get back to their own territory soon. The old man said that the younger men from their home village had all been slaughtered during a Saxon raid the previous summer.

Alan nudged Rhys and smiled.

"There, that's why you have to kill the enemy."

***

By evening, Erc had ordered a change of course to the west, which would mean tacking back and forth into the wind all night.

"We're well south now, men," said Rhys, satisfied that there was no longer any chance of being chased by longships. "If all goes well, we'll start sailing north sometime in the morning, and that means fast sailing homeward."

A cheer went up from the tired men.

Although it was clouding over, the moon and stars gave just enough light for the fleet to be able to stay in a group. At one stage during the night, it became misty and each boat had to signal occasionally to stay in touch. The signal was a sharp blow on the mast, the sound of which carried a long way over the water and gave a good sense of position. Rhys wondered what would happen if heavy rain or a sudden storm enveloped them; it would be terrifying to look around at dawn and find yourself alone on the ocean.

Everybody took turns at fitful sleeping and, after eating, it became apparent that they were running short of water. The extra passengers had needed to drink and Alan said that there was probably the same situation on the other boats. Although some of the men had grabbed food and valuables from the houses, they had not thought of taking water. Unless it rained, they were all going to get very thirsty on the way home.

***

After a long tack to the north, the vague outline of the Syllan Isles came into view on their right. Erc edged the fleet closer, which seemed rather strange as the islands were almost certainly occupied by the enemy. It had been many years since any Britons had dared to venture close and galleys to and from Armorica sailed well out into the ocean to avoid being within sight of the islands. Erc called the boats together as he was hoisted up his mast to scan the horizon.

"There's a light on the shore. I know the islands well. We'll go into a quiet cove and take a look. If it's just fishermen, we'll finish them off and get some water." With that Erc gave the signal to carry on.

This was very alarming – what if there was a longship? Tarou moved aft next to Rhys and Alan to whisper, "I smell a trick, boys. Erc's father and some fishermen on the islands were killed here by the Saxons many years ago. I fear he may be seeking revenge."

Rhys' blood ran cold at the thought of more fighting. They had been lucky with the raid on Saint Brigits; surely they couldn't be so lucky a second time. The other boats unsuspectingly followed Erc towards the islands, but Rhys followed nervously.

It was long before dawn when they neared the rocky shore. The light of a fire on the nearby beach suggested that someone was living there. Erc led the fleet west into a sheltered cove where the water was calm enough for the men to get a hold on the rocks.

"My man here knows the island," whispered Erc. "He'll go and take a quiet look. If there are any longships, we can get away to sea again before dawn breaks."

Erc's man clambered up the rock face like a wild goat and made for a vantage point overlooking the beach. Tarou breathed deeply.

"We don't have much choice now," he whispered to Rhys and Alan.

It wasn't long before the scout returned to report to Erc, who gathered everybody.

"It's going to be all right, men," he sounded elated. "There's just one longship and her crew. This is obviously their summer base for raiding. We've got to kill them. What do you say?"

The soldiers all nodded vigorously at the thought of more blood-spilling. They seemed to be ignoring the risk to the whole fleet.

Tarou put his hand on Rhys' shoulder.

"We're sure to beat them. If we don't attack them now, they'll be killing our people as soon as they get the chance." Perhaps he felt it was better to cheer the boys on now that Erc had given orders.

The approach to the beach was the same as the day before, but there would be only about twenty-five Saxon warriors and a few older fishermen. Rhys felt that even if they were at the ready, they would be no match for Erc's experienced warband. There would be no dogs and no women and children to worry about. The half moon gave enough light for the raiders to sail quietly around the headland.

Garwyn's boat was first and veered off to glide alongside the single longship bobbing quietly in the shelter of the rocks. There was no noise as Garwyn's crew jumped onto the longship, daggers drawn, to dispatch the sleeping crew.

The rest of the fleet glided through the surf and onto the beach. Rhys could make out several huts above the high tide mark and a glowing fire surrounded by ale mugs and rubbish. The Saxons had been carousing and could never have imagined an enemy near their base. A silent walk up the beach to the doorways of the huts gave the sleeping enemy little chance of drawing their daggers or grabbing their swords. The few that did were hacked down by the howling soldiers and in just a few moments it was all over. The colts with swords drawn had been ordered to circle the camp in a group and make sure that nobody got away.

Nobody did. As they came back down to the huts, death

was all around them. Rhys felt almost sorry for the older fishermen, who were grotesquely spread out on the sand face down, but perhaps, they too, had once been murderous warriors.

The victors were already looting the bodies and collecting the best weapons. It was time to load up with food and water. Garwyn, who had not got onto the beach before the slaughter was over, reported that the two Saxon sailors on the longship had been killed and thrown overboard.

"Good. We'll tow their boat out to sea before destroying it. It will never be seen again on our coast." Erc waved everybody back to the boats where the rescued captives had been nervously peering over the bows at the carnage, some cheering loudly.

The anchor line and moorings of the huge longship were cut and Rhys and Garwyn used their boats to tow it out to sea. When they rounded the rocky headland and got into deeper water, the ocean swell rocked them gently. The tow-ropes were hauled in and the soldiers with their heavy axes jumped onto the longship and hacked at the bottom planking, causing fountains of water to spurt upwards. Dawn was now rising in the sky behind them.

Rhys managed to board the longship and cut away and salvage some of its ropes and its sail. He wanted to take a closer look at them back at Caerllion.

"I'd love to sail that magnificent boat all the way home." Rhys said admiring the timberwork and huge mast. "Look at the sweep of the hull and the width in the middle. No wonder they nearly caught us last time."

Before the ocean swell swallowed up the enemy ship forever, there was a muted cheer. Then the fleet rounded the tip of the island and headed north for home. One day and one more night and they should be back at Ynys Ygraine. There was a good breeze from the west: luckily the wind had hardly changed direction since leaving Saint Brigits. Erc decided to tack as far as possible out into the ocean and keep well away from the coast. This would leave an easy run to their home port overnight.

***

After sailing steadily all morning, with the men all dozing, Rhys noticed a slight fraying of the mainstay, the heavy rope that secured the top of the mast to the stern of the boat, just above his head.

"It's not a problem at the moment, Tarou," explained Rhys. "As long as we're tacking into the wind, the strain is on the forestay, but I would like to secure a second rope down from the masthead, just to be on the safe side."

"How can we do that while we're at sea? The boat is rocking all over the place." said Tarou, with concern, looking up at the mast.

"I can get up there," laughed Alan. "If I get an extra rope ready, Rhys, you'll have to throw out a sea anchor and keep us into the wind for a while."

"I'll signal to Erc and see what he says. He won't be pleased, but if the mainstay broke, we could lose our mast in a sudden gust."

Erc came alongside to inspect the stay and agreed that any repair should be done sooner rather than later. The fleet held their boats into the wind whilst Rhys dropped his sails and let his boat ride the waves on their sea anchor. Alan shinned halfway up the mast whilst two soldiers held an oar under each thigh for him to be able to grab the stays and pull himself up the top of the mast. He looped the end of his new rope over the mast head. Then pausing to catch his breath from the exertion, he glanced out to sea back the direction they had come.

"Sail!" he screamed. "Behind us… I can see a sail."

Rhys asked Tarou to signal to Erc, then taking the new rope from Alan, he quickly looped the end through the large cleat on the stern. All eyes were on the horizon as Rhys tightened the extra stay and tied it up.

"Hoist the sails, bring in the sea-anchor," shouted Rhys in a panic. He then realised his mistake in not trimming his craft correctly when the boat swung broadside into the waves and finished up facing south. Rhys cursed and tried to regain his heading. The other boats were now well upwind of him.

Once more under sail, and with the bow crashing into the oncoming waves, he was able to stand up on the stern to scan the horizon. Each time they rose up on a high swell, he could just make out the Saxon sail well to their stern. They had somehow come from the main island, but were still a long way downwind of them. Erc, with the rest of the fleet, was now well ahead of Rhys who desperately tried to make up the distance. He anxiously inspected his stays.

"It's all right, Tarou, they'll never catch us up. They can't sail into the wind. You wait and see." Rhys knew that, as things stood, they would pull away from the longship during the course of the day and hopefully the night would be dark. In any case, if the whole fleet had to fight, they outnumbered the Saxons at least two to one.

"The enemy sail's disappeared, Rhys," shouted Alan who had been hoisted a little way up the mast to report. "I can't see it anywhere."

"Let me see," replied Rhys. "Surely they haven't sunk! Here, take the helm."

Rhys gained a foothold and searched the horizon. Then he spotted the hull of the longship heading directly into the wind; they were rowing into the waves to try and get upwind of the fleet. This could be dangerous. How could they row into such a big swell?

"I didn't think they'd be able to row in a heavy sea like this, Tarou, they must be taking on lots of water, but once they get far enough upwind, they'll be able to hoist their sail and try to catch us."

Would Erc turn, if necessary, for a sea battle? Or would he sail on 'til dark and sacrifice Rhys' boat? After that stop at the Syllan Isles just for revenge, Rhys wondered what Erc's intentions might be. As the longship seemed to get closer to them, Rhys, once more, started thinking again of home and his family. What if he was killed? Was this all a bad dream?

"They're rowing again," said Alan. "I can see their bow crashing up and down on the waves. They must surely be taking on water."

The day wore on with the Saxons playing cat and mouse. They had no fear of the ocean and they were mad for a fight.

"How did they know where to find us, do you think, Rhys?" Tarou was puzzled. "They must have had a signal from somewhere, I'm sure there were no survivors on the island."

"My guess is that they set sail after our raid on Saint Brigits with other longships, then split up looking for us off the coast. I think the captain of this ship went straight to the main island which has the highest ground to get a good view of the sea... and that's when he spotted us."

"You mean, they probably don't even know of our raid last night on the south island?" Tarou stroked his dark beard and shrugged.

"I don't see how they could have got that far west. Anyway, look, they're under sail again." Rhys was now worried that the longship was gaining on them. He had not imagined that they could row so well in the open sea. They all watched as the enemy sail dropped once more and the longship headed into the wind. Twenty oars dipped into the sea in unison. Rhys' boat sped away across the waves; he would have to keep his heading tight to the north west and keep the rest of the fleet in sight. He prayed that none of their boats developed a fault, for the Saxons would pounce like wolves.

It seemed as if the longship captain sensed that in the coming night he might lose sight of his quarry; Rhys could just hear him chanting "pull, pull," in the Saxon language.

"They're a long way off again now, Rhys," smiled Alan as the longship changed its heading once again.

"I'm not so sure, the farther they get upwind, the closer they'll get to us when they turn again."

There was heightened nervousness as the Saxon sail, once more, came into view. As the longship sped over the swell, spray spurting from either side of the bow, Rhys realised that the enemy captain had gone well past their stern and was now turning toward them to try and gain a little more distance. It could soon be his final turn. The longship slowed with sail and rigging straining against the wind.

"Pass me my bow, Alan. This might be our chance." Rhys grabbed his pack and drew out his wedge-headed arrows. He stood on the stern, legs apart and back braced against the stay. The heaving of the boat was regular enough for Rhys to be able to concentrate on the best time to shoot.

The first arrow went straight into the Saxon sail and a small tear appeared. The enemy captain, now quite visible as he stood in the prow, looked up and seemed to laugh at this feeble effort. Rhys shivered in fear as he recognised the stance and the flowing white hair of the Saxon captain. It was surely Cenwulf the Butcher, and he was determined to kill them all. He thought of Ronan and his galley. Was Cenwulf what the Christians called Satan?

"Damn you," hissed Rhys as he drew back his bow once more. He was sure that Cenwulf, in turn, recognised him, for he ducked behind the high-standing prow as Rhys took aim. But it was not the Saxon that Rhys aimed at – he had to try and rip the sail apart. All eyes were on Rhys as each arrow caused another tear in the fabric of the taut sail, but it did not split down its seams as Rhys had hoped. Then one of his arrows hissed through the air and partly sliced through the side stay of the mast. There was a loud crack as the rope parted and the sail shuddered under the pressure of the wind.

"They're going over," shouted Alan. "The mast is splitting."

Saxon soldiers desperately clambered onto the windward side of their ship as a wave caused their sail to dip into the water but it was too late; the weight of the mast held the hull down and sea water from a rising swell cascaded into the ship. They were sinking. Even the bloodthirsty soldiers on Rhys' boat looked aghast at this sudden turn of events.

Instinctively, Rhys murmured prayers of thanks in the Roman language. It was horrific to see so many men about to drown and this was the first time that he had prayed honestly. The Saxons clung to the mast and the part of the hull that was above water, howling in terror, but the distance between the two boats had increased. Rhys wondered why so many seabirds were circling above the wreckage. Then he noticed two dolphins jumping clear of the sea and circling the stricken longship. Were they really the spirits of the dead? Could they even be the spirits of his father and uncle? Cenwulf would be the first to know.

"There's nothing we can do, Rhys, sail on. Don't look back." Even Tarou seemed to be shaken by the sight of drowning men, although the Saxons had been preparing to kill them.

Erc's boats had spilled wind and were drifting back towards them. It was now obvious that Erc was glad to have avoided a battle with the longship, but would he have left them to fend for themselves? There were cheers from the soldiers on the other five boats when they caught a glimpse of the last of the Saxon survivors clinging to the wreckage. The cold water would soon make them loosen their grip.

Erc and the soldiers congratulated Rhys on his lucky arrow-shot; there was no telling what the outcome would have been, had there been a battle, but there would surely have been terrible casualties.

"I can't believe how lucky we've been," said Tarou, slowly shaking his head. "I thought I was going to have to learn to swim."

The crew was silent as Rhys turned the boat to follow the others.

CHAPTER 24

Back to Din Tagell

Evening turned to dusk and Erc gathered the fleet, once more, for a meeting.

"We're well away from Ynys Ygraine and I fear the wind is increasing. We'll sail east to get a landmark and make for Din Tagell. I want to land our wounded and the captives will be glad to get ashore. Perhaps there will be news of Arthur's march to the south. Stay close in the dark."

This was welcome news for everybody; they would make landfall before morning and be able to get fresh food. The soldiers said they were going to lie in the sunshine all day drinking ale and sleeping. Their laughter echoed across the water as the fleet sailed eastwards with the wind now astern.

The last of the food and water was shared out and there was a noticeable improvement in the condition of the rescued captives. They were still huddling under some hides, but now talked of going home. Each member of the crew napped in their seats, feeling exhausted after their hectic few days at sea. They would certainly have stories to tell their children. Rhys recalled the number of times he had had to relate his experiences when he had returned home; next time would be difficult. He would have to consult with Tarou and Alan, who were the only witnesses to his stabbing of the Saxon. Hopefully they would keep it a secret. He dreaded the thought of Helena hearing about it. She would never be able to get it out of her mind.

As the swell lessened during the night, Rhys could make out the distant coastline and soon Erc was able to get his bearings and steer them further north for a welcome landfall.

Excitement grew as the fleet approached the familiar shape of Din Tagell island. They heard the sound of a warning bell as the lookouts spotted them in the early-morning mist, and hoped they would be recognised as friendly. The whole garrison might be roused in a panic.

Erc led the craft into the sheltered cove where they raised their keels and lowered their sails. Everyone felt well-deserved pride as the boats glided in and slid onto the beach. First, the cold but recovering captives and the wounded soldiers were helped ashore and soon the whole town had descended to the beach to give their blessings and offer to help. The fleet of leather boats was much admired; Din Tagell had never seen such craft.

The tide was coming in rapidly, so Erc ordered the helmsmen to moor in the shelter of the rocks. Tarou helped Rhys and Alan with the moorings; this was a chance for Rhys to speak to them together.

"Tarou, I know we can speak man to man. I've grown up a lot since I joined you at Caerllion and, after the experiences we've had together, I feel as if we're comrades. Well, to put it bluntly, I've been troubled since I killed that young Saxon. I can't forget the look in his eyes. It didn't seem to matter when I was shooting to kill with my bow, but driving a dagger into someone is different. I know I shouldn't have hesitated, but, can you both keep it a secret?"

"Of course," said Alan quickly; he seemed to have read Rhys' mind. "I promise."

"It's all right, Rhys," said Tarou. "I know how you feel. Only Alan and I were there and it will stay forever between the three of us. But always remember, Rhys, you were only following orders. It wasn't your fault." Tarou patted him on the back and ruffled his hair.

As he turned away, Rhys was unable to cover up his tears. Why was he suddenly so emotional? He busied himself with the moorings until it was time to join the victorious warband. The townsfolk collected food and ale, and the connecting bridge creaked when the soldiers crossed it to make their way up the steep pathway to the castle. One of the older officers had been left in charge of Din Tagell, when Cai had taken his army to meet King Geraint. There had been no news of the battle in the south, but they knew that horsemen would be dispatched by Arthur as soon as he had taken Caer Durno near the south coast. There were no thoughts of defeat, such was the respect that Prince Arthur commanded throughout the land.

Hot food was being prepared as the soldiers were shown into the main hall. Torches were lit from the blazing fire, then fixed around the walls providing a warm light. Erc stood on the raised section of the hall where Cai normally sat and prepared to give a speech. The depleted garrison and the elders from the town all crowded into every available space, while lesser mortals jostled for position in the corridors and galleries.

"I think that I will first tell you all about our raid and then a messenger can ride at full speed to Arthur and give him the details." Erc nodded to the garrison officer and his young equerry: there would be a change of horses along the route and, possibly, Arthur's own messenger would be on the same road riding north. At the same time the governor of the town would arrange for other messengers to be dispatched up and down the coast.

When Erc related events of the last few days he exaggerated a little now that he was sure of being a famous sea captain, and it was quite apparent that he was going to enjoy his new-found status. Tarou whispered to Rhys that Erc had probably always intended to call in at the Tin Islands if he had the chance – even though landing there just to get his revenge could have been disastrous. The crowd cheered as Erc described the death of so many Saxons, and Rhys was made to stand up when Erc came to the sinking of the longship. This brought gasps of praise, but it was all very embarrassing for Rhys especially when his fellow-helmsmen whooped and cheered.

After a big breakfast, the men just lay on the grass outside facing the warm morning sunshine. Jugs of ale were passed around and it was not long before most of the colts were fast asleep. Rhys, as usual, started thinking of home and Helena, which always seemed to help when his mind was in turmoil. Soon he was slumbering peacefully.

After a while Rhys became aware of Alan's voice. What was he saying?

"Rhys, I'm glad you're awake. Here, meet my parents."

Shaking himself awake, Rhys jumped up and shook their hands.

"I'm so pleased to meet you both. Alan and I have shared a lot of excitement lately. We're fated to be comrades-in-arms I think."

The smiling couple were obviously relieved to see their son safe and well – it seemed that they were not yet aware of the details of the raid. The other colts slowly gathered round to greet them as Alan had to explain that he would not be coming home to the farm just yet. He was off to Caerllion. His father seemed pleased, but his mother looked resigned.

Just after noon, a horseman was seen galloping along the headland to the island's bridge. This brought everyone to their feet followed by a rush into the hall. It was now the turn of Arthur's equerry to make a speech. He clasped the hands of everybody near him while he tried to regain his breath.

"Victory, men, Arthur has routed the enemy at Caer Durno and has pushed further east hunting down stragglers. The Saxons killed many of our men but they were soon put to flight. We learned that your sea raid had been successful when we freed a lot of captives… they told us that large groups of Saxons had been dispatched all along the coast to warn the villages and many longships had put to sea to try and hunt you down. You made our job a lot easier. Well, they scattered all over the place and have now fled east." He thanked Erc warmly, which drew more applause.

The colts were elated at the good news and could sense Tarou's relief at knowing that there would be no more forays from Caerllion for some time. Rhys hoped that Arteg and his men were safe. It would be some days before they could return home.

After answering the many questions that were shouted at him, the equerry was feted with food and drink. Erc called his men together: it was time to make plans.

"I think we should push on immediately to Caer Taf. That is what the King would want us to do. We'll call at Herculis Village and they can send a message immediately to Ynys Ygraine." Then turning to the colts he winked. "I'm sure that your two fleets can call at the island sometime during the summer to make a courtesy visit."

It was time, once more, to man the boats. The hard timbers of the seating reminded everybody that they were still suffering badly from blisters.

"Why are my muscles aching so much?" joked Rhys. "I don't think I'll ever be able to ride a horse again."

The rescued captives, who had now recovered a little from their ordeal, lined the headland as the fleet set off to the north and home. Everybody waved wildly. A following wind made the journey to Herculis Point a pleasure for the soldiers who had never seen this part of the coast. They were going home.

"I'm not sure if I would want to go through all this again, Tarou," said Rhys, slouching on his seat.

"You won't have to, Rhys. I'm going to ask Arthur to lock you up in the monastery."

The soldiers all turned and laughed as Alan shouted, "Me too!"

BY THE SAME AUTHOR
Cunval's Mission